The Alpha Protocols
by David T. Francis

Bloomington, IN  Milton Keynes, UK

AuthorHouse™
1663 Liberty Drive, Suite 200
Bloomington, IN 47403
www.authorhouse.com
Phone: 1-800-839-8640

AuthorHouse™ *UK Ltd.*
500 Avebury Boulevard
Central Milton Keynes, MK9 2BE
www.authorhouse.co.uk
Phone: 08001974150

© 2006 David T. Francis. All rights reserved.

No part of this book may be reproduced, stored in a retrieval system, or transmitted by any means without the written permission of the author.

First published by AuthorHouse 11/27/2006

ISBN: 978-1-4259-5940-1 (sc)

Printed in the United States of America
Bloomington, Indiana

This book is printed on acid-free paper.

Prologue

The wind blew viciously across Lucy Tyler's face. The weather conditions had worsened in the hour since they had arrived at the warehouse and it had now started to snow heavily.

"Typical weather for Chicago" Lucy muttered to herself, trying to keep herself focused despite the cold.

She had come to Chicago with her Department of Planetary Defense Team in search of an infectee. They had been able to trace the individual, thanks to a local hospital reporting that a patient had shown a DNA match against the test devised by the DPD a couple of months previous.

A few days prior to their arrival, Lucy had sent several agents to monitor the infectee's movements and identify who he had made contact with. There was no doubt that he would be making his best efforts to spread the infection.

The reports that came back indicated that the infectee was working on some project in the area. The objectives now were to capture him, uncover his plans and remove the threat. While they knew that many of the infectees they had tracked were working in groups, this particular one had not appeared to have made contact with anyone else during the surveillance.

Despite following protocols, the team had been disorderly on their arrival on the industrial complex, and had alerted the infectee to their presence. He had caught sight of them as they turned up at the gates to the compound and had fled. They were now forced into chasing him around the buildings on foot.

She tried to keep as close to the wall as she could, edging cautiously towards a metal door about twenty metres ahead. It made no difference against the cold; the wind was blowing hard into her face. Thankfully, the beanie hat she was wearing kept her hair from blowing into her eyes.

At the touch of a hand on her shoulder, she stopped as she reached the door. She looked round and was relieved to see her partner, agent Bale, following closely behind.

"Let me go first," he said to her.

Lucy nodded and let him edge past her. He steadied himself, twisted the door handle with his left hand and let it fall open.

Peering into the dark, they could see the warehouse was full of crates and boxes, but it looked like many of these had been here for some time. Everything was covered in dust and looked like nothing had been disturbed recently.

Despite being ordered by their operation commander, Al Johnson, who was monitoring the operation from back at DPD command, not to enter the warehouse until back up could arrive, Lucy was determined they move in immediately. She felt that as it was not a large building they could easily manage this job between the two of them.

As Bale edged his way in, she followed him closely, carefully watching the area for their target.

He made his way to the right side of the door as he entered, checking behind it as he advanced. Lucy moved to the left, keeping tight against the wall. She raised her gun to an alert position, catching her partner's eye and nodding the silent signal to split up. Although the situation was highly hazardous, they knew they would cover more ground working separately.

They edged around the walls of the warehouse, each making their way to different corners of the building. Lucy could see clearly down the side of the warehouse to a set of stairs that led up to what she suspected were offices. This, she thought, might give her a good vantage point and allow her to guide Bale to the location of the infectee.

She had made her way quickly along the wall to the stairs, checking down each of the four aisles between the crates as she went. Arriving unhindered, she quickly surveyed her route and edged her way up the stairs.

On reaching the top, she carefully opened the door and moved stealthily into the first office. To her left was a large window over-looking the main warehouse floor. Straight ahead was another door which led in to a second office. Taking a quick look through, she saw there was another similar room beyond it, but this one had a door leading out onto a balcony. She made her way through and into the second office, making sure to leave the door ajar so her exit was clear.

A creak and a click made her spin round to see the door she had just come through close, apparently of its own accord. Her heart beating furiously, Lucy scanned the room for any signs of life.

Nothing.

She turned back and continued into the second room. Another sound off to her right caught her attention, but before she could act on it, she was thrown across the room and landed against the bank of filing cabinets.

Momentarily dazed, she realized she had dropped her weapon from the force of the impact. It was in front of her by a couple of feet, just out of arms reach.

In the corner of her vision, she saw a large pair of black boots approaching.

Not recognizing them as ones worn by Bale, she raised her head to see who they belonged to. As she did, a powerful kick connected with her jaw, sending her slamming back into the filing cabinets. Hovering near to unconsciousness, she felt two strong hands wrap around her throat and squeeze down forcefully on her windpipe.

She guessed, correctly, that these hands belonged to the infectee who they had pursued into the building. His grasp was getting tighter around her neck. Each breath was hard won and her vision was starting to fade.

Lucy flailed frantically against the infectee's grip. He was obviously bigger and stronger than she was, and the desperate struggle was useless. She just hoped Bale had heard the commotion and had been able to catch up with her in time.

Then, as quickly as it had come, the pressure around her neck was released and Lucy slumped to the floor, gasping to get some air back into her lungs. Her vision had not cleared enough to see what was happening, but she guessed that Bale had got to the room to rescue her.

Lucy slowly began to make out two blurred figures in front of her. She could feel the impact as one of them smashed into the wall next to her. He then rolled himself forward, back towards the other who had started to direct another attack at him.

A gun shot sounded, followed by the violent flash and crackle of the stun charges the team used to incapacitate an infectee. As suddenly as it had all started, it was over.

Relieved, Lucy started to sit herself up. The remaining blur helped her into a sitting position and a hand was gently placed on the side of her face. Her head was raised up and she could see the outline of a man's face was looking into her eyes to see if she was okay.

As her eyes came back into focus, she realized it was not Bale with her. Although groggy, she instinctively went for the gun at her hip, and froze when she realized it wasn't there.

"You'll be alright," he said to her, a voice she found strangely comforting. "I'm guessing you'll have just a few bruises and probably the mother of all headaches tomorrow."

This was a dark haired man, probably in his mid-thirties she thought. It was not someone she recognized at all.

"Who..." Lucy started to ask.

"Am I?" he finished for her. But a loud crash caused him to snatch a look behind, before turning back. "A friend. You are not alone. We are all fighting the same enemy"

Lucy looked at him, still disorientated. "I don't know what you mean?"

"You have a new ally, Dr Tyler. Everything will be made clear to you very soon"

There was a second loud crash, and Bale burst through the door into the offices.

Lucy turned back to the stranger as he pointed his weapon at the window overlooking the warehouse. A gun shot rang out and the window shattered into a thousand pieces, and Lucy realized her rescuer was preparing his escape route.

The stranger turned back, pointing the gun directly towards her face as he edged his way backwards, turning his focus towards Bale advancing on him. This caused Lucy's colleague to hesitate at the door, ready to dive in to save his partner, poised for the inevitable shootout.

Suddenly the stranger turned and ran towards the window, and Bale saw his opportunity to burst through the door and into the second office. He levelled his gun at the stranger, who jumped over the balcony and disappeared back to the ground floor.

"Stop!" Lucy yelled, only now finding her feet. "Let him go!"

Bale moved out on to the balcony and watched as the stranger disappeared across the warehouse floor. His gun followed the stranger, but he could not get a clean shot off. The stranger made his escape out of the door they had entered only a few minutes before.

As Lucy laid her hand on his shoulder, he turned to look at her. Before he could say anything, she answered the questioning look on his face

"I think our cause has gained a new friend."

Chapter 1

"Come in," a voice said loudly in the room behind the door Harry had just knocked on.

As the door opened, the middle aged man walked in carrying a number of beige coloured folders. He was very apprehensive about the meeting he was walking into, especially as what he had to tell the Prime Minister was not likely to make him very happy. He tried his best to hide his nervousness, hoping the Prime Minister would not pick up on it.

"Thank you for seeing me at such short notice Sir," Harry said as he made his way across the room. He had been to 10 Downing Street on several previous occasions and already had the chance to meet the Prime Minister once before, although he had not been formally introduced.

Tonight however, he had come to Chequers, the Prime Minister's weekend residence. It was a Sunday night and at four in the morning, he was not relishing this particular meeting. He observed that the Prime Minister was still wearing his pyjamas and dressing gown, so this confirmed to Harry that he had probably had him woken up when he called to arrange the meeting just over a quarter of an hour ago.

"Come and sit down," The Prime Minister said, gesturing towards a large leather seat as Harry walked across the room. "I'm more than a little intrigued to know what you have had to wake me up for and tell me about so urgently at four in the morning".

"Yes Sir. Please accept my apologies for the hour I have to come to you with this news, but this matter has become most urgent."

"And please, call me John," the Prime Minister said with a gentle smile, aimed at helping his nervous guest feel more at ease. It was a trait that he had become renowned for over the past three years in the job. "It's too early in the morning for all that formality. Please forgive me, it is Harry isn't it?"

"Yes Sir." Harry replied. After a slight pause, he continued "Sorry John, Sir," struggling to sound as confident as he wanted to. He wasn't nervous about meeting him, but the news he carried was going to change the way the Prime Minister viewed a great many things.

Holding out the first of the folders he had arrived with, he offered it for the Prime Minister to take. Harry Wheelhouse started to explain the situation.

"This folder contains the details of an event that occurred in Rendlesham Forest, near Woodbridge in Suffolk, on the night of the twenty sixth of December 1980. Maybe you may remember it yourself anyway."

"I admit that I do vaguely remember something about this," the Primer Minister responded as he flicked through the folder which contained a variety of photos and reports that had been collated after the event. "I was of the opinion that it was always a hoax, perhaps something to do with a group of US airmen who had got drunk and were looking to try it on with the public. At least, that's what I remember from some documentary I saw about it."

"That's what was passed to the press and we have continued to let everyone to believe that ever since," Harry continued. "The first folder is the information that is freely available to the public, but if you look through this folder," handing another of the folders to the Prime Minister, "you will see actual statements from those involved, further photographic evidence, radar imaging and so on that actually confirms this event really did happen."

"Can you explain from where these records come from then? If they are not publicly available," The Prime Minister asked, a slight hint of suspicion creeping into his voice as he spoke.

"Some have been stored at GCHQ, while others have been stored elsewhere as part of a project I will outline and hopefully make clear to you as we go on."

"This next folder contains records concerning an event which occurred on October twentieth last year. This incident occurred over a section of the M25 around northern London. A number of unidentified objects were observed along a twenty mile stretch, and we have collected reports made by multiple witnesses."

"So basically, you've woken me up at four am to come and tell me UFO stories?" the Prime Minister asked, sounding a little frustrated.

"No sir, I've had to wake you to tell you that we have a serious problem," Harry said, trying to sound more serious as he felt he was not yet convincing the Prime Minister. "But, yes, in essence the problem is basically based on UFO stories."

"Do you want me to believe that aliens have landed? Or perhaps that we have made contact with them?" The Prime Minister had started to add a bit of sarcasm to his voice as he spoke. He had expected to be presented with news of an Al Qaeda attack or another tragic natural event, like the tsunami that had occurred in Asia just over twelve months previous, not some unknown advisor spouting stories of UFOs.

"Do you want to get to the point and tell me what has happened?" the Prime Minister stated.

Harry, realising that he would have to try harder to convince the Prime Minister continued to push on with what he had to say. This was not the first time he had told this story, having made the same presentation to the heads of MI5 and MI6 when they had taken up their roles during the recent changes within both agencies. Harry certainly remembered how he had doubted everything himself when he had first heard it a little over twelve months ago.

"Sir," Harry stood and presented the Prime Minister with a fourth folder. "The most recent, and proven, contact was made on March sixteenth this year by the crew on board the Space Shuttle Atlantis. They encountered what they reported as an unidentified craft passing the planet. Several unidentified objects were dispatched by the craft and shot into the planet's atmosphere."

"So why do we have no records of this event then?" the Primer Minister asked.

"We do," Harry stated. "NASA reported the event as a meteor shower, with six objects hitting the planet in different locations. One landed in the United States, one here in the United Kingdom. Everyone accepted the story and life progressed as normal. However, we had an agent on the inside as we have suspected for sometime that the Americans were trying to hide the truth, even from us."

"Let me guess," the Primer Minister asked, shaking his head again. "You're going to tell me that Area 51 really does exist next."

"It does," Harry replied, watching the Prime Minister's face react with disbelief. "But not where everyone believes it to be. You can read those reports at a later date Sir. As it stands so far, we are aware of six people having been killed directly at the site of the impact in the United States, but they have been trying to capture six more. These were able to escape and were known to have been on the run within the US."

The Primer Minister looked at Harry, still looking far from convinced. "What killed them then?"

"As we believe from the DPD records," Harry started.

The Prime Minister put his hand up to stop Harry. "The DPD? I've not heard of them."

"The Department of Planetary Defense," he said. "They are an agency jointly run by Homeland Security, NASA but who report solely to the Secretary of Defense. Their public mission is the detection and tracking of space objects that threaten the earth, but they began covertly dealing with this alien threat shortly after the object hit the planet."

Giving the Prime Minister a few seconds to take in the revelation of another covert government agency, he continued the original explanation.

"The evidence we have gathered shows that they were infected by something emitted by the object. Our source has been able to report back that this by way of some advanced nano-technology modifying the human genetic code. Those that died were killed when their bodies did not survive the effects of the nano-probes trying to modify their key abilities. The nano-probes are able to increase a subjects strengths, for example raising their intelligence, increasing their strength or making them faster. The problem is some people's bodies cannot take the modification and we have seen examples where their muscles themselves explode from within."

"So," the Prime Minister then interjected. "You said six of them escaped and were on the run. What happened to them?"

"We have been able to confirm that the team sent out from the DPD to investigate the initial incident were able to capture a member of the public who had been subsequently infected. They have been holding him in custody with at least two others we know they have also captured since. I do have to admit that once they were taken into their secure facility in Washington, we have had no further credible updates on these prisoners."

"Facility? How did the US government manage to keep this all covered up for so long?" The Prime Minister's interest was finally starting to grow in the conversation.

"Our agent inside was able to keep us informed that contact with an extra terrestrial object had been made and we have also been able to confirm, that they are struggling to contain the problem. In fact, I believe this problem could get out of control here if we cannot begin our response soon."

"As mentioned just now, they have been able to capture several suspected infectees. But they do not seem to be able to contain the spread of the nano-probes. Further reports from our sources in the field have confirmed that it appears that they have even been imprisoning people who appear to have become infected by a virus modified by the alien nano-probes."

"If you look through the file I just gave you, it contains confirmation of the information I have just told you."

Harry watched as the Prime Minister opened the folder and started to review the contents. Harry remembered the moment he had reviewed the evidence for himself and wondered if he had reacted in the same way. The Prime Minister had started to go slightly pale and his hands started to slightly tremble.

After a couple of minutes, the Prime Minister stood and walked across to the cabinet by the window. Opening a bottle of whiskey, he poured himself a large glass. Having taken a swig and composed himself again, he turned to look back to Harry and asked "What's the best case scenario?"

"The Americans and their DPD can regain control of the situation, contain the threat and, hopefully, even remove it all together." Harry replied, but was not able to portray any level of confidence in his answer to the Prime Minister. Because of his lack of belief in the American's capability to contain the threat, he was unable to honestly look the Prime Minister in the eyes as he spoke.

"Seeing as you have woken me at four in the morning and I strongly suspect from the lack of belief in the statement you have just made, I assume we do not believe that they contain the problem?"

"Then our worst case scenario is the Human race is now under a real and serious alien attack."

For a couple of minutes, the Prime Minister stood looking out of the window collecting his thoughts. He had not been in the job on September eleventh 2001, but wondered if this was a similar feeling his predecessor had experienced in learning that terrorists had launched a daring attack on a democratic western country.

Looking towards the stars in the sky above, he just had more and more questions forming in his mind, but realised he would probably not be getting all the answers he felt he wanted tonight. Maybe he could call the president of the United States and ask his friend to give him some more information.

Turning back to face Harry, the Prime Minister asked "It is nearly five months since the first encounter happened in America, how long have we known about this? Why has this not been brought to my attention before tonight?"

"We received the original intelligence reports the night of the encounter on board the Space Shuttle. Satellite telemetry showed multiple objects were tracked entering US airspace at a similar time on the night in question. Initially, we thought little of it given the American's history of secret projects."

As Harry spoke, the Prime Minister walked back to the chair behind his desk and sat down. He leaned back in the chair as he listened, but maintained his focus on his guest throughout.

"Within a few hours, reports were being filed, but as would be normal with this type of report you would probably never have seen these."

"However, we started getting reports that a small group of prominent 'experts' had suddenly appeared to vanish from their normal lives. But we were able to use our sources to find out that their bills were still being paid, as if someone was managing their lives for them."

"Sounds like a normal undercover operation procedure for the CIA or NSA then," the Prime Minister chipped in. "Certainly would not have been the first time of this happening either."

"Yes, that is exactly why we again did not see the need to respond. However, we started getting reports and details of strange incidents and events going on within America and contained within these reports were descriptions of several of these people."

"None of the details we were getting from our sources suggested that the DPD team were looking outside of the United States with regards to the events that had occurred. While this might be the case for this incident, we have tracked encounters before and our team are convinced that they are linked. The incident in 1980 was the first one that we in the UK have providing documented and credible evidence. With the event in October last year, it confirmed that we are as involved as they are."

"What concerned me most was that the reports we were submitting to our superiors here in the intelligence services were appearing to go un-noticed." Harry knew the accusation would shock the Prime Minister further, but this had been one of the key reasons for taking the action he had tonight.

"These reports would go where then? Who would they be submitted to?" the Prime Minister questioned Harry further.

"Through the intelligence agencies, to three high level security chiefs - the heads of MI5, MI6 and the Home Secretary. One set would also be passed to Dave Hunt who is head of the Alpha Team as you will find outlined in the Alpha Protocols we will discuss shortly."

"This is where it gets even more worrying. We strongly believe that someone was intercepting and destroying these reports. As only three people outside of the Alpha team have ever received these reports, the limit of suspicion is to them alone."

"You're saying a member of my cabinet or top security chiefs are destroying reports that concern the safety of our country?" The Prime Minister became very concerned. He was well aware that there was always going to be reports passed through government departments that he would never be privy to, in fact there were going to be many he would never want to be privy to, so was not overly surprised that he had not heard about this before. What did concern him greatly was that he was now being told that one of his ministers, whom he had come to place great trust in to allow him to do his job as Prime Minister of the United Kingdom, was not only hiding information from him, but in all probability destroying information vital for the protection of their country.

"Why would a member of my cabinet be doing that? I just can't accept that someone I have chosen to put in such a position would do such a thing."

"Unfortunately, we think that there is more to this than someone just destroying the reports," Harry said. "We think that we are dealing with an alien infectee. While the nano-probes work quickly to modify the genetic code of an infectee, we have been afraid of people possibly collaborating with others within parts of the US government who see this as a possible weapon to be developed"

"You are now saying that the US government have formed this Department of Planetary Defense to fight the threat," the Primer Minister questioned, "but they are also trying to use the threat to develop new weapons? Just as I think I am forming a good, open relationship with the president, someone always throws up something new. I'm going to have to talk to him and get to the bottom of this."

"I'm sorry Mr. Prime Minister, but you must not divulge any of this information to anyone, especially the president of the United States. We need you to immediately activate the Alpha Protocols so we can address this problem, protect our country and help the US push the alien threat back."

The Prime Minister asked suggestively, "Who else knows you are here then?"

Harry gave a slightly embarrassed look as he admitted "No one I'm afraid, well no one above me in the regular chain of command anyway."

The Prime Minister stood up and leaned across the desk as his mood darkened suddenly. He continued, "My question in that case is, how is it you been able to get a meeting with me at all without your superiors knowing?"

Harry was ready for the question but had been expecting this to arise earlier during the conversation. He had been able to take control of the conversation and had been getting into a flow.

"With all due respect Mr. Prime Minister, there are channels within your government that even you do not know exist. The reason I have been able to come and meet you in this way is because we have had procedures and protocols prepared for such an occasion."

With a heavy sigh, the Prime Minister sat back down and took another swig of his whiskey. "How many of these protocols am I not aware of then?" he asked. Quickly, he added, "Ignore that remark, that's not important right now. What is it that we need to do now then?"

Harry passed over the final folder he had been carrying as he entered the meeting. This was labelled with Top Secret classification on the cover. As he took the folder, the Prime Minister opened the front cover.

"Protocol Alpha One?" the Prime Minister read questioningly. "Defence and Containment Against Extra Terrestrial Threats."

"Yes sir." Harry replied. "Protocol Alpha One is our response to an Extra-Terrestrial contact. We must activate the team with immediate effect and begin our preparations to protect our country. "

Chapter 2

Walking from the Prime Minister's office, Harry made his way out of Chequers and returned to his car. He found that he was escorted the whole way back by one of the Prime Minister's security team.

As a result of his promotion to the newly created role of the Prime Minister's liaison to the Alpha Protocols, he had just become one of the most important people within the government. As he looked over to his escort, he was amused at still being shadowed around the Prime Minister's residence. He knew that was all due to change once word was out and he would have relatively free access to contact the Prime Minister from this point on.

Having left the building, Harry's mobile phone started to ring the moment he turned it back on. He had thought it would probably be rude if it had started to ring while he was in the meeting with the Prime Minister. He took a look at the name on the screen and saw it was the Home Secretary.

"Interesting," Harry thought. "I wonder just how would he have found out so quickly?"

Deciding to play it carefully on the phone, Harry pressed the green button to answer the call and. There was no point in letting the Home Secretary know more than he needed to know.

"Wheelhouse here," he said confidently as he climbed into the driver's seat of his car.

"Harry," the voice said. "I hear you have woken the Prime Minister up. I really hope that is not just so you can tell him stories about UFOs and aliens?"

"Not exactly Sir. I was briefing him on the issue of the Alpha Protocols." Harry responded calmly. He was trying very hard not to let his distrust of the Home Secretary creep in to his voice.

"Is that not something that could have been done during normal hours Harry?" the caller continued to say to. "And surely, would it not have been better coming from a member of his cabinet, not a lowly advisor such as you?"

"Well Sir, we believe we risk loosing control of the situation faster than we originally realised. We need to protect the United Kingdom from any potential threat that spills over," Harry explained. He paused for a couple of seconds before continuing "or do you see it differently Sir?"

"You've overstepped the line this time Harry. Don't even think that you'll be in your job tomorrow morning," the Home Secretary spat out. "I don't think there'll be anyone who will trust you after what you have done tonight. I promise you, I shall make sure of that."

"I'm afraid that's not your call any more Sir." Harry's confident and steady tone broke slightly as he let a hint of the building adrenaline in him cause him to react.

"And what do you mean by that?" came the reply, starting to sound increasingly angry.

"The Alpha Protocols have been activated with immediate effect," Harry stated. "Therefore, I now report to directly to the Prime Minister. We shall remove the alien threat from our country and then we will turn our attentions to help the rest of the world protect the entire human race." Harry smiled to himself as he finished his retort.

"We shall see about that Mr Wheelhouse."

"Good night Sir," Harry said calmly as he cut off the conversation, ending the call. He knew this would leave the Home Secretary seething and took great delight in making the first strike against the aliens and their allies.

Harry was still sitting in his car on the driveway of Chequers five minutes later, as he started to dial a number he knew well. For reasons of security, it was not stored on his mobile. He had kept it memorised until such a time that he needed it. That time had finally arrived.

"Hunt here" a very sleepy sounding voice answered at the other end after six or seven rings.

"Dave, its Harry," he said, quickly realising that he was starting to become a little bit excited by the situation. "I've just come out of a meeting with the Prime Minister. Protocol Alpha One has been activated. I need you to report to Alpha Command as early as possible this morning, at which time you will assemble your team for immediate duty."

"Alpha One?" the voice repeated sleepily. After a few seconds, "Protocol Alpha One, activated for real?" the voice continued. This time it sounded more responsive and lost the sleepy tone behind it.

"Dave, as you have seen with your own eyes, the Americans are loosing control of the threat. We have now got confirmation of a breach within the government here in the UK. We have got to activate the Alpha Team immediately to prevent falling to that threat ourselves. Sorry if I sound like I am teaching you to suck eggs, but the severity of the situation is greater than we thought. I will meet you at Alpha Command in four hours time."

He waited a few seconds for a response, but when there was none coming, he added "Dave, we've just become the most important people in the country."

"I'll see you soon Harry" Dave replied, now sounding completely awake. He disconnected the call, leaving Harry to start his journey to Alpha Command.

Having put the phone down, Dave rolled over onto his back again. With a deep calming breath, he lay staring at the ceiling.

He had worked on the Alpha Protocols for several years, but had never really expected anything to actually come from the work. It was one of those jobs that nobody in the country should ever have known existed unless the worse case scenario ever occurred.

He had seen the plans for the UK's responses to a nuclear attack, a terrorist attack with a chemical or biological weapon and even one for an asteroid impact. He had not been directly involved with writing any of those plans, but had been given the opportunity to review them as part of preparing the Alpha Protocols.

That had been until about six months ago. It was at that point they had become fully aware that the United States government had activated a set of protocols in response to a substantiated sighting by the Space Shuttle crew.

These were pretty much the same as the United Kingdom's Alpha Protocols, but from their contact within NASA, they did not appear to be containing the threat to the extent that they had been created for.

He had just returned from a hectic trip to America a day and a half before, and had still not got over the jet lag. He debated whether or not to try and go back to sleep in an attempt to grab an extra couple hours now.

In reality, he thought, I'm not going to be able to get back to sleep now.

Looking over at the clock on the bedside cabinet to his right, he saw that it was still only five in the morning. He should have guessed that when the call came, it was not going to be at a civilised hour. When did disasters ever happen at a civilised hour?

Dave decided he might as well get up and begin making the preparations at Alpha Command. This was one of many secret bases that the United Kingdom's government operated around the country. It was always fully prepped and manned twenty-four hours a day.

Only two people knew the true purpose of the base as the command centre for the Alpha Protocols in the event they were to be activated. The plan which had been released to the relevant parties contained a false location for security purposes. The fact they did not know the real location would only be revealed at the relevant time and only to the members of the Alpha Team.

He and Harry had regularly made visits to the base to ensure that it would be ready to be activated at less than four hours notice. He had inspected it himself on his return from America only the previous evening. He knew they would be fully operational within a matter of hours to begin working.

The question was what was waiting for them when they did? Dave had a strong suspicion it was not going to be good.

As he started to get dressed, he tried to resist the urge to rush as he felt a rush of both excitement and fear run through him. That had been one of the reasons he had chosen to live where he did. The drive to the command centre would only take fifteen minutes if he drove directly to the base.

He remembered one of the orders that had been recommended in an early draft of the protocols. Harry had believed that members of the Alpha Team should not follow the same route to the command centre on more than one occasion in each monthly period. That was something he didn't think he would have been able to abide by as easily living this close.

As he finished getting dressed, he caught sight of himself in the mirror. He just stood for a few seconds, trying to compose himself, taking deep breaths to help calm down from the growing excitement.

He was about to face what was likely to be a life changing moment. He was about to embark on something that most people never believed would happen at all, let alone during their lifetime. He believed that he was the best person for this job, otherwise he would not have been taken on for it.

Giving himself a little smile to reassure himself, he turned towards the bedroom door and set off towards Alpha Command.

Three hours later, Dave stood in the command room at the heart of Alpha Command.

The room itself was very well lit. The walls were painted in a clean, white colour. This left Dave feeling that it made the place feel very sanitised.

The central area of the room was taken up by a large table, surrounded by twelve chairs. Built in to the table were various monitors and keyboards, all of which could be moved up and down, with sliding covers. This meant that the table could become completely clear for use during meetings as well as serving as the main command centre during operations.

Off to his left were a number of monitors and screens hanging on the wall. Currently, they were displaying a map of Europe with three flashing points, each one representing a member of the Alpha Team about to receive activation orders.

Behind Dave, Harry entered the control room. He had made good time travelling to the Command centre and had arrived earlier than he had intended. He was glad to see Dave already working on assembling the team.

"How's it going then?" he asked as he stood next to Dave. "Have you made much progress on assembling the team yet?"

Turning to look at Harry, Dave replied, "Agents should be at the teams homes within the next hour or so and begin transporting them all here. Then we can brief the team and initiate stage one of our plan."

"Good work," Harry said. He rested his hand on Dave's shoulder and said "Let's go and get some coffee while we wait. I suspect you'll be spending enough of your time in here very shortly."

Chapter 3

Carla Wilson stood looking out her bedroom window towards the beach. She knew that she was not a morning person. She had been having problems sleeping for several years and always thought she was probably the most temperamental person when she got out of bed each morning. Maybe this was why she had never met anyone who would stay with her for all that long.

For this reason, she had chosen to live on her own. She was now forty five years old and already had one failed marriage behind her. That had lasted for a little over three months and had been a very violent affair.

Carla now lived in the town of Aberystwyth on the west coast of Wales. This suited her fine. It meant she could work from home for a marketing company based in London, but continue to maintain the high level of privacy she enjoyed.

She had so enjoyed the academic part of university life that she had completed two courses. The first had been in psychology, but she then followed this by undertaking a degree in Biology.

When she had finished university, she had worked for the government in a range of studies in relation to how the public would respond to a major incident. A couple of the most recent studies had involved incidents such as a major terrorist attack or biological event within the UK.

These would establish as to how the country would react to such attacks. They had been given a range of scenarios to propose plans on how to deal with each on for rural and urban areas through out the UK. Each study was then taken by other government departments so they could develop control plans should such an event occur.

Before she had taken her current job, the final scenario they had been presented with had her thinking that they were being set up with. They had been asked to prepare a plan in relation to how the population should be controlled in the event of an alien encounter. This included what information they could supply without causing a panic, how to supply that information and so on.

She had actually found this quite a bit more difficult than a scenario such as an outbreak of Small Pox. Those were realistic scenarios and did not need to include a plan to convince the public that the threat was real. She had written a note that even if televised pictures of a UFO landing on the Buckingham Palace front gardens were broadcast around the United Kingdom, the majority of people would still not believe it. At least with a disease like Small Pox, the reality of the situation was clear for anyone to see.

About a year ago, she had taken a role away from government work. Her current job was an easy role in a marketing company. To her, it would allow her to have a private life back. Time to do what she wanted, when she wanted.

Shame things had not worked out exactly the way she had planned them. Especially since leaving a classified job within the government did not actually mean you were free from working for them again in the future.

Draveak Bill woke with a groan. He knew he had to give up the drinking as it was getting harder and harder to get up each day.

Glancing at the clock on the wall, he could see that it was only just after nine. For what reason had he woken up early today? There were more and more days that he just could not remember what he was meant to be doing until the daily hangover cleared.

Rolling off the bed, he made his way to the kitchen and flicked on the kettle. Might as well get up anyway he thought, but to do so he was going to need a very strong, sweet coffee.

Draveak stumbled through to the toilet, but caught sight of his the message light on his answering machine flashing. He stabbed at the play button as he passed and then completed his stumble into the toilet.

"Hey Draveak," the message started. The voice was that of his lawyer. "How are you doing? Your case is due next week and you've not been returning my calls. Will you give me a call tomorrow, or knowing you, today when you get this message? Speak soon."

Finishing off, Draveak stepped over to stand at the sink to wash his hands. He looked in the mirror as he washed them, realising what a bad state he was looking these days. How had he fallen so far in such a short period of time?

It had only been a few months ago that he had been working at the European Space Agency. It was a job that he had enjoyed immensely and had still been thrilled with since the day he had started.

However, trouble with his wife had lead to serious arguments at home. Those arguments had led to her leaving him and going back home to London.

At the time he found solitude in the bottle. It would never argue with him and it never talk back either. However, the only drawback was that it did have a kick in the morning.

He thought he had kept control of his drinking so as it was not affecting his work, but after a couple of months his colleagues around him realised that it was no longer the case. Several of them had tried to encourage him to give up the drink, go for counselling, and even take some time off from work to go after his wife.

He had taken none of this advice and the drinking continued. He had been called in by his boss on several occasions and had got used to hearing the same speech at each time.

"Draveak, you are one of the best engineers in the world. You know you could be the best and you should be working with the best. You know how NASA has been after you for some time, but as long as you keep this drinking up, you are not going to be going anywhere."

It had been the same speech each time. On the fifth occasion, it had become more serious. This time he was given a written warning, told to take a week off and ordered to get off the drink.

It was at that point that Draveak had lost his temper and thrown a punch at his boss. With him left lying on the floor with his nose broken, he had then walked through to his lab and smashed the place up.

It had taken six security guards to control him, two of which were left with broken bones. It was that incident that had led to his up-coming court appearance.

Draveak was now stood in the kitchen, coffee cup in his hand, as he gazed out the window across the river. He still could not work out how he had dropped so low, something that had not helped him in trying to beat the drinking.

In just over a week he was due in court to answer charges of assault and causing bodily harm. He knew he that he did not have a leg to stand on. One way or another, he was going to be giving the drink up.

Austin Newton stood on the balcony and looked out over the sea. It was a clear, sunny day, but already the temperature had already started to creep up.

He did not like it too hot, but living here certainly beat being stuck in the UK during the winter months.

Austin came out to Gran Canaria for a few months every year, normally returning to the United Kingdom at the start of May. The rest of the year was spent working in the lab or behind a computer typing up some sort of research he'd been working on.

This year, he had been tasked with writing a number of documents which meant he had been able to stay in the Canaries during the summer months as well, an opportunity he had quickly jumped at.

He would still work while down here in the Canaries, but he wasn't put under the same pressure here. He could spend the day lounging around, take a dip in the pool to cool off, take a walk along the beach, and then work through the evening.

He could find it just as easy to work all day and then spend the evening at leisure. He knew people thought he could be so laid back in his attitude, but he found he had a lifestyle that he was more than happy with.

One thing that many people did not realise about his trips down to the Canary Islands was that it allowed him to spend time with his real passion. Space. He really enjoyed sitting behind a telescope and watching the sky at night.

Whenever he got the chance, he would take a trip over to La Palma, another of the Canary Islands, to spend time in the observatories and with the guys working over there.

Austin had written a number of short stories about alien life and alien invasion on Earth, many of which pulled upon his knowledge of physics to give them a true to life feel, something he had once been told people did not want to read in science fiction writings.

However, it had meant that his writings had been read by someone at government level and he had been asked to help write a theoretical document on how the country should respond to an alien attack.

At the time, this seemed like a bit of fun, a chance to live out bit of fantasy, but as time progressed he had become a little worried by how serious some of the people working with him had been taking this. It was as if they believed an alien invasion on Earth could actually take place.

When he had finished this project, he had spent several weeks researching into aliens and reported encounters on the internet. The more he researched the more he believed that there were some really mad people in this world.

He was happy to live in his own world of physics and science fiction writings, a world he understood and was able to accept as real.

A knock at the door caused Carla to groan out loud to herself. She had just sat down to proof read a new brochure which was going to take her most of the day and had always hated being disturbed once she had started anything.

As she walked from the living room through to the front door, the visitor knocked again. This resulted in making Carla even more agitated.

"I'm coming," she shouted as she reached the door and opened it.

"Good morning," the voice said behind it as she realised it was the local postman. He had always been friendly and courteous to her since she had moved here, especially as they had enjoyed several chats during that time. She felt sorry for having taken her frustration out on him now.

"Morning Freddy," she responded. "Sorry to shout at you like that, but you know what I'm like when I sit down to start my work."

"No problems," said Freddy, chuckling. "I've got a parcel for you today. Feels fairly heavy if you ask me." Holding out a parcel wrapped in brown paper, Carla could see that it had a hand written address on the top, along with a number of assorted stamps.

"Thanks. Do you need me to sign for it?" she asked.

"No. There's no need to sign for this one. Just been sent as normal mail for you. Always amazes me people still do that given the value of things sent by some people."

"Thanks Freddy. See you later" Carla said as she closed the door. She had to smile to herself as she heard Freddy walk back down the pathway, whistling a tune she could not place.

Making her way back to the living room, she turned the package over in her hands trying to figure out who it might have come from. She knew it was unlikely to be the office as they would never send her anything with it being signed for.

She could count her friends who might send her something on one hand, and it certainly wasn't her birthday for a few of weeks yet. She also counted her family out as she had not been on speaking terms with most of them for several years.

Carla placed the parcel on the table in her living room. As she did, her attention was caught as she noticed that the stamps used on the parcel had not been franked. Perhaps she could peel them off and use them herself later on. It would save her a few quid at a later date.

Hearing the clock in her hallway chime the hour, she took a quick look up at the clock on the wall in front of her. The time was now just after ten in the morning. She'd got a few more minutes until she had to make a call for work.

Removing the tape used to seal the parcel at one end, she quickly peeled off the brown parcel paper. Inside was a metal tin, with clip fasteners at each end to hold the lid on, like some of the food storage tins she had in her kitchen. She was growing in both puzzlement and intrigue as to who this parcel was from.

But she found that there was no note or card included within the parcel. Carla assumed that who ever had sent her the parcel must have put it inside the tin.

Opening the two catches on either side of the lid, the contents of the package made a faint, but audible click. Before she could even move to take the lid off, the whole package exploded with such force and heat all the windows in the room were blown outwards.

The explosion left a scene of devastation as the table she had been stood at with the parcel, was against the front wall of the house. From the force of the explosion, the front wall of the house collapsed on top of Carla.

Even if she were to have survived the initial explosion, her body would have been covered by enough rubble to make it hard for anyone to have got to her quickly enough to save her.

Draveak had just finished a call to his lawyer's secretary and took a look at the clock. It was now five to ten, so he would have to leave immediately if he was to get into town in time for the meeting.

He walked from the kitchen back into his bedroom and grabbed some socks from the drawer. He sat himself on the side of his bed as he pulled them on, before he pulled out a pair of black shoes from under the bed. He was still suffering from yet another handover and bending over just made his head thump even more.

Draveak sat for a few seconds with his head in his hands. He felt awful, but he had to go out and meet with his lawyer. He had liked the sound of the new secretary's voice when she had called just a couple of minutes earlier. He'd even tried a bit of flirting with her and she had sounded like she was not rebuffing his attempts. A smile crept across his face as he tried to picture what he hoped she would look like.

He took another look at the clock in front of him. He saw it was now one minute before ten in the morning. He would soon see if his luck was in today when he got to the office. Not that he could be interested in starting a new relationship with anyone other than his wife, but sometimes he just wanted to satisfy his male urges.

Draveak stood up to leave his bedroom and headed to the front door. As he passed, he took his jacket off the coat rack in the hallway and slipped it on. He leaned over to his left and grabbed the set of keys from the phone table.

Just as he opened the front door, the telephone began to ring. He looked at the display panel and it showed the phone number of his lawyer's office.

Deciding not to answer it as he would be there in the next thirty minutes or so anyway, he turned to continue opening the front door and walked out to his car. He heard his answer phone kick in as he closed the door behind him.

Draveak glanced around his front garden as he made his way over to his car, a red Ford Mustang that he had only just had imported from the United States. He shook his head slightly as he saw how wild he had let it get over the past few weeks. It hardly surprised him that the neighbours had started to complain about the state of it.

He paused to take a look across the road as he caught sight of a strange vehicle he'd not seen around his neighbourhood before. All of its windows were completely blacked out and it somehow seemed to be a little out of place for this area.

He shook his head as he decided that this was nothing he needed to worry about. It would only make him late for his appointment if he were to go and check it out. Even as he unlocked the car and opened the door, he watched as two men wearing dark grey suits climbed into the car. However, he didn't really pay enough attention to notice how both of them looked as if they were in a rush to be getting somewhere.

He would be rushing himself soon if he did not get a move on, so Draveak opened the car door and climbed in. As he sat down, he watched the strange car disappear down the road, but the nagging doubt at the back of his mind continued. He couldn't put his finger on what it was that caused him to worry about their presence.

He put the key in the ignition of the car and turned it.

As the key turned and the engine tried to start, the car exploded into a fireball which lifted the car several feet off the ground. Parts of the car and glass from the windows were blown across the garden, into the neighbour's garden and the road.

At the same moment, the sound of car and house alarms joined in as the force of the explosion sent a shockwave out and triggering alarms within two hundred feet of the explosion.

Austin Newton looked at his watch and saw it was now five minutes before eleven. That meant it was five to ten back in the UK and he ought to call back to see how his mother was doing.

She had been taken into hospital the week before for an operation on her knee and everything had gone as well as can be expected for such an operation. However, he knew she liked to be treated as if it hadn't gone so well and enjoyed the fuss he made of her.

Austin picked up the phone, starting to dial the number as he put the handset to his ear. He stopped dialling as he could not hear the normal dial tones of the numbers he was dialling.

He put the hand set back down and lifted it to his ear for a second time and found there was no dial tone either. Having replaced the handset again, he followed the cable from the phone, along the wall and towards the socket by the bottom of the hall, only to find it was still plugged in.

"Got to be the flaming Spanish phone company again," he remarked to himself, shaking his head in disbelief. "They never seem to get it right around here."

Austin walked through to the kitchen to find his mobile phone, which he normally left on top of the fridge. It was exactly where he expected to find it. He reached up and picked it up.

"Damn it," he spat out as he checked the screen on the mobile phone. "No signal"

Frustrated, he threw the phone across his kitchen on to the worktop on the opposite side of the room. As he paced back into the hallway, he remembered there was a pay phone across the road from his house. He could go and use this to make the call instead.

Austin grabbed a pair of flip flops and slipped them onto his feet. He grabbed his wallet from beside the phone, strolled out of the house and across the road to the telephone.

"At least this one isn't vandalised," he mumbled to himself picking up the handset and checking for a dial tone. "And it is working too."

He propped the handset between his shoulder and head so he could open his wallet to look for some coins to use to pay for the call and took out a couple.

As he fed them into the slot on the phone, he felt a hand on his shoulder. Taking the handset in his left hand, he looked round to see a stranger behind him.

Before he could say anything, he felt a strange feeling round his neck, like something hot sliding across it. At the same point, he found he could no longer breathe. Looking down, he saw blood running down his front, just as he started to feel faint.

The last thing he saw as he slumped to the floor was a man run off down the road ahead of him, wearing what looked like a dark grey suit. As he started to feel increasingly faint and his vision began to blur, he tried to call out for help.

He did not know if anyone had heard his shout. He was not even sure if he had made a sound as he had tried.

As Austin tried to lift himself from the floor, his strength disappeared and he collapsed. As he tried a final attempt to lift himself again, he heard the sound of a car stopping nearby, followed by the sound of someone getting out of it.

Darkness quickly followed as he started to slip into unconsciousness. The last thing Austin would ever hear was the scream from the lady driver who found his blood soaked body as he died on the footpath outside his home.

Chapter 4

Harry strode into the command room with a purpose. He was trying to find where Dave had disappeared to after he had left him getting a coffee a little over half an hour before.

"Where on Earth is he then?" he asked, partly to himself, but also in part to the two guards stood either side of the doorway.

Neither guard responded, as per their orders, until Harry addressed them directly.

"Have you seen Dave come in here recently?" he asked them directly.

"No Sir," the first soldier responded abruptly. "Not since he left with you Sir."

"Then where the hell he is?" Harry repeated. "He's not answering his phone either. I'm going to make him read the bloody protocols again from cover to cover for that. He should know better than anyone."

Harry knew that Dave was clearly aware that he should have his mobile with him and turned on at all times. It was outlined in the Alpha Protocols quite clearly, especially with respect to him being the team leader and probably the most important person within the entire operation.

He needed to find him urgently as things had not been going according to plan with regards to assembling the team. They needed to try and prevent the situation from rapidly falling into disarray. Harry walked back out of the command room and headed towards the heart of the command centre to continue his increasingly urgent search.

Walking down the main corridor, Harry could reach almost all the rooms in the complex on this level. As he walked down, he passed the various labs, computer rooms, communication rooms and the main break room area. There was still no sign of Dave in any of these.

At the end of the corridor, he had reached the complex's gym and could see someone moving through the frosted glass wall. He could tell by the shape and size, it was definitely a man in there. Given the height, he was fairly certain it had to be Dave.

"Where is your mobile then?" he asked gruffly as he entered the gym. "You should know better than…." He trailed off before finishing "You look knackered."

"Just my way of keeping busy Harry," he replied. Looking around the room as he ran, he continued by saying "My phone is, um, back in the changing room."

Dave stopped the treadmill and came to a gradual halt. He was an especially keen runner and was regularly found spending time in the gym on the treadmill. Over the years, he had run the marathon on several occasions, along with a host of half marathons and shorter distances.

Although not the fastest of runners, and definitely not with the physique of an average runner, he was extremely fit. Harry had known him for a couple of years now and did not know too many people outside of the military units they dealt with who could show similar levels of fitness.

Dave had been running for just under twenty-five minutes and had run just over four miles. Sweating profusely, he took his towel from the rail next to the treadmill and started to wipe himself down.

Harry's phone started to ring.

"Wheelhouse," he said answering the phone. As he listened, his head dropped and he brought his other hand up and covered his face.

"Thanks," Harry said to the caller, failing miserably to hide his concern from Dave.

"What is it?" Dave asked, "What's wrong?"

"We've just been alerted to a problem with Carla Wilson. The system has picked up a report of an explosion in her road and our agents cannot get to the house at the moment. That was one of them who is trying to get through and see what is going on as we speak."

"Give me a moment, I'm getting changed," Dave responded. "I'll meet you in the command room."

Harry turned and started towards the door of the gym as Dave headed in the opposite direction towards the changing rooms.

"You better make it quick though." He said as he stopped and looked back at Dave. In an attempt to lighten the moment, he tried to say jokingly "You better shower as well, you're going to stink!"

As Dave entered the command room, he could see a live news feed on one of the screens across the wall. It looked like a bomb scene with a view of an extremely badly damaged property behind the reporter and quite significant damage to the houses near it.

"What's going on?" he quizzed Harry, crossing over to get a closer view of the report on the screen.

Turning so he was able to face Dave, Harry looked paler than when he had left the gym. As Dave looked away from the screen and back to where Harry was sitting, it became obvious something was drastically wrong.

"That's not Carla's place is it?" Dave continued, pointing at the pictures on the screen. "Please tell me that she was not in there."

"I'm afraid so. They have pulled a female body out of the house, but no-one has confirmed the identity yet. Our agents were able to get through and they have spoken to the postman who was still delivering mail to the houses further up the road. He reckoned that something exploded in her house. He also reported having delivered a strange parcel this morning, but didn't think much about it at the time."

Dave put his hands to his head in frustration. "Damn" he shouted loudly. "Damn, Damn. Damn. Carla was a key part to this team. I really hope that isn't her."

Harry's phone rang again. "I hope this is better news" he said, putting the phone to his ear.

While he listened to the phone, Harry did not saying anything. He leaned over the table and with a few key presses, changed the channel on the screen from Sky News to the BBC 24 hour news channel.

A second scene of devastation was being shown, with a news reporter outlining how a car in this quiet neighbourhood had exploded with a single occupant in. There were eye witness reports of extensive damage to properties along the road. Police were also reporting at least five casualties in the immediate area.

"Something is going very wrong here" Harry said solemnly as he ended the call, looking directly over at Dave. "It looks like Draveak is dead too. Agents are now arriving on the scene to pick him up, but they found the emergency services were already attending the site. It looks like his car has exploded, initial signs show a large scale blast occurred on the driveway where he was parked."

"One could be an accident," Dave said. "Two is just suspicious to say the least."

Harry's phone rang again. "This had better be good news or I'm going to scream"

As he sat listening to what was being said, Harry sank back into his chair, the look of horror etching deeper into his face.

Within a few seconds, Harry quickly stood up and threw the phone across the command centre.

With that, he angrily shouted out "For the love of God."

Dave, becoming increasingly concerned walked closer to Harry. "Austin. Tell me he is okay." He laid his hand on his colleague's shoulder offering some comfort to his boss.

"Dead. The whole team is dead." Harry was obviously upset by the events going on. He did not really know the team in the same way Dave had come to know them, but had formed a sort of bond with them when they had previously met.

"Austin was found with his throat slashed outside his home. Agents are waiting for the Spanish police to arrive. One of them has taken a look around the house. He found the phone line outside the front door was cut. There is something that really does not add up here."

Dave pulled a seat out from the table and sat down. None of the information regarding the team had been included in the Alpha Protocols plan that had been distributed. This meant that there were only a few people who knew who the members of the team actually were.

He should have been the only one to know where the team members lived until such a time as the protocols were activated. Then he would release the information to the relevant parties to collect the team members and bring them all Alpha Command. He was aware that even Harry would not have known where they lived until that time.

Dave had kept the information secure on the Alpha system and only he had the passwords. At least he hoped he did. He had to check to see if anyone else may have had access without him knowing.

Swinging round to face the computer screen on the table, he started to log on to the system.

Harry had walked back over to the screens on the wall and was watching the news reports closely. He was trying to see if there was anything on the screen he could see that might give them some hint as to what might have happened.

Dave logged on to the system and began to access the security logs for the Alpha system. He did not expect to find any accesses to the team data files prior to this morning for anyone but himself.

His eye was caught by an interesting entry shortly after five am that morning. As he scrolled further through the list, he was able to find additional discrepancies in the logs.

"Harry, come and take a look at this" he said, a slight hint of surprise entering his voice.

"What is it?" he replied, leaving the news reports so he could view the screen over Dave's shoulder.

"It looks like someone was trying to access our systems this morning. Someone with clearance to most of our systems has tried to view the team's records. They have then tried to delete the log entries to cover their tracks. They've made a good job of it too, except there is an entry from the system confirming deletion of the records."

"So who would have that sort of access to the systems?" Harry started to ask.

"You mean other than me and you?" Dave finished. "The team would not have done until they had arrived here anyway, and certainly never from outside of Alpha Command either. That leaves just our three overlords. Or someone smart enough to break in through the triple firewall system that we have put in place and show no trace of doing so."

Harry pointed his finger at Dave. "You better not let them hear you calling them that. But I will have to agree. One of our superiors is the most likely candidate. In fact, one of them called me as I left the Prime Minister's and before I called you this morning."

Dave closed down the connection to the system and turned in the chair so he could look up at Harry. "Let me guess, the Home Secretary?"

Harry nodded to show Dave had guessed correctly. "I'm afraid so. It appears the breach goes deeper than we discussed only yesterday. We need to regain control of this now."

Dave decided that it was time that he had to take control of the situation. After all, that was why he had been chosen to do this job. He turned to Harry and started to issue his instructions.

"Right, I want to get the agents currently there to stay at each of the incidents sites and have them thoroughly investigate each one. Get them anything they need to do this. Tell them to leave no stone unturned. I want the proof of who did this and how. We have got to preserve any evidence before the police or anyone else gets in the way."

"Get Draveak's car impounded and back here as soon as possible. There must be some clues on there somewhere. Even if it only gets us whoever planted a device on it, I want to know. That information might be able to lead us back to the source of the attacks."

Harry nodded his agreement and started to move across the command room to where he had earlier thrown his mobile phone.

Dave had stood up from the chair and was looking over Harry. There was a determined look replacing the shock that had been there only minutes before.

"I'm going to stage two of the Alpha Protocols. We're going to make contact with the DPD. We're going to need their help more than ever now."

Chapter 5

"We might have a little problem Lucy," Bob Forster announced as he entered the DPD command room.

Lucy Tyler and Al Johnson were stood together looking at the screens across the wall of the command room. On display was a map of the United States, along with profiles of two suspected infectees they had been trying to locate.

Lucy turned to face Forster, and then noticed Bale was following closely behind him. The look on his face showed he was more than a little concerned.

"What do you mean by a little problem?" she asked both men quizzically.

Forster offered her a sheet of paper. "Make of it what you will, but some guy wants to talk to you. He asked for you by name. He wants a video call in five minutes"

"Dr Tyler," Johnson said in his authoritive voice, but allowing a hint of sarcasm to creep in. "You, as team leader, should know better about that. You don't just go giving some guy your phone number here."

Lucy looked back over towards Johnson, putting an equally feigned look of hurt on her face. But before she could say anything in response, she was interrupted.

"I don't think that would have made a difference," Bale said. "It appears this call came in over one of our secured channels. We could not even track the call so I cannot say where it came from other than it was not a standard US accent."

"Right. Definitely not American." Forster said while looking at Bale. Turning back to face Lucy, he continued "It was a British accent. Quite plain, but definitely British. English if you want me to be a bit more to the point."

Lucy looked at the details on the piece paper Forster had passed her. There was little information regarding the call other than the date, time, who received it and a message. The message read "Be ready to take my call in five minutes."

"You'd better get your best people onto this Bale" Johnson ordered. Pointing directly at the agent he continued. "I want to know who this is, where he is from and what the hell he wants."

Just a couple of minutes later, the computer on the table in front of Lucy flashed up a message to say a video call was waiting to connect. She looked at her boss, who nodded back that they were ready. She clicked on accept call.

On the screen to the side of the command room where they had previously been viewing the map, the face of a young man appeared. Lucy guessed at early thirties, but there was something familiar about him. She just could not put her finger on it, but she was positive she recognized him.

Alongside the image of the caller, there was an image of the command centre as it would be view from the other end. Lucy knew this was so they could view the images they were sending on a video call, but this never made it any easier to deal with. She never liked to see herself on TV or in the paper. When she did, it normally meant their cover was in danger.

Lucy stood and walked to stand closer to the screen. It was a move to make herself the focus of the caller's attention.

"Good morning. My apologies for not addressing you by name, but I'm afraid you have all of us at a loss," she announced.

"First of all, thank you for taking this call. Secondly, Mr. Bale, you can stop your people tracing this call. Mainly, because you won't be able to. Also, by the end of this call you will know as much as you need to make a decision as to trust me or not."

Pausing as he switched his full attention back to Lucy, he continued. "Thirdly, I am guessing you have a vague recollection of me Dr Tyler. Am I right?"

"I have to admit I do," Lucy replied. Shaking her head slightly, she said "You are very familiar but I just cannot seem to place you at all"

"My name is Dave Hunt, and we have met twice before Dr Tyler. Firstly, I was at your presentation on planning for an outbreak of a deadly contaminant last year. It was in this you outlined scenarios to frighten us all. Unfortunately, it had no such effect on me. I must apologise for the rather directed questions after the lecture."

"I do remember that," she said, partly turning back to address the others at the table. "That gentleman was the one I had a few things to say about following that lecture."

"None of them good, I take it?" Forster added quietly towards Bale, with an element of sarcasm involved. He did not like this man they were talking to and he had never been one to shy away from hiding his feelings.

"I'm not surprised by that. My questions were directed for a reason, one that is about to become plainly obvious very shortly. The second time we met was a week ago. I hope the bruises have cleared up by now?"

Lucy paused before answering. She quickly thought back to where they had been the previous week. The one event that jumped straight to mind was the incident in the warehouse.

"Chicago," she exclaimed. "That was you? You told me that we were not alone in this fight. Help was at hand. What did you mean by that?"

"All shall be clear very soon. Does the name Alpha Protocols mean anything to you?"

"No I can't say it does." Lucy replied honestly. Her interest in this guy was definitely captured. "Al, what about you? Anything you can provide information on?" Lucy turned to face Johnson as she asked.

"Sorry Lucy," he replied. "That means nothing to me at all."

"Okay then," Dave interjected. "Perhaps the date of the twenty sixth of December 1980 might ring any bells with any of you?"

Lucy looked at the others again, all of whom shook their heads. Turning back to the screen, she shook her head and replied "I have to say no to that as well."

"Okay. Does Atlantis, March 16th 2006 mean anything to you?"

Forster looked to Bale, noting that he was still maintaining focus on the screen, before turning back himself. Lucy maintained a composed appearance, knowing that it appeared this guy was obviously already up to speed on their operation already.

"Given that reaction, I think my question is answered. My sources have kept me informed of the events of the past five months or so. Starting with the encounter by the Space Shuttle Atlantis and the subsequent events. We have been able to monitor how your Department of Planetary Defense is struggling to cope with the alien threat. As you are now probably now starting to realise, we have been observing your team's activities at close quarters."

"Why?" Lucy asked. "What do we have of interest to you then?"

"The story starts about twenty four years ago in eastern England. The Alpha Protocols were initially formed in 1981 following an incursion in to UK airspace by an unidentified object around a couple of our country's joint airbases in Suffolk. Since then, we have developed the Alpha Protocols to where they stand today. I am pretty sure we are probably following similar procedures to each other, but as you must also be realizing, you have not been able to contain the threat as intended."

"How do you know your sources are correct Mr. Hunt?" Bale asked.

"As part of the Alpha Protocols and thanks to British intelligence at MI5 and MI6, we have been able to keep an extremely close eye on occurrences and events around the globe. We in the UK were able to put together an extremely good team. Many of these people are working in other governments and agencies around the globe. While they know they are working with or for the British agencies, they do not know what the purpose of the information is really for."

"Initially, the protocols were developed under the control of the UK government. But about six months ago, we had to become our own separate agency. We gathered a small team of experts, whom we called the Alpha team. Each was the leader in their field. Each was told that they were part of a project looking into extraterrestrial research, but that is the extent of their knowledge of what was happening."

"I guess that was sort of the same process we had here," Lucy interrupted with. "But not all of our team were necessarily volunteers from the start. Given circumstances, not everyone gets the choice to not be involved. Please go on."

"Well, once we got word of an impact in the United States shortly after the encounter, we started to receive reports from many of our various sources. While many of our top intelligence people initially washed over these reports, many were soon passed to me here. At this point I arranged for you, and as we became aware of them, your team members to be shadowed."

Lucy took a quick look over her shoulder to her colleagues. Bale gave a quick shrug suggesting that they had not been aware of being watched. She turned her attention back to the screen as Dave continued.

"This was not the easiest assignment some of our guys have had. Therefore we have had to piece together some of the information. One of you in particular has been extremely hard to find background information on."

Lucy again looked back to her team members sitting behind. She stopped at Bale, knowing that it was most likely him that they could find limited information on, especially as she could not do so herself either. Maybe this would be a chance for her to learn more about his elusive background.

"So is that why you were in Chicago then?" Lucy asked as she turned back to address Dave again.

"Yes. But there is more information that we need to share first. Basically, on October 20th last year, we received multiple reports of a number of unidentified objects observed over a twenty mile stretch of the M25 motorway around London. These were reports that our experts in the UK were able to supply evidence and cover stories to prove it as a hoax."

Bale stood up and asked "You said that these objects were proved to be a hoax?"

"No, we supplied evidence intended to make people think it was a hoax. I am sending you copies of the records we have collated of this incident – photos, videos taken by observers, interviews, radar records. I would hope you can check these against any records you have. We may be able to work together to help build a better picture of this particular event."

"I have also included a recording of multiple transmissions picked up at the time of the appearance of the objects during October. As is a transmission that was intercepted in the encounter in 1980, along with the relevant files we still hold on the event."

He looked down to something away from the screen and Lucy saw movement as if he was typing on a keyboard. After a couple of seconds, Dave added "the data should be arriving about now."

Lucy walked back around to where Bale was sitting and looked at the monitor in front of him. She could see that they were receiving the data

"Can you give us a minute please Mr Hunt?" Lucy asked looking back up to the screen. "I need to speak with the rest of the team while we take a look at this information."

"Please, drop the Mr. Hunt. Just call me Dave. Keep the line open, but feel free to cut the sound and video if you wish" he replied.

"Cut the feeds" Lucy said to Bale. Once he acknowledged the feeds were cut, Lucy addressed the whole team by asking "What the hell do you make of this?"

"I think we all knew that at some point this would come out, especially after last weeks little incident in Chicago. I think we're lucky that these people appear to be on our side," Bale replied. "We have received the information from him and I am just going to check our records for any information on these Alpha Protocols."

"These guys sound pretty keyed up on us, so I really hope someone in our intelligence services is as keyed up on them," Johnson added. He realised he did not need to make the point to Lucy or their team, but felt he had to make it anyway. "This is a serious lapse which makes 9/11 pale into insignificance. I'm especially concerned if he is right that people in our own agencies might be feeding information to them."

Bale had turned back to face the computer console on the table as Johnson spoke. With a few keystrokes he initiated a search on the term Alpha Protocols. Only one entry was returned, which he opened.

The entry returned stated very little beyond what they had already learned during the conversation with Dave. Their records told him that the Alpha Protocols were indeed a response to a possible alien threat, initially developed in the early 80's. It did appear that the United Kingdom had been ahead of them in preparing for such an event.

Frustratingly, the system contained no more information other than two lines of text entered at the bottom of the screen. The first line contained the phrase 'Current Status Unknown'. This was followed by the date and the agency responsible for the entry. To Bale's surprise, this showed that the entry had been made by a director of the NSA only yesterday.

Bale switched the display to show on the wall monitor in the room for the rest of the team to see.

"Well it looks like this is something our data guys here at the department have missed if the NSA is making new entries on this," Bale announced.

"Try looking up that date he gave us. October twentieth 2005. Let's see what we have on that," Johnson instructed.

Bale entered the date and started a search. An extensive list of results was displayed, none of which in the top selection looked likely hits. Bale then entered London as an additional search word. This resulted in cutting the list of results by about a third. Next, he added a third search criterion of the name M25.

This resulted in cutting the list to eight different entries. The top entry looked like an intercepted report about road traffic incidents on the road on the date in question. The second and third entries looked like reports involving road works and maintenance reports from the UK agencies.

The fourth entry grabbed everyone's attention. It had been taken from N.A.S.A. and had been filed three days after the event. Opening the related data files with the report, maps of the UK appeared on the screen, along with what looked like flight paths across the southern part of the country.

At the monitor next to Bale, Lucy was searching through the records they held to see if she could find any reference to Dave Hunt. Despite his obvious suggestion the British agencies had been able to gather rather too much information about them, they should have been able to do the same as well.

After a few seconds, a file was returned showing a profile of Dave Hunt. The picture matched the person they had been talking and information from a number of American agencies had indeed been collated.

"It looks like our friend is above board then," Forster said as he looked over Lucy's shoulder. "So, are we going to get back to him then?"

"Open the feeds again," Lucy said to Bale. "Let's get some more information from Mr Hunt."

"Sorry about that Dave," Lucy said to him once the feeds had been re-established. "I just wanted some verification on what you are telling us. Please feel free to continue where we left off."

"No problems, I know our Prime Minister needed a little convincing before he signed the activation of the protocols a little over twelve hours ago. The team was to be activated as it was now felt the threat to both our country and the planet was at its highest level we had ever seen. Little did we know that the threat went as high as it did within the UK government itself."

"Two days ago I arrived back in the UK from my stint observing you and the team was activated this morning. None of them made it to Alpha Command, our control centre here. Initial reports indicate that they were all murdered at their homes before our agents arrived, but investigations are still going on." This was the first time in the duration of the meeting that any real emotion was visible on Dave's face. It started to show that he had obviously endured something pretty traumatic in the past few hours.

"I'm really sorry to hear that," Lucy said.

"We are working to get new members promoted to the Alpha Team. They will have been fully briefed on the situation and will be aiding the search for what we believe is an infectee infiltrating our government."

"Did you just say an infectee is in your government?" Lucy asked, her interest suddenly caught as the potential escalation of the threat hit her.

"Yes. I do believe that would be the only way the information on the Alpha team could have got out. As well as me, only five people are aware of the Alpha Protocols. They are the Prime Minister, the head of MI5, the head of MI6 and Home Secretary. Then we have Harry Wheelhouse, who actually has overall control of the operation."

Behind her, Lucy could hear as one of her team began to type on a keyboard to find more information on the names they were getting. She hoped that Dave did not see, but she knew that she would have expected the same if the conversation had been in the opposite direction.

"I do not believe that the leak would have been the Prime Minister as he was only made aware of the protocols when he signed the activation order earlier this morning," Dave explained. "At no time were the names of those involved given to him."

"The head of MI5 and the Home Secretary could both have gained access to the information if they knew where to dig. From our system logs whoever it was obvious they knew where to look and how to cover their tracks. Other events occurrences point us directly to one of them, but we need concrete evidence before we can justify any action."

"And you believe that this was why your team was not able to be assembled as you planned?" Lucy asked.

"As I said, it appears each team member was murdered," Dave said abruptly, the pain of the loss evident in his response. "We believe they where taken out by military strike teams, and we believe one had been sent to take me out as well. However, I was already at Alpha Command. Our agents have worked with the local authorities and cover stories were given as to how and why the team members were killed."

"Our command centre is well hidden, so much so that even those within in the team would not know its location until the time was right. We took the precaution as part of the protocols to have multiple centres on standby. This meant that should anyone be able to uncover the location of one base, we could quickly relocate. However, the actual location of our primary command centre was only known to two people at any one time."

"However, the new members of the team are obviously not going to be familiar enough with the threat or ways to defend against it. We need your help in trying to establish the complete picture here in the UK."

"What do you think we can offer you then?" Johnson asked. "You seem to know as much about things as we do."

"Dr Tyler, that's what." the answer came. "I realize that you have plenty of problems going on your side of the Atlantic, but we could do with some assistance. Plus I would also like to see how we can work together to improve a global approach to preventing this alien threat."

"I don't think we can really allow this," Johnson stated firmly.

"I think we have something that will make your mind up. Do you recognize this image?" Dave asked.

On the screen appeared a picture of what looked like a virus, but its outer skin looked metallic. The detail was incredible, especially when compared to some of the images they themselves had collected.

"A copy of this image was intercepted as an attachment on an email two weeks ago," Dave outlined. "We believe that the images that were intercepted on the same message prove that someone is attempting to modify this nano-probe so it can be used as a weapon. We think that the original version came from the US, but as yet we cannot track where from. Someone has covered their tracks sufficiently to give us a problem, but our systems were able to break their encryption keys quite easily."

"Modified so as not to infect people?" Lucy asked. "We've been able to analyse the nano-probe, but no more than that yet."

"As I said, we suspect someone is working on modifying the nano-probe for purposes other than trying to protect ourselves against its danger, but as yet, we have still not been able find out who or how."

"To be honest," Lucy said, "That does not come as any surprise."

"If they can modify it so that it does not infect people, is it possible that its effects can be controlled?" Dave asked.

"It is possible, but we're no where near that level of success in breaking the signal down," Forster responded. "If someone was trying to do that, I would expect to see a lot more infectees running round."

"That leads me on to the big topic we need to discuss with you is how we think we have discovered a way that might be able to limit the genetic mutation of an infected person."

"How?" Forster asked, pretty much jumped up out of his seat at the news. "I've not found a way to do that yet, and if I might say so myself, I am probably the best person in the world to be solving that."

"Please don't get too upset. We are still going to need your help and resources to complete our work, and then we need to run any number of tests. You probably hold more infectees captive than we do, unless I am very much mistaken."

Forster sat back down in his seat, mumbling to himself. He really could not see how someone else would have been able to beat him to finding a way to prevent the genetic mutation within an infectee. There was no one better than him in the world with regards to alien viruses.

Lucy, ignoring Forster's reaction, turned to Johnson and said "I think I have got to go. Bale and Forster can look into the source of that email from this end. I guess it might take them a couple of days to get to the bottom of this. Forster can talk with the relevant people once I can establish who that is. I think that there is a great deal we can learn from them when I get over there."

She turned to Bale putting her back to Dave and said to him quietly "I want you to find out who is leaking information to them. But keep it quiet from these guys okay."

"Lucy, we can't really spare you at the moment," Johnson stressed. He was far from happy at letting Lucy go for any length of time.

"I think we need to utilize any friends and resources we can at the present moment. This is by far the best lead we have had yet. If I go tonight, I can be back in four days. I'm positive the guys are more than capable of dealing with any issues that come up."

Lucy held up her mobile phone and finished by saying "And I am only on the end of this."

She turned back to face the screen and continued "I will get a flight to the UK tonight, but where's the best place to fly into then?"

"Heathrow. Use a commercial flight. I'm afraid that we need to maintain a certain level of secrecy, so contact me with the details as soon as possible. I will also give you secure numbers for lines we know are not tapped in any way."

"Okay. I'll speak to you shortly then." Lucy turned and said to Bale "Cut the feeds. Let's get organized."

Chapter 6

Arriving at Heathrow airport, Dave casually made his way from the car park and into Terminal three. Lucy Tyler's flight was not due to land for another twenty minutes or so. Given the amount of time it took for flights to taxi from the runway, he knew that he did not need to rush to the terminal gate.

He walked towards the arrivals gate, making his way through the regular airport crowds who were arriving back from holidays or business trips. A security guard stepped out in front of him and blocked the way through.

"No way in here Sir," he announced, placing his hand on Dave's chest to stop him. "This is the way out of the airport for those arriving. You can't come through here."

Dave took a badge from his pocket and presented it to the security guard.

The guard took the badge and examined it closely. The name given on it was Dan Livermore and his job was Terminal Security Liaison Manager. He looked sceptical but given the size of the airport, he knew he did not know all the staff. The badge was certainly one he recognised as the official identification for airport staff.

"I'm sorry Mr. Livermore," he said, passing back the badge. "Please go through, but you really must wear your identity badge while you are in the terminal building to save any problems."

Dave nodded his thanks to the security and pinned the badge to his jacket lapel. He turned to continue his way through the arrivals gateway and into the terminal. He made it through the baggage halls and customs areas without any further delays, although he did notice several of the airport staff glancing towards the badge as he passed.

The flight that Lucy had arrived on was due to arrive at gate 22, one of the furthest from the main terminal building. Before leaving Alpha command, Dave had ensured that he was familiar with the layout of the terminal building, just as was outlined in the Alpha Protocols with regards to mission preparation. With a sigh, he started the walk out to the gate.

On the way, he took careful note of the people around him. He knew that observation and analysis of situations, surroundings and people were key skills needed by members of the intelligence services, let alone the members of the Alpha team. There were times that their lives would depend on those skills. If you were to let your awareness of your surroundings drop, then you might not get a second chance.

The majority of the people around him were heading for the customs and arrivals halls, but there was also a steady flow of people heading out to gates, preparing for their departures.

Smiling to himself, he remembered how several visits ago to the airport he had been here to get on a flight to the Canary Islands for a two week getaway. Now, nothing more than a memory, he wondered if he could get away like that again any time soon. Maybe not very likely he thought, snapping his thoughts back into the present.

Looking at his watch, he noted that Lucy's flight should now have landed and would now be well on its way taxiing towards the gate.

As he passed gate seventeen, Dave noted a couple of armed police stood to the left of the hallway. Further up on the right, there was another pair chatting between themselves. Still, this was a typical site in most airports around the world since the events of September eleventh 2001. Visual displays of security were as much a part of reassuring the public as it was a deterrent to anyone wanting to cause problems.

What definitely appeared not to be normal around the terminal were the eight smartly dressed men loitering around this part of the building.

Taking a quick look at them, Dave noted that all were wearing smart grey suits, light grey shirts and black ties. Dave guessed that each one was also likely to be armed, although the guns were obviously kept out of sight from ordinary passengers. They probably had small arms weapons concealed under their jackets, as was typical of this group of agents working out of MI5.

Dave took the mobile phone out of his pocket and quickly dialled Harry's number.

"As expected," he said to Harry as he answered, "the party has been gate crashed. Best notify the other guests to be ready."

"Will do," Harry replied. "Good luck Dave."

Dave pressed the button to disconnect the call and slid the phone back into his jacket pocket. Casually glancing around, he made a quick check to satisfy himself that none of the agents had reacted to his presence.

As he approached gate twenty-two, the airport staff were walking around preparing for the arrival of the passengers about to leave the plane. Through the window, he could see that the aircraft was making its final movements into place for the doors to open and allow the passengers to disembark.

Dave watched closely as the eight agents were making their way closer to the gate. Two of them headed beyond the gate itself and stood about fifty yards from the far side of the gate. Two more had made their way across to the gate opposite and were loitering amongst a growing crowd of passengers gathering for their flight.

A further two had stopped and were stood talking about fifty yards back down the corridor. One was stood looking back down the hallway idly chatting to the other, who was himself trying to not look as if he was watching the gate area itself too closely.

One of the remaining agents had made his way to sit on a seat just outside the gate. As he did so, he picked up a newspaper left on the seat next to him. From his actions, Dave could see he was also trying to casually watch the gate area over the top of the paper.

The final agent had a quick word with one of the staff members on the gate before being guided on to the gantry and towards the aircraft door.

Looking around the terminal area, few, if any passengers, had even noticed these extra men around them. Most probably took one look and put them down as business men. Why should they think any different? Many of them are on their way to their holidays, Dave thought. They would not be interested about suited men who are probably off on some business trip.

Suddenly passengers started to make their way off the aircraft. Being an overnight flight from Washington, many appeared to be tired, just wanting to get out of the airport and on to their destination. Others, who were probably even more tired, just wanted to stay out of the way of those behind who were rushing to get out of the airport.

A vibration in his pocket alerted Dave to his mobile phone going off. Taking it out of his pocket, he took a look and it displayed a new text message had just arrived.

Opening the text, it said "Just arrived, waiting at gate 18 now."

Dave, taking a quick look at the men stood around the gate smiled to himself. Guessing the reception that might have been arranged to greet Lucy's arrival, she had booked a flight from

Washington under her real name. However, she had actually taken a second flight from Washington under an alias.

If someone at a high level in either of their governments was in deed aiding the alien threat, then they fully expected them to be monitoring any activities by either of the two agencies. Any meeting between members of either team could pose a serious threat to their plans.

As Dave turned to walk back towards gate eighteen, he failed to notice one of the agents who had taken up position at gate twenty-one turn to watch as he walked away. After a quick whisper in the ear of his partner, he started to say something into his jacket lapel.

Initially, none of the other agents moved to follow him, but they all closely watched Dave as he walked back down the hallway.

Approaching gate eighteen, Dave saw Lucy, briefcase in hand. She was waiting to one side of the gate as the last few passengers from the plane filed past her. She stood looking down the terminal building, opposite to the way he was approaching her from.

He paused to allow himself to take a good look at her. While he had seen her during his turn for surveillance in America, and again during yesterday's video meeting, the only time he had been closer than this, he had been forced to make his escape before Bale had tried to shoot him. This was the first time he had been able to view her as close up as this in more normal circumstances.

She was looking smart, but casually dressed in a pair of black trousers and a loose fitting, dark blue top. Thinking back, Dave actually could not remember a time when he thought she had not appeared smartly dressed, even when she was in action out in the field.

"Good morning Dr Tyler. You're looking a bit better than last time I saw you in the flesh" he said, smiling gently as he finally approached her. "I hope you had a good flight?"

"Yes, thank you. Is there much of a reception waiting for me then?" she asked as she turned to face Dave.

"I estimate there are eight. Not a bad count for someone who is meant to be a friend. I dread to think what reception you would get if you had been a terrorist or an alien," he said jokingly.

Dave took a quick look back over his shoulder as he noticed Lucy's glance beyond him, back where he had come from. "Oh shit," he said. Turning back to face Lucy, "Walk with me now. I think we might have been spotted."

Lucy took another look over his shoulder as he put a hand on her arm and started to guide her down the hallway. She saw that four of the suited men had started to make their way from gate twenty two towards them.

As they started to walk down the corridor away from the on-coming agents, she noted the two armed police officers on the opposite side of the corridor had also turned their attention towards them.

"It looks like our little surprise is no longer a surprise," she said sounding slightly concerned. Despite having been having been shot at before in the line of her duty, she had been able to carry her own weapon. Here she felt more vulnerable than she had done for some time.

"It looks like we might need to make a run for it," Dave said, continuing to lead her along the corridor as they started to pick up the pace. Looking down towards her feet, he added "I hope you have got the right shoes for it Lucy."

As they made their way up the hallway, Dave started to drift towards the left side of the corridor, heading towards the t-junction they were approaching. Lucy followed him. As they turned the corner, he took Lucy's hand and they broke into a run.

Lucy kept close behind him and could hear voices behind them starting to shout orders for them to stop. As they ran, she took a quick look over her shoulder again to see six of the suited agents in pursuit behind them. They had their guns drawn and were picking up their speed to keep up with them. As Lucy dropped back slightly, Dave had to let go of her hand. However, she was still able to keep pace with him.

Around them, alarm started to spread amongst the people in the in corridor. Most stood looking around to see what the source of the commotion was, while others were moving towards the walls to keep out of the way.

As they approached the end of the corridor, two more agents stepped into the corridor in front of them. One stood on each side, both had their guns drawn and pointed directly towards them. Lucy felt this did not look a good situation.

Suddenly, she saw two flashes coming from just ahead of Dave, followed by two familiar sounding shots. At that instant, almost everyone in the corridor around them dropped to the floor, leaving them and the six suited men behind standing. Some people started to scream and shout as they became more unsettled by the events.

As they passed the two suited men, both of whom were now sprawled on the floor, she slowed as she wanted to stop to see if they were still alive. Dave grabbed her hand and urged her to keep on running.

"They're just stunned," he shouted to her. "But we need to get out of her now."

Entering the baggage hall, Dave led her towards the customs area beyond. They were still running as several of the security personnel in the customs hall reacted to the growing commotion approaching them. They started to move as if to block their way out.

"Security," Dave shouted, waving them out of the way with the hand holding the gun. "Get out of the way. Now!"

One of them was the guard who had spoken to Dave earlier when he had first made his way into the arrivals area. Instinctively, he stepped aside to let them through and waved to his colleagues to do the same.

"What about my bags?" Lucy asked.

"We'll sort them out later," Dave replied. "I'll get someone to pick them up for you."

Still running, they quickly cleared the customs hall. They left not only confused passengers behind them, but also stunned security and police. Many of the passengers were starting to panic at the sudden events going on around them, and in particular the appearance of several armed people. A number started to move towards the various exits around the area, which included the passageway they had just come from.

This confusion was what Dave had hoped for as the agents ran straight into a crowd of people blocking the customs hallway. This allowed Dave and Lucy the time they needed to head across the terminal entrance hall and turn towards the exit to the car parks.

Waiting members of the public reacted in a similar way to the passengers who had been in the baggage halls. Screams and shouts started to fill the air as panic started to spread amongst the crowd.

As Dave considered the growing panic and confusion behind them, he knew the longer it will take the agents to catch with them. The more time they could gain, the less risk they would face of a possible shoot out with the agents in a public place.

The passage leading towards the car park ran up a slope, but luckily there were few people around at this moment in time. There was a row of luggage trolleys at the top of the ramp.

As they reached them, Dave stopped and twisted the front one away from the wall. The rest followed as part of the trolley train. Lucy had to step aside, watching as he moved the trolleys and pushed them back down the passage way.

The slope of the passage caused the trolleys to pick up enough speed to roll quickly down the slope. As Dave headed past her and towards the car park, she saw the first of the agents appear at the bottom of the passage. He had to dive out of the way through the doorway he had just entered through as thirty or so trolleys came crashing towards him.

"That will give us a few seconds more," Dave said leading the way towards the car park. "Now come on."

As they ran along the next passage way, Dave took a headset out of his jacket pocket and put it on over his left ear.

"Alpha five, this is Alpha Lead," he said into the radio.

"Alpha Lead, do you have the package?" he heard back through the headset. He had to hold his left hand to his ear to steady the device he had hurriedly put on.

"I've got her. We're on our way to the carriage now," he continued. He did not catch Lucy's glare as she took being called a package as an insult.

"Your carriage is compromised," Alpha two reported. "Make way to the alternate vehicle."

"Shit," Dave shouted. Still moving quickly, he turned to look back and said "Come on Lucy, we need to take the stairs. Our original transport out of here has been compromised."

Looking at the sign by the exit, Lucy saw they were on floor five and followed as Dave started to head down the stairwell. While Dave had warned them of a possible reception at the airport, this was not at all quite what anyone back at the DPD had imagined. She noted that the Alpha Team had obviously expected a lot more than they had.

Four floors down, she followed Dave into the main car park area. Suddenly she froze in horror as Dave stopped by a car about twenty spaces from the stairwell.

"How the hell do we get away in that thing?" she asked with real surprise. She knew that her voice carried a disgusted tone, but she could not believe her eyes.

The car that Dave had brought her to was bright metallic orange in colour. It stood out like a sore thumb amongst the other cars in the car park. She could see the Ford badge on the front of the car, but this was obviously not a model she was familiar with back in the United States.

A gun shot sounded from behind, making her jump. The subsequent crack against the nearby concrete pillar brought her attention back to the current situation.

"Get in now!" Dave ordered from inside the car as he leaned over, having opened the passenger door. "We've got to go."

Even before she had closed the door properly, the car was moving and travelling towards the exit. Flashes on the windscreen indicated where bullets were bouncing off from the shots fired by their pursuers. They continued down the side of the car as Dave turned and raced on. Obviously, the car had been fitted with bullet proof glass. She wondered what other surprises there might be for her.

All of a sudden, Lucy almost screamed with shock as the car park barrier was shattered against the windscreen and the car lurched violently to the left. Her eyes took a few seconds to adjust to the change in brightness outside compared to the dark car park they had just left.

"Alpha Two, we have are making our way out of the airport and will rendezvous with you in just a couple of minutes" Dave was saying, but obviously Lucy could not hear the response he got back.

What Lucy found most disconcerting, having never been to the United Kingdom before, was that everyone was driving on the wrong side of the road for her. As they speed through the tunnel leading our of Heathrow airport, weaving in and out of the traffic, she could not help but flinch each time they passed a car on the right hand side.

With the honk of horns and a screech of wheels, the car suddenly cut from the right hand lane and across several other lanes of cars as it headed towards a slip road to their left. With speed picking up, Lucy really wasn't sure what she had let herself in for.

Chapter 7

Dave really pushed the car as they accelerated up the slip from the airport exit towards the motorway. The traffic around them was not excessively heavy, much to his relief. He had been to the airport in the past and had many memories of sitting in long traffic queues just to leave the area before.

Glancing in the mirror, Dave could see at least three, possibly four plain looking Jeep style cars had followed them out of the airport. These were quickly joined by several police cars, lights and sirens blaring in an attempt to encourage people ahead to move out of the way.

As pointed out by Lucy before she had got in, the car was painted in bright metallic orange, and was going to stick out on the road. Very few other cars around them were painted as brightly as this particular vehicle. This was part of the plan the Alpha Team had come up with in case someone tried to interfere with Lucy's arrival in the United Kingdom.

Dave glanced over to Lucy, who by this point was starting to look a little rattled. From his past experience, Lucy was a very strong and capable person who was able to take control of most situations. Right now, this was one situation she was not in control of and it had started to show.

"You okay?" he asked her.

She looked over at him with a look of cynicism. "More or less," came her reply. "Bit of a wake up call after a long flight."

"As we discussed before you left, we expected some form of reception, but there was more than even we had planned for," Dave explained. "We have prepared a few tricks which should be able to get us out of this."

Dave had turned back to concentrate on the road as he spoke, but Lucy sat looking at him for a few seconds more. Although there was an air of urgency in his approach, there was no panic. Even after just a few minutes with him, this was something she had to admit to already starting to admire.

This was something she knew was also one of her main strengths. It was vital in a job like they were both doing, especially as they had the responsibilities of some many other people's lives in their hands.

Given the events that the Alpha Team had faced during the past twenty four hours and the losses that had they had already suffered in its personnel, it was obviously going take a strong person to keep the level of control like he was doing. She could not imagine the impact of loosing any of the members of her team back in the DPD, let alone the whole group in one day.

Before she looked back at the road in front, she caught a glimpse of the speedometer on the dashboard. It was showing that they were travelling at over a hundred miles an hour. While she knew that the speed limits were set higher in the United Kingdom than back home, and Dave would be more than capable to cope, she still found herself a little shaken by it. A raised eyebrow gave away her surprise at how fast they were actually going.

Dave, noticing her reaction out of the corner of his eye as he looked in the rear view mirror, commented "Bit faster than you Americans are used to I guess?"

"Funny," Lucy said sharply. "It's more being on the wrong side of the road that is the part I find the worst."

As Lucy sat holding on to the handle on the door, the car had weaved through the traffic and was currently in the right hand lane of the three spread across this road. A lot of cars were moving out of their way ahead of them. Lucy thought this was probably due to the police cars with their sirens and lights flashing behind.

Suddenly, their car cut across the two lanes to her left and dived very late into a slip road she had not seen. This resulted in the police cars, several of which had been able to close up tightly on their tail, all shooting past the junction and continuing along the road they had just left.

However, the four unmarked Jeeps, which had been sitting slightly further behind the police, had been able to follow with more ease. With the slip road being empty of traffic, their pursuers were able to pick up some speed in an attempt to close the distance between them and the orange Ford Focus ST.

Lucy tried to note the road signs they had passed. These indicated they were going to be heading north. None of the names on the sign post meant anything to her other than two she had recognised. Birmingham, the United Kingdom's second city and Oxford. She had known several people who had studied at the university in Oxford, but little more than that.

"Where are we heading then, besides north?" she asked.

"Alpha Command is based outside Ipswich. It will take about eighty minutes from here," he said. "Depending on any delays we may experience. We will travel round the M25 for about forty minutes or so first."

"Alpha Leader here," Dave said as he had to shift his focus back to the headset, obviously as one of his team members had contacted him. He then looked over his right shoulder and continued "I see you Alpha Two."

To their right, the slip road they were on was merging with a four lane stretch of motorway. This was the M25, the main motorway around London. Despite the stories Lucy had heard about it being an over sized car park, she was surprised at how empty it was.

After a couple of seconds, he spoke again as he kept taking glances in his mirror. "And Alpha Three coming up right behind you Two. Form up on me and prepare for some real driving. There are four Jeeps behind we need to loose, plus any police we pick up on the way."

"Copy that Alpha Lead," Alpha Three responded as he pulled up next to Dave's car.

Looking over, Lucy could see two more cars exactly the same as the one they were in. Taking a look at Dave, she could see he was checking the rear view mirror for the Jeeps who should be appearing just behind them at any second.

"Here they come," he announced, partly to Alpha Two and Three, but also to Lucy. "Better hang on tight," he said gently, this time aimed solely at her.

As they finally joined the main carriageway of the motorway, Dave increased the speed again. The three cars were now travelling at just over a hundred miles an hour again, but the Jeeps were now easily closing up on them.

Traffic was quite light on this part of the motorway, so while it was going to prove difficult to loose the following cars, there was less danger to members of the public. This allowed Dave to move across to one of the central lanes.

As they travelled, she watched as the two other cars passed them to their left. She looked in each one as they passed. She noted that in each there was a passenger as well as a driver. Each car looking pretty much identical to the one she was in she realised.

As the second car passed, she also noticed that they both had the same number plate.

The next thing she realised was Dave had switched to the left lane, just as the second car to have passed moved into the lane they had just pulled out of. As they pulled past this car,

Dave swung back into a gap between the other two cars which Lucy thought was just over a couple of car lengths long.

"That one's got the same as our plate hasn't it?" Lucy asked, realising she was stating the obvious the moment she had spoken.

"Sure has Lucy." Dave replied. "Now are you concerned about the colour of the car?"

Lucy smiled to herself. She now knew why he had been so confident about how they could escape in a garishly bright orange car. As there were now three of them, all identical, the job was just made all the more easier.

She was suddenly bought back to reality as a blaring of car horns started off to her left. One of the Jeeps had started to cut up the inside and had cut in front of a small red car, again another model she could not recognise. The driver had been left with no option but to pull onto the hard shoulder to get out of the way.

As she checked out the Jeep, she recognised a familiar style to the vehicle. It had blacked out windows all round and dark grey body paint. That was standard CIA styling back home in America, but she did not know if it was the same for the respective agencies over here.

Approaching a junction, Lucy saw the hard shoulder narrowed as the motorway passed under a bridge. At that moment Dave swung his car into the same lane as the closest Jeep. Immediately at the same time, the car in front, Alpha Two she thought, had made a similar move.

The Jeep swerved left in reaction so as to avoid a collision and drove directly into the crash barrier where the hard shoulder narrowed. She watched in the mirror as the Jeep's speed caused it to tip and barrel roll across the motorway, narrowly missing two of the other Jeeps that were following.

The fourth one was not so lucky and veered off to his right to miss the incoming vehicle. As he did so, he cannoned off the crash barriers in the central reservation, he himself loosing control of his vehicle. As he rebounded in the main carriageway, it appeared the driver was in all likelihood now unconscious. His vehicle headed straight across all three lanes and into the crash barriers on the other side.

"Two down," Dave said.

"Two to go?" Lucy finished off for him.

"Actually, we've still got four to go." Dave pointed towards a slip road joining the motorway, on which was two further grey Jeeps approaching at high speed. Both pulled onto the motorway, each quickly taking up separate lanes ahead of them. With two behind them, Lucy expected them to try and box them in, in an attempt to stop them.

As Alpha Two moved alongside them in the third lane, making an attempt to get past, the right hand Jeep moved to block the lane. Alpha Three had pulled alongside in the lane to their left, meaning Dave had to slow slightly to let him in ahead of them. They were now following behind the other two orange cars.

The left hand Jeep pulled into the middle lane as he fast approached a lorry in the left hand lane. Both Jeeps then started to slow down now they were next to each other in the right hand two lanes, making an attempt to use the lorry as the missing part of their trap.

Alpha Three moved up behind the left hand Jeep and made a move to try and pass between the lorry and the Jeep. Dave had tucked in behind Alpha Three enough to minimise the view of him from the Jeep ahead.

Off to their right, Alpha Two was making similar move between the right hand Jeep and the crash barrier of the central reservation. She watched in surprise as both Jeeps moved across the road to prevent either of the Ford Focus's making any progress past them.

Suddenly, Lucy was thrown back in her seat as Dave accelerated away and towards the gap that had just opened between the Jeeps. Given that the Focus was a smaller and lighter vehicle than the Jeeps, they were halfway through before either driver had realised.

The Jeeps tried to move together and crush Dave's car as it passed between them, but his speed was too great. The two came together and smashed into the side of each other.

Alpha Two and Three both used the gaps to the side of each of the Jeeps to swing past. However Alpha Three, passing on the left side, had not left quite enough space and his wing mirror was ripped off as he passed the Jeeps.

Unfortunately for one of the following Jeeps who had picked up speed to try and attempt to follow Alpha Two, one of the leading two Jeeps had swung out from the collision and clipped him. The driver lost control of his vehicle as it ended up ramming into the crash barriers of the central reservation at speed. The impact caused the car to explode.

There were now only two Jeeps remaining in the pursuit. They were trying desperately to close the gap between them and the Alpha Team as they approached the next junction.

Lucy jumped slightly as her mobile phone began to ring in her jacket pocket.

"Tyler," she said as she answered the call.

"Hello Lucy," the voice on the phone said. "Harry Wheelhouse here. I hope you are well."

"Perhaps now is not the best time for introductions," she replied.

"I need to speak to Dave, we can't receive their signals on the radio," Harry said.

Lucy held her phone out to Dave and said "Harry Wheelhouse for you."

Trying not to take his eyes of the road, Dave grabbed the phone in his left hand and put it to his free ear.

"What do you want Harry. I'm kind of a bit busy right now."

"I know. What the hell have you got into there Dave? We're tracking you here at Alpha Command. We've been able to keep the police out of the chase. We've have had to convince them that you have a bio weapon in your car and that MI5 are dealing with it."

"Cheers Harry, I thought they were missing from the party," Dave said, as he tried to hang on to the wheel as he weaved around another car that had pulled out in front of him. "Now, what can you do about these Jeeps for us?"

"They were sent from MI5, but I've ensured there will be no more."

"We've still got two Harry, but we shall loose them very soon I hope. You better get some decent cover stories for the three we've already left behind."

"I'll sort it out. Just try and keep damage to a minimum from now on Dave." Harry finished the call and Dave passed Lucy her phone back to her.

"Alpha Two, Alpha Three, just these two and I think we will be clear. I want Alpha Two to take the next junction and hopefully one will follow, then Alpha Three repeat at the junction after. We're running out of motorway."

Almost immediately, they were upon the next junction. Alpha Two was still in the right hand lane, so dropped his speed slightly and cut behind the other two towards the junction.

Almost instantly, one of the Jeeps also peeled off and followed him up the slip road.

"What's going to happen to them then?" Lucy asked.

"If the guys in the Jeep catch them, then they will be taken to MI5 to be dealt with. Once there, Harry will be able to get them moved round so we can get them back out. More likely, once the message filters through to the head of the agency of our involvement here, he should be able to get his agents called back to base."

Lucy nodded as she listened. Where as the DPD had the full support of the heads of the various agencies through to their government, the Alpha Team still had to work outside of the normal channels for the time being.

"Our main concern would be if they were to get hold of you. I'm sure you are aware that once the secret services and agencies get hold of someone, it is easy to make them disappear in one of so many different ways."

Dave's attention was drawn off as someone contacted him on the headset.

"Thanks Alpha Three, report back to Alpha Command for debrief," he said into the radio.

He then dropped the speed they were travelling at considerably and turned his head to take a quick look what was behind them.

Lucy turned to see what he was looking at. She could not see the remaining Jeep she expected to be following behind them any more.

"What happened?" she asked. "Where did the last one go?"

"Not sure, but Harry must have made the right noises," Dave replied. "It looks like we will probably have a clear run through to home now."

Lucy turned back to face forwards. With a sigh, she leaned back in the seat.

"I'm glad that is over then," she said.

"If you're glad, then imagine just how I feel right now," Dave said. "Much as I get a thrill from driving, that is not something I want to do too often I can tell you."

Approaching another slip road, Dave gently drifted across the left hand lane of the motorway and onto the slip road. Looking at the sign posts they passed, Lucy still did not recognise any of the names of the cities in this direction.

She wished she had taken more time to familiarise herself with UK geography on the flight over. Hopefully the rest of the journey would be more subdued and she could take the opportunity to talk to Dave in more detail. She had a lot of questions she wanted to ask.

Chapter 8

Having left the M25 motorway, the journey had turned into a more peaceful and relaxing drive. It had allowed Dave the chance to give Lucy a thorough introduction to the Alpha Protocols. Lucy was then able to outline some of the more intimate details about the DPD that Dave and the Alpha Team were not aware of.

She was also looking for the opportunity to dig for information as to who was leaking information from with the United States government, security agencies or even her own DPD staff. She knew well that if anyone linked to the alien threat was able to intercept the same information, then they could be fighting a lost cause already.

Without being pursued, Dave had informed Lucy it would take them about three quarters of an hour to travel the fifty or so miles from the motorway to the outskirts of Ipswich. Travelling at a more subdued speed of seventy-five miles an hour, Lucy was able to let herself relax a little. As she listened to Dave talking, Lucy leaned back in the seat and watched out of the window.

For some reason, she had not expected the United Kingdom to look quite so different from the United States. She had grown very used to spending her time in Washington with the buildings and the hustle of city life all around her the whole time.

Despite having to go out on missions in the field, most of these were also in cities or towns around America. Very few actually took them into open countryside for any length of time.

Most of the time they spent travelling around meant they would take some sort of flight from city to city. Rarely did they go by car, so this was a novelty for her in some respects.

Here in the United Kingdom, all she had really seen so far from the road was countryside. Even the two towns they had passed along this road, known to the local residents as the A12, she had got the impression that there was nothing was on the same scale she was used to back home.

"Do you mind if I ask you a personal question?" Lucy asked Dave, bringing herself back to the present.

"Sure, ask anything you want." Dave gave her a quick glance before turning back to concentrate on driving again.

"As I am sure you are probably aware, my job in the United States sort of meant I was the logical choice for running the Department of Planetary Defense's response to the alien threat. But, how did you get involved with all this?" As she asked, she twisted herself round in the seat so she could comfortably look at Dave.

Taking another quick look back at Lucy before returning his concentration to driving again, Dave answered her question.

"Basically, my background is in computer and information security. Not to blow my own trumpet, but I had become a leading expert in securing systems and networks. This raised interest in my skills about two years ago when I was asked to work for various government agencies here in the United Kingdom to help increase the security of their systems."

"One such project was to manage a team who were assigned the task of attempting to break into one of the systems at GCHQ. They assumed this was one of the most secure systems around. However, my team found a back door to a part of the system that contained a host of classified information regarding alien encounters and technology. While they were able to hide our tracks, I had obtained enough data and information to pull together a number of experts to look into the issue."

"I was able to continue monitoring these systems without being traced for a further six months or so. During that time, we were able to intercept and decrypt a number of documents and transmissions regarding a covert operation within the DPD. We knew nothing about this other than a word used in secure circles within your government."

"However, about a year ago, my searches were discovered. Partly, this was down to me and my colleagues asking too many questions in the wrong places. However, one of those questions had attracted the attentions of the right people and I was summoned to appear in front of a panel of top security and intelligence ministers to explain what I had been doing and why."

"I thought that I was going to be in a lot of trouble and I am sure you are aware what that can mean whether here in the United Kingdom or in the United States – people are known to have disappeared and the truth disappears with them."

"Anyway, the session took a different direction as it transpired that our government had begun planning what turned out to be the Alpha protocols. And my snooping around had meant that my knowledge and skills were to be used to improve them to where they are today. They also wanted my team of contacts to form a response team in the case that alien contact was to happen again within the UK."

Lucy injected another question. "So at what stage did you learn that we had initiated our team at the DPD?"

"We were aware of the existence of the team for about eighteen months as I said, but it was not until about a week or so after the Space Shuttle encounter that we realised you had actually activated the team and what it really meant. As soon as we realised this, we checked our records and were able to confirm that you had encountered an alien craft via access to records at NASA."

"And it was at this point you started to monitor my team?" Lucy pushed.

"Yes. But as I said yesterday, it was not the easiest assignment some of my guys have had. Mainly this was down to the secrecy you were working under. As I am sure you are aware, not many secrets are normally kept that well in D.C."

"I get that all the time from the likes of the government boys," Lucy retorted, shaking her head "and still don't know what they mean by it."

As she spoke, she noticed they had started to slow down. As they did, she turned her attention to their surroundings.

"So where are we headed then?" she asked realising they had reached a major junction. Having now seen a couple of these junctions in the United Kingdom, she was amazed their road system worked as well as it did.

As they stopped at a red light on the junction, she looked around and saw a large retail complex off to one side. It was comforting to see one or two names that she recognised from home around her.

"In about fifteen minutes you will see our centre of operations here in the United Kingdom," Dave started to say. She could detect a strong element of pride in what he was saying as he mentioned about their base of operations. "We find it best to keep out of London as there are a lot less people watching what we do. Plus, as you will see shortly, we have quite an extensive operation."

Pulling off from the lights, they headed down another slip road and onto another main road. Looking at the clock, Lucy saw it was just after twelve.

"No wonder I'm getting hungry," she thought to herself. "I hope I can get something eat soon, or at least a strong coffee. It's been a long day already."

Leaning back in the chair, she closed her eyes for what she thought was a few seconds, but suddenly opened them again as the car felt like it dropped out from underneath her.

"What the…" she said, realising it was closer to a scream than anything else.

Around the car it had gone dark. All she could see ahead were three lines of lights stretching out ahead into the darkness, green to the left, red to the right and white down the middle.

"Nothing to worry about," Dave said trying to reassure her. "Just the back door into our base. Just in case we think we are being tailed or need a quick getaway, we have a back tunnel. I also need to get this car back in to be checked over."

As the road turned a bend, they were still travelling at about seventy miles an hour. The car began to slow down as the tunnel started to lighten up. Within a few seconds, they had entered a large, brightly lit hall.

As they entered the hall, the car really slowed down and Dave pulled into a bay of about fifteen or so vehicles. As they started to turn into one of the empty parking spots, Lucy looked over at the car next to them.

At least, it used to be a car at some time. She wondered if this might be the remains of the vehicle one of the Alpha Team members had been killed in just days ago. However, she would not push the issue for now.

"Welcome to Alpha Command," Dave said as the car came to a complete stop. Undoing his seatbelt and getting out of the car, he said to Lucy "hopefully, you'll be impressed with what we have brought together here."

Lucy unfastened her seat beat and also climbed out of the car. She was quite relieved to be able to stand up and stretch her muscles again. It had been quite a tense drive, especially after a long flight from the United States.

Looking around, Lucy could see they were in a completely covered hall, probably three to four stories tall. Although tall, it was not overly large area in floor space that was covered.

She was now able to take a better look at her surroundings. They were currently stood in a bay which was obviously a parking area, with a range of cars, motorbikes and vans of varying types, including what she thought must be a police car.

Noticing Lucy looking around the cars, Dave explained about the collection to her. "Basically, we only activated the Alpha Protocols a couple of days ago, but for the past year, we have been working on preparing for such an event. We just plan for as many eventualities as we can and felt we needed such a range of different vehicles to cover these."

"Most are normal vehicles so we can travel around to investigate reports, visit witnesses etc, but obviously the vehicles like the vans tend to be kitted out with all the latest surveillance kits."

She pointed to the vehicle remains behind her and ventured to ask "Is this the car that one of your team was killed in?"

"I'm afraid so," he replied, sounding a little mournful. "We got it moved here so one of the lab guys can analyse to see what clues we can get. I don't think they have found anything conclusive yet to be honest."

At the end of the bay, there was a stair case leading up to the next level. Along the length of the wall, there were windows overlooking this area, but only the one doorway at the top of the stairs.

Having made their way up the stairs, Dave waved the back of his hand over a panel to the side of the door. After a second or so, the door swung inwards and opened into a large hall area and Lucy followed him in.

"All the doors are controlled and secured by micro-chips inserted under the skin of everyone working here. Not only does it act as a security pass here, but we use them for tracking our people. They also come in useful for identifying bodies as we found out a couple of days ago in verifying two of my team's bodies."

"We realise that you may only be here for a few days so will provide you with a security card, but would rather give you one of the chips in the back of your hand. It will be quite easy for our doctor to remove this before you leave anyway."

"That's fine," Lucy replied. "Just gives me another one to the collection." She pointed to the back of her neck. "We would ask the same if you were to come over to our operation."

The hall area was fairly open. On the opposite wall were what she thought were two doors, but as they walked closer she realised they were doors to a couple of lifts. In front of them was a large desk which had a lady sitting at. There was a guard beside each lift door, both in army uniforms.

"In front of you is the main way in and out of Alpha Command. We are currently six stories below ground, although the base is only four stories itself. This is the second level, with one above and two below. We came in on level one, and as you saw, it gives us a second entrance into the base. There is another tunnel similar to that which leads up to the ground level and onto the site above."

"Did you say the site above? What's up there then?" Lucy was already reasonably impressed with the size and scope of the centre.

"It's a research park for hi-tech industries," Dave said. "It's been there since the mid sixties and has been a leading research facility for communications, hardware and software industries. It has been used for top secret research and testing over the years, so it was the ideal place for us to put this centre."

"They have a range of satellite dishes on their site for communications, many of which we have been able to tap into and use for our own systems. I shall take you up there shortly, but first I need to introduce you to Harry and then get you your ID badges and so on."

Dave led her up another flight of stairs and into a corridor. Looking to her left down the corridor, she could see various doors on either side, leading down to a frosted glass wall at the end.

She looked back and followed Dave as he headed right down the corridor. About forty or so yards, he stopped by a double sized door, at which two armed guards stood either side at attention.

"Bit like home this" she remarked, smiling slightly.

As Dave swiped his hand over another panel and the door swung open to reveal a large, brightly lit room, he said "Welcome to the Alpha Command room" and followed Lucy in.

Chapter 9

As Lucy entered the command room, she strangely felt right at home. Although the room was different from other command rooms she had been in, there was a reassuringly familiar feel about it.

Something she had thought having been in several of this type of room back in Washington, and having seen many films attempt to recreate them, there was just something about the air of the room that made it feel the same.

Off to one side on her right were a number of screens of varying sizes mounted along the wall. In the centre of the room there was a large table with twelve seats around it, one of which was occupied by a middle aged man.

Over to her left, the entire side was a large glass wall with a number of computers, monitors and maps along it. The wall itself was clear and looked over an area of labs of some description.

Lucy turned to Dave, pointing to the glass wall. "What goes on in there?"

"Research mainly. I shall introduce you to the guys in there shortly. When we go the other side, you will notice that it is a one way mirror, although most of those who work in there won't even be aware that we can watch them from in here."

"But for now, we don't need to see them," the man by the table said, pressing a button on a control panel next to one of the computers on the table. The window then darkened and Lucy could see nothing of the lab next door.

"You must be Harry Wheelhouse," Lucy asked, turning to fully face him. She held her hand out for him to shake.

"It is nice to meet you in person at last, Dr Tyler," he responded, shaking her hand firmly. "Please call me Harry. You'll find we are all pretty informal around here. When the shit hits the fan, you don't have time for pleasantries anyway."

Lucy smiled. Thinking about working back home in the United States, she never seemed to call most of her colleagues by their first names very often. She knew them all by their surnames. She put it down to just one of those culture differences she could not have prepared herself for.

"Lucy's fine for me," she responded, trying not to sound uneasy about it.

"Please, take a seat," Harry said, as he pulled one of the seats out from the table for her. "Can we get you a coffee or something else to drink?" Harry asked.

"I'd love a coffee." Looking back over towards Dave as she stepped towards the seat, she continued "It's been a bit stressful for the past couple of hours."

Dave pulled an expression on his face as if to say "it's not my fault". He turned so he could look towards Harry. As Harry smiled back with a slight nod of his head, Dave turned to the door and headed towards it.

"Don't worry, I'll get the coffee," he said in a defeated tone, throwing his hands up in the air in mock defiance.

As Dave headed out the door, Lucy was making herself comfortable in the seat Harry had pulled out from the table. She laid her briefcase on the table in front of her. Harry took the seat next to her and sat down himself.

"How much has Dave been able to tell you about our operation here?" he began by asking.

"Some, but I expect seeing it for real will probably be better than any talk in the car on the way here," she answered. "From what I have seen already, you appear to be pretty well prepared for some of the problems you might be about to face."

"That probably comes from having closely monitored your operation and having been able to adapt our plans to reflect what we have learned," Harry said. "As I am sure Dave will have explained, we are quite a way from London, so our operation is less noticeable than some of the security agencies in the United Kingdom."

"Yes, he did explain that on the way. I have to be honest that I am not entirely familiar with your security agencies here. I am aware that MI5 and MI6 are the main two that we, sorry our intelligence services, interact with most. Personally, I have not had any dealings with them since joining my government."

"Correct. There are others, as well as the police, other emergency services and so on. What we do not have is a federal law enforcement agency like you do, although we have created a new unit called SOCA which many see as a first step to implementing an FBI style agency. This can make it difficult to take control of any incidents we have had in the past."

"However, as part of the Alpha Protocol, we have been able to issue a new directive to all the police forces across the United Kingdom, called Order Alpha One. That means we can take control of an incident and this removes the requirement for services like the police to be there if we deem it necessary."

"What about cover stories then?" Lucy asked. "How do you explain such a change to the relevant parties or the general public?"

"As I am pretty sure you are aware, since the introduction of your own Department of Homeland Security, terrorism makes a great excuse for this sort of change. Plus it always acts as a great deterrent if they suspect there might be bio-weapons or nuclear agents involved and we need to test the area."

Dave entered the room carrying a tray with three coffees on. He placed them down on the table and took a number of packets of sugar out of his pockets and put them on the table as well.

"I didn't know how you would like your coffee," he said. "So I got you white, sorry if that is wrong. Just help yourself to sugar."

"White is fine for me," Lucy said, taking a sip from one of the cups. "I guess at least there is something about me you haven't been able to learn."

Dave and Harry exchanged glances, although Lucy could not tell if her intended rebuke at them having been spying on her for so long had had the intended affect.

"In case you might not have noticed," she said as she decided to continue talking, "but I am starting to feel a little tired at the moment. It has been over thirty six hours since I got some proper sleep and I could really do with something to eat right now."

"Fair enough," Harry said as he stood up and walked over towards the glass wall. He picked up an envelope from the desk and passed it over to Lucy. "In here are your ID badges for the site above, one for within the command centre here and papers for the hotel we have booked. Dave will now take you up top and show you round STAR Park."

"STAR Park? Is that the technology park you mentioned earlier?" Lucy asked as she turned her attention to Dave.

"Yes. It actually stands for Science, Technology And Research Park. It is a little bit of a corny name really, but they thought space based names gave it technological feel back in the sixties. You'll get to see around it and some of the things that we run up there as well. I suspect you might even like to see the canteen first though."

At the mention of food, Lucy really felt her hunger take over. It had been twelve hours since she last ate anything. She never enjoyed airplane food, so had not eaten a great deal on the flight.

"I wouldn't say no to something to eat right now," she exclaimed.

"Okay. Give me five minutes to grab a couple of things and I'll take you up top. You can finish your coffee in the meantime. If you want to make any calls, there's a phone under this panel on the table." Dave opened one of the panels to reveal a phone.

"Obviously, calls to your department in Washington will be over a secure channel, thanks to our security guys. And with Forster's help, we have been able to utilise a new encryption protocol for any data we send back and forth."

"That's my boys," Lucy chuckled. "They're always willing to get stuck in."

As Dave returned to the Command room, Lucy was making a telephone call. He stopped at the door and gave a little wave to her to signal he would give her a bit of extra time. She smiled and gestured it was okay for him to wait while she finished her call.

Dave walked over and took a seat across the table from Lucy. He leaned right back in the seat, taking the chance to examine Lucy's face as she spoke. He did not pay any attention to what she was saying as he tried to look her over without making it obvious to her.

Lucy stood up from her seat as she started to end her call. With a laugh, she said "Just make sure someone is feeding my animals while I am away."

Dave looked at her as she laughed at the response from the person she was speaking to.

Looking slightly embarrassed as she noticed Dave now listening to her, Lucy then said "Okay, okay. I'll stop worrying."

Dave shook his head and laughed. He had to admit that he was no better than Lucy. He had got several pets at home and had been known to phone home to check how they were doing while he had been away.

Living on his own, they offered him some company. Company that would not answer back. Company that would not nag at him because he had left his clothes on the floor. Company that was pleased to see you again after time away, whether you left them for a couple of days or a couple of weeks.

But then there were times you needed more than that sort of company. Times you came back from a tough trip and needed someone to talk it out with or to be comforted by. In this line of work, that was certainly a rarity.

"Bye Claire," Lucy said ending the call and putting the phone down. "Ready then?" she asked standing up.

"I thought I was waiting for you?" Dave retorted as he stood up and started to head towards the door.

As Lucy walked alongside him, she put her hand on his back and said "I'm just waiting for something to satisfy my need for food right now. Then let's get up to speed on everything."

"Got your STAR Park badge on?" Dave asked, taking a quick look across Lucy's front.

The badges were attached to a clip she had fastened to a belt loop on her trousers. She lifted the badge up to show him she had put it on.

"You could have got a better picture you know," she said, complaining as they made their way towards the stairs down to the main level.

"It's the one we got from your system records while you were on your way over." Dave gestured for Lucy to walk down the stairs ahead of him. "Best you blame Johnson for that."

"That's exactly what I mean," she quipped as she passed him and headed down. "I never liked it back home either."

"I didn't think there was anything wrong with it," he muttered to himself quietly. He realised immediately that he had said it out louder than he had intended, hoping Lucy had not heard.

Lucy turned her head back to face him and asked "Sorry, I missed that."

"I was just saying that I've never been happy with my pictures either," he replied quickly, trying to cover a feeling of embarrassment at the fact Lucy might have overheard a comment he should have kept in his head.

Once they reached the bottom, Dave stopped at the reception desk at the bottom of the stairs. There was a quick exchange of words between Dave and the girl at the desk. She stood up from the desk, as Dave turned so they could both take a look at Lucy.

"What?" she said, feeling a little self conscious as both Dave and the girl looked her up and down.

"Just trying to decide what size you are," he replied. "Your suitcases still have not shown up, so I'm just arranging for Nikki here to get you some new clothes, shoes and so on."

Lucy stepped forward to talk to Nikki herself, but before she did, she said to Dave "Give me a few seconds here please."

Dave did not move, so she looked back again and added "Alone please."

Dave then took a few steps away to give her a couple of moments to discuss what she needed to be bought for her.

As soon as she was finished and turned back to him, he ushered her towards the lift and pressed the button to call the lift. As the lift was already on their floor the doors opened straight away.

"How many stories below ground did you say we were?" Lucy enquired as the doors shut behind them.

"We are currently six floors below the main building on the site." Dave pressed the button marked G and the lift started to head up. "You'll notice from the controls here the main building has eight stories above ground. To access the lower levels, you need to use the chip in the hand again. This means that there is no visible panel or controls to anyone else using the lift in the main building."

"So the workers here don't know about this place?" she asked, intrigued.

"No, not at all," Dave replied confidently. "There have not even been any suspicions yet either as far as we are aware. There have been secret projects and research going on here for years, and with so many rumours already doing the rounds, we don't even have to work hard to hide the place."

"What sort of rumours?"

"The main one is about the top floor and how secret work for the government has been carried out up there since the seventies. Aspects of it are true and there are aspects of these rumours that we can play on to help it along." Dave continued to explain as the lift came to a halt.

"Like what?" Lucy asked as the lift doors opened. As they did, she saw several people outside waiting for the lift, chatting amongst themselves.

Dave did not answer, but just walked out of the lift. Nor did he look at any of the people waiting for the lift. As Lucy followed him out, a hush had ascended over the group until both of them had exited the lift, and the doors begun to close.

She followed him towards the main doors to their right and they made their way out of the building via a glass surrounded corridor.

After quickly checking no one else was within ear shot, Dave turned to look at Lucy as they walked down the corridor.

"As long as we keep the myth about secret projects on the upper floors, we can help keep prying eyes and ears from our secrets. One of these myths has always been how people working on the upper floors suddenly go quiet when other people get on the lifts. This gives us excellent scope to keep this myth going."

As they exited the glass corridor, Dave held the doors open and Lucy got her first look at the site above ground. She could see the main building stretch off to her right, beyond which, she could see an array of fifteen or so satellite dishes of varying sizes.

As she followed Dave across a large area of grass, they made their way towards another building which was constructed of black and blue glass around a white steel frame. She could see around the area another ten or eleven buildings of varying sizes and designs, including a few she thought looked a bit like aircraft hangers. She noticed that most of the people walking around the site were also heading towards the same building as they were. The rest seemed to be heading away from it.

"There are all sorts of companies based on this site, a number of which we have got links or connections with. In fact, most of them will not even know about it. If we find that they are working on things we think we could use, then we are able to take what we need."

"That's a bit sly, isn't it?" Lucy asked. "Do you get much from that arrangement?"

"Yes, we've gained incredible software advances from some of these guys. We need to keep as ahead of the game if the things you have experienced are anything to go by."

As they reached the door to the glass building, Lucy reached to open the door. This gave her the opportunity to take a look back the way they had just come, back towards the building the command centre was located under. She wondered how many people worked on this site and hadn't got an idea what was going on under their feet as they walked about, as they worked.

For the first time, she started to think about if this was how people behaved around the various government buildings in Washington. While it was accepted that the running and protection of their country happened there, they still tried everything they could to mask their activities from prying eyes.

Despite that, she had heard of rumours starting to do the rounds in Washington as people began to question what the DPD's real function was.

For now, hunger was getting the better of her, so she followed Dave through the door and into the canteen.

Chapter 10

As she entered the building, Lucy was impressed to see that the site was well served for everything somebody might need during the day. There was a small bank, a couple of little shops selling magazines and snack foods. There was even a dry cleaner available here.

Off to her left was a food court offering a range of food for all tastes. To her right appeared to be what reminded her of an airport waiting area, an open plan space full of seating and tables for people to spend some time away from their work. There was also a small coffee shop off to one side. It seemed to be quite popular by the size of the queue.

"What do you fancy then?" Dave asked her.

"So what's the pizza like here then?" she replied jokingly.

"Favourite of yours is it?" Dave said quizzically.

"Sorry, just something the guys back in Washington complain about all the time. It seems to be the staple diet for them these days." Lucy could not help but smile as she spoke. "Is there a salad bar here then? That will do for me."

Dave directed her over to the salad bar at the far end of the food court. He left her to make her selection while he went over and opted for the pizza himself. Surely, he thought to himself, they had not eaten pizza quite like these ones. Looking at the plate he had picked up, he wondered if it was the best choice after all. Not that there was anything else that seemed to be any more appetising than the pizza.

Having queued while Dave paid for both the meals, Lucy followed him to a small table in the corner of the seating area. It was located against the window with a view of the main security gate area. There were fewer people sitting around this part of the canteen so they could talk while they ate.

"So, just what have you had to give up to live this life?" Dave asked Lucy as they started to eat.

"Everything it seems," Lucy replied, taking a quick look around to reassure herself about how much she could say. "It seems I am not able to go anywhere at home without at least one of department's agents guarding me. I accept now that they are there for my protection, but it means you don't get to have a private life any more. That's if you even had the time to have one. You should have seen the arguments about Johnson not sending one over with me on this trip."

"What about the rest of the team?" Dave questioned further. "How do they cope?"

"Some of them have adapted better than others. Bale has obviously had this type of life for some time. I'm absolutely sure there are things in his past it would probably be best for me to never know about." She paused slightly so she could take a sip of her drink. "To be fair, I don't want to dig into any of their pasts too much as long as they are getting the job done."

"I guess for those who have always worked within government departments or the military, they learn how to deal with keeping secrets," Lucy continued. "With all the hours this job takes, there are times you don't get home for days at a time and having to explain that to an unappreciative partner is not easy. I'm sure you will soon appreciate the hours this job will bring with it."

"We'll see," He began to respond before his attention was distracted by a couple of people approaching them. As he looked up to address them directly, Lucy turned to see a young girl and a middle aged man, each carrying a tray of food, stood next to their table.

"Hello guys, how are you then?" He had switched from a very serious tone in his voice as he talked to Lucy, to a much more casual one.

"I'm fine Dave," the girl replied. "Where have you been the past couple of weeks then? We've missed seeing you around here at lunchtimes."

"I've been away on business in America pretty much most of the time," he replied. "Do you want to join us while we finish eating then? We're not going to be too much longer though."

As they newcomers placed their trays on the table and sat down, Dave introduced both of them to Lucy. "Helen, Jack, this is Lucy. She has come over from a sister operation in Washington to help with a project that we are currently working on."

Lucy found herself shaking both of them by the hand and greeting them as Dave continued. "Helen and Jack work for the company I left before I started working on our current research. I've not seen them for the past few weeks while I was in America. It may even be longer than that by now thinking about it."

"How is the work going then?" Helen asked. "It certainly sounds like it is keeping you rather busy these days."

"It's going okay I guess," Dave told her. He looked over to Lucy, before returning his attention to Helen as he spoke. "Most of it is research and writing various papers. You know what it's like when you work with the Americans and across different time zones. Most of my days seem to start and finish at night. I might not even get to see the daylight for weeks at a time."

"Lucy," Helen started to ask, "so, how have you found England so far?"

"Truthfully, I only flew in this morning, so I've not had the opportunity to see anything yet really." Pursing her lips slightly, she added "I am hoping that the rest of my stay is as uneventful as the trip here. However, I suspect Dave has got a fair bit of work for me to keep on top of."

"I'll let you in on a little secret about Dave," Helen said, leaning forward slightly. "It will only take a smile from a pretty lady, much like yourself, and he'll just forget what he was asking you to do. It used to work for me all the time." She gave Dave a quick smile to show she was just teasing him.

Lucy looked at Dave, with a slight grin forming. "I'll keep that in mind if he starts to try and push too much work over to me then," she said. Her amusement grew as she noticed Dave had started to turn slightly red with embarrassment.

"How long have you known Dave?" Helen continued to question Lucy, not noticing Dave's reaction to her previous statement.

"We've only been working together a few days really," she replied, starting to feel a little uncomfortable at the questions aimed at her. "But we've already known each other a few weeks now." She looked over to Dave again for a bit of support, becoming increasingly uncomfortable.

"I don't want to sound rude guys, but we've got to get back to prepare for a meeting shortly," Dave said before Helen could quiz Lucy any further. He knew she was just being her normal self, but they weren't in a situation to be making friends everywhere.

"That's okay," Helen said. She turned to face Lucy and smiled. "It was nice to meet you Lucy and I hope you get the chance to see some of our country while you are here."

Dave and Lucy rose from the table, picking up their trays and left Jack and Helen to finish their meal. On the way out of the cafeteria, they deposited their trays in the trolleys at the exit.

As they walked out of the building, Lucy said "Thanks for that. While I know we don't need to tell people the truth, I still feel uncomfortable about having to do it."

"No problems," he replied. He put his hand on her shoulder as they walked. "I completely understand where you're coming from, especially as I know how hard it can be talking to your friends and not being able to tell them what you actually do for a living."

"I've had to cut off any contact with all of my friends as it's not worth the risk of an infectee finding out about them and trying to use them against me." She felt comforted by his hand and felt surprised how disappointed she was when he removed it again. "Plus it means I don't have to lie to any of them."

Dave started to laugh as he added "Even if I could tell them what I do, I somehow think many of them won't even believe it."

Arriving back at the lifts in the main building, they were on their own as most people around the site were currently back at work following the lunch break. Taking a look at her watch, Lucy saw it was now just after two o'clock.

Entering the lift, she started to question Dave about the environment of the Alpha Command. "Doesn't it bother you working underground at all?"

"Not really," he replied. "I'd rather be down here than in some sky scraper somewhere if I was to be totally honest with you. Since September eleventh when I was meant to be in the World Trade Centre, I've been a bit jumpy in tall buildings. I know I should be grateful that I should not have been in there, but I was left thinking that could have been me."

Lucy looked at him with a puzzled expression. "Most people would have taken the positive view about not being in there," she said.

"Strange as normally I would pick on the positive aspects of things," Dave said with a hint of regret in his voice. "But with regards to that one big event, I just got hung up on the negative side. I still cannot put my finger on as to why to this day."

As the lift doors begun to open, Lucy said "You'd be okay in Washington then. Most buildings have only got the fourteen levels above ground, so we don't go that high. Still, it is higher than many of the buildings around us here from what I have seen."

They made their way up the stairs to the level above and headed towards the command room. Dave was going to give Lucy the full and official tour of the base, so where else was better to start than the centre of operations.

As Dave and Lucy arrived outside the command room, they were greeted by Nikki, who Lucy had talked to before they had left for lunch. She was carrying an assortment of carrier bags and bits for Lucy. These were the clothes that she had been sent out to buy as they had been unable to locate the missing suitcase at the airport.

This had not been located on the luggage carousel or at the lost property areas. They had put two agents on to the task of looking for the case, but Dave suspected that other parties were also looking for it in the hope that they could find anything of use from it.

In reality, they would not find anything in the case. All Lucy had brought from the United States was her clothes, towels and make-up. Everything else of importance was able to be transferred to the Alpha system through the encrypted channels they hard worked with the DPD to set up overnight.

Dave asked her to leave them all in his office so they could pick them up before he took Lucy to her hotel. For now, he had to finish showing Lucy round Alpha Command.

"Once we've done the full tour, I'll take you to your hotel so you can get some rest before we start getting to grips with everything tomorrow. I guess it's been a long day for you so far."

"Pretty used to living on two hours sleep a day," she said with a tired smile. "Let's take a look at what you've got in place here then."

Following the tour of the base, they finished back in the command room, each with a coffee in hand.

"One thing that is definitely the same here as back home," Lucy said. "We all probably drink too much coffee in this line of work. But I have to say it tastes better here than it does back home."

"One of the perks of not relying on government funding," Dave replied, holding his cup up in much the same way as toasting a bride and groom. "We get to afford proper coffee. But you're right, we do seem to live on this stuff some days. Other than the coffee, would we pass your assessment?"

"I'm impressed with your operation, I must admit. I suspect there would be a lot we could learn from you. However, until you start to deal with the type of problems we have had to, you will not know if your operation is truly ready and able to cope. But with the correct staff, I do believe you have the best facilities to be ready."

"As discussed yesterday, we are working to get the extra staff in shortly," Dave said. "You know what happened with our team, but I don't think myself and Harry have been able to fully come to terms with it. It certainly brought home the severity of the issue to us and how deep the problem runs."

Lucy placed her cup on the command room table and tried to fight back another yawn. Despite having his back turned to her, Dave heard her fail to hold it back. Much as he was enjoying her company, he knew she needed to get some rest.

"Anyway, you ready to go the hotel?" he asked as he turned back to face her. "Before it gets too late and we have to fight through rush hour traffic."

"Sure, getting some sleep sounds a good idea at the moment," Lucy replied. At the thought of sleep, she was unable to hold back yet another yawn.

The hotel was located about ten miles from Alpha Command on the southern side of Ipswich. It had only taken about five minutes to get there. As Dave had explained, the traffic round the town always became very heavy after five each evening as the rush hour started.

Lucy had laughed and responded by telling him how bad a city like Washington was at the same time each day. Because most people only worked in the city and lived away from there, the roads were chaotic to say the least. She could recall many evenings having been spent sitting in queues of traffic just to get home. She also said how she had been grateful for the mobile phone as it was a chance to do some extra work instead of when she did finally get home.

Having parked his car outside of the hotel reception, Dave collected Lucy's belongings from the back seat of the car as she went ahead to check in. There were quite a few bags, even after they had tried to pack things into fewer bags before leaving the command centre.

It reminded him why he had hated, with a passion, going shopping with women in the past. They always seemed to buy far more than they needed to. As he thought further, he had quite often never even seen them wear half they clothes they bought anyway.

This was slightly different in that Lucy had been forced to leave her suitcase behind at the airport as they were pursued by the men the Home Secretary had sent to ensure she did not meet up with the him and the Alpha Team

As he caught up with her, she had been given her door card and was ready to go straight to the room. She offered to take some of the bags from Dave, but he responded by saying that he was happy to carry to the room for her.

As they reached the room, Lucy opened the door and entered the room to put her coat and bag on the chair as Dave waited at the door to the room. She turned back to see him waiting and laughed.

"Do you want to bring the bags in for me or shall I take them from you?" she said.

"I'll bring them in," he responded, slightly embarrassed. "I'm just not someone to walk straight into a ladies room, even if it is just a hotel room."

"You Brits do seem to be big on manners don't you," Lucy said, amused by his actions.

Putting all the bags on the bed, Dave then turned to Lucy and asked, sounding slightly embarrassed by Lucy's assessment of him, "Is there anything else you need, or I can do, before I go?"

"No, I'm fine thanks Dave," she replied. She started to say something else, causing Dave to pause. She then paused, unsure why she did not just come out with what she wanted to ask. Taking another breath, she tried again. "Unless you want to get a beer or something with me before you go?"

"I would love to, but should really let you get some rest. I'll be here to pick you up at about half eight tomorrow morning then." As he said the words, he knew he might come to regret not taking the chance of some private time with Lucy. He could feel an attraction to her developing, but doubted she could ever feel the same about him.

Trying not to give away his sudden rush of feelings, he gave her a friendly smile and said "Good night Lucy."

As he made his way out the room, Lucy said "I'm looking forward to getting some time with you tomorrow. I'll see you in the morning then."

Closing the door behind him, Dave walked along the corridor towards the hotel reception area, shaking his head.

"I must be mad not taking her up on her offer," he said to himself, reaching the door into the main lobby. Looking back along the corridor towards her room door, he muttered "Completely mad."

Chapter 11

Suddenly, Dave sat bolt upright in bed. There was a familiar sound, but he could not place what it was. Feeling like he was still asleep, he wasn't sure if he was dreaming or awake at present.

He wiped his face with his hand and decided he was actually not dreaming at this point in time. He leaned over and fumbled on the bed side cabinet for the source of the noise. The first thing he found was his alarm clock.

After pressing the snooze button on the clock had not stopped the noise, he moved his hand to turn the bedside lamp on. However, as he did, his hand moved over something vibrating which felt like it was more likely to be the source of the noise.

Looking closely, he realised it was his mobile phone he had left next to the bed that was ringing.

As he picked it up, he took a closer look at the alarm clock on his bedside cabinet. The display read 2.32. No wonder it was still dark and he was struggling to wake up.

"Hunt here," he said as he answered the call. He was trying his best to sound more awake than he actually was. However, he failed miserable to do so.

"Alpha Lead, you're to report to Alpha Command immediately," the voice on the phone said. "You will need to pick up Doctor Tyler on your way. We have an emergency situation that has occurred in the past half hour."

Dave, now almost fully awake at the impact of the news, instantly recognised the voice as that of Harry Wheelhouse. "What's happened?" he asked. "What do you mean a situation?"

"This is not a secured line Alpha Lead. Report to Alpha Command immediately." Harry sounded considerably more serious than Dave had ever remembered him. This was the second call he had received in the middle of the night during the past three days, but this time it sounded like something major had happened.

He put the phone down, leaned over to turn on the lamp beside the bed and swung himself out of bed. Grabbing a pair of jeans and white t-shirt from the chair next to the door, he quickly threw the clothes on.

Still not being one hundred percent awake, and trying to find his way around his dimly lit room, he kept tripping on last night's clothes that he had left strewn across the floor. Eventually he gave in and turned the overhead light on.

Sitting on the edge of the bed, he pulled on his socks, followed by a pair of trainers. As he did, he wondered if this was going to be too casual a look. Especially if they were to go somewhere that they might meet the public, he might need to make an effort to look more presentable. That was why he also kept a wardrobe of clothes in the command centre, just in case.

With a final wipe of his eyes, he got up and walked out the room and headed downstairs. As he got to the bottom of the stairs, he remembered he had left his mobile phone upstairs. As he made his way back up to his bedroom, he was greeted by his cat, Hammond, at the top of the stairs.

The cat had been named so thanks to a previous girlfriend's obsession with car programs and a bizarre crush on one of the presenters. The cat itself was a small and scrawny looking animal, so was quite aptly named.

Leaning down to stroke it on the head, he said "Sorry mate, I've got to go into work."

The cat followed him into the room seeking attention having been woken up by Dave moving round. As he grabbed his phone from where he had left it on his bed, he turned back round and fell over the cat as he walked towards the door.

"Hammond," he yelled. "Sorry, but I'm in a hurry here mate. I'll get someone to pop in and feed you later." He followed as the cat ran down the stairs and disappeared. Dave shook his head decided he would worry about the cat later on. There were more important things to be dealt with at the moment.

As he got back downstairs, he grabbed his car keys and wallet from the table next to the front door. He also picked up his STAR Park security badge as he was going to have to go in the front way tonight.

Once he had got in the car and pulled out of his driveway, he plugged the phone into the hands free kit and dialled the number Lucy had given him during the afternoon. This would allow him a secure connection to her mobile.

"Better try and wake her up before I get there" he said out loud to himself. "At least it will give her a small chance to get ready."

There was no answer as the phone diverted to a voicemail. Lucy's message just stated her name. Seeing as this was a secure line only used by the members of her team, there was no need for it to be more than just her stating her name. He did not bother to leave a message as it was only a couple of minutes drive to the hotel. He would just have to wake her up when he got there.

Opening her eyes, Lucy found herself sitting up in her bed. Sweat was pouring down her face. She had just had another dream, like so many others that she'd had before. Often she could not remember her dreams at all. In the past she had put this down to probably something she had eaten during that day, but she became less certain of the cause as the years had passed.

It did not help that she had always had trouble sleeping in strange places, particularly while travelling. Having not slept for almost two days as she had travelled over to the United Kingdom, she had been keen to get some sleep during the night.

She took several deep breaths as she tried to calm herself, gently wiping her hand across her forehead.

A loud banging off to her left caused her to focus her attention back to the present. That was probably what had woken her from her dream in the first place. As she took a few seconds to look around the room around her, she remembered she was staying in a hotel in the United Kingdom. Leaning over, she turned the lamp beside the bed on.

"Lucy, I need you to get up," she could hear a voice saying on the other side of the door. It sounded like someone was trying not to shout while also attempting to be heard through the hotel door.

Lucy, only wearing a short, white satin nightdress, scrambled out of the bed and half stumbled over to the door. Checking the security chain was in place, she opened the door so she could look out and talk to who ever was outside.

"Lucy, it's me." Dave said. She picked up on the agitation in his voice as he spoke quickly. "There's been an emergency. We've been ordered to get ourselves to Alpha Command straight away."

"Okay," she said. "You'd better come in and wait. I will need a couple of minutes to get dressed."

"Thanks Lucy," Dave said as Lucy closed the door to so she could release the security chain again. She then completely opened it again so she could let Dave in to the room.

As he passed her, she noticed him take a sly look at her in her nightdress and she felt slightly embarrassed.

Normally, she would have felt completely embarrassed to be caught by a stranger while she was wearing so little. Yet the feeling she got with Dave was very different. It was not the fact that he had taken a look at her dressed like this that embarrassed her, but it was the feeling of being flattered that she knew he had.

Ever since she had first learnt about him, and as she spent more time with him, she was starting to feel a stronger attraction towards him. But now was not the time to think about that.

Closing the door, she grabbed some of the new clothes by the bed and headed into the bathroom. As she did, she said "give me a minute or so to change." She pulled the door too behind her, but she did not close it completely.

Dave walked into the main area of the room and found a chair next to the window, upon which he sat down. He took a look across the room and saw the various bags from the replacement clothes they had arranged for Lucy carefully lined up next to the bed. It looked like she had probably put most of the clothes she was likely to need in the drawers and the wardrobe already.

On the bed itself, the covers were thrown back across it. This was obviously from where she had just got out in a hurry to answer the door just those few seconds before. On the far side of the bed was a bedside cabinet, upon which he saw Lucy's mobile phone, her purse and other personal belongings.

"I hope you got some sleep," he called out towards the bathroom.

"A bit," Lucy replied. "Like I may have said before, you get used to the hours of the job and the lack of sleep that comes with it. Also, I never sleep well the first night in a different place."

"I notice that you looked a bit hot just now," he asked.

"Excuse me?" she called back quickly, surprised by the question.

"I mean, is the room too warm for you?" he responded as he realised he had probably picked the wrong words. "You looked like you might have been a bit too hot."

Before she could answer, a noise from the cabinet behind him made Dave jump, catching him by surprise after being so engrossed in the short conversation. Realising it was Lucy's mobile phone, he picked it up and looked at the display.

"It looks like that someone at the DPD is calling you," he said towards Lucy.

"Can you answer it then? I'm not quite decent yet," Lucy replied hurriedly.

Dave pressed the button to answer the call. "Doctor Tyler's phone."

"Who is this?" a strong, male sounding voice asked at the other end.

"Hunt. Dave Hunt from Alpha Command," Dave said. It was a line he had always wanted to use ever since he started working for secret agencies and this seemed like a moment for it to cause amusement. He smiled to himself as he spoke. "Is that Deputy Director Johnson?"

"Where's Doctor Tyler?" Johnson asked. He had obviously not picked up on Dave's attempted humour. "I need to speak to her immediately."

"I'm afraid she's getting dressed still," Dave replied. "You'll need to give her a couple of minutes yet I guess."

"What do you mean…? How come you are answering her phone?" he started to enquire. After a slight pause, he continued "No, I'm not going to ask. I take it the two of you are aware about what has happened then?"

"No, not really. I was on the way to Alpha Command and I had to pick up Lucy from the hotel. What can you tell us?" Dave had walked towards the bathroom and peered into the room just as Lucy, now fully dressed, opened the door. She glared at him, more out of show than actual irritation.

"Just get yourselves to Alpha Command as quickly as you can. How long will it take you to get there?" Johnson asked.

"Ten minutes, maybe fifteen absolute tops. I take it this must be serious then." Dave eyes followed Lucy as she walked past him and back through to the bedroom area. She was now dressed in a pair of blue jeans and white t-shirt. She was still pulling on a black fleece jacket as she sat on the edge of the bed.

"Not since the night of the Space Shuttle encounter have we had such a serious incident. I suggest you hurry Lucy up and get going immediately." Dave realised that Johnson was quite concerned about the situation, whatever it was that was happening. "We'll speak shortly."

Dave pressed the disconnect button and ended the call. He held the phone out to Lucy.

"Looks like the shit has hit the fan," Dave said grimly. "I think we better get a move on."

"We better get going then," Lucy replied. As she continued to speak, she held her hand out towards Dave. "Let me put my watch on, and I'll grab my ID cards from the table." She put her watch on, having taken it from the desk next to the TV as she had passed Dave and picked her ID cards for STAR Park up from the table.

As Lucy made her way towards the door, she turned back to Dave and continued. "Let's go and find out what's going on then."

As Dave and Lucy entered the command room, they took a quick look at each other. They quickly realised how severe the situation must be. For a start, Dave knew the doors were never normally sealed shut behind them as they entered the room. He also felt a different air around the place as they had made their way up from the lifts.

On the monitors across the wall were TV screens showing images of what looked like an airplane of some description on fire. To the left, the next monitor showed what Dave thought was an infra-red image of the same area. Various other images and displays were across the remaining screens around the room.

"I've seen images like that before," Lucy said, looking back at Dave. "It's pretty much like the one I saw from shortly after the first impact when the shuttle had encountered that alien craft."

"Lucy, it is considerably more serious than that event," Johnson's voice said across speakers in the room. "I can confirm that another unidentified craft has been monitored as it approached the planet during the evening. This time we had a better idea of what we were tracking than we did back then. It was tracked to about thirty miles from where you are presently."

Harry Wheelhouse stepped forwards towards the monitors.

"Just over an hour ago, we started getting reports of an unidentified craft from the United States Air Force radar stations as it entered our local airspace. Within minutes, the US air force scrambled four F15 jets from RAF Lakenheath."

Harry looked directly at Lucy, "That's the one of our local air base round here. The United States Air Force has a large force based there."

Johnson took over describing the events of the evening so far. "It appears that as the fourth jet was taking off, it collided with something as it left the end of the runway. The pilot had started to report something appearing in his flight path before the personnel in the control tower reported seeing an explosion on the jet's flight path."

"Are you trying to say the jet actually hit this craft?" Dave asked.

"If one of the jets hit it, what happened to the craft?" Lucy added interrupting Dave before he could finish.

"That's what the makes the situation quite urgent that we get the both of you out there as fast as we can." Johnson said. "The craft is still there."

Harry used pressed a button on the control he was carrying and one of the screens changed display to show an over head shot of the airbase.

"This is live feed from a US spy satellite from the Defence guys we have been able to link into. As Lakenheath is a military base, the incident site has been secured around the jet aircraft itself."

From the image on the screen, they could clearly see where the airplane had crashed. It was still surrounded by flames and smoke. As Harry pressed another button, another image appeared showing an area just off to the west of the runway. Along one side of the image ran a white line, Dave instantly realised this was the security fence surrounding the airbase.

"The alien craft has been reported as crashing several hundred yards outside the base limit. While the military have moved to surround the crash site, we need to recover the craft as soon as possible."

"We want the two of you to go to the site and find out what's left of the craft. Early reports have raised concerns that we may have an intact alien vessel to deal with. We also need to know what has to be done to move this thing and bring it back here to Alpha Command," Harry explained. "This could well be the best piece of alien technology that has come into our hands yet."

Lucy stepped forward and addressed Johnson. "What did the craft do before the crash? Do we know where it's been?"

"I've got our guys working on that right now. They are already reviewing the satellite reports and information collated at Cheyenne Mountain, along with the information we are collecting directly from the airbase." Johnson said sternly. "I've got the team here trawling the internet for any talk of sightings or stories so we can keep a lid on this issue. Now get yourselves moving and get to that crash site."

"Remember," Harry added, "the crash may have been on an American airbase, but it might not stop our opponents from taking control given the chance."

"As the craft has crashed outside, you will be responsible for the alien vehicle until we can decide what to do with it," Johnson said. Quickly he added "Not that I doubt your team's ability to deal with this Mr Wheelhouse."

"There's a helicopter waiting on the pad up top," Harry said, not responding to the previous comment from the American. "Take the Taser guns with you, just in case, and keep in contact."

"Good luck and let us hope this is the breakthrough we need," Johnson added.

Dave looked over at Lucy with a determined look but she recognised the excitement behind his eyes. This was something she had seen in her team on their mission out in the field. They both turned and headed out of the command room, Lucy closely following Dave. The time for action had arrived for the Alpha Team.

Chapter 12

Sitting on the helicopter as it lifted off from the ground, Lucy sat looking out of the window. It was going to take less than twenty minutes to fly from the Alpha Command Centre in Ipswich to the crash site. Flying in planes had never bothered her, but she was still to get used to helicopters.

A lot had happened during the past few months and not for the first time she caught herself asking how she had got involved with all this. Sometimes she wished it was just a bad dream, but if it was, it was one she could not wake up from.

She had never imagined when she had joined the DPD that she would ever have been trying to save her own planet from aliens. She knew the threat from asteroids or such like was real and the Earth had been hit before, but she had never accepted the possibility of another species visiting the planet.

She had been on many flights such as this when they had been investigating a case back home in America, but not since the first flight had she felt so nervous. Sitting on another helicopter, heading out to another encounter with another alien craft, but in strange country this time, it really hit her hard how far the alien threat had been able spread in such a short time. She wondered if this meant they were starting to loose the battle, or if this were to just be a minor set back.

While her heart was telling her that they would win the war against the alien threat, her head was starting to question how much they could really control the situation. With people like Dave, she felt they might have the right people to deal with the problem.

She looked over to Dave, who was talking to someone through the microphone on the headset he was wearing. She could not help but wonder if between them, Dave and Harry had grasped the seriousness of the situation. For them to become actively involved in the fight against the alien threat, they were going to have to learn very quickly that it was a major step up from just watching the DPD in the background.

She caught Dave's eye as he continued to talk and he gave her a reassuring smile. She felt she could trust this guy, even though she had only really just met him properly the day before. Maybe that was because he had already saved her life once, but she already knew deep down that they would be able to work well together and lead their respective teams to defeating the aliens.

Dave pulled the headset off and leaned over to talk her. He passed her an envelope which contained an ID badge. She took the envelope, opened it and turned the badge over in her hand. It displayed her picture and her name, Dr L Tyler, World Health Organisation.

"The US military do not yet know what caused the crash, only that an unidentified air craft entered their air space," Dave shouted over the noise of helicopter. "Harry said the cover story is that someone had flown a Predator type drone into the country from a vessel just off the coast. We have also told them that we suspect a biological contaminant may have been on board. The area is to be secured as such while our advance team check it out."

She looked at Dave cynically and asked "Don't we look a little unprepared for a biological incident?"

"We'll be landing at the entrance way to the airbase where Harry has arranged for a bio-hazard unit to set up," Dave explained. "When we land, we will meet with the advance team in place who have begun investigating the site. They should be able to provide the 'confirmation' that it is safe for us to access the craft."

"Technically we are here as part of the World Health Organisation to seek reassurance of the United Kingdoms response to a suspected biological attack," Dave continued. "But, we should have a small military team of our own from Alpha Command arriving shortly after we do. They should be able to secure any wreckage for retrieval and delivery to our base."

Lucy smiled. "I like the cover story, but do the military buy it? What about the base personnel?"

"Johnson confirms that non-essential personnel on base have all been confined to their residences. As this has happened at night, most of them would have been asleep and those who live off the base are already at home. That just leaves the night watch, but being at night time and fairly dark, we don't think they actually saw much other than enough for them to make their own stories up."

"And the wreckage, if we do find anything?" Lucy asked. "What's the plan with that?"

"I'm hoping you can help advise us on what we need to do when we get there," Dave replied. "As you say, if we actually do find anything that might be of use to us."

In front of Dave, the pilot waved his hand to get their attention. Dave put his head set back on and listened to what he was saying.

Lucy looked back out the window of the helicopter. She could see that they were now on the final approach to the airbase. The helicopter had started to bank slightly as they circled the site, and out of the window she spotted the two crash sites.

"We're here," Dave said leaning in close to talk to her again, but also to look out of the window. "Just in case, you hadn't already guessed."

Lucy smiled to herself at his comment as she continued to look out at the scene below. On the actual air base, towards the end of the runway, she could see the remains of the crashed jet. There was still a fire burning around the wreckage, but the fire engines and emergency vehicles surrounding it seemed to be gaining control of the situation in comparison to the pictures they had seen back at the command centre.

Outside of the base, as Harry and Johnson had already outlined to them earlier, a second site in the woods was lit up. She could see where the craft had entered the woods by the path of trees which had been knocked down. In the middle, she could see something silver on the ground.

As the helicopter lowered closer to the ground, she could see the control site outside the main entrance to the base was made up of three main tents. It looked like a decontamination area with water sprays and equipment she had seen in emergency drills back in the United States. She noted that there were at least ten people wandering around, most of them dressed in red haz-mat suits.

The helicopter touched down just inside the base perimeter as close as the pilot could get to the main entrance. There were two armed soldiers quickly approaching the helicopter before they had opened the door.

"Dr Tyler, Dr Hunt," the first of them said as they started to climb out of the helicopter. He closely examined their ID badges that they both held out before he continued. "If you'd like to follow me, I'll take you to the base CO. He's waiting in the command tent the other side of the base entrance."

Dave and Lucy followed the soldier who had spoken to them, as the second one followed closely behind. They didn't have to go far to reach the command tent. The leading soldier opened the tent door and let them in.

"Sir," the soldier said loudly as they approached an older man in a USAF uniform. As he looked up, the soldier continued. "The World Health Organisation experts are her as requested, Sir."

As the General saluted him, the soldier returned the salute and then turned back and made his way out of the tent.

"Dr Tyler, Dr Hunt. I'm glad you could make it. My name is General Mitchell." He walked over and shook both Dave and Lucy's hands.

"Thank you General Mitchell," Dave said as they shook hands. "What's the current status of the situation?"

"We have actually got the fires at the crash site of the F15 under control right now. We expect to have it completely out within the next thirty minutes or so."

"What about the pilot?" Lucy asked, sounding genuinely concerned. She thought she knew the truth, but wanted to hear it to be sure.

"I'm afraid he never had time to eject. He died in the crash," the General explained. We currently believe it was immediately on impact with the unidentified craft. As for the second, unidentified craft, I sent six of the base guards out to investigate."

"You sent out six guards?" Lucy asked.

"However," General Mitchell said before Lucy could follow up on her question. "I received a call from the National Security Advisor back home who instructed me to setup a perimeter around the site and secure it. I was to then await contact from you, Dr Tyler, or from a Mr Wheelhouse of a UK/US joint response force."

"We did that, and about ten minutes ago, the guys with hazmat suits entered the secured site and began investigating the craft. Can you enlighten me as to what is so special here? Why would the World Health Organisation have an interest?"

"I'm afraid that is classified information at this stage General," Lucy replied. "Who's in charge of the operation here then?"

"This way please, I shall take you to him."

General Mitchell led them across the tent to a table, over which was spread a large scale map of the area. On this map, there was an outline of where the craft wreckage had fallen. It confirmed what they had already been told about there only being the one piece of wreckage.

Next to the table stood a man, dressed fully in a red hazmat suit, who was in the process of removing his helmet.

"Dr Hunt, I'm really pleased to see you again," he said, sounding quite enthusiastic. Turning to General Mitchell, he continued "Thank you General, I can take it from here."

As the General moved away, Dave moved round the table and walked over to greet the other man. As he did, they shook each other's hands to make it look they were old acquaintances meeting up again.

"How are you doing Stuart? Is everything secure?" Dave asked.

"By the book, or rather by your protocols," Stuart replied. "No-one is allowed to go near the wreckage without one of the Alpha guys being with them."

"What about the guards that the General said had been sent out to it earlier?" Lucy began questioning him as she made her way around the table to join them. "How close did they get to it? Where are they now?"

"We have taken them to the med-tent, isolated from anyone else," Stuart started. "Following the experiences we have learned from your team Dr Tyler, we ensure anyone who might get close to any possible alien artefact that we know little about will be isolated until we can get them tested for any possible effects. I've got one of my medical team running the first set of blood tests as we speak."

"Have you been able to test the site and the craft using the nano-probe scanner?" Dave asked. "Is there any immediate threat when we go up there?"

"Yes, while the count is higher than normal, it does not appear to be all that high. I'm almost certain you will be fine not wearing a hazmat suit as long as you are only exposed for a relatively short periods." Stuart paused, catching a look form on Lucy's face as if to question his certainty. "As I say, I am as certain as I can be given the results from our scanner. We've not exactly been able to test it up close before."

Lucy did not say anything, but held his gaze for a few seconds more before Dave asked another question to break the moment.

"What is up there then?" Dave questioned.

"You'll be amazed by what we found," Stuart said. "There's nothing like this craft as we know it. And I'll save the biggest surprise for you for when you actually see it."

As Stuart started to lead the way out of the tent, Dave's mobile phone began to ring. He quickly grabbed it out of his jacket pocket and answered the call.

"Dave, it's Harry," he heard. "You may want to get a move on and return to Alpha Command with what we can. We have intercepted a call from the Home Secretary. He has issued an order for the army to take control of the site outside the airbase. They will be there in less than twenty minutes."

"Shit," Dave said loudly enough that everyone in the tent heard. Almost everyone there stopped what they were doing and turned to look round at him. "Thanks for the heads up Harry."

He disconnected the call and turned to Lucy. "We need to move the wreckage now, or else we will loose it to who ever the Home Secretary sees fit. I seriously doubt that it would be either the Alpha or the DPD teams. How have you ever had to move one of these things before, bearing in mind that by road might not be an option here?"

"We have been able to produce a material that reduced the emissions from infected items," Lucy tried to explain, "but we have not got any of that here. Let's go and see what we are looking at. Maybe we can load it on to the chopper we flew in on."

"Follow me," Stuart said, starting to head out of the tent again. "It will be a bit big to put in the helicopter you came in though."

As he led them out of the back of the tent, they headed towards a pathway into the woods. Two guards stepped forward to block their way along the path, but Stuart waved them aside. He confirmed with them that Dave and Lucy were with him, letting them check their ID badges before the three of them proceeded towards the crash site.

It only took them a couple of minutes to approach the piece of wreckage. Stuart had been spot on. It just looked like an elongated metal cylinder, but to their surprise, there wasn't any sign of damage to it at all. The object appeared to have its outer shell section to be intact.

Before they could get right up next to the wreckage, Lucy stopped and stood, staring at it. This was nothing like the probe that had been reported by the crew on board the shuttle. That had been a spherical shape.

This seemed to be very different, yet there was something very familiar about it. She just could not understand why she felt that so strongly, but suspected she must have dreamed about this at some point.

"Given the size of it, I reckon we could secure it to the underside of the helicopter and have it out of here in ten minutes," Stuart said to Dave. "What do you think?"

"Obviously, I would rather be studying it here and finding out what it is before we move it." Dave was walking around the craft as he spoke. "I guess that we really have no choice given the circumstances. Let's use one of the tents to cover it. We can then strap it to the helicopters landing pads, as long as the pilot can hover for a couple of minutes."

"The clearing here is definitely large enough," Stuart said, quickly looking around the area of woodland they were stood in.

"Go back and get a tent, ropes, whatever you think we need. Get the pilot to fly over here now. I'll go and check over the craft with Lucy while we wait." Dave started to head back onto the same side of the wreckage as the others, but turned back to Stuart. "Best you get a move on as well."

Bending down, Dave was running his fingers along the side of the craft. He then laid his whole hand against the side and rubbed it up and down further. Although he did not know what to expect, he was completely surprised by what he found.

"Lucy, feel this. I can't believe how smooth the side feels," he said.

When he did not get a reply from her, he stood back up and turned around.

"Lucy? Where are you?" he called out, looking around for her. He stepped forward, looking everywhere around him, but could not see anyone. "Lucy!"

As he continued to step forward, he noticed that something was not right. He took a closer look at the trees. All around him, the forest started to burn. He could feel the heat against his face as flames engulfed everything he could see.

An eerie voice sounded over the noise of the fire. Dave could just make out the words as they were whispered from all around him.

"This world is ours."

"Hello. Who's there?" he shouted out to it as he continued to try see whatever it was that was speaking. As he did, something dark moved through the flames to his side. He turned and stepped towards it as it seemed to move further into the trees, still trying to hide from him.

As he stepped closer, the flames grew higher. Dave had to raise his hand as the heat started to burn his skin. He put his hands to his face to feel as the skin started to blister away from him.

He jumped as he felt something touch him on the shoulder, causing him to look round at what it was. To his complete surprise it was Lucy, laying her hand on his shoulder. She was stood over him, looking down, as he was still squatting beside the alien craft.

As he looked up at her, he lifted his hand away from the craft. He suddenly felt very strange, like he had lost his way and did not know where to turn. He touched his face with his right hand as he realised what he had just seen was not real.

He was still in the forest by the craft. There had been no fire and he had not been burning.

"Dave, what happened? Why did you not respond?" she asked, sounding more than a little concerned. She squatted down next to him, running her hand over his sweat covered face. He felt cold as she touched him.

"I'm not sure really. It appeared to look so real," he answered, looking a little confused. "The forest. It was all burning. All around me, fire. Then there was something off in the distance. There was someone or something in the distance, moving in the flames."

"Did it say anything to you," Lucy said, looking him straight in the eyes. She recognised the look of dread in his expression as one she had seen in soldiers returning from survivors of the World Trade Centre attacks back home.

"How do you know that?" Dave asked shakily. "How can you know what I saw?"

"I've heard the voice in my dreams," she answered. "I've seen the fire. I'd initially put it down to being spooked by what had happened. I think it proves we have made contact with whoever sent this thing. I think you have also seen their plans for our planet."

"That is something I am going make damn sure they cannot do, is destroy our home," Dave told Lucy, extreme determination coming into his voice. "We're going to get this thing back to Alpha Command and do everything we can to beat them."

Chapter 13

"The helicopter is on the way up here," Stuart called as he ran back up towards Dave and Lucy at the crash site. He found it quite hard going as he had several ropes thrown over his shoulder and a piece of tarpaulin in his arms. "But I think we have another problem."

"What now?" Dave said, standing up from where he had been squatted down, talking to Lucy about his vision. "You go first, but we've also got some bad news to tell you."

"Those six soldiers we tested for infection," Stuart said. "We got their first set of test results back and they were more than a little worrying. Four of them show increased theta waves and two show sign of mutation of their DNA. I've arranged for them to be transferred to Alpha Command for extra testing. They'll be following us in a second helicopter."

They heard the sound of the helicopter approaching, as Stuart threw the ropes over to Dave. He began throwing the large piece of tarpaulin he had brought up with him over the craft.

"Don't touch the sides, whatever you do." Lucy told Stuart. She started to ask him "do you know if any of the soldiers touched the craft when they were up here earlier?"

As she talked to Stuart, her attention was drawn away as she caught sight of Dave wandering away from them. He was walking towards the trees, searching across the ground. He was kicking bits of stick and logs as he went.

"I don't to be honest. I should think we need to get you to be involved with questioning them back at base later." Following Lucy's change of attention, Stuart had also started to watch Dave, trying to make out what he was looking for.

"Stuart, get over here," Dave called, as he leaned down and was moving something around on the floor.

Having finished putting the tarpaulin over the craft, Stuart quickly made his way over to where Dave was. He was surprised to see that he had found and was closely looking at two very large, sturdy branches. He looked at his boss, puzzled as to what Dave was thinking.

"Grab one and I'll take the other," Dave said as he bent down to grab the first of the two branches.

"Why? What do we need these for?" Stuart asked, still not able to figure out what Dave was intending to do. He looked back towards Lucy and shrugged his shoulders towards her.

"We can use these to lift each end of the craft, while Lucy feeds the ropes round. We then won't have to touch the craft as we try and secure it to the helicopter," Dave explained.

"So, what happens then if you touch this thing?" Stuart questioned. "I take it that it isn't something good."

"You don't want to know," Dave said, looking Stuart straight in the eyes. "Just believe me when I say that I'm still more than a little freaked out from when I did just now." He started to make his way back towards the craft with his branch. "Let's just get on with getting this thing out of harms way as quickly as possible. We don't have much time left."

"Why, what's the sudden rush to move it?" Stuart was well known for asking a lot of questions, which Dave had sometimes struggled to keep his patience with when they had worked together before. This was one of the occasions that it would be best to pull Stuart back into line.

"Will you stop asking questions and get on with helping us move it," Dave said facing Stuart. The look he gave Stuart would be enough to tell him they were not messing around here. "When Harry called, it was to tell us the army are on their way with orders from the Home Secretary to take this thing back with them. They will be here in a matter of minutes. They won't be in a mood for asking questions either."

With a sigh, which was more as a show of attempted defiance than anything else, Stuart grabbed the second branch and followed Dave. They quickly dragged them back over to where the craft was. As they did, Dave noticed that while they had been talking, Lucy had already placed the ropes next to each end of the craft.

They each slid their branch underneath the craft, one of them on each side of it. Between them, they were able to lift it about half a foot or so off the ground. This would be enough gap for Lucy to feed the ropes around it.

Quickly, Lucy took the rope and fed one end underneath, before moving round behind Dave and pulling the end through. She then threw the rope over the top of the craft and ran back round behind Stuart. She repeated this several times so the rope was wrapped around the craft three or four times.

In the meantime, she was battling against the growing wind that the helicopter lowering itself above them generated. She kept having to shake her head to stop her hair blowing across her face.

By the time she had finished wrapping the rope around a third time, the helicopter had lowered itself over the craft, but the pilot waited for further direction from the ground to ensure he did not get too low. It was just above their heads, so Dave and Stuart lowered the craft back to the ground.

Dave waved the pilot down further so that it was low enough to reach the foot rails underneath it. Both he and Stuart grabbed the ends of the ropes and begun to tie them to the rails, pulling the ropes as tight as they could around the craft.

At another wave from Dave, the pilot lifted the helicopter slightly, raising the craft further of the ground. Grabbing another piece of rope, Dave and Stuart pulled it underneath the craft and worked it along so it was as close to the opposite end as they could get it.

Again, they started to pass the rope around the craft several times. Dave tied his end of the rope securely around the foot rail, as Stuart threw his end over the craft. Lucy ducked under Dave and threw the rope back under the craft to Stuart.

Lucy paused for a couple of seconds as she saw a number of lights appearing in the woods behind Stuart, coming up from the control area at the air base. Obviously the army team had arrived and were now headed after the craft themselves.

"You better get a move on," she shouted towards Dave, trying to make herself heard over the noise of the helicopter. She pointed back towards the approaching lights. "We've got company heading our way and fast."

Both Dave and Stuart looked in the direction Lucy was pointed and could clearly see at least twenty separate lights coming up the hill. They were running out of time.

Turning their attention back to the craft, they tied the rope round the craft about three times again. Stuart securely tied the other end to the other foot rail of the helicopter. At least, Stuart hoped it was going to be secure enough to hold until they got back to Alpha Command. He gave the end of the rope a couple of tugs to reassure himself. He looked up and gave Dave a quick thumbs up to show he was done.

Now with the craft secured to the bottom of the helicopter, the pilot lowered it down as low as he dared, allowing Dave to climb up into it. As soon as he had scrambled on board, he turned and offered Lucy his hand to help her up. Stuart stood behind her and by placing his hands her hips, helped lift her to make it easier for her.

Once they were both in the helicopter, they both reached down to grab Stuart's hands. Despite the two of them holding him, they struggled to pull him into the helicopter.

"Go" Dave shouted at the pilot, even as they were still helping Stuart into the helicopter. "Get us out of here, now."

They finally pulled him in with them literally as the first soldier burst into the opening, shouting at them to stop.

As the pilot lifted the helicopter further from the ground, gun shots began to ring out from below them. The first of the soldiers arriving in the clearing had begun to open fire on the helicopter. Dave ducked as one of the bullets cracked through the window on the helicopter door as he pulled it shut.

As the pilot flew the helicopter forward, he was only just able to gain enough height, scraping the craft below them across top of the trees at the edge of the clearing. The sound of gun fire dropped off as they left the crash site below.

The pilot circled over the air base as he begun to head back towards Alpha Command. Within a few seconds, a second helicopter started to fly alongside them, also having just taken off from outside the base. The pilot held out a head set and waved it at Dave. He moved so he could take this from him and put it on.

"Hunt here," he said speaking into the microphone.

"This is the pilot of chopper two," the voice said over the radio. "We will follow you in to Alpha Command. I have six passengers on board, as requested Sir."

"Thanks. Stay tight on us and keep an eye out for company." Dave was trying to look out of the helicopter to see how far behind them the second one was. He could see as it moved from being alongside to flying just off their tail.

"Alpha Command, this is Alpha Lead here," Dave said over the radio. He knew that Harry would be listening in to them on the agreed frequency. "We have two birds incoming, both with cargo."

"Alpha Command confirms," Harry acknowledged over the radio. "The landing pad is cleared and ready for inbound birds."

Dave took the headset off and laid it on the seat next to him. Both Lucy and Stuart were sitting opposite him, looking out of the windows on either side of the helicopter, watching from where they had just left.

"Won't they learn the whereabouts of the command centre when we land these two helicopters?" Lucy asked Dave, turning to face him. "Even if they do not follow us, they can track us on radar."

"Pilot," Dave called as he twisted in his seat and looked forward. "Switch to silent mode. Signal the other bird to do the same."

The pilot waved back his acknowledgement as he flicked a couple of switches on the helicopter's flight panel. Instantly, the noise from the rotor blades became considerably quieter.

"Now they won't be able to." Dave turned to face Lucy, with a slight grin forming across his face. "We are now silent and should be undetectable to radar. We'll take a slightly longer route to Alpha Command than we took to get here as we do have an alternate site just in case they have sent someone after us."

"Just sit back and enjoy the ride home," Stuart said, leaning back in the chair. He tipped his head back slightly and closed his eyes.

Lucy sat just looking at Dave. She had been impressed with his quick thinking, especially once the pressure had started to increase. She was concerned about the effect that the craft might have had on him, especially as she had only ever had the dreams while asleep. Never had she experienced one while she actually awake.

From the moment they had approached the craft, she had found that she had started to develop a head ache. Even now, she could feel it beginning to pound. As she started to look away and back towards the window, she moved her hand to her nose. Something felt cold across her top lip.

As she looked at her fingers, she realised her nose was bleeding. She looked back to Dave, who had turned from looking out of the window and back towards her. She saw a look of surprise on his face as he too noticed the blood trickling out of her nose.

"You okay?" he asked as he quickly moved over to kneel on the floor in front of her. He pulled a handkerchief out of his pocket and gave it to her.

"I think so," she replied, holding the handkerchief up to her nose. "I've got a thumping headache coming on and now this."

"I've read reports before where people who claim to have been abducted talk about head aches and nose bleeds. Do you think it's the craft affecting you?" Dave asked. He was becoming increasingly concerned for her safety this close to the craft, if it was actually the cause of the problem. He knew full well, there was not way to get her away from the craft until they landed back at Alpha Command.

"It must be," she continued. "How long will it take till we get back to the command centre?"

"About ten minutes or so," he said, putting his hand on the side of her face. He smiled back as Lucy relaxed at his touch. "Are you going to be okay for that long?"

She nodded back and was about to say she would be, but was cut off by a frantic wave from the pilot up front. She pointed to him so Dave would turn his attention towards the front of the helicopter.

As he turned around, he picked the head set up from the seat and put it back on. As he listened, he quickly moved to press his face to the window and look out towards the second helicopter.

"We're going down," the pilot yelled though his microphone, albeit muffled as someone tried to take the headset from the pilot.

Dave kicked out to get Stuarts attention and shouted out "the second helicopter's going down. The pilot was cut off. What can you see out there?"

All three of them looked out the windows of their helicopter, trying to see where the second one was going down. It was still quite dark outside, so they were trying to look for the various landing and rotor lights that would be visible on it.

After a few seconds, they could see the brightness of the explosion as the helicopter crashed just off to their left. It had lost height fairly quickly and collided with what Dave suspected was an electricity pylon.

The pilot of their helicopter had to adjust his flight path a little as he had been distracted by his fellow pilot's demise.

Dave started to speak into the microphone, his voice full of urgency.

"Alpha Command, come in. We have a bird down. I repeat, we have a bird down. Crash site is four miles from Alpha Command. I repeat again, we have a bird down."

"Do you want me to put down?" the pilot asked over the radio.

"No, get us back to base," Dave responded. "The cargo is too important to risk. Alpha Command, can you get some assistance to the site."

"Do you expect any casualties Alpha Lead?" Harry's response came back over the radio.

"Negative, size of the explosion makes it look unlikely," Dave reported. "But we will need to get the bodies back to Alpha Command inside the hour though. Lead Out".

He began to take the headset off and place it back on the seat next to him as Lucy leaned forwards and beckoned Dave to do the same.

"Are you sure there won't be any survivors?" she asked, sounding more than a little sceptical. "If what we have seen before by these nano-probes increasing their abilities, they might be a bit stronger than you think."

Dave looked at Lucy for a few seconds, before putting the headset back on.

"Alpha Command, get someone to the crash site immediately. Make sure they are armed. Be prepared for hostile survivors." Dave sounded despondent as he spoke. "Our situation might be worse than I first thought."

As Dave entered the command room, Harry was already taking a call from the unit he has sent out to the crash site over the loud speaker system.

"He's just arrived," Harry was saying. "Please repeat your last statement."

"Sir, we have recovered six bodies, all are very badly burnt. Two are still alive, but only just."

"What about the pilot?" Dave asked, looking slightly concerned as he glanced at Lucy next to him. Both immediately realised that there was a passenger not being accounted for in that count.

"He was in the six we found on board Sir," the reply came back.

"There were six soldiers on board as well as the pilot," Lucy said sternly. "There should be seven bodies. You better be count them again and I want you to be absolutely positive about it."

After a pause of a few seconds, the voice came back over the radio and said clearly "I can confirm we counted six bodies, including the pilot."

"I suggest you and your men arrange for those to be delivered here immediately." A touch of urgency started to creep into Lucy's voice as she spoke. "You will also detail some men to find and recover that seventh body."

"Sir, no one could have survived the crash," the soldier continued to argue. "The helicopter was pretty much wrapped around the pylon Sir."

Harry jumped in to take control immediately.

"Captain, you have your orders. You will send a team to search for the seventh body immediately. He may still be alive and mobile. You have authorisation to shoot to kill."

As the line was cut, Dave was sure he could hear mumblings in the background as the soldier and his colleagues were surprised by their new orders. If they only knew what they might have to deal with, then they would not be so willing to complain.

"Don't say it," Dave said, pointing to Lucy.

"What?" she replied shrugging her shoulders, an innocent smile forming.

"You were right back there on the helicopter. It looks like we have our first infectee on the loose. That changes things for us a little bit." Turning to face Harry, Dave asked "Have you been able to get the personnel records for the six soldiers from the air base?"

"I'm just waiting for them to be sent over to us. I had to get Johnson to request them for us," Harry explained. "Have you got any ideas about what happened on the helicopter before it crashed?"

"From the communications we got from the pilot, it sounded like there was a struggle on board." Dave said. "I suspect that one of the infected soldiers must have tried to take the helicopter over. When the pilot resisted, they lost control and crashed. Maybe even on purpose."

"Talking of infectees, shouldn't we be getting your blood tested fairly quickly?" Lucy asked Dave.

Just as she asked the question, Stuart entered the command room. He was carrying what looked like a doctor's briefcase. When he put it on the table and opened it up, she saw that it contained equipment to take blood samples and what looked like a fancy notebook computer. It was obvious to Lucy that the Alpha Team had been monitoring them closely and had developed some of their tools further.

"Already on to it," he said. "Hold out your arm then boss." There was an excitable tone to his voice, which instantly raised Lucy's suspicions that there was something going on.

Dave held his arm out, rolling the sleeve on his top up, so that Stuart could take a blood sample from him. As Stuart got the syringe out to take the sample, Dave pulled his arm back slightly.

"Hey boss, we've been through all this before," Stuart said. "I thought you had got used to having needles stuck into you. Or was that treatment all for nothing?"

Lucy looked Dave in the face and tried hard not to laugh at him. So far she had seen this all action, no fears type approach to things, but this fear of needles amused her.

Holding Lucy's gaze, Dave held his arm out so Stuart could take the blood sample. Lucy was able to keep a serious look on her face until Stuart had finished taking the sample. However, she could not help but laugh out as he removed the needle from Dave's arm.

"Sorry," she said, trying to control herself. "Just we can try and save the world, but you can't face a needle." She looked away. "Sorry, I really am."

"Thanks," Dave said, sounding very hurt by her reaction. "I know who not to turn to when I need support then."

As Stuart put some of the blood he had just taken into the sample tray on the testing device, Dave moved over and stood next to him to watch. Lucy moved alongside him and put her arm around his shoulders. He looked over to her and she smiled to show that she was sorry for having teased him. He smiled back to show that he was okay about it.

"It will only take a few seconds to see, but we will need to do another test in a couple of hours to be sure. Plus, I need to run through some of the new tests that our boys here have been developing. We now have a sample of blood that we can observe any possible alien infection develops." Stuart told Dave.

"I think you probably ought to have some tests as well Lucy," Stuart said turning towards her. "Given the nose bleed and headaches you talked about on the helicopter, I just want to be certain that you aren't affected by what's happened today."

"No problem. I really should have suggested it myself," she replied.

"As I said, with what you said on the helicopter," Stuart said, "I think it is doubly important that we get you tested to make sure that there are no problems from that encounter."

A sharp tone from the testing device got all their attentions back to the test. Stuart pressed a few keys on the laptop and a window displayed showing red blood cells, along with some graphs outlining cell counts.

"Okay then boss, do you want the good news or bad news first?" he asked, sounding very worried in deed.

Chapter 14

"Just tell me where I stand," Dave snapped sharply. "Don't mess me around here Stuart."

"I'm glad to say that you are clear of any signs of the nano-probes in your blood at the moment," Stuart said, a relieved smile appearing on his face, shortly followed by one of relief on Dave's face. "Well, that's the good news."

"So what's the bad news then?" Lucy asked.

"The bad news is that I'm going to have to do another blood test in a couple of hours. That will allow me to make a hundred per cent sure that there is definitely no nano-probes or signs of genetic mutation." Stuart answered, grinning insanely.

As Stuart started to put the testing kit away, Dave picked up some papers that were on the table in front of him. He quickly rolled them up slightly and whacked his colleague around the side of his head.

"You're a real ass you know," he said. "That wasn't funny at all."

Ignoring the banter between the two of them, Harry took a look over at the clock on the wall behind and noted that the time was now just after six in the morning. That would mean that Dave would need to have his next set of tests at just after about eight o'clock.

For now, they had a number of issues to be dealt with. They had two survivors of the crash on the way to the Alpha Command, along with four dead bodies, some of which were known to be infected by the genetic mutation caused by their encounter with the alien craft just hours before.

There was one infectee apparently on the loose somewhere in the Suffolk countryside, trying to evade soldiers who seemed to be unable to believe that anyone could possibly be fit enough to be on the run, let alone survive the helicopter crash.

One of the better pieces of news from the morning's events, Harry thought, was they had an actual alien craft to investigate and experiment with. This was something that they, the Alpha Team had, not their counterparts in America. While he knew they were fighting the same threat, there was a feeling of 'getting one over the competition' in the back of his mind.

Granted they had the head of Department of Planetary Defense working with them here at the moment, but Doctor Lucy Tyler was providing superb knowledge and experience to their new team. He was willing to accept that over the long term that the two teams would have to work together if they were to have any real chance in defeating the alien threat once or for all.

In reality, they were going to need help from other countries and people around the globe. The situation was far from United States Government's original view that this threat was an America only problem. This had developed into a global threat and could still prove to lead to humankind's demise.

As he had been watching the spirit amongst the three team members working together out in the field earlier that morning and again here in the command room, it was easy for him to forget the tragedy of three days before. The loss of the original three members of the Alpha Teams who had been brutally killed in their own homes was starting to become a distant memory.

So far, Stuart had fitted into the team very well. Stuart had been a forensic detective they had been able to obtain from the metropolitan police force. He had a PhD in biological research and had written a paper about the possibility life on Mars before he had joined the police.

While Dave was an expert with computer hardware, networks, security and general software, his key role was to run the Alpha Team and would likely to be on operational duty much of the time. Going forward, they would require someone who could assist with hacking into systems. While they could use their position in the intelligence services to access banks, the police systems and government records with impunity, they needed someone who could get into systems that they were not meant to have access to.

He was expecting a new member of the team to arrive some point during the morning. He was hoping that he would also fit in with the team as quickly as Stuart had, but he knew the new member was not necessarily a people person.

For now, he needed to get the team ready to crack on with all of the various tasks at hand.

"Right then all of you," he said abruptly, causing the team to stop talking and all look at him together. "It's time we got started on some of these jobs at hand I think."

Dave nodded and stepped away from the other two.

"Stuart," he started to say. "I want you to go and start running the various tests on those two survivors we brought back. Figure out if they are infected or not. They are certainly extremely lucky that they survived if they aren't. Then, check the bodies and perform autopsies, whatever you need to do."

"Yes boss," Stuart said.

"Lucy," Dave continued. "I need you to liaise with Johnson so we can sort out a cover story as to how these soldiers died, even those who are survived, while I will begin the investigations and looking into that craft."

"Is in here okay?" she asked.

"Yes," Dave replied. "Use what ever you need."

Harry interjected to say "Then I want you, Lucy, to get your guys to get in contact with Dave and help out with this craft."

Lucy nodded to show she was happy to do so. "I'm sure they are itching to get stuck into an opportunity like this."

"Oh, and all of you, remember to get that blood check done on Dave," Harry finished. "I don't want to miss any possible effect this craft has on him, or on Lucy for that matter."

"I'll need to do a scan of your brain waves, repeat the blood tests and some other ones so we can get a full picture of your status," Stuart said. He changed the tone of his so it sounded like he was now addressing a child and said "But remember I'll be testing Lucy as well, so you won't be on your own."

"Stop teasing him, will you," Lucy interrupted. Turning to Dave, she finished with a smirk "don't worry about Stuart. I'll hold your hand while the nasty man sticks the needle in your arm."

"Get on with it you lot," Harry ordered sternly, to which the team took their leave from the command room and made their way around the base to begin their various tasks.

Stuart quickly made his way over to the labs located next to the command room. His task for the moment was to start the examination of the bodies and the survivors they had brought back from the helicopter crash.

"Some real work to get stuck into," he thought, resisting the urge to rub his hands together in glee. He was raring to go on this work, realising he was one of just a handful of people who even knew about this threat. He felt that this was his calling in life and he would be the best at it.

As he entered the lab, he found the four body bags were just being delivered by some of the base soldiers. Each one was brought into the labs on a trolley, escorted by two soldiers to each one. This was something that he found quite strange, as they were meant to be dead bodies.

Each body was then transferred from its trolley and placed on a separate bed along one side of the lab.

He was more than little unsure as to what he was going to find in each of the body bags. For the first time in his life, he actually found himself hoping that he was just going to find a badly burned body of a human being in each of the bags.

"This doesn't feel right," he said to himself as he moved to the first of the body bags. As he took the zip in his hand, he paused and started to take a deep breath.

"What doesn't feel right?" Harry asked behind him, the result of which was to Stuart jump slightly.

"I was just thinking that I am hoping to find burned humans in the bags," Stuart answered gingerly. "I've never wanted to find a person in a body bag before, so this just feels a little bit weird."

"I did tell you when you signed up for this that you would not be dealing with the ordinary," Harry retorted. "Perhaps now you will believe what I told you."

"I didn't really doubt it, but even this is quite beyond what I was expecting. Let's have a look at the first one then shall we?" Stuart said as he took the body bag's zip in his fingers again.

Looking at Harry, he slid the zip along the body bag about a quarter of the length of it. Taking a deep breath, he carefully peeled open the top of the body bag and took a look inside.

Harry moved so he could stand alongside him, also taking a close look inside the body bag. He could see that as Stuart peeled the plastic of the bag back, skin and burnt flesh peeled away from the body inside.

"Is that what you expect to find then?" Harry enquired, finding himself squirming at the sight of a badly burned body.

"Sure looks like a human to me," Stuart replied. He reached over to the small trolley next to them and picked up a syringe. "Let me run a couple of the DNA tests to make sure. Then we'll run the same checks over the other bodies."

One by one, they checked the remaining body bags and took blood samples from each one. Stuart was relieved to find that they all contained the badly burned remains of humans, or at least they appeared to still be human. Until Stuart was able to perform the complete DNA test for the effects of the nano-probes, they couldn't be certain that these men were not infected.

"At least these ones were dead," Stuart said to Harry. The two survivors from the crash were more of a worry. They had been brought in badly burned from the crash, which in itself was not a problem. The lack of broken bones on both was of surprise to everyone who had dealt with them.

What was the most worrying fact to Stuart was that their wounds had started to show signs of healing. They knew from Lucy that infectees captured back in America showed an increase in strength, but also a marked increase in the ability for their bodies to be able to heal themselves.

And it was because of that information he had issued the instruction for the two survivors to be taken down and secured in the cells on level four. There they had a small number of cells which had been prepared for the event that they needed to hold injured captives.

While he would bring them up to the lab for their examinations, they had also learned from Lucy that they needed to take extreme caution with the infectees at all times. Throughout the time they would be out of their cells, they would be secured in specially built medical trolleys which would ensure they were locked down.

For now, he had arranged to have them sedated. It seemed the most humane thing to do while they were so badly injured. Problem was he wasn't even sure that they were still completely human.

Besides, he was going to need the room in the medical lab so he could perform the tests on Dave and Lucy to see how the recent encounter with the alien craft affected both of them.

Lucy had reported that she experienced a reaction to being in close proximity to the craft they had returned to Alpha Command. Where as, Dave had said he had a vision after he had touched the craft, Lucy had mentioned that she had also experienced a similar dream. There was something happening to both of them that he needed to get to the bottom of.

For now, the samples he had taken from each of the dead bodies needed to be tested so as he could check the DNA, before he headed down to the cells and repeated the process on the two survivors.

"I better go and see how Dave is getting on downstairs," Harry told Stuart. "It will be the first time I have seen an alien craft before for real." His voice gave away the underlying excitement at getting to see an authentic alien craft for himself.

"It's the first time almost any of us have seen an alien craft before," Stuart retorted as he turned his back on Harry. He realised that looking at dead bodies was not as exciting as an alien craft, but he was happy with that choice. "And I am seriously hoping it will be the last time as well right now."

As he left the lab and headed towards the stairs to the lower levels, Harry met Lucy as she was coming out of the command room.

"How are things going back in America then?" Harry asked.

"As well as can be expected really," Lucy replied. "I've been checking the reports filed for the past day or so and they've captured another three infectees. The medical team have been able to make some further progress on a method to block the effects of the nano-probes for short periods, although they are still hoping we can share more knowledge before I leave. I have given him Stuart's email and said they need to get together to discuss this further."

"Any feedback from them about the craft and cover stories?" Harry questioned.

"As you guessed correctly earlier," Lucy replied, "there are moves being made to get the craft moved from here to our team at Area 51. We want to have the NASA guys involved with investigating it, but obviously, we could struggle to allow any of them to come over here at the moment and keep it under cover."

"You know I would find it very hard to make the decision to release the craft and send it over to Washington. Besides, you saw the problems we had in getting it here. As soon as the military get wind of it being moved, they will be making moves to take possession of it," Harry tried to explain.

"That's exactly the reason that there has not yet been a concrete request made. So at least it gives you time to take an opportunity to prove your creditability to the powers that be in my government." As she spoke, she could not hide a hint of cynicism

"From your tone of voice, I doubt even you believe that we'll get to keep the craft without an argument," Harry retorted. "I'm afraid we both know what certain elements of either of our governments would do if they could get hold of this craft, let alone any of the research either of our teams were able to undertake."

"You don't need to tell me that," Lucy said, slightly annoyed at the feeling of being lectured to. "I've had many an argument with various liberal members of our government who are familiar with our real work who feel exactly the same way as you do. While my concern is to work within the DPD to stop the alien threat, I wish we had built in more provision to control the flow information. But it's too late for that now."

Harry did not want to get into an argument with Lucy about this now. He was certain that this would be a discussion he would have with other members of both his government and her government in the coming hours.

"I'm going down to see how Dave is getting on with the craft while we still can guarantee having it here. What are your plans at the moment?" Harry asked Lucy.

"After I get a coffee," she said, "I've got a few more calls to make back home. But I would like to go and talk to the prisoners."

"Stuart's got them sedated at the moment," Harry interjected, "So you might not get much out of them for now. He'll be going down to run some tests on them shortly, so perhaps you could check in with him."

"I will. We were never able to get much response from any of our captives anyway," Lucy started to explain, "but I hope I can help you try and get something out of these two. Certainly, we need to find out how much contact they had with that craft before we got there. Although if I am perfectly honest with you, I have my doubts that they will be able to offer us much information."

Harry nodded his approval and started to walk down the hallway towards the stairs. As he reached the top of them, he stopped and turned round to shout back to Lucy before she disappeared into the ladies toilet.

"Lucy!"

Lucy's head appeared around the door to look back at him.

"Don't forget." Harry started to say.

"To go and see Stuart in an hour or so, I know" she replied, shaking her head. As she turned back and continued into the toilets, she called back "Will you stop worrying."

Harry smiled as he turned and continued on his way, leaving Lucy to get on with her business.

———————

As Harry entered the lab on level three where they had brought the craft for investigation, he took a deep breath. He had not been prepared for actually seeing an alien craft. He had not even known how to prepare for seeing it. Come to think of it, he thought, would anyone actually know how they would react to such a sight?

The craft was suspended from the ceiling so that it was raised off the floor by about two foot. This was obviously to allow them room to work all around it.

There were currently only the two people in the room, Dave and himself. While he could see Dave was recording the dimensions of the craft, he wondered if he had the skills and knowledge to investigate this craft sufficiently. Not that he wanted to doubt Dave's abilities, but he was sure this was not one of his more natural ones.

Harry was well aware that a request to move the craft to America was likely to appear at any moment, but he wanted to see if his team could find out anything first. He was hoping to be able to get some help from the European Space Agency later today, someone who could come and assist with the technical side of things. He felt that would then help almost complete the Alpha Team to a fully operational level.

He would not find out till later in the day if his request for the additional resources had been accepted, so for now, it was up to Dave to work on this alone.

"How are you getting on in here then?" Harry asked him.

"Slowly. I have to admit that it's not like this is the sort of thing I ever thought I would be doing everyday," Dave replied, scrambling out from underneath the craft. "I've got it all measured up, logged on system and documented. But we're going to need some help to analyse the data. We're going to need to compare this to the records at NASA to see if we can make any comparisons between the two craft."

"What about the casing? Have you looked into that any further?" Harry asked as he moved to rub his hand over the side of the craft.

"Stop," Dave said firmly as he grabbed Harry's hand and pulled it back away from the craft. "Don't touch it. We still don't know for certain if that was what affected me back at the airbase."

Harry looked slightly embarrassed, realising he had nearly put himself at risk. Without taking the matter any further, Dave started to say "Well, take the hammer over there and hit the craft with it."

Harry, giving Dave a sceptical look as he turned to pick the hammer up that was being pointed to. He moved closer to the craft and hit the side of it with the hammer.

"Harder than that," Dave said, smiling. "Really hit it hard. Hit it like you really want to damage it."

Harry did so, this time taking a really big swing as he hit the craft again. To his surprise, there was not a mark left on the metal casing. Even more surprising was that there was literally no sound made as the hammer struck.

"That's incredible," Harry exclaimed. "I have to admit I did not know what to expect, but that was certainly one of the things I would not even had considered. It should have made some noise with me hitting it that hard."

"I've tried various cutters and a whole range of tools so far," Dave explained, pointing to the work bench behind them. "I've not been able to mark the casing with anything. As you have also noticed, you can't hear a thing as you hit it. You can't even see where the thing was hit by the jet during the crash. There are no obvious signs of seams or joints anywhere on the craft. I can't even see any signs of engines or propulsion systems."

"Have you been able to find anything out then?" Harry asked, hoping he could come up with some reason to justify keeping the craft here at Alpha Command when the request finally arrived.

"All that we do know so far is that when I touched the side of the craft, I had that dream," he said. "You know that vision of the fire."

"I'm trying to arrange for an extra member to join the team later today. I've asked for someone to come over from the European Space Agency who might be able to help assist us with this work. I know it's technically your team and your protocols, but I think we are all flying by the seat of our pants right now. And with an infectee on the run, the Home Secretary to deal with and now this, I think we need all the help we can get."

"I can't agree more," Dave replied. "There are better things, and I am sure there will be more pressing things, that I will need to deal with than spending my time down here. Especially if things progress the way Lucy suggests they will."

"Talking of Lucy, you better go and find her shortly," Harry said. "You've both got to go for those tests with Stuart. Can't have you getting infected on us already now can we."

Dave put down the tools and walked over to the computer terminal.

"No arguments from me Harry," Dave said, ensuring he had logged out of the terminal and shut it down. "Besides, it gives me the excuse I need to go and lie down for half an hour, although I doubt I'll be getting any sleep."

Chapter 15

Harry walked into the Command room to find that the team were already waiting for him. Lucy, Dave and Stuart were all seated at the table, discussing something amongst themselves.

He had called a meeting to get some updates on the progress they were all making at their various tasks, but also had some bad news he needed to break to the team. He was certain that it would not go down well with Dave in particular.

"How did the tests go?" Harry asked, taking a seat at the head of the table.

"Lucy's test showed there was no change from the records that Johnson had sent over for me to check against," Stuart replied. "But for Dave, there does not appear to be any mutation or signs of any infection. However, I have been able to confirm that he is definitely showing a worrying increase in brain wave activity. They appear to be at a significantly increased rate than even Lucy's which concerns me greatly."

Leaning forward, Harry asked "Can someone just outline to me what that really means? Not being a medical expert or such like, what's the issue with brain waves? I've read various medical reports from the DPD, I've heard you talking about it around here, but I just haven't got a clue what you guys are really on about or what it means for any of these guys."

Stuart took the question as his cue to demonstrate his expertise. He flipped over one of the monitors on the table and lifted the keyboard out. He quickly logged himself into the system and found a set of data files he had stored. He switched the display to the wall monitors for everyone, but especially Harry, to see.

"Basically, our brains generate electrical activity all the time, which is what we refer to as brain waves. The waves that we can measure at any one time depend on the state the brain. That state varies from being drowsy or asleep, through to being fully awake and focused. When we engage in different activities, the electrical activity of the brain also changes. There are four different brain wave types that we classify, these being alpha, beta, delta and theta."

Switching the display, he showed four different graphs, one highlighting each of the different waves he was trying to explain.

"Alpha waves tend to show the brain in a relaxed or calm state. Examples where we can see these include preying or meditating. Another, but simplistic example would be when you close your eyes."

"Beta waves are associated with arousal, problem solving, attention and concentration. We can break these down to two different levels of beta waves, but that's not for this conversation."

"Delta waves occur when we actually are asleep, and finally, theta wave activity generally occurs during dreaming. You would rarely find theta waves in a person who is awake, but when they are present, we often see such a person suffering from anxiety or conditions such as epilepsy."

Harry, who had been leaning back in his chair as he listened, moved so he could sit up. He then asked a second question, partly aimed at Stuart, but also looking to Lucy for a response.

"You say that those subjected to the nano-probes, or as it now looks likely, from contact with our alien craft, will suffer from increased brain waves?"

"Yes," Stuart replied. "The type of brain waves that we see increase seems to be determined by the change the person endures thanks to the nano-probes. For example, someone who sees their physical strength increase also seems to have a large increase in beta waves. Someone like Dave who has reported dream like experiences should show an increase in theta waves."

"So why do we not see them suffering from anxiety or epilepsy as well?" Harry asked.

Lucy raised her hand from the table slightly to signal to Stuart that she would answer this question.

"The spikes in the theta waves tend to register when the subject is actually having a dream or a vision. Even if they are awake, the visions are generated in the same part of the brain as when dreaming while the subject would be asleep. Why or how, we do not know."

"I'm starting to think that when we see large increases in theta waves, this is just the brain trying to integrate the contents of the dream further into the person's subconscious," Stuart continued. "I would go so far as trying to implant something to the human mind."

"Thanks for that," Harry said. "I think that makes it a bit clearer for me, but I will probably ask that you give that little talk again a bit later today."

"As Harry just said, I'll need you all to be giving the talk to our new team member who will be joining us very shortly. He should be arriving within the next couple of hours," Dave explained. "Let me give you the heads up on this guy now."

Dave stood up and handed out a folder to each of the others. Inside the folder was a profile of the new member.

"Joining the team we have Dan West," Dave started to say, handing the last of the folders to Harry.

"You are joking aren't you," Lucy said questioningly. "A convicted hacker?"

"We're going to need the best people to be on this team, and Dan is definitely one of the best with cracking software and breaking into systems anywhere in the world," Harry stated.

"If he's the best, then why did he get caught then?" Lucy asked with a wry smile. "And how on Earth can you guarantee his loyalty to the team?"

"Because, he knows that he will never see the light of day again if he screws up," Dave said bluntly. "He will be left to rot in jail for the rest of his life. Technically, he is not a bad lad, just needs to be given some direction."

"If you say so," Lucy said, unable to hide the scepticism from here voice. She felt it probably best to change the subject at this point. She did not want to argue with Dave over a difference of opinion about someone's background, especially as it was not her team after all. "What progress have you been making on that craft then Dave?"

"Well," Harry said before Dave could answer, "I'm afraid things have changed with regards the craft. It will be on its way to America within just a few hours."

They all looked straight at Harry, each with the same look of extreme surprise. While they had been expecting that piece of news to be broken to them at some point, it had not been as early as this.

"You what?" Dave asked angrily. Turning to face Lucy, he continued to say "Just what strings have you been pulling to make that happen?"

"It was nothing to do with me," Lucy replied, sounding hurt by the accusation. "I've been with you pretty much most of the time since we found it."

"Not when you were on the phone to your goons back in America," Dave pointed out. "I'm sure you had plenty of time to make the arrangements for this."

"I promise you Dave," Lucy pleaded, "this is nothing to do with me. I suspect it has come from higher up, but I really have not even discussed the craft with anyone other than Johnson and Forster."

"Enough," Harry said standing up before Dave could start another attack towards Lucy. "It's nothing to do with Lucy. It's all to do with our friend in the Home Office I'm afraid."

"What do you mean?" Dave's anger did not subside, but a sound of suspicion crept into his voice. "Surely in that case, it would be moving to somewhere that he would have more control over it was him and not over to the DPD. He'll have even less control of it there than he does if we were to keep it here."

"As long as that craft is here, we cannot guarantee keeping this base as secret as we need to. The Home Secretary will have his men watching us all like hawks and as soon as they find out where we are, they will be here in force," Harry explained.

"Wouldn't that be difficult for anyone to hide? A full on attack here would reveal both ourselves and threaten their cover within the government." Lucy asked.

"You should know as well as anyone the effect an anti-terrorism story has on the public when a government tries to cover something up," Harry said. "We're making arrangements for the craft to be moved up top, packed into a container and moved to Felixstowe docks."

Harry watched as Dave was still not placated by the explanation, but his anger towards Lucy seemed to have disappeared. He was certain that she would probably not hold that outburst against Dave given the apparent relationship forming between them. He wondered if their feelings were going to develop to more than just a working relationship, but he was concerned that if they did, it would not be beneficial to the team.

"Once it is there and loaded," he continued to explain despite his thoughts, "the vessel will head on a commercial route to international waters, at which stage, it will be met by a couple of US naval vessels and escorted back to the United States. It's all been arranged between me and Johnson. I must apologise for not keeping you and Lucy in the loop Dave, but this is the only way we can ensure that the craft is secured."

"Don't you think it's time we tried to eliminate the problem of the Home Secretary?" Stuart asked, knowing that asking would more than likely result in annoying Harry. But the response he got was not what he would have expected.

"Much as I know you want me to react to that question, I am not able to give you that satisfaction this time Stuart," Harry said. "This time I happen to agree with you. Tomorrow lunchtime, he is due to be giving a speech to the country about the recent events they have blamed on terrorist activity and how they intend to deal with it."

"What's the betting that Al Qaeda will get the blame for the mess we're leaving behind?" Dave asked. He had intended to try and come up with some witty remark to lighten the mood, but realised he had failed miserably.

"As you know, we believe that he has been infected by the nano-probes," Harry started to outline. "We also believe that he is going to try and spread some form of message through the press conference. A message we believe may contain subliminal content. We need to come up with a plan to remove this threat before he gives the conference. I want the team to come up with a plan by the end of today as I can tell you he is due to arrive at the Eastern hotel at eleven thirty tomorrow morning. Do what you need to do to find a way in and either capture him or kill him. And without implicating us in it in any way."

"Sounds like it's going to a challenge Harry," Dave said. "Who knows we're going to do this? I take it that you must have run the idea past the powers that be?"

"I have the Prime Ministers approval on this and he, along with elements within MI5 and MI6 will be doing what they can to provide us with any support we need to complete the plan. We will then work with them all so as to cover up as best as possible afterwards."

"What about the Home Secretary's involvement with the agencies?" Stuart asked. "Surely he will know what is going on within either one if we are working with them?"

"That's why we are only working with small elements," Dave replied. "The heads of each agency have been fully briefed on the threat now and will ensure as best they can that nothing gets reported back to our friend at the top."

"So what are our priorities then?" Lucy asked.

"I can give you the information you need to know," Harry responded. "Then it is up to Dave to take control and ensure the plans meet the protocols. I do feel I have taken a bit too much of a hands on role than I would have liked because of some background dealings, but now I have go to hand more control back to Dave."

"It is now just after nine in the morning," Harry said as he looked at the clocks on the command room wall, "so you have three hours with the craft still here. It is scheduled to be moved to the Felixstowe at that time and be at the docks within an hour."

Harry paused to look round the table at the three team members just to see if there was to be any questions.

"I want you and whatever agents you need on site to ensure it does not get intercepted. Then, as I said, you need to be in place to remove the Home Secretary at half past eleven tomorrow. I suggest that you now get on with it."

"Where will you be?" Dave asked. "We will still need some bits you might be able to sort out quicker than we can."

"I won't be going anywhere, but have some other tasks I need to deal with. Just give me a shout when you need me." Harry got up and collected his papers from the table. "I'll be in my office for now, but the new guy will be here shortly, so make sure you make use of him as soon as he has been briefed."

As Harry walked out of the command room, Dave stood up and stretched. He slowly moved to stand closer to Lucy, who had also taken the opportunity to stand up and stretch. He placed a hand on her shoulder and started to apologise.

"I'm sorry for having a go at you back then Lucy," he said, with a strong hint of regret in his voice. "No excuses, I should have known it was not you pulling the strings, but I was so angry."

"No problems," she replied, putting her hand on the side of his face. While she was still annoyed that he had accused her of having been pulling strings in the background, she found it was very hard for her not to forgive him so easily.

As she dropped her hand away from his face, she realised Stuart was watching them closely. She had wanted to keep her growing feelings in check, but felt she might have taken things a step too far with the last gesture.

She smiled at Dave and hoped the subject would drop. As she did, Dave then took a step back, pulled out his mobile and started to dial a number.

When it was answered the other end, he said "It's Hunt. Get me all of the maps of the area we have. I want the plans of Felixstowe docks and the water channels that surround it. Send them to the command room when you have them, but make it as fast as you possibly can."

Putting the phone down and turning to the others, he said "I don't know about you guys, but I think we should go get some coffee because we've got a lot of planning to get on with this morning."

Chapter 16

After the meeting with Harry had ended, the whole team made their way through to the refreshment room with the aim of getting themselves coffee. The room itself was a windowless, square room with only the one door in and out.

Across one wall was a large worktop upon which the coffee machine sat. Beneath the worktop was a fridge alongside a dishwasher, while along the wall there were a number of shelves with a range of cups, cutlery and assorted tins of snack foods.

The room also had a couple of tables, with four seats around each one for people to sit and relax at. They also had a canned drinks machine and a confectionary machine along another wall.

While Lucy was pouring her coffee, Dave was leaning against the worktop, flicking through the channels on the television mounted on the wall. As he changed through them, he stopped on channel 501, Sky News.

His attention had been grabbed by the breaking news headline "PM v Home Secretary." The presenter who was interviewing the Prime Minister was questioning him closely about his relationship with the Home Secretary.

"Over the past few days, rumours have surfaced that there is a widening gulf between you and your Home Secretary. What is your reaction to this accusation Mr Prime Minister?" she asked.

"While I am happy to go on record to say that myself and the Home Secretary may not agree on every subject discussed, there is no rift forming between us. I hold every member of my cabinet in high regard and they have been chosen for their particular jobs because I feel they are the best person to be there," the Prime Minister answered. As he spoke, he gave the impression of honesty and his complete belief in what he was saying.

"What about the rumours that have also begun to surface that a secret agency is being set up within the country's secret services as a result to the recent prominent events, such as on the M25 a couple of days ago, to deal with a growing terrorist threat within the United Kingdom?"

"As you are well aware, nearly the whole of the western world has been faced with a new type of threat since the events of September 11th 2001. I cannot give you any details of any projects, agencies or such like that we have considered, let alone committed to, because it could put many of our valuable intelligence resources at risk." The Prime Minister started to sound tired as the interview progressed, but continued to answer the question.

"We place great faith in the traditional intelligence services of MI5 and MI6, who work closely with the other intelligence agencies all around the globe to share information. Many of these rumours about a secret new agency probably stem from details emerging of small task forces or units within these services who are working to protect our country against the threats that we face daily."

"How do you respond to the issue of an alien threat to our planet, stories of which have started to leak out from the United States in the past few weeks?" The reporter asked, with a slight hint of scepticism entering into her voice.

The Prime Minister gently smiled, shook his head slightly as he answered her question.

"I'm sorry if I seem a little unenthusiastic in my response to these suggestions, but I think these are stories that originate from conspiracy theorists that are looking for explanations that are just do not exist. Again, we only have to look back to the events of September 11th to see that for obvious reasons, governments around the world are working to protect their people from those of our own species who seek to destroy our way of life, not from an alien threat."

Dave looked over to Lucy, who had stepped over and stood next to him as the news report continued.

"What do you make of that then Lucy?" he asked her, turning so he could face her.

"I'm definitely intrigued to know where they might be getting reports of the alien threat from," Lucy replied. "But I have to say that I thought your Prime Minister handled that interview extremely well. From my point of view, he certainly did not appear to give away that he might know anything about this. Guess that is part of the reason we try to keep the politicians and our President out of the loop as much as possible. They are just too eager to use it for their own gain."

"Whatever we do, we need to try and keep our operations a bit more discrete than perhaps we have done up to now," Dave said. "However, we are going to need to create a damn good cover story for removing the Home Secretary tomorrow."

"Shame we haven't got Bale here to help with that sort of operation," Lucy said wistfully. "He's pretty good at those types of operations. I'm sure he would have you in there in the blink of an eye."

"Well, I can certainly plan how to get in and out of the hotel, and we do have a number of good special ops guys here who I am sure could do the job pretty well," Dave responded sharply at Lucy's comments regarding wanting to bring one of her own guys in. "We have a number of ex-SAS and SBS personnel, I'm sure many of who could give you special ops guys a run for their money."

"If you say so," Lucy replied backing down on her suggestion, not wanting to start an argument. "Perhaps we better go and get started then."

Dave noted as they left the refreshment room, Stuart had already left them alone and was just heading into the command room at the end of the corridor. He had caught the look in Stuart's eye as Lucy had touched his face earlier and knew that there would be trouble brewing if Stuart felt like stirring it up. Stuart was the joker of the group and never needed much encouragement to try and wind someone up.

As they reached the command room themselves, they were met by an internal courier who was carrying a bundle of papers, including a number of what Dave was expecting to b the rolled up plans of the area and the docks he had requested only ten minutes or so before.

"Are those for me?" Dave asked.

The courier nodded and held them out for Dave to take. Dave passed his coffee to Lucy before taking them from him. With his arms full, they then turned and headed quickly into the command room, the door sealing shut behind them.

Everyone working at Alpha Command knew about the command room and held it in high regard. It was seen as a room many of them would probably never see the inside of. Many of the staff had been taken from various intelligence agencies around the country and were well aware that most of the agencies had these sorts of rooms. Only those with the highest level of clearance would ever be permitted to enter.

This did not stop many of them from trying to steal a quick look inside these sorts of rooms when ever they got the chance too.

As the courier was about to find out, it was going to do him no good at all in trying, as there was just a second set of doors inside this set, preventing him from seeing anything at all.

"Oh well," he thought to himself. "If I keep my head down and work hard, maybe I can get to join a team such as theirs and get to see what goes on in there." He turned back down the corridor and headed back to his room on the third floor.

"What makes you think they will be expecting us to move the craft through the docks then?" Stuart asked Dave.

The table in the command room was covered by various maps of the local roads, plans of the docks and pictures of various points on the maps. Some of the images were also being displayed on the monitors along the wall at the side of the command room.

They had been looking at this and trying to formulate the plan to move the craft for about half an hour now. They had already had a call with Johnson back at the DPD to throw some ideas around for a smooth transfer of the alien craft.

"Much the same reason as Harry wants us to move it," Dave said as he paced around to the opposite side of the table. "They have figured out that we are based some where around this area. They also know that for us to move it, it is going to have to be by one of two methods. The first is by air, starting its route through one of the US airbases. The other option is for it to be sent by sea. Where else is there round here that we can use to send it by sea?"

"There are plenty of other ports around the country," Stuart added. "Why not somewhere like Liverpool instead?"

"Because," Dave said trying to make Stuart understand his reasoning, "we would still need to get it there by road in the first instance. We would also need to invest considerable resources into ensuring it was well protected during the whole journey. At least if we can get it to Felixstowe and onto that ship, then that reduces the amount of time we need to guard it. The docks are fifteen miles from our base here, while Liverpool is at least six hours."

"Okay, point taken," Stuart conceded with a shrug of his shoulders. "But even when we get it there, how's it going to be protected on the ship? Harry talked about getting it onto a commercial vessel and then once in international waters, it would be escorted by US warships."

"We have made alternate arrangements for one of the US naval frigates currently on route to escort the craft across the Atlantic to dock at Felixstowe. They will then make a request, as an ally of the United Kingdom to be allowed to take on emergency water supplies," Lucy said. "The USS Pacific was one of several of our vessels on exercise and travelling close to the UK over the past couple of days. As soon as the alien craft was first reported, the US navy were ordered to get the ships in to positions around country should the threat have developed further. As long as we can get the container to the dock front, it can be loaded onto the vessel and out of the docks in a matter of minutes."

"I'm sorry to be asking so many questions," Stuart pushed, "but how do we get a container to the dock front when, as you quite rightly fear, they will be expecting us. And surely, having a US naval vessel sitting in docks is bit of a give away?"

Dave turned from the command table to look at the maps they had on the wall monitors. Holding his chin with his left hand, he stood, thinking.

"You're right with what you are saying, Stuart. We have got to make sure that we throw them off our trail as early as we possibly can." he said, deep in thought. "We said that we would send three different lorries, each carrying its own container to the docks. What if they insist on stopping and searching each and every one? Then we still may not be able to get the craft to the dock front at all."

"So why not send it another way?" Lucy asked, as she moved round the table so that she could stand next to Dave. "Why not move it in a smaller vehicle. That might be quicker to transfer to the vessel anyway. It would certainly give us extra mobility if it came down to getting out of there quickly."

"You're a genius Lucy," Dave said interrupting her, getting a little over excited with the situation. He took a couple of steps closer to the screens, pointing at an image of the dock front. "You are definitely right to say that loading a container just arrived in the docks onto the USS Pacific will take time. It will need to be hooked up to a crane, swung on to the ship and unhooked again before the ship can set sail. That leaves to much time for it not to be a risk."

Stepping closer still to the largest monitor and pointing to the dock map where the USS Pacific was going to berth, he suggested "what happens if we have the container on the dock front, already hooked up to a crane and ready to be transferred to the ship?"

Stuart made his way around the table to join Lucy as they continued to listen to Dave outlining his new plan.

"As Lucy suggested," Dave continued, "we load the craft onto a smaller truck or van, obviously the smaller the better. Then, should we run into trouble at the docks, we can try and get the vehicle into the container and moving without any delay."

"Therefore, as soon as the container is on board, then the US naval vessel can up anchor and leave the docks," Stuart finished.

"Better still, if the ship has a crane or hoist that we can utilise, it could even be moving the container as it starts leaving the docks." Lucy added. "I can check with one of our defence guys that the vessel being sent in to the docks will have some form of crane on board. He will be able confirm if this part of our plan is possible or not."

"Lucy, I need you to get Johnson on the phone again," Dave said as adaptations to the plan raced through his head. "We're going to need a cover story prepared as to why the vessel was leaving the dock so suddenly and I am sure he can pull off that one for us."

"It's a good plan," Lucy said cautiously, "but I can't help but think that there is still something we are missing. What of our missing infectee? Could he pose any threat to our plan?"

"None of our agents or soldiers has been able to find any sign of him since the crash earlier this morning. Who knows where he will head or what his intentions will be," Dave replied. As he continued, he looked to Lucy for her advice. "How can he even know we would be moving the craft anyway? He should have even less knowledge of us than our friend in the government?"

"Lucy," Stuart enquired. "I've seen mentioned somewhere on the DPD notes that infectees have the ability to sense one another, maybe even communicate non-verbally."

"Yes," she replied, turning to look at Stuart. "We're not sure how much they can sense and possibly share between each other, but you are right on that. As to the true level between full on infectees, I can't provide an answer about that for you."

"Even if that were true," Dave added, "none of our infectees down stairs know what we have planned either."

"But you two do," Stuart responded. As he saw that both Dave and Lucy were about to argue back that they would never reveal their plans to anyone else, he decided he would answer first.

"I'm not saying that you two would willingly share the information, but someone more tuned with the alien infection may be able to detect and read minds more than we think. I'm just trying to think of all options here."

After a slight pause, Dave replied "Fair point. There is still so much we need to try and learn. Something we need to find more time to make happen."

"What about that craft down there?" Stuart said as he continued his with his current line of thought. "Lucy mentioned earlier that she had started to suffer from a head ache when you got close to the craft. Now, while I know that she is not infected like some of these guys are, do you think they can sense where the craft is?"

"Hold on," Lucy said. "I might not be able to answer that for you, but I know someone who should be able to." She turned back to the command table and started to dial Forster's phone number in the med-lab back at the DPD.

"Forster here," he answered abruptly.

"Good morning Forster, its Lucy," she said. She took a quick look at her watch and realised that it would only be about five thirty in the morning in Washington. Somehow, she knew he would still be doing some sort of research in the lab at this time of the day. She had even caught him going to sleep on the autopsy tables a couple of times. "I hope you are all coping without me there to keep you all in line."

"We're coping just fine here," Forster answered, giving away the fact that he had indeed been asleep by his weary voice. "It's good to hear from you Doctor Tyler. I would ask as to how things are going over there, but then you wouldn't be calling for my help at this time if they were fine, now would you?" he asked.

"You're the same as always when we have to wake you Forster, but we haven't got time for that right now," Lucy said, fighting the urge to snap back at him. He always seemed to know how to antagonise her at the best of times. "As you know, we have been able to capture this alien craft. The decision has been made for us to move it over to our guys in NASA shortly. I want to get your opinion on something."

"I told you Lucy," Forster responded smugly, "even over there, you cannot do without my expertise. Go on, ask away."

Lucy looked at Dave as Forster spoke and rolled her eyes. He just seemed to do it every time he spoke and it drove her mad. Dave gestured with his eyes towards Stuart and smiled.

She held back her own smile, realising he felt the same way with his colleague at times.

"Remember how we discovered that the infectees could sense each other," Lucy started to explain. "From what we have sent over to you and the other guys already, what do you think the chances are of an infectee sensing the craft itself?"

The response that came from Forster was silence. Lucy gave him a few seconds before asking "Forster, you still there?"

"Yes, just let me think a few seconds," he snapped. "I want to give you a concise answer, but it's not something we can exactly check to be certain, now is it?"

"Just give me your best guess then," Lucy snapped back, her patience finally running out. "Do you think it is something that we need to be worried about?"

"I'd just like to add something in here Rob," Stuart interjected. "We found that Lucy started to suffer from headaches when she got close to the craft out in the field. We've tried to keep her away from it since though."

"Yes, yes, I know. I've seen the information already," Forster sounded short tempered, but Lucy was never surprised by his attitude any more. "And I know about the effect it had on Dave. So I would have to say that yes, someone infected by the alien nano-probes could well be able to sense the craft. How much, I don't know until we get it back here and can start running tests on our infectees here. All I can really suggest is that you go and try it now and scan Lucy's brain waves to see what happens."

"Thank you for your input Doctor Forster," Lucy said. As she leaned over to the phone to end the call, they all heard a couple of voices in the background sound like they were claiming a victory on getting the alien craft sent to them in America.

Catching Dave's eye, she hoped that this was not going to spill over into another argument about the location of the craft. She saw instantly that the focus was truly on getting the craft to NASA, not the blame game which it had been earlier in the morning.

As Lucy closed the call, she added "See you in a few days' boys."

"Well, that probably answers one question I was going to raise," Stuart suddenly added. "I guess that all drivers will have to be armed then?"

"Yes, it does look like it," Dave replied. "We've still not been able to get the ammunition we use in the stun guns so that they don't just kill a non-infected human. I'm led to believe some of our techs are finishing the testing on the new ammo, but it won't be ready for this mission today."

"But if we take traditional weapons with us, then we run the risk of not stopping an infectee," Stuart said. "I know which one I would prefer to take to get us through this. It's down to the level of risk you want to take boss."

"What about cover?" Lucy questioned. "While we can arm the drivers and ourselves, have we got anyone providing support on route or at the dock area?"

Dave changed the monitor displays to show a larger scale map of Felixstowe docks and the area surrounding the river estuary. The area was a meeting of two rivers, the Orwell heading east, the Stour north east. As well as the container port of Felixstowe on the north side of the estuary, there was also the passenger port of Harwich on the southern side.

In between the two rivers was a peninsula with a large marina at the tip opposite Felixstowe docks. Exactly the place for a couple of snipers to be situated Lucy thought. Obviously, she noticed, so did Dave as there were two points highlighted on the map.

"As you can see," he started to explain. "We have two snipers, one here and one a couple of hundred yards further round, giving good coverage of the vessel and the dock front. We will have a small team in the dock area, which will get into position as we arrive at the docks."

"Sitting off the mouth of the estuary, we have a four man team waiting in a small boat. Should we need additional backup, they have a high speed dinghy which can get them to our aid within a matter of minutes."

Lucy studied the map for a few moments longer, checking if the plan was as good as anything she could have come up with. She was fairly certain that they had covered as many possibilities as they could, but there was still a nagging doubt at the back of her mind. What if they had missed something?

Most of the operations carried out by her teams had been reactionary missions, responding to an alien infectee or escaped prisoners. This time, they were preparing to try and face one of two enemies, perhaps even both, as they tried to get the upper hand. Perhaps this would be the first time they could really take the fight to the aliens.

If they could successfully complete this mission, then they would have an incredibly valuable piece of the jigsaw in their hands. The advances and research opportunities that this offered to them were immense. It was too valuable a prize to loose now.

"I just feel we're missing something," Lucy said. "Something obvious. We can't afford to loose this craft, it's too important to us. We've got to get this right. Are we sure we are prepared to fight on two fronts? What if our escaped infectee is not working alone?"

"I can't see how he would be working with anyone else yet," Stuart said. "It's only been a few hours and I doubt he'll have made contact with anyone else yet, if he even knew who else to contact."

"I know it's a huge risk," Dave said, "but we really have no choice but to follow through with the plan. I'm sorry guys, we are running out of time I'm afraid. We need to get the craft ready to move and start loading the vehicles up. We're going to have to hope that Lucy is wrong and that we will only have to contend with one of our friends. Now let's get ready."

Chapter 17

Just under an hour later, the team were stood together above ground looking at the final preparations for the mission.

Three lorries, each with a freight container loaded onto their trailers, were sitting on the roadway within STAR Park. All would look identical to anything but the closest examination, except for their number plates. Each container had been sealed and displayed labels suggesting that hazardous substances were contained within each one.

In each lorry cab sat one of the Alpha Team's agents. Each had been hand selected from one of several the Special Forces groups in the United Kingdom, so should be able to deal with almost anything that might be thrown at them on this trip.

Behind the three lorries stood a smaller, Ford Transit van. This was painted up in the colours of a local plumbing company which was known to have various contracts on within Felixstowe docks. This would allow them easy access around the dock area without causing too much suspicion.

Dave and Lucy were stood behind the transit chatting between themselves, watching as Stuart ensured the doors were securely closed and ready for the trip to Felixstowe docks. Once the doors were secure, Stuart threw the keys over to Dave and started to head towards the main building, back in to Alpha Command.

Dan West was now walking over towards them to join the group, fresh from his final briefing with Harry. Smiling at Dave and Lucy as he passed them, he walked straight up to the back of the transit and tried to peer through the window.

"Not fair," he whined. "You've blacked the windows out. I can't see through to see what the thing looks like for real."

"You've seen the pictures of it already," Dave said abruptly. This close to a mission, he was not ready to start messing around. He also knew that putting the craft on display in public areas was not exactly a recommendable course of action. "That's the closest you're getting for now I'm afraid. Go and get back to the command room. It is up to you and Harry to observe all the communication channels to see if anyone picks up on us. Give us feedback the moment you hear or find anything."

"Sure thing boss," Dan replied, seemingly unbothered by the reprimand he had just received from Dave. "I'm looking forward to getting stuck in to it". He turned and walked quickly back to Alpha Command.

Dave watched Dan and was amused by the enthusiastic bounce to the new team member's walk. He wondered to himself if he had been as obviously excitable the first time he discovered the truth about alien life already being here on Earth.

He was holding a headset in his hand, which he now placed around his ear. It was time that he addressed the other team members and got this mission on the move.

"Alpha Lead to Alpha team. We are ready to go, Alpha four will leave on my mark, five and six will follow at intervals of five minutes. You have your orders, so good luck to you all."

All three team members reported in and confirmed their readiness to get into the action.

"Alpha four," Dave announced over the radio, "you are good to go. Good luck. We should be seeing you at the docks shortly after you arrive."

Dave watched as the first lorry started his engine and started the journey to the docks. He turned round to see that Lucy was already making her way around the transit van before he had the chance to ask her if she was ready for them to take their place in the plan.

As she opened the door to the transit, she watched down the road behind them to see a familiar orange car pull up behind them. The driver was revving his engine as he stopped. Stuart then pulled himself out of the window of the car and sat on the door frame.

"Ready then boys," he said with a grin as he rubbed his hands together with pent up excitement. Catching Lucy's raised eyebrow in response, he smiled back as he added "and girls."

"We're ready, Alpha three," Dave said sternly, starting to wonder if he was the only member of the Alpha Team wanting to take this mission seriously. He knew that they all had their own ways to deal with what was happening and he had to let them get on with it. It did not stop him making sure he took his role of team leader in what he felt was the best way. "Remember your orders and keep to the agreed distance. Should one of our friends show themselves, be ready for anything."

"Okay boss," Stuart replied. As he slid himself back into the driving seat, he put on his headset and reported back to Dave "Alpha three is ready to go."

"His cockiness is going to get him into trouble," Dave said to Lucy as they settled themselves into the transit. Turning to face Lucy, he said "And you thought Dan would give us trouble. He can't be any worse than Stuart."

Lucy, also fitting her radio earpiece, laughed. "I was just thinking that all he needs is a couple of numbers painted on the door and he'll think he can start jumping that car."

Dave looked at Lucy with a look of puzzlement on his face.

"Have you not seen the Duke's Of Hazzard then?" she asked. "You're the right age to remember that show you know."

"Okay, I do know what you mean," he replied, shaking his head and laughing. "Just don't go suggesting that comparison to him or he will think he can try that. He doesn't need much encouragement at the best of times."

After checking his mirror on the driver's side, Dave suddenly swung back towards Lucy and said "What do you mean that I'm about the right age to remember that show? I'm not as old as I look you know."

"I'm only a couple of years older than you," she replied smiling. "And I remember quite well. Besides, I'm not the one with grey hair am I?"

As they laughed and talked for a further couple of minutes about everything and nothing, Dave watched the minute's countdown before Alpha Five was due to leave. He then spoke into the headset again.

"Alpha Five, you are clear to go."

"Alpha Five confirms departure," his voice came back over the radio. "Good luck Alpha Lead."

They watched the second lorry drive up the road and turn out of the park. As it made its way through the park security gate, Dave turned the key in the transit's ignition. The engine started and Dave gave it a couple of quick revs to reassure himself.

He just had to roll his eyes as Stuart in the Ford Focus behind also revved his engine. He then contacted Stuart on the headset.

"Alpha Three," he said. "Alpha Lead is leaving the park."

"Copy that Alpha Lead, see you shortly," Stuart radioed back.

Dave pulled off and passed around the remaining lorry that sat in the road in front of them. As they passed it, he gave the driver a thumbs up signal, which was duly returned to them.

They made their way to the park exit, before heading towards Felixstowe.

This was the second full mission that Dave had been on for the Alpha Protocols and could feel the excitement within him growing. He that found he had to try and calm himself more than he had expected to. He knew that being over excited could affect his awareness of the situation.

They passed through STAR Park exit and onto the road outside the park. It was only a few hundred yards from the exit to the roundabout on to the main road. As they reached the roundabout, traffic was slightly heavier than they had expected for late morning.

Turning left on the roundabout, they joined the main road and begun to head in a southerly direction. In about three miles or so, they would join the main road, the A14, which would pretty much take them directly into Felixstowe docks.

Dave knew the roads well, having lived around this area for around twenty years. There were five junctions between them and the docks, which were the points they had suspected as danger points during the journey. Locally, it was well known that the final stretch before entering the dock area was a common point for lorry hijackings.

Checking in his mirror, Dave could see Stuart joining the road at the roundabout they had just turned on. He estimated that he was about four hundred yards or so behind them as they had agreed in the plan.

"Alpha Six to Alpha Lead," a voice came over the radio. "I'm about to leave the park and enter the game."

"Acknowledged Six," Dave responded over the radio. "Good Luck."

"Thank you Lead," the voice said over the radio. "Six Out"

"We're all go now," Lucy said having received the message in her headset as well. "Let's hope it finishes as well as it has started."

Dave looked over at Lucy and nodded in response to her statement.

"So do I, but I still have a bad feeling about this," he said. "Too many people want to take this thing from us. It's not easy to try and keep it away from all of them."

They were approaching the first of the five junctions on the route. This was another roundabout where two minor roads joined the main one that they were currently driving along. Sitting on one of the hard shoulders to the left was a police car, marked in the typical yellow and blue checks that signified a Suffolk police force vehicle.

Dave had expected a car to be sitting at this point of the route as it was a favoured place for the local police to sit and provide a strong visual presence to motorists. It was common to find youngsters using this stretch of road to race along as it was quite straight for about a mile or so between the roundabouts.

Traffic travelling along the main road and passing over the roundabout was flowing steadily despite the amount of cars. Dave was relieved to find they passed over the roundabout and along the main carriageway without seeing any suggestion from the police car's driver that they might decide to follow them.

Lucy took a look back in the mirror and watched as she saw Stuart pass the police and onto the main carriageway behind them as well. She looked for a few further seconds to make sure before saying "It looks like the police car has not moved."

"Let's hope Dan and Harry are keeping an ear to the police channels to make sure they are not relaying any information," Dave said. "We can always bring down the police communication network, but that would always be a last resort action."

Back in Alpha Command, Dan and Harry were sat in the command room. As Dave had requested as part of his plan, they were monitoring all the emergency service channels. The police reported through to the Home Secretary, so they instantly became a source of concern.

Up on the monitors across the wall was a large scale map of the area between the docks and STAR Park. Along the main roads were five flashing dots. The three red one represented the three container lorries - Alpha Four, Alpha Five and Alpha Six. They were spread out across the map at regular intervals, which meant that so far, everything was going according to plan.

Between the markers for Alpha Five and Alpha Six were two blue flashing dots. The first of them represented Alpha Lead, the vehicle Dave and Lucy were driving, which also contained the alien craft. Just behind them was Alpha three, Stuart, in one of the team's cars running point for them.

On the map, there were three additional sets of flashing markers showing. Two were based on the bit of land across from Felixstowe docks and one was sitting just out of the main waterway, about half a mile out from the river estuary.

These were called the Gamma teams. They consisted of highly trained special ops soldiers, who had been transferred to the Alpha Protocols task force to provide military advice, cover and support for any missions that they were to undertake.

Currently, there were sixteen of them in the team. Eight of them had been handpicked from the SAS, the United Kingdom's elite army unit, while the remaining eight had been picked from the SBS, the elite naval strike team. They were viewed as some of the best soldiers in the United Kingdom's armed forces.

Harry hoped they were not going to be needed, but this mission posed too many problems for them not to be used. He hoped it did not come down to them getting involved because the more times they did, the harder it would be to provide adequate stories to cover up any events in front of the public

"Sir," Dan said suddenly, attracting Harry's attention back to the problem at hand. "We've got a hit on the police communications. They've just reported Alpha Three's location. It looks like they now know we are on the way."

Harry, leaning across the table, flicked a switch to open the radio link so they could hear the team over the loud speakers in the command room.

"Alpha Lead, come in," he said clearly.

"Here Alpha Command, go ahead" Dave came back over the radio.

"Alpha Three has been identified," Harry announced. "Be on your guard for trouble."

Dave looked back in the mirror to see if Stuart was still behind them. They were now on the approach to the second junction which was where they would change from a southerly direction. They would switch to the dual carriageway, leading them east and towards the docks at Felixstowe.

He was happy to Stuart still about four hundred yards behind them, but there was something he just did not feel comfortable with. While they had not travelled very far, he realised that there was another car following just behind the orange Ford Focus. He'd recollected seeing it parked at the edge of the road as they had pulled out of STAR Park, but he had not taken any notice of it as they had left the site.

Perhaps there was nothing to it. Maybe it was just someone who had got a bit tight to Stuart's tail. But he needed to check with Lucy to see if she could sense anything or if it was just him becoming overly cautious.

"Lucy," he asked. "Can you sense anything unusual at the moment?"

"No, just a slight headache," she replied. "It is a bit like when we found this thing. Why do you ask?"

"It's nothing probably. I hope." Dave decided to keep the possible problem to himself after all. He would check after the next junction to see if the car was still there.

As they approached the roundabout, he slowed the vehicle and checked the road was clear. Seeing that it was, he started to speed up so they could pull onto the junction and towards the slip road. Catching him slightly by surprise, the radio crackled into life, but the message was full of static.

"Alpha …… Four has enc ….. had to stop …"

The transmission was cut short, but not before a gun shot could be heard.

Dave looked over to Lucy, who had also heard the same transmission over the radio.

"Alpha Command, this is Alpha Two. What can you tell us?" she asked.

"Nothing yet I'm afraid," Harry replied. "Alpha Four's vehicle appears to have stopped three minutes short of the target. I have sent air support on its way to the site."

As part of the plan, Dave had arranged for a helicopter at STAR Park to be available on standby to provide air support and video feeds back to Alpha Command in case something was to happen. It would only take the helicopter a couple of minutes to get to the site to report back.

Alpha Five was still a few of minutes from the reported location of Alpha Four, so hopefully, the helicopter could provide feedback before he arrived. They might have the opportunity to amend their route prior to arriving themselves should the threat still remain at Alpha Four's location.

Checking back in the mirror, Dave could see that both Stuart and his shadow were still present. Why was he not radioing in the problem Dave thought? Had Stuart just not realised? He should be more observant than that. There was no way he should have not noticed someone so obviously tailing him. He decided it was time to let Stuart know, so he spoke into the radio again.

"Alpha Three, are you there?" Dave asked.

"Yes Alpha Lead," the reply came back. "What's wrong?"

"Have you checked what's behind you recently?" Dave asked sharply. "You've got yourself a shadow. You had better keep an eye on them."

Lucy turned in her seat as she listened to Dave. This allowed her to try and get a better look back in the mirror on the door. She was still not used to being driven on the wrong side of the road despite having now been driven round several times. Perhaps it was something she would never get used to she thought.

"Which vehicle am I looking at?" she asked.

"It's the grey one right behind him," Dave said. "Medium sized car."

"Got it," she said as she caught sight of it despite being quite a distance behind them. She was impressed that Dave had spotted it so easily despite being focused on everything else that was going on. "Is there any where we can try to loose him before we get to Felixstowe?"

"Not with Stuart on our tail," Dave replied. "We've got four miles to the junction that we will need to take to get to the docks, so it gives me a couple of minutes to think of a plan."

"Also gives us two more junctions to encounter any more problems," Lucy retorted. "Can we get Stuart to drop off and see if he follows? Like we did before couple of days back?"

Dave looked thoughtful for a couple of seconds, obviously thinking about the best way to deal with this situation.

"Alpha Three," he said into the radio. "I've got an idea. Two miles up, slingshot junction."

"Copy that Alpha lead" Stuart replied. "Two miles it is."

Lucy looked over to Dave, puzzled. "And what the hell is the slingshot junction then?"

Smiling, he turned to look at her as he replied. "You'll see shortly. It will prove if he is tailing Stuart or not."

Sitting back in Alpha Command, Harry was watching the video feed from the helicopter. The first of the lorries was now heading back along the A14 in the opposite direction to the route it was meant to be following.

From the first set of pictures received back from the helicopter, he had seen a body moving on the side of the road. This he assumed was that of the driver. It had the hallmarks of a lorry-jacking, something that had happened quite frequently on this piece of road.

It was well known that many drivers were getting tired by the time they reached Felixstowe docks making them an easy target. There was rarely a week that went by where someone did not try to hi-jack at least one lorry. Most were taken when the drivers stopped for a quick break in the lay-by, but others, like this particular event, were more daring.

A car would pull up in front of a lorry, cause them to slow down and stop. They would then remove the driver from the lorry cab and steal the lorry.

Normally drivers were not hurt in these types of attack, let alone get shot. However, seeing as most drivers were not normally armed, things had obviously turned a lot nastier than normal.

Harry remembered that they had armed the drivers with the stun guns they had been working on for the past few weeks. If they had also taken the regular guns, then they could well have a serious problem on their hands.

He was certain that your normal lorry-jacker would not find it easy for just anyone to reverse engineer the weapon, and it only had a limited number of bullets loaded. However, should they realise how much they could get on the black market or selling to, god forbid, a group such as Al Qaeda.

"Alpha Lead, It's just a hi-jacking by the looks of it," Harry reported to Dave over the radio. "Medical attention is en route to Alpha Four. Alpha Five has now passed and reports that he is approaching the dock gates."

"Received Command" Dave's reply came over the radio.

Dave looked back in the mirror and saw Stuart gaining on them as they approached the junction. As they passed the three hundred yard marker, he had closed up to about five car lengths behind them.

The tailing vehicle was still behind Stuart's car, trying to maintain it's proximity to the Ford but was now failing not to make it look too obvious.

Passing the hundred yard marker, Lucy turned so she could watch out the windows on the passenger side of the car.

They were still driving in the left hand lane at about sixty miles an hour, well within the United Kingdom's speed limits. She estimated Stuart was obviously now nearing about eighty miles an hour.

As Dave and Lucy passed the end of the slip road and continued down the dual carriageway on their current route, Stuart's Ford suddenly dived at the last moment across the chevrons and into the junction.

Almost instantly, the following vehicle left the dual carriageway and followed him up the slip road.

"I don't think he's aware of us then," Dave commented, taking glances out of the window on Lucy's side as the two cars passed them on the slip road. "We shouldn't need to take the alternate route by the looks of it. Watch ahead."

Lucy moved back round in her seat so she could see straight ahead. As they passed under the bridges of the junction which crossed over the road, she saw the slip road from the junction sweep back down to the main carriageway.

Flying down the slip road at an increasing speed was a familiar orange Ford Focus, closely pursued by the grey vehicle. As it passed them on the inside and headed towards the road, she got the chance to take a good look at it.

It reminded her of many of the vehicles they used around the US when they had to go on missions or investigations. It was a typical plain, grey colour with slightly tinted windows.

If she were back home, then she would have assumed this was a CIA type vehicle.

She tried to get a look at the driver, but was unable to as it was already pulling away from them at some speed. As she watched, the two cars joined the road and began to leave them behind.

"How far have we got to go now?" she asked.

"The next junction is a large roundabout," Dave explained. "The main road heads off to the right and down towards the main dock gates."

"Alpha Five reports having passed through the dock gates successfully," the radio announced. "He is heading towards the rendezvous point. He reports no contact so far."

"Command," Dave said as he reported back their progress. "Alpha Three has made contact with, and is hotly pursued, by a suspect vehicle. He has diverted any possible interest from us for now."

"Copy that Alpha Lead," Harry's voice said over the radio. "Report in as you reach the rendezvous point. Good luck."

As they reached the junction, locally known as the Dock Spur roundabout, the road split into two. The first headed into the town of Felixstowe, the other took the A14 around the edge of the dock area and towards the main gate as Dave had explained to Lucy.

Watching across the roundabout, they could see Stuart disappearing towards the docks area, still being hotly pursued. They followed at a more leisurely speed, allowing the pursuer to be taken away from them.

As they left the roundabout, following the road in the direction of the docks, Dave took a quick look on the roadside at an ambulance attending to Alpha Four. This had obviously been sent from the ambulance station at the hospital just on the edge of the town.

He knew the lorry was now on its way somewhere else, but Harry would have sent a team to recover it as quickly as possible. Each vehicle had been fitted with a GPS tracker, so they would easily find it before the thieves could get too far.

Passing under another bridge, Lucy noticed that it had a large sign painted across it. In big letters, it declared "Welcome to the Port of Felixstowe."

"Guess that means we must be here," she commented towards Dave. She looked at him and was not surprised to see him roll his eyes in response to her obvious statement. She then looked beyond Dave in the driver's seat and could see the main dock area spread out to the side of the road.

Despite having seen the maps and some pictures back at Alpha Command, she was surprised by the area covered. She remembered Dave had mentioned that Felixstowe was one of the largest container ports in Europe, so she started to wonder what the larger ones at Rotterdam and Hamburg must be like.

She could see the cranes lined up along the dock front in front of about five different ships. Four of these were container ships, while the one in the furthest berth looked like the pictures of the USS Pacific Johnson had sent over to them earlier in the day. At least the ship was waiting for them she thought.

The road started to dip down as they had reached what would be the last junction on their trip. The slip road leaving the main carriageway would take them down to dock gate number two. The plan was for the lorries which successfully made their way to Felixstowe were to head towards the dock front and prepare to be unloaded on the third of the four ships currently berthed. The containers would then be loaded on to the waiting transatlantic ship.

Should there be interest in any of them, then this would deflect the interest from the transit so they could move the craft to the USS Pacific. The hope was that there would be little or no interest in the dock area, but they also had a couple of further surprises planned should someone decide they wanted to cause trouble.

As they pulled up to the dock gate, the traffic was split into two lanes. The left hand lane took the lorries and vehicles destined to be loaded onto the ships so they could be logged on the system and directed to the correct place within the docks.

The second lane, the one that Dave had selected, allowed traffic to flow more freely in and out of the docks. This was primarily for the dock staff, dock vehicles and other people visiting the area for operational tasks, such as the plumbing company whose name was painted all over their vehicle.

They joined a queue of about three cars and one other transit, each one in turn stopping at the security gate. Dave hoped Dan was as good as his records showed and he had got their details added to the docks security system so as to allow them to pass through easily.

As they pulled up to the security gate, a guard stepped up to the window. He signalled for it Dave to lower it so he could speak to them.

"You know where you're going?" he asked, even before Dave had finished winding down the window on the transit.

"Yes, I've been here enough to know the place like the back of my hand," Dave replied, as he handed over a couple of security passes they had brought with them. They were Port of Felixstowe passes that were given to their regular suppliers and contractors for quick access to and from the port area.

"Off you go then," the guard said as he handed the passes back to Dave.

"Cheers mate," Dave said, starting to wind the window back up again.

Dave checked the lane ahead was still clear and pulled away from the security gate. They started their way into the dock area and head towards the dock front. He made contact back to Alpha Command to report in.

"Alpha Lead to Alpha Command. We have arrived and are now heading towards the rendezvous point."

"Copy that. Alpha Three has not reported in yet. Alpha Six is three minutes away. Please Hold Alpha Lead," Harry said.

As the radio went quiet, Dave looked toward Lucy and said "I'm not sure I like that please hold we just got from Harry."

Harry's voice came back over the radio. He sounded slightly concerned this time. "We've just got a new update. We have eighteen contacts at the party, I repeat eighteen contacts."

"Alpha Five confirms visual," a different voice said as it came over the radio. "All armed and appearing to attempt to stay out of sight. Looks like a mix of normal soldiers plus a small number of Special Ops. I recognise a couple, so they have sent some pretty tough cookies. They are ignoring the target for now though."

"Thanks Alpha Command, Alpha Five" Dave said, sounding disappointed. "So much for a simple transfer then."

Lucy shrugged her shoulders and looked back out the window. She hadn't thought this was going to be easy. This just proved how determined their enemies were in trying to get hold of the alien craft.

Making her jump, Dave's attitude changed dramatically from one of mild disappointment to one of excitement. He was talking partly to her, but also to those on the other end of the radio.

"All right then boys, let's get this party started and show them what we are made of."

Chapter 18

As Dave and Lucy made their way through the docks, they drove past various areas of stacked containers and buildings. They were heading towards the dock front as quick as they could go without making themselves conspicuous. As they crossed the railway line which ran through the heart of the docks, Dave spotted the first of the enemy soldiers.

Lucy had also spotted another soldier who was lurking around a couple of parked vehicles off to the side of the road they were currently driving along. She carefully pointed him out to Dave, keeping her actions to a minimum so as not to make someone checking the vehicle's occupants suspicious of them.

As they reached the end of the road, Dave signalled his intentions to turn left. This would allow them to follow the dock front along to where the USS Pacific was waiting for them. Stopping to check the traffic, trying to ensure they looked as normal as possible, Dave took a look and saw Alpha Five's lorry being moved into position under a container crane to lift the load off and on to the ship alongside him.

As they moved off from the junction, he saw in the mirror a group of four dock workers heading towards the vehicle. They were all wearing high visibility jackets and safety hats. They were waving at the crane driver to stop what he was doing. One of them separated from the group and made his way over to the lorry cab and opened the door.

They were closely followed by what looked like three armed men. It looked like the diversion had proved to be effective.

After about three hundred yards, the USS Pacific came into view at the far end of the dock front. Despite it still being a short drive to the vessel, a surge of relief fell onto Dave as they approached their target.

That was until two armed and uniformed soldiers stepped out from the road side and into their path. Both had their guns drawn and pointed directly at them. A third stood slightly off to the side of them and was waving for him to slow down.

"Best play it cool," Lucy said. "Remember no-one on board the Pacific can actually help us here while the craft is on UK soil."

Dave nodded and slowed as they approached. He carefully moved his hand so as to flick the lock on his door and allow the central locking to secure all the doors. He did not want to risk anyone trying to get in to their vehicle.

Lucy wound her window down so they could hear what the soldier that had waved for them to slow down had to say.

As they reached a stop, one of the guards walked around towards Dave's door. The other stood in front of the Transit, holding his gun ready. The third soldier, who had been stood off to the side, walked up to the window and leaned down slightly.

"I'm going to have to ask you to leave the vehicle," he said

"Why is that then?" Dave asked as he leaned across Lucy to address the guard. "We're here to fix some pipes up in the canteen building over there."

Lifting his gun to point the barrel into the car, the soldier repeated the theme of his last statement with more emphasis.

"You will exit the vehicle immediately and you will be taken into military custody."

"I don't think so," Dave said abruptly.

With a screech of wheels, Dave threw the Transit into reverse and pulled away, back the way they had approached.

Despite being thrown back into her seat, Lucy ensured that her window was closed again, but kept watching the soldiers to see their reaction to the situation.

As if expecting the move, the two armed soldiers raised their guns and began shooting directly at the transit.

Lucy found that she ducked as bullets ricocheted against the windscreen, just before she realised it was actually bulletproof. Before she could sit back in an upright position, she was thrown against the side of the Transit as Dave put it into a spin and put the vehicle back into a forward moving direction.

More soldiers began to appear in front of them, also firing machine guns towards the Transit.

However, their attention suddenly became split between Dave and Lucy racing directly towards them and a second small team of soldiers emerging from the container on the back of the lorry that they had just stopped from being unloaded.

Dave put his foot to the floor and continued to speed up as they hurtled into a right hand turn and back in the direction of the dock gates they had come through as they arrived.

People were now starting to run away from the dock front in panic at the outbreak of shooting and vehicles racing around. There were dock workers, drivers, anyone who did not want to be caught in the middle of a growing gun battle.

"Alpha Six is through the dock gate and on approach to the rendezvous point, ETA thirty seconds," Harry announced over the radio.

"Where are we going?" Lucy asked.

"Another way around," Dave replied. "Let's hope our guys can distract some of them for long enough, if not remove them all together."

Having crossed back over the railway line, Dave went into a right hand turn on a road running along side the track.

Behind them appeared a camouflage coloured Land Rover, a soldier hanging out of the passenger side with a machine gun spraying them with bullets.

Lucy found herself being thrown around in the passenger seat, grateful for the safety belt still trying to hold her in. The noise of the engine was in competition with the noise of bullets bouncing off the sides of the transit.

She took a look at Dave to see a face of concentration as he focused on trying to get them to the dock front again. Her admiration of him was growing and she found herself regretting that in about than two days time she was going to be heading home to America.

If things were different, maybe she could have got to know him better. Perhaps they still could, but would their commitments in different countries be just too much for anything to happen. Then again, it was these commitments that had meant they had been able to meet.

She was brought back to reality with a bump as the Transit was thrown into another corner. It was as they started to turn that she saw another Land Rover coming head on towards them. As with the vehicle pursuing them, there were soldiers leaning out with several guns firing at them. Sparks caused by bullets ricocheting off the windscreen appeared once more.

Dave had opted to use the railway line to try and cut through towards the dock front with more speed than taking on the Land Rover head on. As the rails were laid within the concrete roadway at this point, it would not cause them too many problems, unlike if it had been a standard railway line with sleepers and shale.

Taking a look behind, she saw the Land Rover, who had been in close pursuit on their tail, cut in to follow them. However, in doing so, he had pulled across the path of the second one. In swerving to miss the other vehicle, he clipped the road kerb and flipped his car on to its side.

Lucy found herself having to look away as she realised that there was one of the soldiers who had been firing on them now trapped underneath the vehicle. In all likelihood he was now crushed and unlikely to survive.

Swinging onto another roadway and with the dock side appearing in front of them, they were now heading back in the right direction. In front of them, another lorry appeared and pulled across the end of the road.

Although it appeared to now be blocking their way, she noticed that it had actually parked at an angle. This meant that it was blocking the roadway along the dock front, but left the way clear for them to turn to the left and head towards the USS Pacific. She realised that this was Alpha Six arriving to help out.

The doors at the rear end of the container opened and another group of six armed soldiers started to jump out and take up positions around the lorry. The majority of them began to open fire on the soldiers who had earlier been hidden, but were now making themselves known as they attacked the Transit. Meanwhile two of them had taken up a position to shoot towards the Land Rover which was following Dave and Lucy in their Transit.

As Dave swung the vehicle into the left hand turn and onto the road along the dock front, the driver of the Land Rover was hit by a shot from one of the Alpha shooters. On the passenger side, two soldiers who were passengers decided to leap for their lives, one breaking his leg on impact with the road due to the speed they were travelling at.

Despite slowing slightly, the vehicle continued in a straight line. It clipped the front end of the lorry across the road causing it to turn slightly from its original path. This only left it with one direction to go as it over ran the dock front. It was thrown into a barrel roll, lifting it into the air slightly as it hit a mooring point on the dock side.

The resultant explosion as it hit the side of a container ship, which was docked in front of it, threw debris across the area. Crew on board the boat had to scatter as the Land Rover hit and flames spread up the side of the vessel to where they had been leaning over, watching the events that were unfolding below them.

Straight ahead was their target, an open container alongside the USS Pacific. All they had to do was get their transit into the container, close the doors and it would then be winched onto the vessel. Their objective was in sight and Dave felt it could not come too soon.

That was until two cars appeared in front of them around the container, one on either side. Both Dave and Lucy recognised the two vehicles the moment they saw them. However, Dave was slightly confused as to why they should be appearing at this moment. It started to cross his mind that Stuart should not have been heading in this direction with someone on his tail, but there was not time for that now.

"Stuart!" Lucy said surprised, as the orange Ford Focus raced towards them, as the same grey vehicle that been following him when they had become separated earlier, swung in tightly behind him.

"Hold on," Dave ordered, trying to make a decision quickly as to which way he should move aside to let them pass. He decided he would swing to the left, hoping Stuart would at least continue in a straight line and not think he should move to his right.

Narrowly missing each other, Dave and Stuart passed one another in opposite directions. As they did, Dave swung the transit slightly towards the grey car, causing him to swerve towards the dock front. However, they clipped the rear end of the vehicle at the last moment.

This resulted in the grey car to start to loose control and run straight into a warehouse wall along the side of the road.

The car continued to scrape along the building until it came to a halt, hitting another wall several hundred yards on.

Further up the dock front, Stuart put his car into a controlled spin and sped back towards the way he had come.

At the same time, Dave had lined the Transit up to enter the container. A loud thump from underneath the vehicle sounded out as the front left tyre of the Transit exploded.

Out of the corner of her eye, Lucy saw one of their attackers fall having been shot by one of the Alpha soldiers. As he fell, she thought that it was his gun that had been pointing at them and it must have been him who shot the tyre out.

Dave was struggling to keep the transit straight with one tyre missing, but was doing his best to keep on target with the container. With just under one hundred yards to go, Dave put his foot hard on the brake, slowing the Transit.

As they entered the container, the vehicle began to skid. With a thump, it hit the end of the container, throwing both Dave and Lucy forward with a jolt.

Although shaken, both Dave and Lucy pulled themselves out of the vehicle as quickly as they could. Dave had to reach back in to the transit and grab his weapon that he had left in the pocket on the door. Lucy had edged to the end of the container and had taken a careful look out. She looked back over to Dave as he moved up on the opposite side and met her look with a quick smile.

Ensuring that they were able to keep themselves covered, the both surveyed the dock front to assess the situation.

Dave looked along the dock front and saw Stuart getting out of his car he had parked alongside the warehouse. He ran round the vehicle and crouched down against the wall, just by the corner of the building. Behind him, three of the soldiers from the Alpha team were closing up on his position quickly. One of them was making a brief check of the bodies as they went.

Off to their right, there were at least four other soldiers taking positions amongst the containers that were being stored on the dock side. They were all aiming their guns towards the container doors. One took a couple of shots at Dave, forcing him to duck back into the container.

"We've got to get out of here and the doors shut, then they will load the container," Dave said to Lucy as he moved across to stand next to her.

"We need a distraction," she replied as Dave leaned across in front of her trying to find possibilities. "You got any ideas?"

Dave continued to peer out of the container and searching the area around them. He could not see anything that they could obviously use as a diversion. Stuart looked over at where Dave was hiding and they acknowledged each other with a quick salute.

Behind Stuart, as they passed the grey car, one of the Alpha soldiers had stopped to check the state of the driver. He suddenly collapsed backwards as the occupant climbed out the car shooting at him. In total, he let off four or five shots into the soldier.

He then turned to begin shooting at the other two soldiers who still had their backs to him. The first fell just as the second turned and tried to take a shot, narrowly missing his target as he too was hit. Just to make sure, the assailant calmly placed a bullet in each of the soldier's heads as he walked past them.

Stuart, realising the occupant of the car should not have been up and walking following the crash he had just been through, urgently looked at what was above him. He saw that just behind him was a window into the warehouse, so he grabbed a discarded broom that was lying on the floor in front of him and smashed the glass.

He stood up and pulled himself through the window just as several shots hit the concrete wall where he had just moved from.

On the dock front, four newcomers suddenly appeared from the waterside. They were scaling the dock wall and climbing on to the dock side. Each one was fully armed and ready for action. The lead member spotted Dave just inside the container and signalled to him.

"Lucy," Dave called to get her attention, having moved back to the other side of the container to see how the soldiers in the containers were shaping up. As she looked round towards him, he continued by saying "It looks like our diversion has just arrived."

"Looks like we have two then," she replied. Pointing across to where Stuart had been, she continued to say "as it looks like our infectee has arrived as well."

"When I tell you to, get out and round the side of the container on the dock side," Dave instructed Lucy. "Keep yourself under cover. We need to get this thing moving."

She nodded to show she understood his instruction and that she was ready to go on his signal.

Peering out round the door, Dave could see the infectee was heading their way, making his way straight towards them. It also brought him straight into the line of fire of the soldiers around the docks, both from the Alpha Team and their enemy's.

As gun fire started to ring out, the infectee's attention was drawn away from the container and towards the new group of soldiers who had only recently appeared from the waterside and had taken positions behind vehicles or crates. They were trying to pick off the enemy soldiers beyond the infectee and the container.

"Now," Dave ordered as he and Lucy made their move to get out of the container. Keeping down, he grabbed the door on his side and swung it shut as quickly as he could. It resisted him to begin with, but with a hard push he was able to get it to move and closed.

To his side, Lucy was trying to push the other door shut, but was not finding it as easy. Her smaller body and lack of weight in comparison to Dave meant that she was going to struggle to move the door on her own. Dave moved over and added his efforts to help close it.

Along the inside of the door rang the noise of bullets ringing against the metal panels, causing them to duck back around the side of the container.

Looking up, Dave saw a number of crewmen standing on the USS Pacific, waiting for them to sort out the container so they could start to move it. One of them gestured to Dave that he should look back around the container.

In doing so, he could see that most of the shooting was between the various groups of soldiers, where as the infectee had made his way to the container. He had now stopped outside and was stood looking in the opening at the craft. His prize was in his grasp.

Dave turned back and leaned against the metal wall trying to think of a plan quickly. They needed to deal with the infectee first, leaving the various groups of soldiers to fight it out amongst themselves. As for Stuart, he had not seen where he was at the moment, so could not count on his involvement for the time being.

He took another look around at the dock side battle just to confirm the locations of the various soldiers, before turning back round and drawing his weapon. He held the gun in his right hand and flicked the safety off. With the left hand, he placed it on Lucy's shoulder and leaned in to quickly tell her his plan.

"When you hear my shout, move around the container," he said to her. "Take the shot as soon as you can. Just get him out of the game. Don't try it before you hear me though."

He waited for Lucy to show that she was happy with his plan before he ran along the container and disappeared around the end.

Lucy edged her way towards the end of the open door and waited for the signal from Dave. She looked down towards her feet, realising that there was a gap between the metal door and the floor which left her feet an open target. She could also see the shadow of feet moving the other side of the door.

They started to move away from the container, so she started to look back up. However, she was distracted by someone waving at her from the USS Pacific. She looked up towards them quickly, before she realised she had made her mistake.

With her attention distracted, she was caught by surprise as an arm reached round and pulled her back around the door. She found herself being held against someone, who she suspected was the infectee, and could feel something cold pressed hard against the side of her head.

She started to scream but found the grip tightened around her mouth and the gun was pressed harder against her. She thought better of trying anything else given the situation she now found herself in.

"Drop your gun before you step out," he commanded, roughly turning Lucy to face the side of the container where they both were expecting Dave to step out from. "Drop it or I will shoot her."

Dave stepped slowly round the corner of the container, holding his gun at head level. He held his aim at the infectee as he slowly stepped forward.

"I said drop it. I will shoot her, I can promise you that," he ordered.

As the gun was pressed even harder into the side her head, Lucy's normally confident appearance was breaking and she looked as if she might break into tears. Because of the way she was being held, she could not twist her head in an attempt to move away from the gun.

Giving Lucy a push as he took a small step towards Dave, the infectee shouted loudly, "Now!"

Chapter 19

As he found himself caught in two minds, Dave dropped his aim slightly. He could not take the shot as the electric charge from their ammo was likely to cause Lucy serious harm, if not killing her instantly.

But he could not risk letting the infectee take further control of the situation. As long as the craft remained on the ground, the risk of it falling into the wrong hands grew.

"Drop it," the infectee ordered again. "On the count of three, you will drop the weapon or I will kill her. One."

Dave looked at Lucy and saw the tears in her eyes. He could see how much she was shaking and realised just how scared she was by her current predicament.

"Two."

Dave flinched slightly as the radio in his ear crackled. He let the gun drop to the floor and held his hands up.

"Okay," he said, sounding defeated. "You win. Now let her go."

The infectee took a step to his right and towards the container doors. He was still holding the gun too tightly to Lucy's head, just as a shot hit the back of his heel. This caused him to stumble backwards slightly.

At the same instant, Dave launched himself forward. As he did, he grabbed Lucy, throwing the pair of them to the floor. He rolled slightly, so he would take the brunt of the fall on the concrete instead of her, wincing in agony as they hit the hard surface.

A shot flew over their heads and the crackle of electricity sounded as the infectee fell in a crumpled heap against the door of the container. Looking up towards the warehouse, he could see Stuart standing on the roof, pointing his gun back down towards them.

With a grateful wave, he signalled to Stuart that he and Lucy were okay. As he started to sit up, he looked at Lucy who was in his arms, still shaking. She looked him in the face and let Dave wipe the tears from her eyes.

"You're safe now Lucy," he said comfortingly. "But you're going to have to move out of here just in case."

As he spoke, one of the Alpha soldiers ran up beside them and took Lucy by her arm to help her up. Even before she was fully on her feet, he was leading her back under the cover of the container.

Dave stood up and grabbed one of the arms of the infectee and dragged him clear of the door. He then put his weight against the door of the container, finally getting it to close.

He quickly moved to slide the lower bolts on the door shut and secure the container. At the same time, the container started to rise from the dock side.

Dave looked up behind him and waved his acknowledgement to the crew of the USS Pacific. The crew that had been gathered on the decks watching the events below had all disappeared as they had all returned to their duties as the ship began to move out of port. The craft was finally on the move and was now in the protection of the US navy.

Causing Dave to spin round and look back towards the buildings, gun fire rang out as two remaining soldier appeared from the containers. They were aiming at the strapping which attached the container to the crane, but this left them in the open and an easy target.

Dave quickly dropped to his knee, grabbed his gun from by his feet and with one shot, took down the left hand one of them. The second fell as another shot rang out from the top of the warehouse behind them.

Dave knew that as the two soldiers were unlikely to be infected, the shots would have killed them instantly. He would regret killing soldiers who were only following their orders, not knowing that they were from someone being controlled by an alien nano-probe. But for now, that was not a train of thought he needed to be following.

Dave turned to look up and see Stuart was still stood on top of the warehouse, gun still raised. He was still aiming to where the second soldier had just fallen to the concrete. Slowly, he lowered his weapon and relaxed. Seeing both Dave and Lucy still alive on the dock front, he gave a quick wave towards them. He then turned and started to make his way down to where they were.

Dave turned around and Lucy was running back over towards him. The soldier who had helped her was following closely, gun raised in anticipation of any further trouble.

"You okay?" she asked as she reached him.

Dave wiped sweat from his face and nodded. "I think so. That was harder than I imagined it was going to be. What about you?"

"I'll be fine," she replied. "Did get a bit frightening back there, but I should have had more faith in you."

With the noise of gunfire and shouting having now dropped away and the battle drawing to its conclusion, the sound of sirens started to appear in the background, gradually getting louder. That was until they were drowned out by the sound of a car engine as it approached them.

Dave spun round and saw the orange Ford Focus pulling up along side them. The window already down, Stuart leaned out and shouted to them.

"Get in, come on. We don't need to be dealing with cleaning this lot up. Let's leave that for Harry to sort out"

"Help me with the body," Dave said to the soldier. "We need to take him with us."

Lucy quickly climbed into the back of the car, while Dave and the soldier grabbed the stunned body from the floor. They bundled it into the back of car next to her, making Lucy squirm as the limp body fell against her.

The soldier climbed in next to it and closed the door. He then lifted the body away from Lucy and held it so it looked like it was sitting upright.

Dave took the front seat, closing the door behind him with a slam. Stuart put his foot down to the floor and the car accelerated away, just as a number of police cars appeared on the dock front behind them.

Dave opened the glove box and grabbed a couple of leather pocket wallets. He threw one back towards Lucy and held on to one himself. He also threw a pair of handcuffs into the back towards the soldier and pointed to the infectee.

"Put them on him," he ordered.

Lucy helped hold the infectees hands up so the handcuffs could be securely put around his wrists.

As they approached the corner to turn away from the dock front, there were more police vehicles arriving. They were moving to block the roads in and out of the dock area.

As they approached the police cars, a couple of officers had stepped into the road in front of them. Stuart stopped the car as he reached them and leaned out the window to flash his wallet at them. Looking in the window, both Dave and Lucy also held up the ones they had.

The policeman looked at the soldier, then to the body between them and saw the handcuffs on him, with Lucy holding a gun against his chest.

"We need to get him into custody and some medical attention immediately," she told the policeman. "We're not sure how long he might have."

"Do you need an escort?" he asked.

"No, we'll be fine," Dave said. "We just need to get going."

He nodded to show his understanding, stepped back from the car and shouted some instructions to one of the other policeman to move the cars blocking the road. As the cars moved, he then gestured to Stuart that he could now move on and on their way.

Stuart pulled away and made his way through the police cars. A number of ambulances and various vehicles were also starting to arrive as the Alpha Team were making their way out from the docks.

Dave started to talk into his radio so he could report back to the command centre.

"Alpha Lead to Alpha Command. Package is posted and delivery has commenced."

"Congratulations," Harry replied. "You had better all get back here and we can get on with covering up this mess. Any ideas on how many dead we have got?"

"I think we have probably lost as many as six of our soldiers," Dave responded. "But I think I can help with the cover up story."

As he spoke, he pulled a mobile phone out of his jacket pocket. As he opened it, he scrolled through to find a number and dialled it.

Behind them, a large explosion on the dock front sent flames and smoke billowing up into the air. Everyone in the car, except Stuart who was trying to concentrate on driving, looked back to see what was happening.

"What was that?" Lucy asked. Even she was a little shocked by the size of the explosion behind them.

"A little failsafe plan," Dave said. "I'd arranged for one of the containers to be filled with explosives and set to detonate on my signal. It will also leave a covering of cocaine powder within the blast area making this look like a drugs raid gone wrong. Harry should be able to help convince the local authorities that was the truth of what happened here."

Lucy leaned forwarded and laid her hand on Dave's back gently. As she did, she noticed him twitch slightly for the first time. In all likelihood, this was probably because he had taken a knock during the fighting and as the adrenalin of the situation dissipated, then pain would start to take control. She realised if that was the case then he might need some attention. A second thought jumped into her mind as she hoped it was not just medical attention that he would need.

"I think you would be a great asset to us back home if you wanted to come and join us," she said. It was partly to get her mind back on their current situation but also because she felt that the time was right to allow a close friend to be around, not just to help with the protection of her country, but to help her personally.

"It's a shame our problems are not over here yet," he responded, looking back over his shoulder towards her. "We've still got a Home Secretary to deal with tomorrow. Then, maybe, we can make some plans about where we go from here."

As he turned back to face forwards again, he noticed the grin starting to appear across Stuart's face. Dave then added "As in how we save the world I mean."

As they were driving back to Alpha Command, the soldier who had joined them on the dock front leaned forward and tapped Dave on the shoulder.

"Excuse me Sir," he asked.

"You don't need to call me Sir," the reply came. "Dave is fine."

"As per your position on the Alpha team," the soldier explained, "my orders dictate I should address you as such, Sir."

"Very well," Dave replied with a sigh. Perhaps there should have been some flexibility written into the protocols.

"Sir, can I ask how it is you shot this man and there appears to be no visible wounds?" the soldier enquired

"What is your name then soldier?" Dave asked

"Sergeant Gage Sir."

"What about your first name?" Lucy asked.

"Adam. Adam Gage, Doctor Tyler."

"Now his orders do not state anything about you having to address me as such," Lucy said abruptly. "You can call me just Lucy. But in answer to your question, we, as in the US government, have shared a new weapon with the Alpha team that stuns the target."

"But I saw him take multiple shots with my own eyes, and they did not stop him. He just kept going."

"Sergeant Gage," Dave said, turning round to face him directly. "I know the records of each and every one of the guys in our teams. Can you, for the sake of both Lucy and Stuart, tell me your recent history?"

"Sir?" he questioned. "I don't understand what that has to do with the situation?"

"Please just answer my question. It will become quite clear to you very shortly Sergeant Gage," Dave ordered.

"Well, okay then," Gage answered sounding rather sceptical. "I spent two years in Afghanistan during the conflict with the Taliban and then moved to reconnaissance in an attempt to track down and destroy weapons caches. I then was sent to undertake several missions in Iraq prior to the start of the war, and then spent the next six months working on trying to help seek out insurgents."

"So, you would say you were quite adept at covert activities?" Dave questioned.

"Yes Sir, I believe I am," Gage responded, sounding very confident in his answer he gave. "I've been in the special forces for nearly ten years now Sir."

"If I tell you the truth behind this captive, then there will be no going back for you," Dave told Gage. "You will be accepting a mission of the highest priority to this country. The only way out will be to live in a prison cell for the rest of your life. If you're ready to accept this undertaking, then you will find yourself promoted to the Alpha Team."

Lucy leaned forward and tried to ask Dave as quietly as possible "What are you doing?"

Dave looked further round to face her and gave Lucy a quick look as if to say, I know what I'm doing. She leaned back in her seat and waited for Dave to explain.

"Sergeant Gage," Dave continued as he looked back round to him. "The information we are about to tell you is highly classified and as such, you will be placed in a position of extreme trust. This prisoner has in fact been infected by a nanoprobe which is in fact of alien origins."

Sergeant Gage noticeable shifted in his seat, moving slightly away from the body.

"Don't worry," Dave said, with a slight smile, partly of amusement, partly as a gesture to reassure Gage. "It cannot be transmitted by physical contact alone. The infections we are aware of have been by contact with alien items, ingestion of contaminated food and water supplies and also close proximity to known sources. As just mentioned, the nature of the virus is alien, extra terrestrial to be precise."

Lucy watched Sergeant Gage closely as he listened. He looked from the Dave, to the body and then back to Dave, a look of disbelief appearing on his face. The same look she had seen on so many faces of people who learned about the alien threat. One that had stuck in her mind was when Rob Forster had learnt of the threat.

"In fact, Lucy here was partially infected over six months ago when she was subjected to exposure to the nano-probes from an article they found on a mission. We also believe that I have been partially exposed to the virus, although so far it has only caused a vivid hallucination."

"So why does she not have super strength like I saw with this guy on the dock front?" Sergeant Gage asked, looking Lucy up and down, unnerving her slightly.

"The reason for that is as yet not completely understood," she said. "As we have seen with some other people, the exposure was enough to cause me to have some changes with regards to my brain waves, but not enough to infect me or cause a mutation to my DNA."

"Not everyone who is infected actually survives to reach the same state that our prisoner here has," Dave said as he took over from Lucy. "A large number have actually died from horrific mutations and deformations of their bodies. We have some photos and videos back at Alpha Command you can see, but this is sure something I do not hope to show you for real."

"Basically, the infection changes the human DNA so as to increase someone's strength, mental abilities. It all depends on the person's abilities by the looks of it," Lucy added. "As yet, we do not know why. Other than reported visions of the planet being burned, we have no leads as to what the aliens want from us or our planet."

"And you are trying to stop the spread of these probes?" Gage asked. "Trying to stop this change from happening?"

"Yes. The Department of Planetary Defense in America started working in towards the end of last year following an alien craft that was sighted by the crew of the Space Shuttle Atlantis," Dave continued to outline to Gage. "This craft released something towards the planets surface. Lucy and her team have been working to fight this since."

"How long have we known about this over here then?" Gage asked.

"Here in the UK, we implemented the Alpha Protocols just over three days ago as our response to the threat. This is a threat that has happened because a key member of our own government has been infected and is trying to spread the infection. We are not yet sure if this is either by him or as part of a group. It is something we still cannot verify. Our problem worsened over a day ago when a jet taking off from the American airbase at Lakenheath collided with an alien craft."

"You mean that's what was in the container just now?" Sergeant Gage enquired.

"Yes," Dave answered, nodding his head. "Because of dangers here, we took the decision to put the craft in the hands of the DPD team in Washington and with NASA. They have a team there who have more expertise than we do. We had to admit that we believe that they can protect this craft better than we can at the moment."

"So how do I fit in then? Why are you telling me this now?" Sergeant Gage asked.

"Because, I am asking if you would like to join the Alpha team. Harry and I were looking at all the records of the various special ops guys we have brought on board, and your record actually stood out from the rest. Having lost a number of the original team had brought forward the need that we have for someone with military planning and tactics to join us."

"And what if I say no?" Gage pushed. "Are you serious about the jail thing?"

"Why would you want to say no? This is the chance to use some of your experience for work that most people would never even dream of." Dave made it sound like he was making the offer of a dream job, although in reality it would be a mixture of stress, danger and a loss of civil liberties of all those in the team.

Sergeant Gage looked out the window of the car, watching the passing countryside for a couple of minutes. He had just learned that aliens actually existed, they were actually here and he was being presented the unique chance to be able to join a fight to hold them back. But what was he going to be fighting? What was the threat? There was so much he did not yet know that this made the opportunity seem like a chance he could not refuse,

After a few more seconds, he turned back and gave his answer.

"Yes, I will join you. I look forward to the challenge Sir."

"Welcome to the Alpha Team," Dave told him, holding his hand out for them shake. "You will be given a full briefing when we reach Alpha Command. There is a lot more that Harry will need to outline to you. And then we shall put you to work to help with planning tomorrow's mission to London."

"Thank you Sir," Gage said to Dave.

Dave turned forwards and sat back in his seat, but added "One more thing Gage. You don't need to call me Sir any more. You're now one of us."

Chapter 20

Having arrived back at Alpha Command, Stuart and Gage carried the still stunned body of the infectee down to the cells, while Dave and Lucy made their way straight up to the command room.

They were met be Harry and Dan, who had been assisting with the mission over the radios. Both were currently working on providing information for the cover story to the local authorities.

"Thanks for the help back there," Dave said. "We got no trouble from the police as we left and no-one seemed to follow us back."

"No problems dude," Dan replied enthusiastically. "It was great fun being able to do this sort of thing legitimately."

Harry, noticing Dave was stretching his shoulder slightly said "Before you guys do anything else, I suggest you go down to the med room and get yourselves checked out."

"I'm fine" Dave said. "Just a few scratches and bruises I guess. How about you Lucy, how are you then?"

"Same here," she replied. "It could have been a lot worse had you and Stuart not been so prepared to deal with the infectee back there. I'm still not sure how he was hit on the back of the foot there though?"

"Actually," Harry added, "you need to thank Gamma Three for that. He could not get a clear shot from across the river until the last second. It was at that point he hit him in the back of the ankle, not wanting to try and shoot him so as to risk hitting Lucy as well."

Dave turned to look at the maps on the wall. He could see on the map of Felixstowe docks that there were still three blue markers flashing, all stationary, but within the same area.

Across the river were a group of seven flashing purple markers, the Gamma team gathering for their return to base.

Dave turned his head slightly to address Harry. "How many casualties did we actually suffer in the end?"

"Three confirmed dead and two took slight injuries," Harry said as he checked the details on the screen in front of him. "Both should be okay for tomorrow though, but I will get an update once they return. One other was just knocked unconscious when he fell. Not as bad as you initially reported in on the journey back thankfully."

"What about the cover story? Are the emergency services buying into the drug thing?" Dave asked.

Dan pressed a few keys and switched the monitor on the wall to the Sky news channel. A reporter was live at the scene, with the caption "Dock's Drug Battle" across the screen.

"Figures released so far by the police reveal that a massive amount of drugs, primarily cocaine, were found spread by the explosion on the dock front. From evidence they have already been able to gather, the police believe it was smuggled in a container brought into the docks by lorry during the morning. Police have confirmed that there were casualties, with several people believed to have been killed during the prolonged gun battle that was fought along the dock front. We expect more details to be released during the rest of the day."

"What can you tell us about the US navy vessel that was reported to be in the docks at the time," The studio presenter asked the reporter.

"Little is known other than it made a quick departure during the fighting," the report explained. "We do know that the vessel was called the USS Pacific. It loaded a container on board and is currently on it's towards the English Channel as we speak. It appears to be just a coincidence that it was in dock at the time as they had docked to take on some supplies of water after having suffered technical difficulties during a recent exercise."

Dan cut the sound, but left the video feed running with subtitles.

"So far, so good," Harry said. "We appear to have got away with it so far. We need to make sure tomorrow goes as well and hopefully we can get some normality back."

Stuart and Gage walked into the conference room, Stuart carrying a couple of bottles of water with him. He threw one over to Dave before handing the other to Lucy.

"Thought you might like something to drink" he said. "I was certainly dying for one by the time we got back, even if I would have preferred something a bit stronger."

Noticing the newcomer entering the room with Stuart, Harry walked over to Dave and gently pulled him to one side.

"You got him on the team already then?" Harry asked quietly, pointing over to the sergeant. "Gage, is he okay with it?"

"Yes," Dave replied. "But we're going to need you to do the full briefing and bits, but yes, he is now a full member of the Alpha Team. Actually while we are all here, I think it might be a good idea if I do some introductions quickly. The team all seems to be in place now."

Dave turned back to face the rest of the team.

"Please can you all take a seat," he said. "We're just going to take a couple of minutes to make sure you all know each other and an update on tomorrow's target."

Everyone took a seat around the table. Despite the fact that there were now several more members on the team, the table still dwarfed them. Dave did not envision a day when the

Alpha Team would fill the whole table, but was fully aware that there would be meetings that might well fill the room.

"Firstly, I'd like to congratulate you all on a successful mission. The craft is now on board the USS Pacific and is well on its way to NASA." Dave paused so he could turn to Harry slightly and ask "Have you got any update on the progress yet?"

"Let me call Johnson and see what the latest is," Harry replied. He pulled his mobile phone out of his pocket and dialled the number for Johnson back in the DPD. As he did, he stepped across the command room so as to allow Dave to continue talking.

"Hopefully, the team there can shed some light on it really is and what its intended purpose is meant to be," Dave said. "This is probably the most important item to come into the possession of either ourselves or the DPD. While we have passed it over to our counterparts in America, this no way reflects on our abilities or their superiority over us."

Pausing to take a sip of water, he then continued. "Secondly, I want to introduce the two new members of our team. I know you've all sort of met each other during this morning and you will get the opportunity to know them all quite well soon enough."

Dave moved around the table and stood behind Dan. As he did, he started to say "Dan West is going to be our systems expert."

Dan gave a little smile, slightly embarrassed to have the focus of the team on him, even if only for a few seconds.

"But when I say systems expert, I don't mean in relation to our systems. He will get us in to any system we need to get information from, plant false records and so on. Banks, government records, security systems, you name it, and he will break in to it. It took the authorities nearly five years to catch up with him before we pulled him from sitting permanently in a jail cell."

The sideways look he got from Lucy told him she still did not think this was a wise move for them to be taking. But he had already made clear to her that this was his team and his choice. He knew he had to get it right the first time because if he didn't, then the lives of millions of people were at risk.

Actually, he had said to himself on several occasions in the past few weeks, the lives of everyone on the planet are at risk. That put no pressure on him or the team at all.

"Then we have Sergeant Adam Gage, ex-SAS and possibly the best Special Forces expert the UK military," Dave continued as he moved a couple of seats around the table. As he past Lucy's seat, he gently rubbed his hand along her shoulders, causing her to look up at him and smile back.

"He will help us with getting into places we need to be, weapons, the kind of stuff that will ensure we don't get killed, hopefully. I'm sure that the events of today will show why I have confidence in him to join this team and be of vital importance."

As Dave finished, Gage nodded to him and said "Thanks for giving me this chance. I hope I can serve you all to the best of my abilities."

"Please Adam, you're not in the army now. Everyone on this team has equal input and standing, so please don't feel like you still have to call anyone sir."

Harry stepped forward and said "Except me."

Dave continued to look at the team, ignoring Harry. "Even Harry. You'll get used to him."

"We'll talk later Dave," Harry said sternly as he walked around the table to stand next to him. "Seriously, Dave is correct. We are a team and I don't doubt your abilities to work together."

Dave suddenly looked very serious and said "What I would like to add at this point is that while you say you can do the job to the best of your abilities, in all likelihood, there will be times that it is not going to be enough to guarantee success each time we go out. This job is going to push your abilities, your knowledge to levels you've never worked at before. I want you to know that I have chosen you all as the best of the best, so do not let me down."

Dave then paused for a few seconds to allow his big speech to sink in before he finished the introductions. As he did, he looked to each team member to see their reactions. The only one who gave a visible response was Lucy, who nodded at him to show her approval of his statement.

He guessed that she must have given a similar speech to her team at some point. At least they were all on the right wavelength. He took a few more steps and moved to stand behind Stuart.

"As you know, Stuart here is our medical expert and team joker. Just watch out for him." Dave said. He then gestured over the table towards Lucy. "And finally, we come to Doctor Lucy Tyler. She is currently here as a representative of DPD, the Department of Planetary Defense from America, to help us ensure that we have everything in place to allow our teams to work together and prevent this alien threat from taking hold."

"I'd just like to say, I've seen you in action and I think you have a good team here," Lucy said. "I look forward to working with you all."

Dave walked round the table to where Dan was sitting. He leaned over his shoulder and entered some details on to the computer. Changing the display on the wall, a picture of the Home Secretary appeared on the wall. He also picked up a control unit from the table so he could change the images as required.

As he spoke again, Dave walked around the table back to where he had started, standing behind Lucy.

"Tomorrow's target is the Home Secretary. As you might have guessed, this is not going to be an easy target for us, especially being our first target as a team.

"You could have found an easier one for us to start with," Gage chipped in, the tone in his voice full of surprise. "Not that I am complaining about getting a decent mission that is."

"What do you want?" Stuart said, unable to resist joining in any form of banter within the team. "How about an old granny or a nursery teacher to let you practice on?"

Gage was not sure on how to respond to Stuart, but did not get the chance to.

Ignoring the obvious buoyant spirits amongst his team, Dave imposed his authority in the team and continued. "However, tomorrow we have got the best opportunity to remove him as a threat. While capturing him is the primary objective for the mission, we must not hold back if it means making a kill."

Dave could hear a few shocked mutterings from Gage and Dan, especially the latter. However, he was not surprised by the reaction.

"I gather from your reactions," Dave said, "that you are shocked by how we are targeting a member of our own country's government. The Prime Minister has been fully briefed and we have been given a green light to make the hit tomorrow."

Dan piped in and asked "Why? I know the background about the threat, but how does he fit in to all this?"

Pressing the control button, another image appeared on the screen on the wall. This was one that showed two different DNA strands. One was a standard double helix that is found in all humans, the other one was the mutated DNA strand showing traces of the effects of the nano-probes. This was found in anyone who survived the mutation caused by the alien infection.

"As you can see here," Dave said, "the left sample is his known DNA strand. This was taken from a sample we obtained out his medical records from several months ago. The second is from a DNA sample we obtained two days ago. This confirms that he has been infected by the alien virus and is now no longer human. As you should be aware from your briefings, he will now be driven by the desire to infect as many people as possible, in anyway that he knows."

"We believe he will be making an attempt tomorrow at the press conference that he is holding at midday. This is due to be televised live across the country. We also expect this to be broadcast to many other countries around the world, so we cannot afford for him to use this opportunity to try and infect countless millions of people."

"Sorry if this sounds like a loud of fairy tale stories Gage, but," Dave started to say.

"Fairy tales?" Gage jumped in. "More like Nightmare on Elm Street type stuff."

Dave could not help but join the rest of the team in laughing at Gage's response. Not that it surprised him, but lightened the mood slightly.

"Harry will give you the full briefing in a couple of minutes. We have developed a rough plan as to how we will make our move to hit the Home Secretary about thirty minutes before he is due to give his presentation. We know that he will be staying in a room on the third floor of the hotel and we believe he will be there until about fifteen minutes before he gives his presentation."

"How do you know that?" Gage asked.

"MI5 and MI6 are aware of our team here, albeit at only the top levels of their agencies," Dave explained to him. He then returned to addressing the whole team again.

"They have confirmed that he will obviously be well guarded. But I have been told on our way up to the command room earlier that we have now been able to modify the stun shells so that they can also stun humans. The charge modifies its level depending on some chemical in the blood, but you will have to ask the techies how it does it. There is still the risk that the charge will still kill them. At least it gives us the chance to reduce the numbers we may leave dead and need to cover up."

"This is where I need you guys to get yourselves up to speed pretty quick. Dan, I need you to pull up any records or information that will help us. While Gage, I want you to take our plan we have developed so far and figure out how we can improve it further. Is there a better way in or out that you can find? Use Dan to pull any information you need or perhaps even plant to help cover our plans."

"I've got to go and file a report on this morning's mission. Stuart, Lucy, I will also need you to submit some details as well. You know the routine I hope. Shout if anyone needs any help or anything, I will be in my office. Otherwise, we will gather together again at seven tomorrow morning for a full briefing."

Harry stepped forward and said "Gage, if you would stay behind, I shall sort out the business of your briefing. Anyone got any questions for me before you all disappear?"

Nobody had any questions, so they all made their excuses and headed out of the room. They left Gage to his briefing and the realisation that his world was about to change, maybe not for the better.

This was one part of the job that Dave really hated with a passion. Writing reports. He had often wondered why, as a covert operation, they actually had to document and report everything that happened during a mission.

To be honest, he knew where the reports went. They were all copied to the heads of MI5 and MI6 for a start. But he still wondered if they were actually read at all. Given the number of reports from the more conventional parts of their agencies, he suspected that the Alpha Protocols' reports had been given the least priority until now.

What would happen if there was something in a report they did not like? He hoped he would never have to find that one out. The more he thought about it, the more he started to believe each of his reports would fall into that category. Their work was never going to be anything but extraordinary.

Still, up to now he had not had to write too many of these things. And those that had been written tended to be rather short and concise. This one however, was going to take a bit more effort than normal. To allow him to get on with it, he had decided to shut himself away from the rest of the team and in his office. He had thought that there should be less distraction than being elsewhere in the command centre.

He had his own office within the Alpha Command, but he missed the people around him. It was in a fairly large room and could double up as an extra meeting area when the need arose.

As well as his desk along one side of the room, he had a table with four leather seats around it. These were rarely used if he was honest about it. Off to one side, there was a large settee which he often used to lay out on when working late. It was not the most comfortable place to sleep, but then there were times there was nothing else to do but crash out on it.

The walls were covered with maps and pictures relating to events and incidents where UFO's had been sited in the UK. He also had a number of filing cabinets that contained folders of information on the people who had reported many of these events. He had investigated a number of them already to ensure they were not part of the alien's plan already. So far those searches had not turned anything up that they needed to be concerned about.

Dave had often tried to tidy the office up in quiet moments, but had given up each and every time. Papers were stacked up on every spare surface. His desk was regularly covered in notes, photos and research. He was often nagged at by Harry for the number of half drunk cups of coffee left on the desk, so much so that some even appeared to be developing their own alien life forms.

As he sat staring at the screen, his mind began to think about the mission tomorrow and the report he'd have to write after that. He found that he just could not focus on the task at hand, no matter how hard he had tried. His thoughts then led him to wonder if this was a problem Lucy had back home.

Now there was a thought that sidetracked him even further. Here was someone he had admiration for the work she had been doing, some of which he had been watching from a distance. Now he got to see and work with her up close, he felt that his feelings for her were developing. Something he was excited at the possibility that it could develop further, but was reluctant to in case it were to interfere with their work.

A knock at the door broke his thoughts, which he felt was probably a good thing anyway. He didn't think there was any way she would feel the same for him. Besides, she was a few years older than him, so he doubted that would help his cause either.

"Come in," he called out.

The door opened and Lucy walked in, holding a cup of coffee. Even now, as he looked her over as she crossed the room, she was still looking rather dirty from the morning's events. He suddenly wondered if he was staring at her too much as she made her way across his office and found himself shuffling some papers on the desk in front of him.

Her being there, reminded him that he could not wait to get into a shower and clean himself of the morning's sweat and dust from the dock mission. He looked down at his desk, trying to hide a sudden wave of embarrassment sweeping over him. She held the cup out to him, so he had to look back up at her.

"Thought you could do with a coffee," she said. "White with sugar, at least that's what Stuart told me how you took it."

"Thanks, I need it. I just can't seem to get my head into doing this right now," he said. "Report writing just does not seem to be an important job to me."

"I know the feeling," she said offering him a comforting smile. "I'm all done with my details for you. It's on the system when you're ready for it. When you're done, I'll meet you in the break room. I'm going to make a few calls to see how my boys are getting on back home without me."

As he watched her leave the room, Dave smiled. He doubted that the members of her team would ever appreciate being called Lucy's boys, certainly not Bale anyway. Somehow, he didn't think he could even compete with them for her attention.

Sipping the coffee, he turned his attention back to the report. He decided that he was going to get it finished. Then he could go and spend some valuable time with her while he still had the chance.

Chapter 21

Having finally finished writing his report, Dave made his way from his office to the break room. He found that both Lucy and Stuart were already waiting for him, sitting at one of the tables chatting to each other.

As he entered the room, Stuart looked up at him and said "It's about time you finished that report, or were you trying to write a novel about today? I'm sure Lucy is pretty bored of me by now and waiting for you to pay her some attention."

Lucy had to look over her shoulder to smile at Dave as she was sat with her back to the door. Dave was relieved to see that she had to face him because the grin on Stuarts face was intended to wind him up. He knew that his colleague had figured out what he was starting to feel towards Lucy and had set out to make his life hell about it.

He made his way across the room, got himself a can of Coke from the drinks machine and sat down next to Stuart at the table. At least he could be sure that Stuart wouldn't be pulling any more faces towards him with Lucy sat opposite them.

"So what do you guys do on your nights off around here then?" Lucy asked. With a little laugh, more to herself, she added "Not that I expect you will be getting too many of those if our record is anything to go by."

Dave and Stuart both looked at each and started to grin madly, which Lucy found to be a little disturbing. A puzzled look spread across her face, replacing the previous moment of amusement.

"Football" they both replied at once.

Punching Dave in the arm, Stuart said "Shame about that team of Muppets you support."

"There's nothing wrong with them mate. They've just been having a hard time this year," Dave retorted. "At least I support the team where I live, not some glory boy like you and your team."

"Glory boy is it?" Stuart replied loudly. "Don't start me on that one again, I'm warning you."

Lucy was slightly bemused by the discussion. She was not a big sports fan, especially not football. Well, at least American Football. Remembering that from an American point of view, one quirk of the people from the United Kingdom was to call soccer football.

"So do you mean your kind of football or our American kind of football?" she asked.

"Our kind of course. What you guys play is not football, it is more like rugby for ladies" Stuart replied.

"Stop it Stuart," Dave said, pushing him on the shoulder. "It's not really that bad a sport once you get into it."

Stuart just rolled his eyes and shook his head at Dave's response. He knew full well that Dave was not a big fan of American football and suspected he was just trying to impress Lucy. He was also aware that Dave knew what he was thinking and hated the fact that Stuart was pushing his luck with the teasing.

"Tonight, Ipswich Town, our local team, are playing at home against Leeds United. It's going to be a good game, possibly with a few beers as well," Dave said. He changed his tone a little as he asked Lucy "would you like to come along with me then?"

"Well, it sure would beat sitting in a hotel room," Lucy replied. "I think that you might have to explain the rules to me a little bit though. But I would definitely say that a couple of beers really do sound like a good idea, if you really don't mind taking me."

Stuart leaned over to Dave and said in a fake whisper, "You know why we don't take women to football, it's because they can't understand it. And do you know why they can't understand it?"

"Don't even say it," Dave said, wagging his finger at Stuart. They had been through this conversation several times since he had known him. That was normally after a few beers however.

"That's because it's a man's sport. That's why." Stuart could not help but grin from ear to ear. He was always unable miss an opportunity to wind up Dave, although he knew he would probably pay for it at some point in the future. He had been offered the prime opportunity to do so over the past couple of days and was taking more than a little pleasure out of watching Dave squirm so much.

"Ignore him," Dave told Lucy, trying very hard not to show his growing embarrassment at Stuart's teasing. He really hoped that she was not picking up on the truth behind it all. "If you would like to come with me, then I really am more than happy to take you."

"I'd love to come with you," Lucy said with a smile. "We can go and get something to eat afterwards I take it?"

"Sure, there's a few restaurants nearby we could go to for some food after the game. We'll talk about what to eat a bit later then."

"I'll be seeing you guys tomorrow morning then," Stuart said. Seeing Lucy look questioningly at him, he added "I'm not going to go and watch that bunch of no hopers when I can watch my boys on the TV at home, in a comfy cheer, and with a decent bottle of beer."

Dave and Lucy both said their good nights to Stuart as he left them alone in the break room. After taking a swig of his drink, Dave looked up to the clock and saw it was only just after five in the evening. It had been a long day and he definitely needed to get a shower before they went out.

"If I drop you back at the hotel, I can then dive home to get a shower and change into some fresh clothes. Probably take me about an hour or so. Will that give you enough time to get ready?" he asked.

"That should give me plenty of time. I don't need to dress up too smart do I?" Lucy enquired. Other than putting them in the various drawers and wardrobe, she still had not had much time to go through the clothes the Alpha Team had supplied the day before and hoped there was something suitable for her to wear tonight.

"No, just make sure you have something on that will keep you warm when it chills down a bit later on." As he spoke, he started to get up out of his seat. "You ready to go then?" he asked Lucy.

He took a last swig of his drink, crunched the can in his hand and carefully threw it towards the bin on the other side of the room. He clenched his fist in victory as it went in first time.

Lucy looked at him and shook her head. "Typical man," she told him. She just shook her head further when he looked back at her, trying to put on an expression that was as innocent as he could.

Dave turned and headed out of the break room towards the lifts, Lucy following closely behind him. As they walked down the main corridor, they passed one of the offices. Inside sat Dan and Gage, both engrossed at looking through various plans and computer images of the target for tomorrow.

Dave felt slightly guilty that they were going out for the evening. But then they had been through a lot more in the past three days than these guys had. There was nothing like throwing them in at the deep end in the attempt to ensure tomorrow's mission was going to be a success as part of their initiation in to the team.

Dan looked up from the screen and saw them walking past. He smiled and waved, which left Dave thinking that this guy seemed to enjoy any time he got in front of a computer screen, especially when it meant getting into systems he was not meant to.

He had learned that Dan had already obtained the information on the hotel bookings, room and staff schedules, orders and delivery times. Anything and everything that may be of help to them with getting in to the building undercover.

Gage was doing his best to use the plans of the hotel, the local sections of the underground system, services and so on of the area around the hotel to find the best entry points for the team. While the basic plan had been formed, these two would ensure the rest of it was in place by the morning.

Dave gave Dan the thumbs up as they passed and turned down the stairs. At the bottom, they walked over to the lift and waited until it arrived. They stepped in and Dave pressed the button for the ground floor.

As the lift started to ascend, he turned to Lucy and asked "So what do you think of our operation so far? Would we meet with your high standards back home then?"

"Well," she started, "in some respects yes you do. But there are definitely other areas where you go against a number of things I tried to implement quite rigidly. In regards to the command centre here, you certainly manage to out shine our centre of operations. I don't mean just in resources and space, but if you can keep this place secret, then it will serve you extremely well."

Before they could discuss any further, the lift reached their floor and the doors opened. There were several people waiting outside to get in, but they moved aside to let them exit.

"I think we can talk about this in more detail later this evening," Dave said. "We've not really been able to go into much knowledge sharing yet have we?"

As they talked, Dave led the way over to one of the car parks that was at the side of the main building. The car park was still fairly full, but there were quite a few people starting to make their way to their cars as they headed home for the night.

"If I knew it was going to be as exciting over here as back home, perhaps I would have bought some of the guys with me," Lucy said. "I'm sure they would have enjoyed the challenge. Certainly, there are times like this morning that would be just what Bale would want to get stuck into."

"I'm sure they've been busy enough themselves from what you said earlier," Dave responded. There was a slight hint of jealousy creeping into his voice at another mention of Bale from Lucy. "The more we talk and from what I saw in America, I don't see this getting any easier either, for both of our teams. Sometimes I think maybe we are a lot better off on the outside, not knowing about any of these things that are going on. What's the saying, ignorance is bliss?"

Lucy laughed. "I think you might be right on that, but don't you get a buzz from it sometimes? Aren't you glad that you're involved?"

As they reached Dave's car, a dark, metallic blue Ford Mustang, he pulled the keys from his pocket and unlocked the car. This was his pride and joy, despite the fact he got a lot of teasing from his friends. Being an American muscle car, it was not a common sight on British roads and many of them thought he was just showing off with it.

Leaning on the roof, he looked over to Lucy and said "I guess you're right. Besides, I've never had such an exciting time with a lady before. Bet you can't beat that for a first date."

Lucy just shook her head as she climbed into the car. "If only there was some truth to that statement," she thought to herself. "If only he knew what I really felt."

Having dropped Lucy at her hotel, Dave had driven the couple of miles back to his house. He knew he had an hour and he might as well not rush if he understood women as well as he thought he did. Most of the ones he knew needed an hour just to choose the clothes they were going to wear when going out, let alone actually be ready on time.

He stood in the bathroom and undressed. His clothes were a mess from the day's excitement. There was dust and mud all over him, his t-shirt also had blood stains from the number of grazes and small cuts he had picked up. This was not a part of the job he thought he would ever get used to.

He took a look in the mirror and turned side on so he could see what his back looked like. He had a number of cuts down his back, a couple looked quite large. Down the back of his right arm was a large graze. This must have come from when he had saved Lucy and taken the brunt of their fall onto the concrete surface.

Once he had had a shower, he thought it probably would not look quite so bad. It certainly might feel a lot more comfortable when he was clean again.

Stepping over to the shower, he climbed in and turned it on. As it started to warm up he stepped forward into the water stream and stood with his face in the spray, letting it run down his whole body. With the water not being too hot, it felt quite soothing over the skin.

As he poured the shampoo onto his head, he began to wash his hair but found his thoughts kept wandering back to Lucy. He'd really only known her for just a couple of days. Actually, he had known of her before having monitored the DPD team for so long, but had not been able to speak to her until just this week.

In just a couple of days, they had been thrown into some of the most unexpected situations, unimaginable to most people who did not know about the alien threat. Between them, they were leading the front line fighting the prospect of aliens taking over the planet.

Until now, there had only been a handful of people in the country that had been aware of the situation. As far as the guys in the DPD were aware, they had believed that they were the only ones who knew what was happening. There was now a larger group who they could discuss this with, even if they had to carefully select where they could talk.

In about two day's time, the only way he would be able to speak to Lucy was by telephone or video link. As he washed himself, the thought started to bother him, something he had not expected when had first picked her up from the airport.

Tonight would be an opportunity to get to know her a bit more on a personal level, and for him to try to impress her enough that she would at least leave to go home with something to think about.

He remembered back to the moment in the car after the mission in the docks when he realised there was a chance that something might have been developing between them. It was only now that he had the opportunity to think about it that he was able to comprehend the moment.

It was when she had laid her hand on his back. As he remembered the moment, he thought about how he had felt the pain of some of the scrapes and had flinched slightly at her touch. But despite that pain, the touch of her hand, even through his jacket, had been soothing.

When she had asked if he would like to join her in America, he had just wanted to say yes straight away. But he knew full well that his place was here in the United Kingdom. It was his job to help protect his country, much in the same way Lucy's was to protect hers, America. She would not want to give up that fight to come and stay with him here.

Finishing his shower and turning off the water, Dave reached out to grab his towel. He started to dry himself, feeling so much fresher and relaxed physically than he had done ten minutes before. But mentally, he was tangled. How he got on with Lucy tonight would tell him a lot about where his future lay.

At least, he hoped it would.

Lucy stepped out of the shower and wrapped the towel around her body. Hotel showers were never as good as the one at home, where ever in the world you went she thought.

She picked up the second towel and started to dry her hair. While she had been out on missions before with the DPD, she had rarely got as dirty as she had done today. She remembered telling Dave that Bale would have had a field day with what they had been through. It was his sort of work for sure.

Had that been a hint of jealousy creeping in to his voice as he had responded to her?

As she walked through from the bathroom to sit on the bed, her thoughts continued to move back to Dave. She felt attracted to this guy in a way she had not felt for any other guy for some time. There was a definite chemistry between her and Bale, but there was something more developing here with Dave.

She felt torn between her loyalty to Bale and her growing feelings for Dave, suddenly finding herself feeling very alone. She looked over to the bedside table and saw her phone.

She picked it up and searched through the stored contacts. She found her mum's number. She knew she could always talk to her mum when she felt like this. She dialled the number and waited as it rung.

"Hello" the reassuring voice at the other end answered.

"Hello mum. It's me," she said, trying to sound positive so as not to worry her too much.

"Hello me. How's the trip going then?"

"Fine. It's just fine. It's definitely keeping me busy anyway." Lucy's voice started to tremor slightly, something that had often happened when she confided in her mum.

"Come on Lucy dear," her mum said, filling Lucy with relief that she could talk to her so openly. "I can hear in your voice something is not right. You know you can always talk to me."

"Oh mum," Lucy said, as she found herself starting to get a little bit tearful. "I'm okay, it's just I think I've met someone who I think I might like."

"That's wonderful isn't it?" her mum asked softly.

"I'm not sure, I thought everything was going just right in my life, but my job, this can't work because of my job."

"Why can't it work dear? Why won't your job let it work?"

"You know I can't talk about my work," Lucy replied. "I can't tell you why, but it's so complicated. I'm only here for two more days and then I might not see him again."

"Do you want to see him again once you come home?" her mum asked.

"Yes, but that will just complicate things at home." Lucy paused for a few seconds as she thought about the time she had spent with Dave all day. "You'd like him mum, you would approve of this guy."

"You mean he isn't like your last boyfriend Lucy?"

At her mum's comment, Lucy shivered. She had wanted to shut out the pain from that time, hence the reason she had thrown herself into her work for the past five years. Lucy paused again before saying "You know I don't like to talk about that mum. Let's just stick with you would like him when you get to meet him."

"Listen Lucy, perhaps you are reaching a point where you need to decide what is more important to you. Your work or your life? You don't need to answer that now, just think about what you want. It's not like giving your job up would endanger the planet, now is it?"

Lucy completely froze for a second. Could her mum know more than she thought? Was she trying to push her into revealing more than she wanted to let on? No, don't be daft she told herself. She was just trying to tell Lucy what she thought was best for her daughter.

"I know mum. Listen, I've got to go. I'm going out for the evening."

"With this guy," her mum asked interrupting.

"Yes mum, with this guy." She found that she had to smile to herself, or rather at her mum's intuition. After a slight pause, she then said "Thanks for being there for me."

"As I always will be my dear," her mum replied in the comforting tone Lucy had been looking to hear. "Love you Lucy."

"Bye mum," Lucy said, pressing the button to finish the call. She looked at the phone in her hand for a few minutes, not sure if having spoken to her mum, she really felt any better about things.

Catching the time on the display panel, she realised she only had ten minutes or so until Dave would arrive to pick her up for the evening. She better get a move on so she would be ready in time.

Remembering that Dave had said she ought to wear something warm for the evening in case it got chilly, she rummaged through the clothes in the drawers that she had got from Alpha Command. She pulled out a pair of jeans with a light blue knitted top and got dressed.

Once she had put the clothes on, she took a light jacket from the wardrobe that she had asked them to pick up for her. It had been one she had chosen on the internet site before they sent one of the staff to get the clothes.

She had been frustrated at loosing her case at the airport, but they had certainly helped her to take care of things since.

Dave had made sure anything she wanted or needed would be covered.

Standing in front of the mirror, tying her hair up, she took a look at herself. Pleased at being showered and changed, she hoped she would do. She hadn't had the chance to go out like this for some time, and was feeling slightly nervous about it. She wasn't sure if it was nervous at being able to go out again after so long, or at the fact she was going out with Dave. She took a deep breath and tried to clear the thoughts away.

Gathering her bag, along with her purse, phone and hotel key, she made her way out of the room and headed towards reception to meet him. Whatever happened, it was an excuse for a couple of beers and a chance to relax before they threw themselves into another day of danger tomorrow.

Chapter 22

As Lucy walked into the reception area of the hotel, she saw Dave pull up outside the main doors. The blue Ford Mustang he drove was a car she was very familiar with from home, but also easily recognisable here. She walked outside to save him having to come in.

However, before she reached the car, he had already climbed out and made his way round to open the passenger door for her.

"You look a lot better than you did earlier," she remarked as she approached him. She leaned in to give him a friendly kiss on the cheek.

"I could easily say the same about you," he replied, giving her a warm smile as he looked her up and down. "I am really hoping that we don't get too many days like that. I'm going to need to get some sleep tonight."

Before she got in the car, she looked him in the eye and said "You'll forget what sleep is before this is all over. Trust me, we learnt that one the hard way very quickly."

Closing the door, Dave muttered to himself "Great."

Since arriving in the United Kingdom at Heathrow airport, this was the most Lucy had got to see of the area. So far, most of the travelling they had done had been by main roads, but now she was getting to see some of the town of Ipswich.

It suddenly struck her how different the United States was from here. Having travelled in and out of Washington every day, they were surrounded by a variety of tall buildings. Yet here as the car crawled through the traffic towards the town, she could see that there were only a couple of buildings anywhere near the scale she was used to.

The road headed down a hill giving her a good view of the town. Ahead and just off to their right was a prominent structure that stood out because of its strong glow against the darkening sky. This, Dave had told her, was the stadium where they were heading. Again, compared to the many stadiums back home, this looked quite small. There was something that she felt quite comfortable with here, perhaps this was somewhere she could settle when everything else in her life was settled.

After another twenty minutes or so, they finally arrived at the car park next to the stadium. She looked at the growing crowds around them as she climbed out of the car. She knew she should not have been surprised that it had taken them so long to get from the hotel and into the town.

As they walked from the car park and across the road towards the stadium, she kept as close to Dave as she could. She did not feel like she would want to have to try and find him again if they got separated in this crowd.

He briefly stopped to buy a program from one of the vendors outside the stand entrance, passing it to her for something to read in case she got bored. He seemed so much more relaxed than he had done earlier in the day. In fact, since anytime since they had met at the airport. Being here made her realise that there were times when she was back home that perhaps she needed to try and relax more. Even with the importance of their work, she should also make time for herself once in a while.

As they entered the stadium, Lucy was starting to become affected by the atmosphere. Even though she did not know much about football, or soccer as they knew it back home in America, she found it easy to get caught up in the feeling of the people around her.

With about fifteen minutes to go before the game started, she could feel the excitement in the crowd. The stadium here in Ipswich was not on the same scale as some of the stadiums back in America, but being smaller, it brought the people closer together she thought. There were so many different types of people around, many of whom were with their families and children.

In the same thought, she considered the possibility of an infectee being loose in the crowd. She started to imagine about the many number of ways that they could use these situations to try and infect as many people as possible.

She found herself looking closely at the food stands. She started to wonder how easy it would be for someone to try and infect the drinks or the hot dogs that were being served here. If someone could get infected food in here, there were thousands of potential victims.

Dave placing his hand on her shoulder broke her from her depressing line of thought. He pointed to a stairway to their left.

"Our seats are on the upstairs level," he said. "We will have a good view from up there. Plus it should not be too busy so as we can chat. You might have gathered from Stuart, Ipswich Town are not a big team, so there are still always plenty of empty seats at the games."

"How many people can you get in here?" she asked, her mind still thinking about the dangers of an infectee running loose in the stadium.

"Thirty thousand or so," he replied. As if reading her mind, he said "These are the sort of places that have caused us to begin modifying elements in the Alpha Protocols. We have been able to learn a lot from the things you guys have encountered, so our plans have got to adapt and change rapidly."

As they reached the bottom of the stairway, Dave stopped and waved his hand to gesture at the people in front of them. He said with a slightly sorrowful tone to his voice, "Just imagine if an infectee decided to use somewhere such as this as a target? Just how many people could be infected in one go?"

Lucy followed him towards the stairs, taking one last look back at the food stands and crowds moving around. She had to remind herself that she was not here to worry about work tonight, but that was easier said than done. With a sigh, she started the climb.

After six flights of stairs, they reached a concourse. Along the opposite wall were a number of short staircases leading out into the stand itself, beyond which she could see the glow from the floodlights around the pitch. Lucy also noted another two food outlets and a bar as well on this level.

Looking at Dave as she followed him towards the stairs in to the stand, she realised this might be the best opportunity to start to learn how to relax. At least, in a different atmosphere and away from their respective offices, they could just be themselves as if they might have been had none of this alien problem had started. Even if it was only going to be for a few hours.

Once they had taken their seats, she noticed a strong change in Dave. Being in the crowd, he was instantly even more relaxed, yet she could sense the excitement within him. He obviously enjoyed his football and she realised this might be why the Alpha Team might have a slightly more relaxed approach to their work. They appeared to have more freedom for their staff to live their lives than the protocols the DPD followed allowed. Perhaps there was a lot she could learn to take home with her and improve the life for her team.

Dave turned to her and asked "So tell me, how do you guys at the DPD deal with any spare time that you do get then?"

Even here, she was not comfortable speaking about her work. Not as openly as this anyway as you never knew who was around or listening. She needed to make this point clear to Dave.

"My employers like their staff to be kept on a tight rein to be honest," she explained. "We can't have them going out and talking about their work, not in public because of the threat it might pose to them and their colleagues."

"Sorry" he replied, sounding like a scolded school boy. "Perhaps we should not talk work here then."

He stood up again and asked her "Do you want a drink or something to eat? I'm a little peckish myself and fancy a quick burger before the game starts."

Lucy still had the thoughts about the infectees and the food stalls in the back of her head, so she had to refuse.

"I'm fine thanks," she replied. "We're still going to be eating later anyway aren't we?"

"We sure are," he said enthusiastically. "I should have grabbed a sandwich before I picked you up, but spent longer than I planned in the shower. I'll be back in a minute or two then."

As Dave left her, Lucy sat looking out across the stadium. She was quite impressed with the place as far as these things went. Although the stadium was not full, the amount of noise generated from the crowd to her right was surprising to her. This, she learnt from various announcements being made over the PA system, was where the opposition team's fans were sat. And as they started to shout louder, so the home fans followed suit, each set trying to out sing the other.

Before she had time to really miss him, Dave came back, burger and drink in hand. Lucy had found that she had started to relax slightly and felt more comfortable within the crowd. Despite preferring to be on her own normally, she was happy having normal, everyday people, doing normal things around her.

As he ate his quick snack and drink, Dave was looking between his watch and leaning forward to look towards the corner of the pitch to their left.

"Almost time," he said to Lucy as she again caught a glint in his eye.

She was about to ask him what it was almost time for, when the whole stadium erupted into loud cheers and clapping. Over the PA system, the Guns and Roses track Welcome To the Jungle started to play and she found herself also standing up, clapping with the rest of the crowd.

In front of them, the two teams were taking to the pitch. Ipswich Town were playing in a blue colour strip, while Leeds United were playing all in white. At least she thought that's what Dave had explained to her on the way. She thought she better be certain which team was Ipswich and not cheer the wrong one.

As the teams took their places on the field, the noise around the stadium was rapidly building further. She looked at Dave to see the excitement in his face as he joined in the singing around him. She also got the impression that he might be holding back because she was here, not willing to go over the top.

With a blast from the referee's whistle, the teams kicked off the match. Everyone around them started to sit back down, although many were still cheering and singing. She did likewise, but accidentally brushed Dave's leg with her hand as she did.

He looked at her and smiled. "Are you okay? Not bored you yet have I?"

She shook her head gently. "I'm fine. I might get more into once it gets going. Once I get familiar with the game."

"If you want to leave at any time, just say so," Dave said gently. "I'm happy to do what you want to do this evening. Don't let it worry if you think you might upset me."

She smiled back, put her hand on the side of his face and pushed to so he was facing the game in front of them. She said with a smile "Just watch the game then will you."

Once the game had finished and they were heading out of the stadium, Dave asked Lucy "How did you enjoy that then?"

"Well, it certainly beat spending the evening sat in the office or in the hotel room on my own" she replied. "I'm glad your team won though. I guess that means you won't be grumpy like Stuart said you would be if they lost."

"Huh," Dave groaned. "I'm going to have to have words with him tomorrow. Casting dispersions on my good character like that."

"I'm sure he was only trying to wind you up," Lucy said, wondering if she should not have said anything in the first place. When she looked at him, she saw that he was obviously teasing her.

"Win, loose or draw," he told her, "it's just being out with the crowd that I really enjoy. Why else do you think I have been able to support this lot for so long?"

Lucy was amused to this side of his personality. Someone who looked to be the best at everything he did and had the attitude that loosing was not an option in their work, who now claimed to support the team he did even though they were not the best team around.

"Anyway," Dave continued, "back to more important matters as I am hungry again. What do you fancy to eat then?"

"What have you got that is close by then?" she asked, feeling quite hungry herself.

"There is Italian or Chinese if you want that sort of thing," he replied after a couple of seconds thought. "Both are just a couple of minutes walk from here."

"You choose. I don't mind either way," she replied.

"Italian it is then" he decided quickly, seemingly having made the choice before he had even asked Lucy.

They walked across the road outside the stadium and cut through the car park they had parked in before the game. The crowd was dispersing quite quickly given the number of people who were at the game. Once they were out of the car park and had crossed a second road, there were actually only a few people around.

As Dave had said, the restaurant was only a couple of minutes walk from the stadium. It was more or less just across the road from where they had parked the car earlier in the evening. They were soon inside and seated at a table for two.

Removing her jacket, Lucy was glad she had brought it with her. She had found that it had actually become quite chilly as the evening progressed. Seeing him still in just a t-shirt, she suspected that Dave had not notice the change as much because he had been jumping up and down several times during the game. But she had to give him credit as he had warned her that it would do so before they had left Alpha Command.

The waiter presented them both with the menu, followed by a wine menu to Dave, from which he chose and ordered a bottle of white wine. The waiter quickly returned and brought over the bottle over to them before they could really get comfortable and start to talk. Dave tasted the wine and thanked the waiter.

"We really better not have too much tonight," he said, as he leaned over to pour a glass out for Lucy. "We have got a busy day tomorrow and will need our wits about us."

"Are you trying to tell me that?" Lucy asked, raising her eyebrow. "Or are you telling yourself more?"

In answer to Lucy's question, Dave just shrugged his shoulders at her and ensured his glass was also topped up. Lucy was certain he was just trying to tease her, but she was not going to respond to him.

She paused slightly as she took a look around to see how busy the restaurant really was. Seeing that there were only a few people, she felt reasonably comfortable about continuing the conversation Dave had tried to start back in the stadium.

"You asked me about how we deal with our free time back home earlier this evening," she said. "Well, our rules state that you would not be allowed to eat in here again for several months."

"That's a bit drastic isn't it?" Dave asked, taking a sip of the wine from his glass.

"Maybe," Lucy replied. She leaned back in her chair and removed the tie from her hair as she spoke. She ran her hands through her hair so it was no longer looking like it had just been untied. "I don't like it any more than the guys do to be honest, but it is there for our own protection. What if someone learned your patterns, knew where you would be and when? You then become an easy target."

"I've never thought about it to that detail," Dave said after a slight pause. "But I can see where you are coming from. I guess one way to look at it would be that at least with the football back there, it would take more than three months to sit in all thirty thousand different seats."

Lucy almost choked on the sip of wine she had just taken as she laughed at the last comment. When it was put like that, it sounded amusing, but she knew that Dave was fully aware what she really meant.

The waiter appeared and asked if they were ready to order their meal yet. Given the time of the evening, and it being mid-week, places did not stay open as late here in the United Kingdom as they did in America. This was another surprise to Lucy as she got to learn more about the real differences between their countries.

They just ordered a main course each, Lucy selecting the seafood lasagne while Dave opted for the meat version. The waiter took the order and left them to continue talking while they waited for him to return with their meal.

"How does that work then? Does it give your guys any real problems?" Dave asked.

"Yes and no. They obviously find some places do better food than others and would prefer to stick to those. They obviously get frustrated when the next take away is not as good. There's not much I can do about that, but I think they are beginning to realise why and accept it now." Lucy smiled as she thought back to her boys back home again.

"There are so many things I am sure that we really should be covering in our plan, but currently don't," Dave said. "I don't believe that you can even try to plan for every contingency. It's not like we can just expect everyone or everything to follow the same behaviour. Take our visitors as we tend to be calling them. One plan that would deal with them would not deal with another set of visitors. Perhaps by working closely together, we can bring our two plans together so as we can form a stronger plan that would be better suited to our friends."

"Perhaps you're right. But, let me ask you this. Do you have any family, friends or someone special close to hand?" Lucy realised that as soon as she had asked the question, it was a slightly loaded one. She had not set out to try to find out if there was already someone in his life, someone that might have his affections that she was looking to win herself.

"No, not really," Dave replied quickly. He paused and looked thoughtful for a couple of seconds before he continued to answer. "Well, yes I do have family, but they do not live around here. For the past six or so months while I've worked on the Alpha Protocols, I've actually spent a lot of my time in the US watching you guys. Many of my friends have moved on and are still waiting for me to contact them. Going by what you are saying, perhaps it is best that way."

"It is, trust me," Lucy said.

"The only real friend who I can talk to at the moment is Hammond, my cat," Dave told her. As he spoke, he kept a very serious look on his face. "At least I can trust he won't go telling the stories to anyone else."

Lucy could not help but laugh and added "I know what you mean. Sometimes I am so grateful that I have my pets to talk to as what I would have to say would probably cause my family to run in terror if I ever told them."

As the waiter arrived with their meals, they both waited for him to leave again before continuing the conversation.

"I can understand where you are coming from on this," Dave said. "We just felt that as we had been able to develop quite a close knit team from working on various other projects, there was no need to be so draconian. Not that it would bother me to be fair if we had to be. There are days where I do not get to leave the office. In fact I have been known to work in there for anything up to a week at a time."

"I can relate to that," Lucy said. "Bale compared my office to Alcatraz a couple of weeks back, saying that once I went in there was never any escape from it. I guess it is like that to me in a way as I have been known to sleep in there, not getting home for days at a time."

"The lives we appear to have chosen to follow are so similar, yet so far apart. You mentioned your family, but is there anyone else in your life?" Dave asked, pushing the subject a little. "That is, if you don't mind me asking."

Lucy put here fork down and sighed. This was a subject that nearly everyone she met seemed to keep picking up on. "There was, but he left quite abruptly over five years ago. It's something I don't feel comfortable talking about if you don't mind. Please be assured that this is not just with you, but people in general. Maybe one day I will be able to talk to someone close about it, but I'm not there yet."

"Sorry," Dave apologised, leaning over the table to put his hand on her shoulder. "I didn't mean to upset you Lucy."

She looked him in the face and replied "You haven't. As I said, it's something people always seem to want to ask and I just want to leave the subject alone. Maybe you are the person who I will be able talk to about it, but now is not the time."

Dave pulled his hand back and returned to eating his food. "As for my family, my dad's a nut case. Complete loon," he said, trying to lighten the moment.

Lucy looked serious and asked "Is he in a hospital or something then?"

Dave laughed loudly and said "No, he's just seems like a crazy old man, but is just enjoying his life. It's the same with my mum. They do what they want and enjoy everything they do. Something I want to be able to when I get to their age. Something I think that this might put a stop to if we do not win the fight."

Lucy smiled, amused by the way he talked about his parents. As she lifted another mouthful of food, she thought that maybe this was the person she could finally talk to about her past. She felt very happy to be with him, talking to him and she was becoming more convinced that there was something here to work on.

As they ate their meal, they continued to talk about their families, friends and their lives before the alien threat had emerged. They found they actually had quite a lot in common and were enjoying each other's company.

The waiter appeared and politely asked them if they would mind finishing up because it was getting late and he needed to close the restaurant.

As Dave looked at his watch, he realised that it was half past eleven. It certainly was time to be getting home and some sleep in before tomorrow.

"I'm sorry," he said, apologising to the waiter. "We seem to have lost track of time a little."

"No problem Sir," he replied. "I shall get you your bill."

Dave got up from his seat and put his jacket back on. As he did, he moved around the table and picked Lucy's jacket from her seat so he could hold it and help her put it on.

Having done so, he moved over towards the door where the waiter was stood by the cash till. The waiter gave Dave the bill and he took out his wallet out of his jacket pocket. He passed a number of notes to the waiter, something Lucy noticed straight away.

"No credit card?" she asked, making her way across the restaurant to stand next to Dave.

"It's too dangerous," he replied. "If we can track anyone down by their using a credit card, then there are also people who can track us. Actual cash is not as easily traceable. No one on the Alpha teams is allowed to use a credit card or a bank card while they are working for us. It's just too much of a risk."

"Sounds like one of my protocols," Lucy added as she passed through the door held open by Dave. "So how do they get cash when they need it? I guess you don't just get it from a cash point."

"They have to get it from Alpha command. It's a precaution we have to take for the time being."

As they reached the car, Dave unlocked it and opened the door for Lucy. As she moved round him to get in, she ran her hand down his arm and smiled. Dave smiled back and she now felt confident that there was definitely a growing chemistry between them.

The journey back to the hotel was a quiet one. Neither really spoke as they both found their tiredness starting to catch up with them. Lucy yawned on several occasions, although she did try to not to let Dave realise.

As they pulled up outside the hotel, she released her seat belt and turned to face him.

"Thank you for what was an enjoyable evening," she said. "It's been a while since I had such a good time out."

"That's okay, I really enjoyed spending the time with you," Dave replied. "Hopefully, there'll be plenty more chances to do this again soon."

Deciding to test the water, Lucy asked "Do you want to come in for a drink at the bar before you go home?"

Dave shook his head and, with a hint of sadness in his voice, replied "Although I really would love to, we've got to be up quite early tomorrow. So it is probably best for me to say no. Sorry"

Lucy, although disappointed, knew he was right, but she tried not to show it. Their mission tomorrow was of the highest importance and they all needed to be fully refreshed. She leaned in and kissed him gently on the cheek, but then paused before placing another kiss on his lips. He did not pull away from her and she felt that he wanted this as much as she did. As their lips separated, Lucy did not want it to end.

For what seemed like an age to her, they sat, foreheads touching, looking into each other's eyes. They kissed one last time before Lucy turned and climbed out of the car. Closing the door, she leaned down and waved through the window to Dave. He waved back before he revved the car's engine and pulled away.

As she watched him drive off towards his home, she put her fingers to her lips and felt grateful for grabbing the chance. Perhaps there was an opportunity that things would allow them to get together. For now, it was something positive for her to go to sleep on, perhaps allowing her to have a pleasant dream for the first time for what seemed like ages.

Chapter 23

Dave found himself walking forward slowly, down a light coloured corridor. Ahead of him lay a dark red carpet. As he walked, he passed doors on both sides of him. First one set, then a second, then a third with no end to the corridor in sight.

A sudden noise behind him caused him to stop and spin round to face the way he had just come from.

In front of him was the familiar face of the Home Secretary, stood no more than a few inches away. Dave knew he hadn't been there just now, so where had he come from?

"You!" Dave barked out. "What do you want with me?"

The Home Secretary did not reply, slowly walking around Dave. The whole time, he kept his focus on him. On the second circuit, he stopped beside him and leaned in.

"Do you really think you can stop us?" he asked in a whisper. "Do you and Doctor Tyler think you can prevent us from taking your world from you pathetic creatures?"

Having finished speaking, he started to walk around Dave again.

Dave turned his head to watch the Home Secretary as he walked behind him. As he did, he noticed that they were no longer stood in the corridor. Taking a quick look beyond his companion here he saw that they were now surrounded by growing flames. It was the same as he had seen as he had touched the sides of the craft they had found just the previous night. He tried to keep his focus on his companion.

"We will do what we can to stop you and your kind destroying our world," Dave said defiantly, as he turned his body so he could continue to follow him. "Mark my words, we will win the coming war."

"Defiant words for a species so weak," the Home Secretary stated. He had stopped circling Dave and each now stood facing the other as they continued to confront one another. "From a species who cannot survive against us."

"We don't fear you. We don't want you here at all" Dave shouted at him, thrusting a pointed finger in his direction. "This is out planet and we intend to keep it that way."

Suddenly, he found the Home Secretary's face thrust into his. "We know you're coming" he whispered angrily. Dave found he backed away as the face passed through him. As it did, the flames grew around him. As before, the flames were engulfing him, his skin starting to burn. As the pain was starting to take hold of him and he screamed out in agony, everything went dark around him.

Taking a few seconds to recompose himself, Dave quickly realised that the blackness surrounding him was in fact his bedroom. He was currently sitting up in his bed in a pitch black room, only interrupted by a ringing sound to his side.

He fumbled with the bits on top of his bedside cabinet to find his mobile phone. As he did he turned the alarm clock so he could read it more clearly. He looked at it only to see that it had just gone quarter past three in the morning.

"Not again," he said out loudly to himself, frustrated at being woken in the early hours of the morning yet again. For each of the last three mornings, he had been woken up before the sun had come up.

It was only about two hours ago since he had got to bed. He guessed it was only an hour ago that he had stopped thinking about Lucy and how they had kissed in the car. Or had he been dreaming that bit as well?

Picking up the phone and answering the call, he said "Hunt here." He tried to cover the fact he had just woken up, but realised they were probably well aware that was the case.

"Bad news, we need you to report to Alpha Command immediately," Harry said on the other end. "You'll need to get Lucy as well."

"What's happened now?"

"The press conference has been brought forward by two and a half hours," Harry explained. "We need to bring the mission start time forward I'm afraid."

"Why the change?" Dave started to ask. He wondered whether now was a good time to tell Harry about the events in his dream.

"We don't have time to debate this on the phone now," Harry interjected quickly. "What's done is done. Just get the two of you here now."

Before he could attempt to argue, the line went dead. Dave threw the phone across the bedroom in frustration. He knew he was not going to be able to cope with having to get up this early as often as he had the last few days for too long.

He hauled himself out of bed and switched the bedside lamp on. He went in search of the phone, which had landed in the washing basket, and dialled Lucy's number. She answered it within a couple of rings, which caught him by surprise. Perhaps she had not been able to sleep for the same reason. He knew they would have time to talk about what had happened at a later time, so got straight to the point.

"Sorry Lucy," he said as she answered the phone, "but our mission's been moved forward. I'll be there for you in twenty minutes."

"Before you go Dave," Lucy quickly added, "can I ask if you had a dream just before you woke up?"

"Yes I did," he replied. "How do you know?"

"Because he also told me that he knew we were coming," Lucy told him. "He said he'll be ready for us when we get there. This one scared the shit out of me a little bit more than normal."

"I saw and heard the same thing. I'll be there as quick as I can Lucy," Dave said. Gently, he added "sorry I could not have been there for you."

"I'll see you shortly Dave," she responded. The line went dead again as Lucy ended the call.

Dave moved quickly around the room grabbing his clothes. He wasn't too fussy about what he put on because he knew they would be changing before they moved out on the mission. As long as the clothes were clean and he was able to look presentable, he did not care.

Within a matter of minutes, he was in his car and on the way to pick up Lucy.

Arriving at Alpha Command, Dave and Lucy quickly made their way to the command room. They were met by Stuart as they reached the lift in the main building. He appeared to still be half asleep himself and certainly looked worse than either of them did, much to Dave's delight.

"So was it a good game last night?" he asked, managing to stifle a yawn as he finished speaking.

"Yeah, good result for us anyway. It certainly helped me chill last night," Dave replied. "Not sure if it was Lucy's cup of tea though."

She laid her hand on his shoulder and said "Stop worrying about me will you. I was fine and I enjoyed myself with you." She smiled gently as she spoke, to which Dave could not help but smile back at her.

Stuart, who was stood on Dave's right, looked at him and rolled his eyes. He had known that there was something developing between them, but this just gave him the evidence to confirm it. The fact it had become so obvious meant that it would now take half the fun he out of teasing his boss.

"Anyway," Dave said, trying to change the subject given Stuart's reaction. "I take it you are ready for another fun day in the office?"

"A day in the office is quite appealing right now," Stuart replied. "I've still got autopsies and tests to do, as well as a new infectee to deal with. They are not going to get done with us chasing around the country like this."

"Welcome to my world," Lucy said as the lift doors opened and she stepped out backwards, keeping her focus on the pair of them. As she spoke, she turned to walk forwards again, saying "It's only going to be downhill from here on in."

As they followed, both Dave and Stuart looked at each other and said to one another "great."

They all made their way to the command room upstairs without any further discussion. As they arrived, they were greeted by Harry, Dan and Gage who were already pouring over various maps and images on the screen.

"Glad you could all make it," Harry said. "Get yourselves a coffee each from the tray. You might well need it by the looks of all of you."

He pointed to a tray on the table which had several steaming coffee pots and cups on. Dave moved over and poured three cups out before handing Stuart and Lucy one each. Luckily, whoever had brought the tray in had selected large mugs and plenty of sugar.

"Sorry I've had to call you all in earlier than planned," Harry told them. "But we have been forced into escalating our time table a little."

"That is probably because he already knows we're coming I'm afraid," Lucy said. "He has told both me and Dave that much already."

Harry looked quizzically over at Lucy, looking for an explanation as to what she meant. "What do you mean he has told you that? I don't understand."

Dave stepped in and explained. "We both had exactly the same dream during the night. The Home Secretary was there, he told each of us that he knew we were coming. I can only guess that is why he has changed the time of his conference."

"You say you both had exactly the same dream?" Dan asked sounding confused. "How can that be?"

"Yes, it's appears to be an effect on some of those infected by contact with the nano-probes on a lower level," Dave continued to explain. "We have recorded details of people sharing the same dreams which are often very vivid and lifelike. And they all seem to feature the same theme of the planet being burned, humans being burnt to death. At least we can be certain that our trip to London is not going to be a surprise any more."

"But surely, he must know that by bringing forward the time of the conference, then we would being forward out operation?" Stuart asked.

"I guess he is hoping that we would not get the information quick enough," Dave said, "given that he still thinks he has control of the agencies. That plays into our favour."

Gage stood up and said "Well, I'm confident that our plan should be able to let us get our man and maybe even get him out again in one piece. Even as we speak, the Gamma team are preparing to leave to take up their assigned positions around the hotel and the surrounding area. If everyone is ready, then I shall start the briefing."

Everyone took their seats while Gage took a position in front of the wall monitors. He felt slightly nervous as this was the first task given to him on the Alpha Team. He felt that should he get it wrong, he would be putting all their lives at risk.

Not that he doubted his plan. What he had to admit that he did doubt was the expertise of some of the members of the team. That was mainly because, as yet, he had not seen them in any real action. True, they had carried out the operation in Felixstowe extremely efficiently, but that would have been a day in the park compared to what they might come up against in London.

"With the Home Secretary now due to be giving his presentation at nine thirty this morning, we need to be ready to move in at ten minutes past nine on the dot. This means that we will need to be in position by five to nine within the hotel basement."

"Dave and Lucy will form the first team. Stuart and I will be the second team. Between us, we will be moving in to take the target ourselves. Dan, you will be staying here with Harry, monitoring all the alarm systems, radio channels, basically hack into anything you need."

"Sure will" Dan chipped in chirpily.

"We will leave here and travel to London by train," Gage said. Behind him, a map of the rail system between Ipswich and London displayed on the screens. As he spoke, a visual display showed what he was saying on a map. "Myself and Stuart will get off at Stratford here. We will follow the Jubilee underground line around towards MI5, while Lucy and Dave will continue further along the line to get off the train at Liverpool Street station. They will then follow the underground via a different line to us. All being well, we should all meet up at the forward base at MI5 headquarters at twenty to nine."

"Why MI5?" Dave asked as he stopped Gage. "It's quite a distance from the hotel isn't it?"

"True, but for years the hotel has been used by foreign dignitaries, ambassadors and such like when staying in London." Gage changed the images on the screen behind him to show a map of the area with the hotel and MI5 headquarters. The image changed from an Ordnance Survey map, to a schematic showing what looked like a long tunnel between the two buildings.

"MI5 have maintained a secret tunnel network that's runs between the hotel and their head quarters to allow the covert movement of staff spying on these visitors. I'm pretty certain, even the Home Secretary is not aware of this tunnel, which will get us directly into the basement of the hotel."

Gage changed the image again, this time to show a schematic of the hotel. He noticed Dave lean forward in his chair with interest as he realised what secrets the hotel had been hiding for almost two decades.

"Once inside, we will have approximately five minutes to get from the basement to our allocated floors. Team one will take the fourth floor, team two will be on the second floor. We will reach these through a network of internal passages and ladders. Dan will be here using their system to allow us to use the lifts and stairs without triggering any alarms. We then need to make our way to the third floor, at which time, we will need to disable three or four guards we expect to be in the corridors at either end of the floor. The tricky part is we expect there to be a number of personal bodyguards inside the room as well. If as Harry suggested last night, they might be also infected then we must expect them put up more of a fight."

"Where do the Gamma team fit into this all?" Dave asked.

On the wall behind Gage the vector drawings of the hotel zoomed out and the surrounding buildings appeared. Gage moved closer to the wall to point out details.

"Across the road, here, we will have a couple of snipers on the roof, watching the windows of the room."

Seeing Stuart about ready to ask a question, he said "before you ask why they cannot take a shot from there, the hotel has bullet proof glass and a miss would result in our target escaping."

Stuart leaned back in his chair again.

"There are no fire exits outside the building from any of the floors," Gage added. "So no-one should be able to escape in that direction."

"What about cover at the exits of the hotel?" Lucy asked.

"Here," Gage replied, pointing to the entrance area at the front of the hotel, "we will have three men stationed close enough to be able to pick up anyone trying to leave through the front. Here, at the rear, we will again have a team of three monitoring this exit. There will be two in the underground car park. Finally, we will have a helicopter on standby two minutes away should we need to evacuate from the roof."

"At least they are well covered," Dave said. "What about the police? Surely, we will see them turn up as soon as any alarms go off at the hotel? I somehow doubt we can buy in their assistance until we have removed the Home Secretary seeing as he is still in control of them."

"Dan here will run interference with the emergency services so as to divert them as much as possible without raising suspicion. This should help keep the scent off of our tail as long as possible."

"Sounds good to me" Dave said as he started passing round a number of brown paper folders. "All the information you require is on the system and briefing papers here. If you have any questions or want to speak to me or particularly to Gage about the plan, then please feel free to do so now or any time before we leave."

He paused for a few seconds to allow everyone the chance to ask anything they wanted to. As no-one did, he continued with what he had been saying.

"It is now half past four, you have ninety minutes to familiarise yourselves with the plan before we meet back here promptly at six o'clock. I suggest you also get something to eat as well. See you all soon."

The team all took their folders and wandered off to various parts of Alpha Command to read and thoroughly understand the plan. They would all have their own ways to prepare themselves for the mission, but Dave would make himself available right up to the moment they left.

With the team having left, Dave and Lucy on their own in the command room. He turned to her and asked "Do you think the plan will work? You've more experience of this sort of thing that we have."

"Not in removing serving members of government voluntarily," Lucy replied. "But as it looks, I think we have a fair chance of pulling this off."

He stood up, put a hand on Lucy's shoulder and said "Let's get ourselves ready and get this job done. Then maybe, we can see where this mess leaves us all."

She placed her hand on his and looked him in the face. "I hope so, but I get a strong feeling this may just be the beginning of a long fight for you. I'm just not sure what we might uncover between now and the end of the day."

With a shrug of his shoulders, Dave moved his hand away and headed out of the command room and towards his office. It was time to make sure all the arrangements were in place and they were as ready as they could be in just under a couple of hour's time.

Chapter 24

As per Gage's plan, Dave and Lucy got off the train at Liverpool Street railway station. Due to the early hour, they were able to make their way quickly along the platform.

Taking a glance at the clock hanging above the platform, Lucy saw it was now about half past seven. They still had about an hour or so to get to their rendezvous point near to MI5 headquarters.

As outlined in the briefing earlier in the morning, Stuart and Gage had got off the train a couple of stops before at the Stratford station. They should be well on their way round the underground system themselves and were due to arrive at the rendezvous before Dave and Lucy.

Lucy let Dave lead the way across the platform. Having been here before, and thanks to his thorough preparations back at Alpha Command, he knew the area extremely well. She had learned from a brief conversation with Harry before they left Alpha Command, that Dave was especially skilled at reading maps and recalling directions. It gave her confidence that at least they were not likely to be getting lost.

She looked around, surveying the area as they walked through the railway station. Liverpool Street was one of the major railway stations within London. It had eighteen separate platforms, all of which served the East Anglia region. Lucy had learned on the way here that this was not the largest of stations in London, and certainly did not compare to many back home, but she was still reasonably impressed by place.

As they left the platform and entered the main concourse, there were already a fair number of people moving around the area. It was still early in the morning, but there were people already making their way to work for the day.

Dave headed across the concourse towards a coffee vendor, turning to make sure she was still behind him.

"I need to get something to eat and a coffee" he said to Lucy. "I should have had something more before we left Alpha Command this morning. Do you want me to get you anything?"

"Just a coffee will do me," she replied as they reached the shop Dave had headed towards. Pointedly, she added "I had enough to eat earlier, as per your orders."

With a quick glare back to her, Dave turned back towards the shop. Lucy stopped and waited at the doorway, while he dived in to grab two coffees and a sandwich.

She took a look around the concourse in more detail as she waited. The area had a very open and airy feel to it, probably due to the high, glass roof above. She looked back at the platforms where they had come from and watched the people moving around. Above the platform was an assortment of shops along a walkway, which lead along to a set of escalators on her right.

"Ready?" Dave asked as he appeared beside her again, holding a coffee out for her.

"Yes, thank you," she said as she took the cup. "Lead the way boss."

She again followed just slightly behind Dave as they made their way towards the station for the underground system. She had done a quick bit of research on this before they had left Alpha Command, just to familiarise herself with the route they were taking in case they became separated at any point.

She had hoped that they might have some time to have a slightly longer look around later in the day once their task was complete. She felt that given different circumstances, she would quite enjoy the chance to get to see more of this country while she was here.

However, she knew that she would not be getting to see much of London really. Even after a couple of days here, she had only got to see Felixstowe docks, Ipswich Town's football stadium and bits of the town in the dark. None of these were what a visitor from the United States would have chosen to set out to visit, but they had still been more interesting than just sitting in the command centre or a hotel room the whole time.

They were headed for the Circle Line and their eventual destination was the underground station at Westminster. They would then have about a fifteen minute walk to where they would enter the MI5 building and meet up with the rest of the team.

They turned to their left and down a few steps as they entered the underground station ticket office. In an effort to keep cover in case anyone had been watching out for them, they followed the routines of normal passengers and purchased their tickets from the automated machines. Sticking to his protocols he had outlined the previous night, Dave paid for the tickets in cash.

Dave handed Lucy her ticket as they approached the gates allowing them access in to the station itself. She looked around and noted that there were several security guards wandering around the area, along with a couple of armed police and even a sniffer dog with one pair. Luckily for them, they were heading away from the ticket gates and towards the main concourse behind them.

Dave had outlined to her the events of July the previous year when three suicide bombers had caused havoc on the underground by blowing themselves up. The sniffer dogs would have been trained to react to the scent of explosives carried, which was another reason why Gage had sent most of their kit ahead in an unmarked truck with members of the Gamma team.

Dave looked around as he passed through the gate and caught her eye. Having seen the security personnel, she suddenly became overly conscious of the fact that they were both armed with their stun weapons. Should anyone pick up on the fact, they may have some explaining to do.

Even with the IDs they carried, it was not as normal for fire arms to be carried in the United Kingdom as it was back in America. There it had become part of their everyday life for people like the police and the FBI to be carrying weapons.

Dave had obviously had a similar thought as he nodded back to her as she passed through the ticket gate. He casually adjusted his jacket to allow him to be certain his gun was still out of sight. She then stood next to him as he put a hand on her back and they started to head towards the platform they needed together.

She could sense he was slightly nervous about the situation, much the same way as she had been when she had started to carry a gun on missions in the early days of the alien threat back home. She had now become so used to carrying one that she often forgot it was there until the need arose.

The main difference here was that Dave had been properly trained with firearms already, where as she had been given a gun after she had attacked her outside their own office. Even then, it was several days before she had got any training herself. She remembered how she had been shown how to load and arm the weapon, but it wasn't until she had made several visits to the shooting range that she felt comfortable with it.

While the first experience of combat based missions for the Alpha Team had been only yesterday morning, they had not yet been exposed to too many members of the public. This situation was very different. They had to avoid spreading any sort of panic or unrest by revealing their weapons or the purpose of their being there.

Luckily for them, the crowds were not as big as they were likely to be in just under an hour or so, which would be when the rush hour really took off. This meant they could move fairly quickly and not risk being knocked around too much.

The Circle line was more or less at ground level here, so they only had to pass through a short tunnel to reach the platforms. As they made their way onto their platform, a train was just pulling out of the station. This meant that the platform was now fairly empty. They made their way up to towards the end of the platform where the front of the train would be when it arrived. There was no particular reason for this she thought, but it made sense to keep away from the main crowds as much as possible.

Looking up to towards the ceiling, she saw a display board hanging down. This listed the next two trains due to on route at the station, along with the time till they were due to arrive. This told them they had three minutes or so to wait.

There was a pair of empty seats on the edge of the platform, upon which they sat down while they waited for the next train to arrive.

"We've got fifty minutes or so. Should give us ten minutes spare," he told her, as he drank some of his coffee. "How are you getting on then?"

"I'm fine, just can't get used to the different way of things over here. I'm kind of looking forward to getting home" she said. "I hate to say it, but get back to the normality of Washington and home."

"Oh, okay," Dave said, unable to hide the disappointment in his voice from her last statement. He had hoped she had seen enough to consider staying with the Alpha Team, but deep down he knew that she was going to be leaving for home very soon.

"I didn't mean to make it sound like that everything was bad here," she added, picking up on his sudden disappointment. "There are plenty of reasons why I would rather not be going back if I was honest with you. But until we get closure on our little problem, then there are some things that will have to wait."

Putting her arm around him, she then said "I hope can you understand why we must keep waiting for what we want."

Dave rested his hand on her leg and looked her in the face as he said "I know. I guess you must be feeling the same way as me." With a slight pause, he looked back towards the tracks and continued. "Then again, I'm sure I'll have more than enough going on to stop me from missing you too much."

"Thanks" she said trying to sound hurt, taking her arm from around him and brushing his hand off her leg. She had to look down the platform away from Dave as she tried to hide a smile. He had given her the answer she had wanted to hear, even though deep down she knew how he obviously felt about her.

"Besides, I'm sure that our work will mean that our paths will get to cross regularly. It's certainly not like we won't see each other before we finish our tasks." Dave's response sounded like he was trying to dig himself out of a hole.

Lucy, now able to hold a serious look on her face, turned back to him and said "Don't worry. I do know exactly what you mean."

As she finished, she leaned in and kissed him on the lips. "You've given me even more reason for us to win this fight," she said as she pulled away.

Both turned so they could look down the platform as the noise of an approaching train broke the moment.

"Come on then," Dave said enthusiastically, standing up. "Let's hope we have some time to spare once we finish this work so maybe I can take you to another football match tonight."

Lucy gave him a push towards the door of the train as it opened. "Don't even think about it," she told him jokingly.

As they got off the train at Westminster underground station, Lucy realised she would get the chance to see the Houses of Parliament. Obviously working in Washington she regularly got to see the White House and other United States government buildings from just driving around the city.

But here she was in London and would now be able to have a small chance to see how different it was from her city. She'd seen numerous pictures in the papers and on TV, but she knew they were going to have to walk past the building to get to the MI5 headquarters.

It was not as busy at this station as some of the ones they had passed through on the journey, so they were able to quickly make their way out of the station and back up to ground level. She was glad to be in daylight again as they made their out. Being in any of the underground systems around the world just felt dirty and smelly, and ended up making her feel uncomfortable.

Straight ahead of them was the Houses of Parliament. Somehow the place seemed larger than she imagined. That was a very unusual feeling for her because, much to Dave's amusement in many of their previous conversations, everything else here in the United Kingdom had seemed so much smaller than it was in America.

"This way," Dave said, leading the way towards a road over to their right. As he strode off, she had to increase her pace slightly. Dave, being almost a foot taller than her, was able to walk far quicker than she would normally walk once he had become focused on where they were going.

They reached a pedestrian crossing and had to wait for the lights to change so they could cross. Unlike in the underground station, there were visibly more people wandering around, many of whom appeared to be heading to work. Despite the growing number of people they found they could still move reasonably freely and quickly.

Taking a quick look up at the tower, Lucy saw from the clock that it had just gone ten past eight, so they needed to get moving to ensure they reached their rendezvous point in time. It looked like they might loose the extra ten minutes they had gained at Liverpool Street.

As they walked alongside the Houses of Parliament, Lucy noted the name of the road they were now making their way along was Millbank. She knew from the mission briefing this would lead them directly to Thames House, the building that housed the headquarters of MI5.

However, their exact rendezvous was actually a property located before they would reach Thames House. This provided a front for an undercover entrance to the complex. Like many of the buildings in Washington, you just did not walk through the front doors when you didn't want to be noticed.

They chatted together as they walked along the road. It was not really about anything in particular, but more to try and maintain a casual appearance of two people moving around the city. As they progressed along the road, Dave would point out things occasionally, hoping it would maintain the innocent appearance they were trying to portray.

As they made their way up Millbank, Lucy could see Thames House at the end of the road. Even from this distance she was able to get a feel for the size of the place. At least, the visible parts of MI5 headquarters. Unknown to most people, but suspected by many, portions of the MI5 operations were carried out anywhere but in the building ahead.

They reached the house they were looking for after having checked the numbers on a couple of properties as they passed them. Taking another look at her watch, Lucy saw that it was now twenty eight minutes past eight. By the time they had made their way inside, they would be pretty much on time for their rendezvous. Hopefully Stuart and Gage had already arrived and were waiting for them.

She followed Dave up a set of six steps to the front door. On the wall beside the door was a panel of buttons and an intercom. Dave took a couple of seconds to scan down the buttons. He then pressed a combination of four of them.

"Just like an old secret knock then," she said.

Dave looked back to her and laughed. "Things really have not moved on in some respects, have they!"

The door was answered by a young man in a smartly pressed grey suit, grey shirt and black tie. Lucy recognised the outfit as the one wore by the agents she had seen at the airport when she first arrived. Dave had told her their pursuers that day had been sent by MI5, so it was a turn around to now be working with them.

He greeted them and led them into a smart hallway. As they entered the building, she could see how anyone getting this far in would quite believe that this was actually a dentists as advertised outside. Just off to their left was an open door leading into a room which looked like a patient waiting room along with a reception desk and receptionist.

They followed the young man along the hallway and in to a room in the rear of the house. As they entered the room, they passed through a scanner built into the door frame, which instantly started to cause an alarm to sound out.

One of the agents staffing the room stepped over and blocked their way further into the room. He held his hand out to signal them to stop and said "I need to search you before you can enter the complex I'm afraid."

"That's okay," Dave said as he lifted his arms up so the agent could run his hands along Dave's arms, then down his sides as he checked for concealed weapons. He had to stop as he reached his belt and felt that Dave was in fact armed.

Dave moved his hand so he could lift his jacket out of the way to show the piece at his side. He had no need to hide the weapon here and they had already issued details to MI5 that they would be armed as part of the mission. The agents should have been warned in advance that this would be the case.

"Please can you sign here to confirm the weapons you are carrying," one of the other agents asked, holding out a small PDA device for Dave.

He signed the screen on the device offered to him, but asked "We're still okay to hang on to them? We are a little pushed for time at the moment."

"Yes Sir," the agent replied. "It's just standard practice. Please can you wear these ID badges as long as you are within the complex."

Dave took the badge held out to him and clipped it to a belt loop on his trousers. Once the agent who had searched Dave had also searched her, Lucy then had signed to confirm the weapon she was carrying. She took the badge that she was offered and clipped it to the top of her trousers.

One of the agents stepped across the room, before directing Dave and Lucy to a doorway at the rear of the room. At first glance it had appeared to be nothing more than a simple interior door, but as it slid aside to reveal a set of metal doors to a lift. They were asked to enter the lift as the doors slid open.

They walked into the lift, the doors sliding closed behind them. It struck Dave how silent the whole thing was, but then it had to be as this was a concealed entrance after all.

Within a few seconds, the doors opened again and they entered a corridor. They were now three stories below the ground within the MI5 complex. As they stepped out of the lift, they found Stuart approaching them from their left.

"Nice to see you both," Stuart said. "I hope you had a good trip here after we left you."

"Fine thanks, uneventful as planned," Dave replied. Noticing Lucy taking another look at her watch, he continued by saying "We need to get moving. Where are we going then?"

"This way," Stuart said turning back the way he had come and leading them back down the corridor. "Gage is waiting for us at this end of the tunnel. He has spoken to Harry who confirmed that all our men are in place. As soon as the two of you are ready, we'll be good to go."

"Good," Dave said. "You have got the clothes for us?"

"Yes, hopefully they will be fine for you both," Stuart told them. "Bullet proof vests as requested as well. Again, I think Gage has got the correct size for Lucy, but our military don't tend to have many in her size, or even shape, I'm afraid."

As Dave looked back to Lucy, she smiled back and said "Why am I not surprised by that? I guess whichever country you are in, they have a problem sending a woman to do the fighting."

Stuart looked round to her and said "Well, there is a kitch…"

But before he could finish, Lucy put her hand over his mouth and told him "You don't want to finish that sentence if I were you."

Stuart saw Dave give him a look that he knew instantly that he had stepped over the line this time. He hoped that Dave would put it down to him being nervous about the mission and think nothing more about it later, but he knew he had better tread carefully for now.

As they turned a second corner in the corridor, Stuart opened a door into a large room. Inside, they found Gage making a final set of checks on their equipment.

"Morning again boss," he said. "Lucy, there's a small room behind that door to your right if you want to go and change. Sorry Dave, given that we seem to be a little short of time, you'll have to change out here I'm afraid."

Lucy took the pile of clothes that Stuart had passed to her and walked over to the room. She closed the door behind her and started to change.

Dave took the second pile of clothes and started to change his top. The clothes they were putting on were dark coloured and slightly more appropriate for wearing on such a mission than a suit and tie that he had worn as they made their way here. Besides, he always felt uncomfortable having to wear smart clothes too often.

He put on the black t-shirt before pulling on the bullet proof vest over the top of it. Despite the vests being fairly thin and light, it felt slightly cumbersome and restrictive. However, he knew he would not have it any other way going on a mission such as this.

Having made sure it was securely fastened and comfortable, he punched his clenched fist again his chest and wondered how tough these vests really were. It was definitely not something he wanted to find out today.

He then slipped the jacket over the top. Once he had also changed trousers, he tightened the belt and clipped his gun to it. Also attached to the belt he had a small knife, a couple of additional ammo clips and mobile radio pack.

Gage handed him a radio ear piece for him to the put on. He fitted it and made sure it was securely on. Almost straight away, a familiar voice came over the radio.

"Everything ready then Dave?" Harry asked.

"Yes, just waiting for Lucy to finish getting ready," he said, at which point he heard the door open and she appeared behind him. She put the clothes she had changed out of into a box on the table. She took an ear piece that Gage held out for her and also made sure that it was securely fitted.

"Dan has been monitoring the security around the hotel and everything appears just as we expected," Harry explained. "The first of his little diversions has begun. There is an accident between two cars on Westminster Bridge from when he took the traffic lights out of action. This will also cause the traffic around the area to slow up so any backup being called in should also be slowed down."

"We're just about to leave Thames House. It will take us ten minutes to walk out to the entrance of the hotel from here. We'll radio back in once we arrive so as to confirm we are ready to go." Dave then added "Alpha Lead out."

As Dave had been talking to Harry, Stuart had stepped over to the wall opposite the door they had entered through. There was a heavy steel panel in the wall which Dave had not taken any notice of initially. He now noticed that there was a small key pad to the right of it.

Dave watched as Stuart entered a code using the pad and the steel panel then slid open to reveal a long, concrete passageway behind it. As they began to leave the room Dave let followed both Stuart and Gage, but paused at the doorway. He let Lucy pass him and into the corridor. As he did, she stopped to place her hand on Dave's chest and mouthed good luck to him.

Dave returned the gesture by stroking the side of her face with his hand. With a smile, he dropped his hand and they both turned to begin the walk towards the hotel. They were finally on their way. There was no going back now.

Chapter 25

The team started the ten minute walk from the MI5 headquarters to the hotel through the tunnel. Stretched ahead of them was the drab, dimly lit, concrete corridor. By the look of it, it had been built some time ago, but was well maintained indicating it must be frequently used.

"So how come we know about this tunnel and the Home Secretary doesn't?" Lucy asked as she walked alongside Dave.

"There are many things that members of our government, even those at the highest levels, are never ever aware of," Dave explained. "I'm pretty certain that it is the same in your government. Especially when it comes to one such as your agency. We know that you have kept the situation from even your own President."

"That was not entirely my call," Lucy responded. "While it is stipulated in the protocols that we restrict the number of people who were to be informed of the threat, it was really intended to limit the number of possible leaks into the public domain."

"Put it this way," Dave countered. "Even before we discovered the Home Secretary was infected by the alien threat, we knew that we would need to restrict the number of people we reported too. We are not in a situation to be seeking the approval of several people when we need to act. We don't need to get caught in a turf war between departments or political foes."

"I can certainly relate to that," Lucy said with a sigh. "Washington seems to be bogged down by that these days."

"We now have the full backing our Prime Minister," Dave continued, "but he only learned about the Alpha Protocols less than a week ago. As we were moved to report directly to the Prime Minister instead of the Home Secretary himself at the same time, we were freed from various rules and regulations that are imposed even on covert operations. While Harry still needs to maintain control over the activities of the Alpha Team, we are going to have the freedom to do what we need."

"I know we've touched on this before, but what about money?" she enquired. "Just how can you hide the expenditure? All of our expenditure gets reported to the senate committee responsible for controlling public expenditure. Surely, your operation must be costing you as much as ours is costing us."

"That's because you mainly rely on public money," Dave said. "While we do make use of tax money, it is not the prime source of our income. As I tried to outline when you arrived, we have a number of companies that we have stakes in who will take our work and discoveries to develop into usable products."

"I do remember," Lucy said nodding.

"From there, they then take them to the world to sell. We cream off not only much of this money through various shareholdings and investments, but any other technologies they can develop. This also allows us to keep as much information about our operation away from the public records as possible."

Reaching the end of the tunnel, they were stood in front of another large metal door which appeared to be magnetically sealed. Off to the right was an electronic pad with a flat red panel, on which Stuart laid his hand.

With a click from behind the wall, the panel turned green and the door released. Gage grabbed the handle and pulled the door open. He waited till the rest of the team had passed through and then stepped into the room on the other side himself, pulling the door closed behind him.

With another click, the door sealed shut again. Inside, they had entered a small room which also had a panel on the wall next to the door, just like the one Stuart had just used. Leading up from the room on one side was a ladder, heading up towards the hotel.

This would lead them up and into a complex of shafts and passages around the inside of the hotel. Dave, looking at the ladder, was surprised at how long this little secret about the hotel had gone without being discovered. At least there were some secrets the secret services were still able to keep.

The key reason behind the system had been that it meant when a secret service agent from the guest's entourage carried out a bug sweep in any of the hotel rooms, there would never be anything to find. This was because they could actually have people and monitoring tools hidden outside the rooms, therefore not using any of the traditional methods of microphones hidden in the lamp or the light shades.

Even working within a covert operation which had access to all of the modern tools and resources, such as the Alpha Protocols, he was impressed with the simplicity of this system. There was a very strong argument that the simplest methods were still quite often the most effective.

"Alpha Lead to Alpha Command," Dave said into his radio. He found that he instinctively started to talk quieter than he would normally do, even though it was unlikely anyone outside of the room would hear them anyway. "We have now arrived at the checkpoint. Is everything still going according to schedule at your end?"

"Alpha Five here boss," Dan's voice said over radio. "Two further diversions have been initiated and I am about to kick the final one off. All radio frequencies are clear and we are good to go."

"Thanks Five," Dave said. "We're switching to radio silence from this end until we are in our final positions. Only report anything in an emergency. Lead out."

Turning to the rest of the team, he took a quick look at the watch on his wrist and checked the time. It was now five to nine, which would give them fifteen minutes to get into their final positions, just as they had planned.

"Right then guys," he said as they gathered around in a circle. "We have been given a go. You all know the plan and we must not fail in this. With luck, when we are next all together, we will have completed our mission successfully."

Dave held his hand out, palm facing down. Both Stuart and Gage followed suit and they put their hands over Dave's. Lucy, albeit hesitantly, laid her hand on top of the rest. She cautiously looked at Gage and Stuart, only see they were both focused on Dave. She turned her attention to him as well.

"Let's rock and roll," Stuart said, struggling slightly to hide his nerves before getting into the action.

"Can't wait to kick some butt," Gage said next. He was far more able to keep his feelings under control having been in the Special Forces for several years.

Lucy delayed slightly, before saying "For the team, I guess," feeling slightly embarrassed by the event. She could not question the spirit of the team if some of the rituals were a bit strange to her.

"Let's go," Dave said finally, as they all pulled their hands back out.

Stepping towards the ladder, he said "Lucy, me and you, we're first. We will take the exit on to the fourth floor and head down. Stuart and Gage, second floor and head up. In three minutes, Dan is going to tap into the video feed of the hotel security system and loop the playback for eleven minutes. That will give us all the time we need to get to room 314. See you there."

Dave started the climb up the ladder with Lucy closely following him. They found that the climb to the fourth floor was going to be quite quick. A sudden rumbling through the concrete wall caused Lucy to pause, just as Dave looked down to check she was still behind.

"It's okay," he said, partially whispering again. "It's the service lift shaft on the other side of the wall. Come on, we're almost there."

It only took a few more seconds of climbing to reach the passage way on to the fourth floor. Helping Lucy into the passage from the ladder, Dave leaned over the edge and checked back down the shaft.

Gage looked up, just as he was entering the passage on level 2 and gave him a quick wave. In just over a minute or so, they would be in their respective corridors, making their way to the target room on the third floor.

It was only a couple of hundred yards down the passageway from the ladder to the door. There was enough for them to stand up and wide enough for them move freely, but in single file. They ran down the corridor, still trying to tread softly. As they reached the end of the corridor, Dave checked his watch. They still had about thirty seconds until the cameras switched to Dan's alternate video footage.

This gave them a few seconds to get their breath back. As they did, Dave placed his hand on Lucy's shoulder and they looked each other in the face. They were both ready for action and the determined looks on their faces reassured each other.

Next to the door was a small control panel with a small screen on the top half of the unit. Dave pressed a key on it and a small screen gave a display of the corridor via a small fish eye camera that was hidden in the corridor. From this he could see that it was clear in both directions.

Once they had passed in to the corridor, they were going to need to turn right and head towards the staircase. They were not expecting any company on this level, but both drew their guns out and took the safeties off in preparation.

Checking his watch a final time, Dave held up his fingers to count down till they moved. Three, two, one. Putting his hand against the panel to release the catch on the door, he waited a couple of seconds for the door to release. He then pushed it open and they exited the passage to enter the corridor.

As he passed through first, Dave stepped out into the corridor. Lucy quickly followed behind him, stepped across the corridor and crouched down on the opposite side. Dave pushed the door to so it closed behind them. A click from the edge of it told them it had resealed itself. A panel slid back over the door and the wall now looked like any other wall in the corridor. It was no wonder the guests never even noticed the door was there.

Dave and Lucy quickly moved to cover opposite sides of the door, Dave looking down the corridor towards the target door to the stairwell, Lucy watching the other way back up it. Lucy carefully took a couple of steps back up the corridor, keeping her weapon raised until she stood next to Dave.

"Do you recognise the corridor?" she whispered to him.

"I'm afraid so. It's the one from our dreams" he answered. "Does it worry you then?"

"I'm trying not to let it do so," she replied, taking a look at him to see if she could gauge his reaction. "What about you?"

"Scares the shit out of me, I can tell you," Dave replied. As he did, he took a quick look back and Lucy saw the concern in his eyes. "Come on, let's get moving."

They began to edge their way down the corridor, making their way along towards the door. Lucy ensured she could maintain a view of anyone who might come along from behind them. They only had to cover about three hundred yards from where they entered until they reached the stairwell.

About a hundred yards along, Dave paused and put his hand up against Lucy's shoulder to signal for her to stop. As she did, she crouched down so she could keep facing back down the corridor. She then took a quick look over her shoulder and saw that the rest of the corridor had windows down the length of it on the right side until they reached the end.

To their left were two lifts, the doors to which currently were both shut. The hotel had two sets of lifts, with two in each set at either end of the hotel building.

Dave waved his hand to tell Lucy to keep crouched down and try to edge along the corridor under the level of the windows. Dave did not want to risk them being seen from anyone watching the hotel from any of the neighbouring buildings.

There would have been the Gamma team in various locations around them, but it would only take one sighting of them to raise the alarm and alert the Home Secretary. This was going to slow them down slightly.

As they edged along the corridor, now crouched, they moved to where they were level with the lifts. Again Dave was stopped in his tracks by a mechanical sound beyond the doors. The lift had started to move and as they both looked at the floor indicator they could see that it was on its way up.

Not wanting to take any chances that the lift may stop on their floor, Dave waved Lucy to quickly move past him and signalled for her to move to the stairway door. He edged back from being directly outside the lift so anyone inside could not see him should the doors open, providing the cover that just seconds ago Lucy had been doing.

The floor count slowed as it went from three to four, indicating it was stopping on their floor. Now out of the direct line of the lift, Dave lifted his weapon and pointed it towards the door.

As the doors slid open, he found himself holding his breath. There was movement in the lift, so Dave quickly moved himself to the opposite side of the corridor from where he had been, so he was now on the same side as the lifts. As he did so, he continued to maintain his aim on the lift door.

Lucy had also moved over to the same side of the corridor, but there was a potted tree to provide some cover as she hid behind it. This would allow her sufficient cover unless someone looked directly at where she was attempting to hide. Dave had no such luck and was left pretty open.

A lady in a hotel maid's uniform backed out, pulling a cleaning trolley as she left the lift. Luckily for them, she was turning backwards into the part of the corridor they were crouched down in.

Dave gave a silent sigh of relief as they realised it was only a cleaning lady. However, they could not risk her spotting them at this point. He quickly signalled to Lucy that she should stay where she was by holding a clenched fist in the air.

The maid had stopped in the corridor and appeared to be looking for something on her trolley. As she did, Dave then edged himself closer to her, until he was stood right behind her and quickly stood up.

With his left hand, he quickly covered her mouth tightly and pulled her to the ground. With a swing of the gun with his right, he knocked her out cold without a sound. As he did so, he moved his body to support her weight to stop her from hitting the ground and making unnecessary noise.

Throwing his gun back towards Lucy for her to catch, he then used both his arms to lift her up and place the now limp body on top of the cleaning trolley. Lucy, tucking his weapon into her belt, had now moved up alongside him. They quickly pushed the trolley up the corridor to the first door they came to.

Luckily for them, this was labelled staff only. Dave rummaged in his pocket and pulled out a door swipe card. Another one of Dan's little uses was that had been able to get into the system and prepare them all with swipe cards to open any the doors in the hotel without triggering any of the alarms.

As the door opened into what looked like a cleaning store room, they quickly pushed the trolley into the room. Dave grabbed a sheet from one of the shelves and tore off a couple of strips of cloth. One he tied around the cleaning maid's feet, the other round her hands.

While he was doing this, Lucy had peered back out into the corridor to ensure that there was no-one else, before she closed the door behind her.

Then, he tied a strip around her head, pulling tight into her mouth, so should she wake, she should not be able to make to much noise. Finally, he laid her body in another trolley which contained a load of dirty linen. At least if she started to move and try to roll around in an attempt to break free, the noise was going to be muffled by the contents of the trolley.

"Come on," he said to Lucy. "We've got time to make up. Let's go."

Lucy nodded and opened the door again. They quickly made their way along the corridor, crouched below the level of the windows again. This time, they made it past the lifts with no trouble.

As they reached the door to the stairwell, Dave turned the handle to allow the door to open. While the door was locked from the outside, the handle automatically released the lock when used on the inside.

Silently, they slipped through the door and into the stairwell. Dave ensured that the door had closed without making a sound behind them before they moved to the landing level on their floor.

The stairwell was larger than those Lucy had seen in many hotels, so she thought this was probably used as more than just a fire exit route. The stairs that led in each direction turned halfway between each floor, so they were covered from the guard they expected to be on the floor below.

Lucy crouched down against the wall at the top of the downward staircase so she could observe both directions. As she did, Dave slid a small mirror out of his pocket and moved forward so he could use it to view over the edge of the stairs. He held the mirror over the handrail so he could look down towards the next level.

He twisted the mirror slightly so he could check the landing level below. He then looked back at Lucy, unable to hide his surprise, before silently moving over to squat down next to her.

"Is there a guard down there?" she asked in a whisper as she leaned in close towards him.

"No," he replied. "We've got five of them. This is going to be more of a problem than we expected."

Chapter 26

Both Dave and Lucy were crouched against the wall at the top of the stairs in an attempt to try and come up with an alternate plan to get themselves down to the third floor. They had found that they now were faced with four additional guards on the landing floor below.

Back at Alpha Command they had only planned to find only a single guard, perhaps even two at most, on the landing in the stairwells on the third floor.

Mixed with ideas of how to take on the guards, Dave wondered if Stuart and Gage had encountered a similar problem in the other stair well at the opposite end of the building. If they had, he knew Gage had the more tactical knowledge and experience to deal with this.

He started to toy with the idea of contacting them and Alpha Command for further suggestions, but that would mean breaking radio silence. He stood up and moved himself silently back to the edge of the stairs and took another look down using the mirror.

After a few seconds of watching their movements, he turned to look back at Lucy and whispered "I've got an idea. Come on."

He then stepped silently back over to the door, swiped the card through the lock and opened the door again. He quickly moved back into the corridor, Lucy closely following behind him. She made sure the door closed silently behind them. They made their way back along the corridor and returned to the room where they had hidden the cleaning lady just minutes before.

"You're about the same size as her," he said, pointing towards the still unconscious body of the maid. "Get her clothes and put them on. I'll stand outside while you do. But make it quick."

Lucy was about to start to question why, but Dave had already moved outside of the room and was stood outside in the corridor. He pulled the door to, but did not close it. She did not like the sound of this, but hoped that she might actually be thinking that she might know where he was coming from with the suggestion.

Noticing that she was a slightly smaller build than the other lady, she realised she would be able to wear the clothes over her top and bullet proof vest. This was something she really did not want to take off at the moment. Moving as quickly as she could, it took her less than a minute to change into the maid's clothes and stash her trousers in the trolley so they were out of sight.

She gave a gentle push on the door and Dave entered the room again. He started to empty the laundry cart of enough blankets and sheets so that he could climb inside.

"Cover me up," he said as he scrambled in to the cart. "Then take the trolley to the lift and go down to the third floor. Make your way towards the same location on that floor as we will find another laundry cupboard at the same point. If we can get that far, then we might have a chance to sneak round these guards."

Lucy quickly asked, pointing over to the cleaning maid's body, "What about her, she might well come round soon?"

"We'll have to take that chance because we're going to be running out of time real soon."

Lucy grabbed some of the blankets and sheets Dave had thrown out and placed them on top of him. She made sure they were pushed tight around him in so as to ensure he was completely covered.

As she started to push the trolley, she leaned down and said to him "I think you need to go on a diet, you weigh a flaming ton."

A muffled voice from inside the trolley said "Just hurry it up will you, it stinks in here." He did not sound amused by Lucy's remark, much to hers.

Trying not to look like she was struggling to push the trolley too much, Lucy reached the elevator and pressed the button to call the lift. Luckily it was still on their floor from when the maid had arrived, so she was able to push the trolley in and selected the button for the third floor.

As the doors shut, Lucy noticed a small camera in the corner of the lift. She really hoped Dan had still got his videos playing on the security system as anyone who might take a look at her closely would soon realise she was not who was meant to be there.

As the lift stopped on the third floor and the doors slid open, she was confronted by two armed men, pointing their guns directly at her. She jumped slightly, as they had appeared through the doors even though she had expected them to be there.

"Please, I need to get some supplies from the cupboard," she said, making herself appear as if she was surprised and startled by the presence of these men in front of her. She kept taking short glances between each of the men and their weapons, hoping it would help convince them of her cover.

The left one of the pair looked to the other, who then nodded back to him. With a flick of his hand, he signalled for Lucy to exit the lift. They both stepped back from the lift door to make room for her to push the trolley into the corridor.

Despite struggling slightly to get the trolley out of the lift and over the edge of the floor, the guards, still with their weapons in hand, watched her closely as she made her way down the corridor to where the cupboard on the floor above was.

As she moved up the corridor, she was able to look further up it to see the door to the target room. She made a mental note of the number of guards and their locations as they were likely to need to know in the next couple of minutes. One thing she had learned from working with Bale had been to make sure that she was well prepared with the simple facts before taking on any foe.

As Dave had said, there was indeed a cupboard here. She fumbled in her pocket for the swipe card, hoping the guards believed her nervousness was real. As she swiped the card through the lock, she looked back at the guards and gave a weary smile.

"Thank you," she said, entering the cupboard and closing the door behind her.

As soon as the click of the lock sounded, Dave was silently climbing out of the trolley, wafting his hand in front of his nose.

"That really stank in there. I get the distinct impression some of the people staying here obviously don't know what hygiene is," he complained. "How many guards did you see in the corridor?"

"There's the two by the lift," she said. "And another three outside the target room. We know there are five on the landing outside that door to our left. I would guess the same number round the corner for the other lift and landing. That would make seventeen."

"He's being pretty well guarded," Dave said. As he spoke, he kept looking around the room for anything that might be of use to them. "This is going to be harder than I planned. I was hoping the bulk of the guards would be on the stairs, not in this corridor. I hope Dan's right and these radios are secure."

While they had maintained radio silence so far, they had obviously kept the radios on to receive any emergency transmissions on the Alpha frequency. He put his finger to his ear piece to activate the radio so he could send a message again. He felt that they had no option but to do so now.

"Alpha Three, Alpha Lead," he said, gratefully how clearly the radios could pick up their voices, even when whispering. "Report."

"Alpha Lead, we are in the stairwell," Gage's voice came back to say quietly. "Five guards at our entry point."

"Await further instructions, we're onto it already. Lead out." He took just a few seconds to think as he looked at Lucy who was waiting to see what he could come up with. He then continued on the radio and said "Alpha Lead to Alpha Command, I need a distraction. Fifth floor should do."

"Alpha Lead this is Alpha Command, we're onto it."

Pacing around the command room back at Alpha Command, Harry had started to worry about what might be happening with the team. He had expected them to be entering the Foreign Secretary's room about now and should be getting some sort of a report back from them.

As Dave's message came over the radio, it became obvious that they had encountered something they had not been prepared for. Harry looked over to Dan and said "I hope you can come up with something fast. You heard Dave, they need a distraction on the fifth floor."

"Already on to it," he said, but the distraction in his voice was evident. Dan was already tapping away at the keyboard, bringing up the plans of the fifth floor. The fifth floor mainly consisted of the larger suites and rooms for when guests arrived with servants or staff they needed to keep on hand for quick access.

Within one of the rooms was an ambassador from the United States, who Dan could see from the hotel bookings that he was accompanied by his secretary. Dan found that they had ordered breakfast to be delivered to their rooms at twenty past nine, so he was pretty confident that they would still be in there.

"Got an idea," he said, typing away.

Suddenly he stopped as a flashing marker appeared on the map of the building. As he saw it, so did Harry.

"What's that?" he asked Dan urgently, pointing to the screen. "That's on the fourth floor isn't it?"

"Something has set an alarm off up there. From the information here it looks like it is in a store cupboard not far from the lifts." Typing away quickly, Dan was trying to stop the alarm and amend log entries so as to make it look like a false alarm.

"Come on, come on," he was muttering.

The flashing stopped on the screen and the marker disappeared. However, messages started to appear on the logs on a different screen of the stairwell doors on the fourth floor being opened. As they still had the live video feed supplied from the hotel, Harry was able to see several of the guards from both stairwells were now making their way into the corridor on that floor.

"I've stopped the alarm and I have locked the room until the system releases it," Dan announced triumphantly. "And they won't be able to release it as I have isolated the relevant section of the code. That should be able to give us a few minutes extra."

"Alpha Four here," Stuart's said as his voice came over the loud speaker. "Three confirms the guards are moving to investigate. We only have two at our entry point now. Well done. We can take these ourselves if Lead is ready."

Dan watched on the screens as the guards made their way along the corridor and towards the store cupboard. His fingers sprung into action again as he locked and isolated both doors at each end of the corridors, unknown to the guards now progressing to their target.

"The guards on the fourth floor are now isolated. You're good to go on Lead's mark," he said over the radio enthusiastically.

While they were waiting for Command to resolve the problem, Dave had been looking up at the ceiling and had quickly found what he was looking for. There was a fine grill leading to the air conditioning system.

On one of the shelves he found a number of aerosol cans, and on another there was some string. He grabbed four of the cans and tied all of them together tightly.

Lucy looked on, slightly bemused, as she took the opportunity to remove the maid's clothes and put back on her own trousers.

"Give me your watch," Dave said, looking back at her and holding his hand out. "The one we gave you this morning."

She took the watch off her wrist so she could hand it over to him. Dave took it from her and tied the watch to the set of cans as well. As he did so, he was twisting the outer dial on the watch.

"What are you doing there?" Lucy asked, leaning in so she could get a better view.

"These watches have a built in timer and detonator," Dave explained. "In three minutes, this will set of an explosion in the air conditioning system. Should cause some alarm, but it will also then clear out anyone in the hotel. Therefore, gives us another way to ensure the press conference does not go ahead today, even if we fail somehow."

Lucy nodded to show her approval to plan, although she was now without her watch. She did not think that the success or failure of the mission would come down to her not completing it with her watch anyway.

A loud bang at the door made them both jump. It began to shake as someone was trying to open it from the outside.

"Oi, you in there," an angry voice was shouting from the other side. "Get yourself out here now."

"Damn. The guards," Lucy said, drawing her weapon from her belt holster that she was now wearing again as she looked to see how Dave would react.

"Alpha Three, prepare to move on my mark. We go in five seconds," Dave whispered into the radio.

"Copy that Lead," Gage's voice came in response on the radio. "Five seconds."

"Whose that in there with you," the voice outside boomed through the door as Dave started the count down into the radio. He also drew his weapon and prepared for the door to open.

"Three," he said as he gently pushed Lucy to one side so they could both cover the door. He saw from the look on her face she was ready for action.

"Two," as he leaned forward to release the catch.

"One," as he raised his weapon and he pulled the door open. At the same moment, he heard Gage's voice over the radio signalling they were moving into action as well.

With two quick shots from Lucy, both guards outside the room were caught by surprise as the door opened in front of them. They both collapsed on the floor, stunned by the charges her weapon had released as the shots hit their bodies.

Exiting the room as quickly as possible so they could catch the other three guards outside the target room by as much surprise as possible, Dave threw himself along the floor to roll across the hallway and landed in a squat position facing them.

A couple of bangs at the other end of the corridor signified that there were also shots being fired as Gage and Stuart were entering the corridor from the stairwell. The time for stealth and subtlety had now passed.

Taking two quick shots, Dave was able to take down two further guards, while the third took a shot at him. Just as he did, Lucy stepped out of the cupboard and dropped the remaining guard with a single shot.

Within seconds, the stairwell door behind them burst open and two further guards who had stayed behind after the disturbance on the fourth floor flew into the corridor. Both had their guns aimed and taking shots towards Dave. He had to throw himself forward to avoid being shot from behind.

As they had both been concentrated on Dave, Lucy had time to swing round and take a couple of shots towards them. Both missed and the left hand guard turned his weapon to face Lucy and took a shot at her. This caused her to try and step back into the cupboard again, only to find the door had closed behind her. She ducked back as the bullet hit the door frame just beside her head.

Two shots rang out overhead, each one hitting their targets, causing the two guards to fall as they continued to press up the corridor towards Dave and Lucy...

Looking up in relief, he saw Stuart and Gage stood the other side of the target door, guns still raised.

"Alpha Command, seal all doors on this level. Shut down the lifts. Secure it while we move in on the target," Dave ordered.

Getting up, he stepped over to Lucy. As he stood next to her, he placed a hand on her arm, but she nodded back to confirm she was okay. They both then made their way to the door to room 314. As they did, Dave swapped the clip on his weapon, throwing the old one down on the floor.

Gage was already moving into position in a kneeling stature to provide a quick start to get into the room fast. He had his gun drawn and pointed towards the doorway, having already changed his clip as well.

Lucy reached forward with her left hand to use the swipe card to release the door lock. As soon as the lock released,

Dave kicked the door hard and it swung open. Before any shots could be fired from within the room, Gage had thrown himself through the door and had caught one of the guards by surprise, pulling him to the floor.

In the distraction, Dave had followed Gage into the room. As he did, he fired at the only other guard still standing in the room, who dropped to the floor instantly.

"Clear," Gage called out.

Dave looked back at Stuart, who had already moved to stand alongside the doorway and cover the corridor. Lucy then moved forward to enter the room.

Now they had a chance to survey the room, the sight that greeted them sent a chill up even Lucy's spine.

Chapter 27

Lying on the floor, along with the two bodies that the Alpha Team had already shot as they had entered the room, they discovered the bodies of four further guards. Each of them was hideously deformed, most completely beyond recognition. There was what was obviously blood sprayed across the walls and the furniture in the room.

Even the smell that greeted them was not pleasant at all, causing all but Gage to cover their noses in reaction. He had been accustomed to such scenes is some of the more unsavoury missions he had been on before.

The room itself was of a fairly large size. Unlike the corridor that was decorated in bold reds, the rooms were decorated in more subtle cream colours.

Midway along the wall to the right of the door there was a large bed. To the left was a small arrangement of living furniture, which included a television, a couple of settees and a coffee table. To the right side of the bed, there was a doorway which appeared to lead into an en-suite bathroom area.

Calmly stood in front of the bed was the Home Secretary, his arms defiantly crossed. Gage, having already dealt with the guard he had taken on, had moved so that he could bear his weapon at him.

"I've been expecting you," the Home Secretary said, portraying an even more chilling level of calm.

"What the hell has been going on in here?" Gage angrily demanded, thrusting the barrel of his gun further towards him. "Did you kill these men? I trained with at least one of these guys."

"No, I did not kill them," the reply came, said with a cold sharpness to the voice. "They were proved to be unworthy of improvement. They could not join the ranks of those who will be saved by us when the time arrives."

Gage turned his head to look quickly at Dave and asked "Is he talking about this alien infection? How can he call it an improvement?"

"I'm afraid so," Lucy said as she made her way across the room. She was making a quick check each of the bodies as she went. Even now, having seen so many other people die because their bodies could not accept the mutation, she was still shocked by the scene in front of them. "They see it as a way to improve the human race, an offer to help save us from a coming disaster they believe will happen."

"You have it wrong my friends, our species will not survive the coming events you mention," the Home Secretary continued. "You really do just misunderstand what our work is about. We are using these alien nano-probes to save ourselves from the forthcoming apocalypse."

"I've heard it all before," Lucy said as she stepped in front of him. She lifted her weapon and put the barrel of her gun directly against his forehead. An anger that none of the Alpha Team had seen in her before crept into her voice. "Convince me why I should not shoot you here and now," she spat out.

"Lucy," Dave ordered loudly as he quickly moved to stand behind her. "Lower your gun now. That's an order."

She looked round to Dave, still holding her aim, and said "And what do you suggest we do then? Just take him with us?"

Gage had backed himself towards the window, attracted by the growing level of noise outside. As he peered out and looked down to the road below, he could see that there was a growing number of vehicles from the emergency services pulling up outside.

"Dave," he said unable to hide the slight concern that entered his voice. "It looks like we better get a move on if I were you. We appear to have got company on the way."

As he finished speaking, a loud boom sounded from the direction of the corridor. The vent above them for the air conditioning system blew out of the ceiling and a strong smell of burning started to fill the room. Within seconds, fire alarms around the building started to ring out loudly.

"What the hell was that?" Stuart said, sticking his head in the room from where he was stood on guard. As he did, he tried to grab a quick look around the room. "It sounded like that came from up inside one of the rooms opposite."

"Just a little insurance plan I threw together," Dave said. Looking up at the air vent, grey smoke started to waft out of it. "With all the fire alarms going off, everyone else will be going down to the ground floor to get out. That will allow us to head up to the roof."

Suddenly, the sound of shots started to ring out from the corridor. Stuart dived into the room for cover just as several bullets hit the frame of the door and threw shards of wood out. As he stood with his back against the wall just inside the doorway, he wiped the side of his face. Several splinters of the frame had hit him in the face and he found that there was blood trickling down the side of his head.

"Looks like the fire alarm must have released all the locks Dave," he said trying to keep his focus on the current situation. "I guess they are coming back for their boss."

Gage stepped forward and pulled something off of his belt. As he held it up, he removed a small metal pin. Straight away, Dave realised that it must be a grenade of some sort and there was only one place that was going to be thrown.

"They know we are here, so more noise is not going to hurt anyone," Gage said as he stepped over to the doorway and threw the grenade back along the corridor. Turning back away from the door, he covered his ears with his hands and called out "Fire in the hall."

At the realisation as to what the object just thrown out in front of them actually was, the sound of voices shouting at each other to get back came from the corridor. The three guards who had been approaching them from the stairwell had now turned to try and get themselves back to any cover before the grenade exploded.

After just a couple of seconds, a thunderous boom sounded along the corridor. This was immediately followed by a plume of smoke and dust blown along the corridor, the sound of glass shattering, then silence.

"Three down, three more to go I guess," Gage said, a slight smile of satisfaction appearing across his face. "That will give them something to think about before the others try to make their way down to face us."

"I don't think I entirely approve of that," Dave said as he unclipped a set of handcuffs from his belt. As he turned back to speak to Lucy, he added "Put these on him."

As Dave tossed the handcuffs towards her, Lucy lowered her gun a fraction from where she had been holding it the Home Secretary's head as she put her left hand out to catch them.

Just at that moment, the Home Secretary moved extremely fast to grab the gun, twist Lucy round so he was holding her around the neck with one arm and the gun to her head with the other hand.

As he did, but too late to do anything to help, both Dave and Gage spun round so they could hold their weapons pointed directly at him. Neither would be able to take a clean shot with Lucy in the way, but also they couldn't afford to provoke him while he had her held prisoner.

"Now I have the upper hand," he said. "Unless you arrange a way for me to get out of here safely, your friend here will surely die by my hand. Whilst it makes no difference to our plans if you try and you kill her or I kill her myself, I'm convinced that one of you will suffer the loss far more than we ever will."

"You're not going to get very far by yourself," Dave retorted angrily as he started to slowly step around the room to see if he could get a better angle on their target. "The Prime Minister knows who you are, what you really are. You are being replaced as we speak."

Maintaining a steady aim, Dave lowered the tone of his voice as he changed his focus to speak to Lucy and said "Stay calm Lucy, I'll get you out of this."

"Been here before haven't we," she replied, trying to give Dave a smile to show she was okay for now. This time, she had more faith in Dave to be able to save her, but she was still trying hard not to panic. At least the gun was not being pushed into her head so hard this time.

"Not to worry, this only delays the start of our improvements to our world," the Home Secretary said boldly. "You don't really think I've been working alone do you? You can't stop the inevitable from happening."

"Perhaps you can tell us how you got infected?" Lucy asked from within his grasp. "Or will that ruin your precious plans?"

"You'd like me to tell you who improved me, wouldn't you Doctor Tyler?" he asked taunting her. "You want me to give you a name so you can remove the threat. Just like every other time. This might be one even you and your precious team can't get too."

Meanwhile, Stuart had been taking shots along the corridor towards the remaining three guards who had been approaching the room from the opposite direction to where Gage had thrown the grenade. They had not been put off for long and were putting up a determined fight.

So far he had successfully managed to take one of them down, but the other two had been able to find cover within some of the doorways and side passages off the corridor. This meant that they were able to get shots a number of shots back towards him in response.

Between shots, he had been on the radio trying to report back to Dan in Alpha Command, desperately trying to keep them abreast of the events. He needed to get the doors on their floor locked again before any more guards were able to reach them.

"Get those blasted doors locked," he shouted, leaning out from the doorway to take a couple more shots down the corridor again.

"Alpha Three, I'm trying," Dan pleaded. "The doors on all the other floors are secured, but the doors on your floor are not locking. Give me a chance will you."

"You're not the ones under fire are you," Stuart screamed back, ducking back into the room again. Taking a look back to see what the others were currently up to, he saw the Home Secretary holding the gun against Lucy who he now was holding captive. "You certainly won't want to swap with Lucy right at this moment."

"Got it," Dan suddenly said triumphantly over the radio. "I had to go in and modify the emergency systems code…"

"I don't give a damn," Stuart snapped back as he stepped out from his cover to take another couple of shots. As he ducked back into doorway, he added "Thanks though."

"No problems," Dan replied.

———

"Now," the Home Secretary said, his voice becoming increasingly agitated as he started to run out of patience with the situation. "Get me out of here and she won't come to any harm. I believe you have a helicopter on stand by somewhere near here?"

"Yes, we do," Dave replied, caught by surprise that he would have been aware of that. Pausing slightly, he then followed up by asking "but how do you know that?"

"You shall find out in time," the reply came. "For now, just you get me that helicopter here immediately. You will then escort us to the roof and make sure none of your snipers try to pick me off."

"Snipers?" Dave asked, trying to act surprised by the accusation.

"Don't play me for the fool," the Home Secretary bellowed. "Remember, if you try to shoot me with one of your little 'stun guns' or I hear a shot from a sniper, then you will be taking your dear little girlfriend with me."

Dave caught the look that appeared on Lucy's face as they both realised they might now have one little secret from the Home Secretary. Had he not yet learned of the change they had made to their weapons which now allowed them to stun humans as well as infectees? That would also mean that he was not aware that they had modified the shells so that the charge automatically adapted itself depending on the chemical reaction as it hit the target.

Dave raised his hand to Gage as he realised that they were not the only ones to pick up on the fact about their guns. Before Gage could say anything, Dave ordered "Go and help Stuart clear the remaining problems outside. I'll get on to Alpha Command and get them to make sure the helicopter is on its way."

"You're sure about this boss?" Gage started to question.

"Do it," Dave commanded. He looked directly at Gage, who tried to hold his gaze for a few seconds as he looked back at Dave. "Gage, you just need to trust me."

With a quick glance back to the Home Secretary, Gage then turned and ran across the room to take up a position next to Stuart at the door while they conferred on the situation.

Dave radioed back to base and said "Alpha Command, can you get the chopper in for us? We have a friend who needs dropping off."

"Alpha Lead, Three has kept me informed of the situation," Harry said across the radio. "Your helicopter is already inbound, ETA is as planned."

"Command, you better make that four minutes," Dave said, trying to sound like he was attempting to convince them to get chopper there more quickly. As he watched the Home Secretary, he was certain that he believed the act.

Harry picked up on the response and decided it was best to follow Dave's change of order without question. "Roger that Lead. Inbound ETA is four minutes. All further access to the building has been restricted until you give the all clear."

"Thanks Command. Out," Dave said. "Gamma team, this is Alpha Lead. Stand down, I repeat stand down. Please confirm status."

Over the radio, Dave could hear as each of the Gamma teams reported in. One by one, each of them confirmed they had stood down.

After the final member had radioed in, Dave finished by saying "Gamma team, await further instructions. Alpha Lead out."

Dave turned his full attention back to the Home Secretary and said "As requested, the chopper is on the way and I've ordered my men to stand down. When these two are ready, we will escort you to the roof."

"Thank you," he replied. "May I ask what you think about the things you have seen of the world to be?"

"Pardon?" Dave said. "What do you mean by the world to be?"

"I know we spoke in your dreams last night," he taunted Dave. "I know that you've both seen what is to be, what awaits those who choose to ignore the path of improvement."

"Tell me then, how are you going to spread this infection now? We've stopped your plan to try and spread it via the conference downstairs." Dave walked over to the coffee table and lifted the lid on the briefcase that was sitting on it. "And what have we here. What's on this CD that could be so important to you?"

"You really misunderstand our aims. Now, give it to me," the Home Secretary ordered. After a pause, during which time Dave just looked the CD over, he shouted out "Give it to me or I will not hesitate to shoot her instead."

Dave moved back over towards them with the CD, but as he held his hand out to pass it over, he dropped it. As it landed on the floor, it fell at angle and in a flash, Dave had lifted his weapon sufficiently to shoot the disc. It shattered across the floor as the shot hit it.

"No," the Home Secretary screamed. This left Lucy's feeling half deafened in one ear in the process. "Her blood is to be on your hands."

As the Home Secretary's finger moved further over the trigger, Dave put his empty hand back up and said "You still need her."

He froze, holding his finger over the trigger. "Why do you say that then?"

"If you still want to get out of here alive," Dave answered quickly, "then you still need her."

"True," he replied, releasing the pressure on the gun. "I suggest we better start making our way to the roof then."

Gage had already stepped out into the corridor and made his way down it to make sure that the two guards they had been shooting at were now stunned. As he did, Stuart followed him so he could provide cover, just in case.

Dave let the Home Secretary, still holding Lucy lead the way out of the room and into the corridor. As he followed, he got a signal from Gage to confirm that both guards were neutralised.

"Stuart," he said. "Go and check the corridor ahead. Make sure the stairwell is empty. Gage, cover our tail. We're going to the roof."

Stuart ran up the corridor quickly, but ensured he took enough time to make sure none of the bodies looked like they would recover, get up and shoot one of them in the back as they went. On reaching the door, he found it was locked, but after a quick glance through, he saw that there was no one visible through the glass on the other side.

"Command," he said into his radio, "this is Three. Release the door locks to stairwell B."

"Confirmed Three," Dan said over the radio. "It's done, door should now be open."

Stuart pushed the door to confirm and stepped nervously into the corridor. He had caught Dave's comment that they should now be the only people in the building, but he didn't want to be the one to find out they weren't.

Holding the door open, he looked back down the corridor to see Dave, the Home Secretary and Lucy moving forward as they followed him.

A noise from above caused him to drop to his knee and aim up to where it had come from. The party in the corridor stopped as soon as they saw this and watched as Stuart edged forward slightly in an attempt to get a better view.

They heard two bangs, sounding almost at the same moment, but two distinctive noises. As they did, Stuart fell backwards against the door he had been holding open.

Immediately, Dave ran forwards to help his team member, as he watched Stuart roll onto his side. As he reached the end of the corridor, Stuart was laid on the floor completely motionless.

Chapter 28

Reaching the door to the stairwell, Dave dropped to his knees next to Stuart's motionless body. It had landed and rolled on to its right side and was now facing away from the door leading on to the landing area.

"Stuart," Dave said quietly as he started to fear the worst for his colleague. He put his hand on Stuart's side and tried to gently roll him onto his back. As he felt Stuart resist being rolled over, he quickly shifted himself so that he could move around to the other side of him.

He leaned down to look closely, only find Stuart's eyes partly open and looking directly at him as he lay on the floor.

"You okay?" he asked in a whisper, lowering his head as he spoke so he could make sure his lip movements were not visible from along the corridor. As he asked, Stuart's expression made it clear that he had something planned.

In an attempt to ensure that he did not do anything to give the Home Secretary any indication that they were trying to hide something, Dave put his fingers on Stuart's throat as if to test for his pulse. Shaking his head, he let his shoulders drop and looked further down towards the floor.

"How can I help?" he asked quietly.

"Don't," Stuart whispered back. "Just stick with the plan. Get them to the roof."

Dave then moved his hand down Stuart's face as if to close his eyelids, as was a normal reaction when someone had been killed in action. Pausing for a few more seconds, he stood up and looked back at the rest of the group. They had now moved along the corridor to the doorway and were waiting for him to stand back up.

"Is he..." Gage started to ask sadly, his voice tailing off as he tried to finish the question.

"I'm afraid we've lost him," Dave said, a tremor sounding in his voice as he made out that he was extremely upset, before Gage could finish his question. Pausing for just a couple of extra seconds as he took one last look back at Stuart's body on the floor, he pulled himself together again.

Firmly he ordered the team, "We need to move. Come on."

The Home Secretary did not say a word as he moved through the doorway and onto the stairs. As they moved, he still held the gun to Lucy's head. He took a sideways look towards Stuart's body, but the drive to get to the roof and away from this building meant it was only a cursory glance.

Dave was a few steps ahead and had stopped to check the body of the guard who had shot Stuart. He had been stunned by the round Stuart had got off and he expected that the guard would be unconscious for another half hour or so.

"You better hope that he is definitely the last of your men to give us any trouble," Dave said angrily as he looked back to the Home Secretary. "Come on, keep moving."

He then turned and continued to lead the way quickly up the stairs. He took them two at a time, up to the fourth floor landing. He made a brief check of the door to the fourth floor landing corridor to ensure that it was still looked.

He could see that several of the guards were still pacing up and down the corridor. They were still trapped by the doors that Dan had earlier locked to trap as many guards as possible who had gone to investigate the earlier disturbance. Panic had started to set in with one or two of them as smoke had filtered through the air conditioning and onto this floor as well. Dan had obviously not yet freed the lifts yet either.

Dave noticed a moving bundle on the floor halfway up the corridor. As he took a slightly better look, he could see it was the maid who they had left tied up in the store room. She was now conscious again, but moving very gingerly, sending a small wave of guilt at having hurt her through him. He quickly refocused his mind as that guilt would only prove a distraction.

They could wait until him and his team were clear of the building. If he had remembered the details from the morning's briefing correctly, there had been no guests on the fourth floor anyway. He had no issues with leaving them all as they were for now.

Suddenly, one of the guards, having noticed the movement on the other side of the door, started to frantically bang at the glass. Being a secure hotel, the glass would withstand almost anything he could throw at it. It would also be bullet proof to any of the small arms weapons they would be carrying, so he could pound his fists on the door to his heart's content.

Dave quickly waved at him through the door and grinned so widely it infuriated the guard even further. He was glad that they could not hear anything through the door as the language the guard was mouthing towards him was quite extreme.

As Dave turned to make his way up to the fifth floor, he saw Lucy behind him, still held by the Home Secretary. She looked more relaxed than last time he had seen her in the same type of situation in Felixstowe. Then, she had been held by another infectee during their last mission. However, he could tell by the look in her eyes, she was still scared stiff.

He would have been surprised to find anyone who wouldn't have been scared given the same situation. He knew we would probably not have been as relaxed as Lucy was right now. As their eyes met, she gave him a little smile to show she trusted his judgement, even if she didn't know what he had planned.

On reaching the fifth floor, he tested the door on this level as well. This one was also still locked. The next floor up was the roof. He was hopeful that the helicopter was about to arrive as agreed with Harry back at Alpha Command. He could not hear it yet, but was not surprised by that either.

Dave leaned over the rail on the stairs and checked that Gage was still following behind them. He was a flight of stairs behind, providing cover for them as they made their way up. While he expected that no-one should have been able to follow them up this way, he did not want to take the chance of being caught from behind.

"Move it," the Home Secretary demanded angrily. "You're taking too long. Will you just get me the hell out of here, now."

"We're going as quickly as we can," Dave retorted, finding himself also getting angry as they approached the final landing area and the doorway to the roof. This was only a small landing area, just a few feet deep between the top step and the door.

"Alpha Command, can you reconfirm all Gamma units have stood down?" Dave asked over the radio, waiting by the door to the roof. He had received confirmation earlier that the Gamma team had stood down, but just wanted the importance of the order to be understood by the team.

"Confirmed Lead," Harry's voice came back. "I also have the helicopter on final approach to your location." Harry's voice changed to a softer tone briefly as he added "Take care will you."

"Thanks Command," Dave responded. He had not yet reported in the fact that Stuart was lying in the stairwell below, but he knew that he would be seeing him soon. He wished he knew what he was going to try. "Alpha Lead out."

Dave pushed open the door to the roof and stepped out. It took a second or so for his eyes to adjust from the artificial lighting of the stairwell, to the bright natural light of the sun.

He could hear the distant noise of the helicopter as it was making its final approach to the landing pad in front of them.

Dave continued to hold the door open so that the Home Secretary and Lucy could make their way out onto the roof. She was being carefully held between the two of them, just in case Dave felt he might be able to do something himself to free her. They all knew Dave's growing feelings for Lucy were being used right at this moment

"Come on Gage," he shouted back down the stairway. He watched as Gage made up the distance on the stairs, Dave was able to lower his voice slightly. "Stay here and cover the door. Keep it open in case we need to get off the roof quickly."

As Gage reached the door, he nodded to Dave to show he was okay with the order. Dave placed his hand on Gage's shoulder and gave him a reassuring smile before he then turned to catch up with the other two.

The helicopter was now in sight as they approached the edge of the helipad. To get onto the pad itself, there was a short set of steps which led up to it. The platform overhung the edge of the building a short way. Straight below them was the main road along the front side of the hotel.

Having made his way up on to the pad, he moved to the edge so he could take a quick look down. Below, Dave could see the flashing lights of numerous police cars, fire engines and ambulances. He was also able to see that the number of emergency vehicles gathering below was attracting the attention of everyone around as hundreds of people appeared to be standing along the length of the street as well.

Many were just people coming out of their offices and homes to see what was going on, although the police were trying to keep them at either ends of the road, as far back from the hotel as they could. Dave noted that this provided additional distraction for the emergency services as they would have to be allocating men to controlling the crowds.

Looking across at the various buildings on the other side of the road, he could see that there was a number of people who were watching from their windows as they tried to see what was going on. Some were hanging out of their windows, oblivious to the possible danger that they might be putting themselves in. There some who were just looking out from behind closed windows, while others were even peering around twitching curtains, trying to hide the fact that there were watching.

He could hear the voice of someone using a loud speaker calling for people to keep back from their windows. Most did not seem to be paying attention to the warnings. Neither did they seem to have been paying much attention to the roof area until the sound of the approaching helicopter had started to increase.

Dave shook his head briefly, amazed that given recent events in the world, the public seemed to have a great skill at putting themselves into danger by their sheer inquisitiveness. London still had the memories of the bomb attacks of July 7th and the failed attack within the weeks after, they should know better than was happening in front of him.

As they had taken to the roof, Dave had noticed that smoke was billowing out of one of the vents leading from the air conditioning system, but this would not have been visible from the street level. All the windows in the hotel were sealed shut, bullet proof and totally secure. Therefore, there would also have been no sign of the smoke inside the building from down below.

The fire brigade would have received an automatic alert from the systems within the hotel, but also from witnesses leaving the building. However, Dave knew Harry would have passed on the information to those in charge down there that there was not actually a fire, but a controlled smoke emission on the third floor.

While this was not entirely true, Dave did not believe the fire he had set would cause too much damage as it was intended to generate smoke rather than burn the place down and should have burnt itself out by now. They would hopefully be off the roof in a matter of minutes, at which point, Harry could then inform the emergency services they were free to enter the building.

Turning back to face the Home Secretary, he asked him "Come on then. I've got you here as you requested and the helicopter is literally about to land. So where the hell did you get a copy of that signal from?"

"Like I said earlier," he replied, "it goes higher than you think. I doubt that even Doctor Tyler here and her precious little team would be able to touch the person responsible."

"Well, if we can't touch them as you say," Lucy said, struggling to speak slightly given the tight hold the Home Secretary had around her neck, "why can't you share the information with us."

Taking great delight in squeezing Lucy's neck harder still to show her the effects of being fully infected on his strength, compared to the partial infection she had received from encountering an alien artefact before.

"Who do you want it to be then?" he said, taunting Lucy as much as he could. "Do you want me to tell you we got it from one of your precious infectees that your DPD guys can't catch? Perhaps you even want me to say it's one of you beloved little Team? Perhaps your friend Forster has been feeding me information on the side."

"I'd know you were lying," Lucy spat out.

"So," he asked, lowering his voice, "if I was to tell you that between our two governments we had found a way to modify and control the nano-probes to create a superior army, does that give you any hints as to who it was?"

"Ellis?" Lucy exclaimed. "The Secretary of Defense? I can't see how he would have got involved without us knowing. I may not like the man, but I don't think even he would stoop so low as that."

She wanted to ask him to prove it, but her voice was drowned out by the noise of the helicopter lowering itself down onto the landing pad above them.

Just beyond the landing pad, a slight movement caught Dave's attention. While he had only moved his eyes to see what it was, he had not been the only one to notice it. It had been enough to alert the Home Secretary, who had turned to also look at what it was.

He suddenly moved the gun from Lucy's head and towards the location of the movement. The distraction caused him to loosen his grip on her slightly, allowing her to breath properly again.

Dave was already moving towards them both, aiming to throw both of them to the ground. Before he reached them, the Home Secretary had taken a shot towards the source of the movement.

A familiar sounding shout was heard as one of the stun shots hit Stuart. Having feigned his injury on the stairway, he had taken the opportunity to follow them up to the roof and sneak round behind them on the landing pad with the intention of trying to take his target from behind.

However, he had left himself slightly uncovered as he moved between two of the vents on the roof, which having caught Dave's attention had been enough to reveal his presence. He was thrown back across the flat roof as the charge spread across his body, before coming rest against the brick wall housing the lift mechanisms.

As his target had turned his back on Dave slightly, he had been able to aim his impact so that he would not throw himself against Lucy. The move had successfully caught the Home Secretary by surprise. Before he could move his attention back to Lucy and Dave, the three of them were sprawled across the landing pad floor.

With his grip on Lucy released as they had hit the ground, she had been able to roll away from him.

It was now Dave's turn to be caught by surprise as the Home Secretary's increased strength and speed allowed him to react quicker than he could. He had started to get back up to his feet having rolled after hitting the ground, but a foot forcefully met the side of his head, causing him to fall backwards again.

Lying dazed, Dave could only watch as the Home Secretary moved towards the helicopter and started to open the door. From behind him, a shot rang out and hit the handle. This caused the Home Secretary to jolt back as the charge dissipated through the metal framework.

However, it did not stop him for long. Using the weapon he held to take aim in the direction of the original shot, he started to let off a number of shots himself, hoping this would give him sufficient time to get in the helicopter. As further shots rang out, none of which found their target, he tried to make another move to get into the helicopter.

Gage, having let Stuart onto the roof a half minute or so before, was now making his way around the landing pad. He was looking to get a better shot, while also keeping under cover as shots were being returned back in his direction.

Dave was starting to get on his feet, and saw his weapon lying on the floor just away from him to his right, but could not see where Lucy had gone. He did not have time to look for her until they had caught the Home Secretary. Standing, he began to wave to the pilot to lift off, which he quickly obliged given the shooting taking place.

With the helicopter beginning to lift upwards, the Home Secretary was frantically scrabbling at the door, desperately trying to get inside. Clinging on to the door and with one foot on the foot rail, he dropped his weapon.

Seizing the opportunity and despite the pain he was in, Dave threw himself towards his gun and grabbed it. Rolling, he took aim as his target was lifted off the pad, hanging on to the side of the helicopter as best as he could. Gage then appeared on the stairs leading onto the landing pad, also aiming at the same target.

"I'm taking the shot," Dave shouted. "Hold your fire Gage."

As the helicopter reached about seven or eight feet from the pad, he took the shot. He hit the Home Secretary in the middle of his back as he continued his frantic attempts to climb into the helicopter.

As the charge hit and stunned him, his body went limp and fell. The body hit the landing pad with a sickening crunch of bones. Gage ran over to ensure he was in fact stunned and started to put a set of handcuffs on him. Not that he was expecting the Home Secretary to be getting up again any time soon, but he remembered that the nano-probes in an infectee's bodies were able to heal them quicker than a normal person.

Taking a deep breath, Dave turned his attention to finding the missing Lucy. Looking round, he could not see her anywhere on the landing pad.

"Lucy," he shouted out, the worry in his voice apparent. "Lucy."

"Help me," a strained voice came from over to his right. "Dave, help."

As he quickly moved the couple of feet to the edge of the landing pad where he had heard the voice coming from and looked over, he saw Lucy hanging on for her life. With one hand, she was holding on to a pipe with all the strength she had.

"I'm slipping," she screamed, trying to reach up with her free arm.

As quick as Dave was in moving to try and grab her flailing arm, Lucy's strength left her and her grip gave out.

Chapter 29

Despite having lost her grip on the pipe at the edge of the roof, Lucy found she did not fall as far as she had expected. As soon as her grip had given out, she had closed her eyes and let out a scream.

Something had got a tight grip on her left wrist. She stopped screaming, opened her eyes again, looked back up and saw Dave looking down at her, holding her wrist as tight as he could.

She could see from the look etched across his face that he was struggling to hold on.

"Gage," he was shouting at the top of his voice, unable to hide the sound of the pain he was in. "Gage!"

"Don't drop me," Lucy said quietly to him. She sounded partly relieved at being held, but also petrified at knowing her life hung in the balance for as long as Dave could hold his grip. She was preying he was strong enough to hold her despite the fight they had just been through.

"I can't hold on," he said, tears forming in his eyes. "I don't think I can hold you Lucy."

Tears streamed down Lucy's face as the realisation of her fate started to hit hard. Not only her tears, but she could also feel tears from Dave falling and landing on her face. She used her right hand to reach up to find something to grab and hold onto. There was still nothing within her reach.

For the second time that day, she felt her time was about to end as Dave's grip on her wrist slipped. She closed her eyes again and hoped the end was going to be quick.

As the grip on her left wrist disappeared, she found a stronger grip form around her right hand, the one that she had been using to try and find a handhold. Not only was the grip strong, it was also lifting her upwards, not the fall she had been expecting.

As she opened her eyes again and looked up, she saw Gage holding her by her right wrist and managing to lift her higher. Dave was also trying to reach back down, this time with both hands so he could grab her left arm again.

Despite the exhaustion etched across his face, she knew he had been giving it everything he possibly had in his attempt to save her. She knew he would not have been able to bear it if he had not saved her, something he very nearly failed to do. She hoped it did not affect him, the fact that he had been unable to save her on his own this time.

Under the grip of both Gage and Dave, she was hoisted back up onto the roof top and safety. As soon as she had both feet on the level, she turned and threw both arms around Dave and burst into tears.

She cried tears of both joy and of anguish. Having just faced near death on two occasions within the space of a minute, she was unsurprised that she felt a little emotional. She held Dave tight as she sought some comfort and a chance to try and calm down.

In return, he held her, feeling the relief that Gage had been there to help save her. As he ran his hand over her back, he knew he would not have been able to live with himself had they lost her.

After a few seconds she loosened her embrace around Dave, who let his arms drop from around her, and stepped back. He took a handkerchief from him pocket and wiped the tears from her eyes.

"Thank you Dave," she said, her voice sounding shaky. She could see the relief in Dave's face, as well as in Gage's expression as she turned to look at him as well. She continued to add "Thank you, both of you."

"Any time," Gage replied looking at Lucy. He then addressed Dave to say "Sorry it took me so long but I was checking the body of the Home Secretary and was about to make sure Stuart was okay."

"Did we get him alive then?" she asked, trying to return her full attention back to the situation. Doing so would help give her something to focus on as she tried to calm her nerves further.

"Yes, he appears to be badly injured, but is definitely stunned," Gage said. As he moved towards the body, he added "I think his back might be broken, along with at least one of his legs. He won't be a threat even if he comes around."

"I'm afraid we've seen infectees recover from serious injuries before," Lucy said. She watched as Gage walked past the Home Secretary's body, puzzled as to why he had not stopped. "We're going to need to get him secured back at Alpha Command as soon as we can to make sure that any threat he may pose is contained."

Suddenly realising what Gage had said just seconds before and noticing he that he was making his way towards a second body, Lucy asked "What about Stuart? You said you were about to check on him? Isn't he back down the stairs were we left him?"

"I was about to check on him," Gage said as he reached the second body. He knelt down next to it and checked for a pulse. "He has only been stunned in the gun fight after you fell."

"I thought you said he was dead," she asked, turning her focus to Dave who had finished checking the body of the Home Secretary.

"I did, but only because he told me he had a plan. It certainly gave us an advantage over our friend here," Dave explained. "It was an immense risk, but luckily for us he only took a cursory glance as we made our way up the stairwell. Sorry to have to mislead you Lucy."

Dave looked up to see the helicopter was hovering about thirty feet above them. He waved at the pilot to signal for him to bring it back done and land again.

He turned around and began to make a call back to Alpha Command. He guessed that Harry was probably getting more than a little edgy and would be keen to know what was happening.

"Alpha Lead to Alpha Command," he said. "I can confirm the target has been incapacitated. We will need medical assistance for him so we can get him back to Command."

"Negative Lead," Harry said over the radio. "You have new instructions. The target must be terminated immediately. We cannot take the risk of even trying to keep him here."

"Command, they have been using the nano-probes for research," Dave said. "Who knows what the hell they have done with them so far. We need to get any information we can from him, therefore I want him brought back to base.

"Alpha Four, this is Command," Harry's voice said over the radio. "Terminate the target immediately." From the tone in his voice, there was no mistake this was a direct order.

Gage walked over to the body. He took a standard gun out of a holster on his belt and pointed it at the base of neck. He looked to Dave, with regret showing in his eyes. While he had been in the army, it was drilled in to him to follow an order from a superior. The problem was that he was now torn between orders from two superiors. And as Harry was Dave's superior in the chain of command, therefore his order overrode any that Dave could issue at this stage.

"Command, this is my team, my mission and I make the calls here," Dave said angrily. Approaching Gage, he pointed at him and said "Do not do this Gage."

As he did, Lucy stepped over to try and hold Dave back. She felt that it was not an order she would have given if it had been her call, and she doubted it would be one that Johnson would have given either. But in this case, the order had been given.

"Do it now Four. That is a direct order," Harry barked over the radio. "My call overrides Alpha Lead's here."

"I'm sorry," Gage said before turning his attention to look at the body, as he pulled the trigger. He took two shots into the body, before looking back up to Dave. "I'm so sorry boss, but an order is an order."

"Harry, how dare you over rule my call," Dave spat down the radio loosing his temper. Even though he knew Harry would not see it, he was gesturing with his fist quite wildly. He was oblivious to Lucy's presence to his side as she was trying to encourage him to calm down.

"Just pull yourself together Lead," Harry responded, emphasising Dave's radio title of Lead as if to remind him of protocol on the radio. "We have another option if you would just calm down and listen to me."

"What do you mean?" Dave said, the suggestion of another plan having an instant calming effect on his anger. "You've got another plan?"

"I have ordered a couple of the guys who were not on the Gamma team to go to the Home Office," Harry explained. "I instructed them to gather everything from his office. Computers, papers, absolutely everything they could lay their hands on. It is all on the way to Alpha Command as we speak. However, I need you, Gage and Lucy to go to his home and search that."

Dave's mood had really changed and he was starting to return back to his normal, calm temperament. He turned to look at Lucy by his side as she was listening to the conversation over the radio. She placed her arm further around him, looked him in the face to show her support having been through a similar experience. There were always going to be incidents where their superiors could override their call against their own judgement.

She could see Dave visibly calm as he thought about what Harry had just ordered. The possibility to uncover the Home Secretary's plans another way had a strong calming effect over him.

"To be honest, I would not have made the same call," she said to him, having switched her radio link off briefly. "But there is a lot of risk in keeping these guys alive, particularly one who is so highly placed politically and quite obviously has powerful allies elsewhere."

"I know that really," he replied to her as he tried to explain, having made sure his radio was also off. "It's just I did not like being over ruled like that."

Switching the radio back on, he addressed Lucy again, but was happy for Harry to hear him try to assert his command again. "Still, it looks like me and you are going to check his house over. If I remember rightly, it's about a thirty minute helicopter ride from here. We'd better leave Gage here to get Stuart out of here and back for medical attention."

Dave moved away from Lucy and over to have a quick talk with Gage to outline their plan, while she spoke to Harry at Alpha Command to confirm the change to the plan.

"I've got no problems with that," Harry said to Lucy. "I will arrange for a second helicopter to be there as quickly as possible to pick them up. As for Lead, is he all right in your view or do you think he let the stress get to him?"

"Given the situation we were in a few minutes ago," she replied, "I don't think anyone could blame him for feeling a little bit stressed. I think it might help in some respects when I go home and he hasn't got me to worry about."

Harry let out a sigh and said "It was a worry I was getting that the two of you may be getting to close. I was concerned that this might affect either of your judgements while under pressure, perhaps at the risk of other team members."

"Please don't lecture me Command," Lucy exclaimed. "I helped write our protocols and realise I should have known better. However, there are some things you just can't plan for. I don't regret what is happening between us. But I can promise you that neither of us will let it stop us doing our jobs. We're going to go and wind up this job and get back to Alpha Command. Alpha Two out."

Lucy walked over to stand next to Dave as he had finished issuing his instructions to Gage. She added the news from Harry that an additional helicopter was now on its way.

Dave then moved over to the helicopter so he could talk to the pilot to outline the new instructions as to where they were to be going. Harry had already received approval for them to take a direct flight path across the city.

He swung back round to Lucy, grabbing the handle on the helicopter door, swinging it open and said "You ready then?"

"Ready as ever," she replied as she jumped in to the helicopter. However, she found her body was now starting to ache. It was no wonder after she had been held hostage, hung off the side of a building and nearly fallen to her death several times.

Harry's words were still ringing in her ears with regards to the serious lapse in protocol she and Dave had found themselves undertaking as their affections for each other grew. But she found herself thinking that trying to keep a distance between them was not likely to help matters either.

She now felt too much for him, no matter how wrong it was. It had given her a renewed focus to winning the fight against the alien threat, a focus to a better future that she wanted to work towards. Not that she hadn't been focused on the job before, but that had been for the good of everyone on the planet at the expense of her own life.

But for now, she still had to concentrate on the mission at hand. Turning to Dave, she waited until he had finished a conversation over the radio, apparently getting some information from Alpha Command.

She then asked him over the noise of the helicopter rotors "How long till we get there?"

"It will be about another fifteen minutes," he replied. "It's on the south side of London, in a small village called Eastingham. There's only twenty or so houses there, so we should not see too many people."

"Did Harry say if he would ensure the house was secure by the time we get there?" Lucy continued to ask.

"If he follows the protocols, then it will be secured for our arrival. I would expect that it will be as low profile as possible, but as soon as the press learn that the Home Secretary is dead, they will be at his home rather fast. We will need to be out of there as quickly as we can. We can then leave it to our agents to finish the job."

"What do you know about his family?" Lucy enquired. The more she knew before their arrival, the easier it might be looking for clues and information.

"Dan has been digging to confirm what he can for now. He has a wife and two grown up children. One has left home and is working in the foreign office as a diplomat. I believe he is currently in the Middle East somewhere. The other son still lives at home and Dan says that our information tells us he has been seen around the house the past few days."

"Have you had them under observation then?" Lucy was pretty sure she knew what the answer would be, especially given how well planned the Alpha Protocols had been up to now.

"Yes," Dave replied. "As soon as we began to suspect that he might have been infected, we had the property put under surveillance twenty four hours a day. Satellite feed, phone taps and so on. Not as easy in a small out of the way village as you might think."

Lucy then asked "Do you know if he might have tried to infect them?"

"We do not believe so. Nothing has raised our suspicions anyway." Dave took his weapon out from his holster and examined the ammunition clip. "It looks like I've only got three shots left. How about you?" he asked her.

Lucy took her gun out and checked it. "Same here, it looks like I only have a couple shots too. I'm not sure I can face another fight today to be honest."

Putting his hand on her shoulder and leaning in against her, Dave said "Neither can I, but I wasn't hanging around all morning like someone I can mention."

With a sneer, she pushed Dave away. "I guess you're the sort of bloke who regularly leave a girl hanging on aren't you," she retorted. "Just promise you won't do it again," she finished saying, with a smile.

The last few minutes of the flight past fairly quickly but silently as they watched the landscape passing below them. While they were hoping for less action than in the past hour or so, they were both mentally preparing just in case.

As they left the main urban areas of London behind them and flew further into the countryside, the helicopter turned to approach the village from the west. Just as Dave had described to Lucy earlier, it was a very small village. The houses were all along a single road, with their target the first house in village. The pilot lowered the helicopter until it landed on the road outside the house.

As they climbed out, Lucy saw that the end of the driveway was taped off with blue and white police tape. There were two police cars parked on the road outside of the house.

Looking along the road, there were a couple of people peering out from the end of their driveways, but for now, there was little other interest. Lucy briefly remembered the day she and Bale had visited a small village out in the state of Georgia. That had appeared to be a quiet village like this, but the secrets it hid were beyond what they had expected to find. She hoped this was not going to be a similar experience.

"Doctor Tyler I presume?" one of the police officers asked as he approached them from the direction of the drive way. Looking towards Dave, "and Doctor Hunt?"

"That's correct officer," Dave confirmed. "I presume the family are in the house?"

"Yes Sir. I have two officers inside with Josh Armstrong at the moment. He is aware his father has been caught up with the events in London, but says that he has not been home in several days."

"What about Mrs Armstrong?" Lucy added. "Is she here too?"

"We've not been able to talk to her yet," the police office replied. "Josh has told us she has not been feeling well recently and that she is asleep in bed still."

"I think we better go in and talk to him then," Lucy said, glancing at Dave.

"Of course, you're free to go straight in," the policeman said. "I've also been ordered to hand over control of the situation to you now you are here. My colleague and I will continue to wait on the driveway until further units arrive."

Before Dave could respond, the sound of smashing glass came from the front of the house as one of the policeman who was meant to be inside appeared to land on the front lawn having been thrown through the living room window.

Instantly, Dave and Lucy drew their weapons and prepared themselves for action. This resulted in shocking the police around them who had not expected to be seeing armed personnel. Lucy had dropped to one knee, pointing her gun towards the window where the body had come from.

Dave was stood, also pointing his gun towards the same window, but had moved aside so that he was stood in front of the police officer they had just been talking to.

"Get back," he ordered. "Leave this to us."

"No problems Sir," the nearest one replied as they both started to back away from the driveway and made their way so they could stand behind their vehicle.

A second crash rang out from inside the house and they could see movement in the room beyond the broken window, but could not make out what was actually happening. This was followed by scream that was suddenly cut off.

Dave assumed that had been the scream of the second policeman from inside the house. In all likelihood, they were probably now dead.

"You take the back door," Dave ordered Lucy, pointing towards the side of the house. "I'll take the front."

Before they could move anywhere, a young man had leapt through the smashed window and landed on his feet in the front garden just ahead of them.

As he did, he shouted out "You've killed my father. He was to lead us to great things." There was anger behind his voice as he added "and now it is your turn to die."

Dave let his attention slip for just a second as he checked that the police officers behind him were now out of harms way.

The slip of attention meant he did not react quickly enough as with lightning speed, Josh Armstrong raced towards him. Before Dave even had a chance to take a shot, Josh had made contact with him and they both landed on the floor.

Lucy held her gun up and took aim. She had a clear shot, but she decided to wait to see if Dave could fight his way out as she would risk stunning him as well if she were to shoot now. But she was not sure how long would she have before she had to make that decision.

Given the fact that Josh seemed to have the upper hand of the fight, it wasn't going to be all that long at all. Having been able to get a couple of heavy punches in on Dave, he was now trying to get a grip around his throat.

With a further flail of his arm, Josh sent Dave's weapon flying from his grip. Without the gun, Dave was now able to try and use both hands to fight off his attacker, but the distraction of loosing it had given Josh the chance to succeed in putting both hands around his opponent's neck and squeezing as hard as he could.

Chapter 30

Lucy moved around the pair of Josh and Dave, trying to get herself a better chance of getting a clean shot so as not to take her partner down at the same time. While she knew it would only stun them, she could do without having to deal with this investigation on her own.

Despite the increased strength they knew infectees gained, the Home Secretary's son was not getting as much of the upper hand as she had suspected at first. As yet, she did not know why. If he had been infected then he should have been able to kill Dave with his bare hands, but Dave was now giving as he good as he was getting.

The first thought to cross her mind had her starting to wonder if the effects from their encounter with the alien craft two nights ago were now causing Dave to become infected. She tried to discount the thought as there had not been any other signs before now except the dreams she had also been having. And that was not enough evidence alone.

She found herself having to back away as Dave suddenly threw his attacker off and on to his back against a brick wall along the side of the garden. She raised her gun again to take aim, but Dave had already been able to get to his feet and ensure Josh had no where to go. He had also realised there was something different about this attack.

"Hold your fire Lucy," he said, gesturing with his right hand as he rubbed his throat with his left. His voice was a little croaky after having been strangled. "There's something not right here. He should be able to put up more of a fight than that if he is actually fully infected."

Lucy kept her aim on Josh Armstrong, but took a sideways look across to Dave. "What is it then?" she asked. "He clearly had the beating of you at the start there."

"Thanks for the reminder Lucy," he replied. As Dave carefully approached Josh, who was still lying on the ground, he tried to make himself look as imposing as possible.

The raging man who had confronted the pair just minutes before, was now a cowering wreck on the floor, all his strength seemingly now disappeared. Both Dave and Lucy were caught by surprise when Josh continued to move backwards away from them, sliding his back along the wall.

"Please just kill me," he begged. "I can't take it any more. Someone just kill me now."

Dave decided that taking a softer approach might prove more beneficial here and slowly squatted down just in front of him so he could try to talk to him.

"What can't you take?" he asked gently. "What's happened to you?"

"I don't know," Josh said, tears in his eyes. "I don't feel well at all. I can't take it any more. I just want someone to end it all for me."

Dave moved closer to him and tried to comfort him. As he did, he signalled with a wave of his right hand to Lucy to lower her gun, which she did reluctantly. But she kept it in her hand, ready to protect Dave if this was all a trick on Josh's part.

"Who is doing this to you?" Dave asked. "We are going to need your help if you want us to be able to help you."

"My dad would keep giving me these injections," he started to say. "He said they were for my protection in case we had another attack on this country. Each time he gave me another one, it made my head thump and made me feel really ill. I started to become stronger and would get really angry very quickly."

"Sounds like the typical effects of infection," Lucy confirmed quietly behind Dave so as Josh did not hear her and would continue to keep talking to them.

"But then I would feel weak again, like I do now. I then get hungry, really hungry and I have to eat anything I can find. I can't help it."

Dave looked to Lucy and asked her "Ever heard of that before? That's not how the infection develops is it?"

"No," Lucy replied. "Once they turn, there's no way back. This would suggest he is not fully infected."

Lucy decided that she did not think that he was currently a risk, so she also squatted down next to Dave. She carefully concealed from his sight that she had kept her gun ready just in case. "Josh, when did your dad last give you one of these injections?"

"Only two days ago, we've not seen him since. He hasn't been at home properly in weeks. He killed my mum as well. At least I think it is still my mum."

"What do you mean," Lucy pushed, "when you say he killed your mum? Did he try and infect her too?"

"Infect?" Josh asked. "Dad said he was going to improve us. Help save us from the forthcoming events. What do you mean by infect?"

Dave leaned in towards Lucy and whispered to her. "We need to get him back to Alpha Command. There might be a lot we can learn from him. We might be able to bring him back."

"I agree," she whispered back. "Stuart told me about some theories he has come up with that we might be able to test out if Josh will let us."

"What are you saying?" Josh asked. "Are you going to kill me?"

"No," Dave responded. "We are going to help you Josh. Just wait there a second."

David suddenly stood up and called over one of the police officers. The one who they had spoken to when they arrived, gingerly stepped out from behind their vehicle and made his way over to them.

"Give me your hand cuffs," Dave said as he approached.

The policeman handed over a set of handcuffs from his belt and Dave then turned back to Josh to say "I'm going to put these on you. We're going to help you but we need to restrain you for now. It's for our safety."

Josh looked up at him, reluctantly holding his hands out for Dave to put them on him. As they were clipped around his wrists, he asked "You promise that you will make sure she is buried properly won't you? My mum did nothing wrong, please treat her properly."

As Josh stood up, Dave looked him square in the eye and told him "I promise. I will do that for you. We will be back to help you shortly."

Turning to the police officer again, he asked "Can you stay here with him? We will get someone to come and pick him up for us shortly."

The police man looked towards Josh apprehensively, but Dave noticed immediately. "He won't be any danger to you. It may be best to put him in the back of your car, but he won't cause any problems."

"If you say so Sir," the police officer said as he stepped towards Josh, before leading him back towards their vehicle.

Dave walked over to stand next to Lucy and whispered to her "We better get Harry to send someone out here fast. I'm fairly confident he won't be a threat again until he gets to eat something, but we need to get him back to Alpha Command as soon as we can."

"I agree," Lucy said. Looking over her shoulder, she saw that the number of people appearing from the other houses in the village had increased. "Well, if they have heard the news about his dad, then you can bet there will be press making their way here as we speak. And with that last incident, they may well be on the way anyway."

"We need to get him and what ever we find in there under wraps pretty fast. I'm going to look in the house while you get the message back to base." Raising his voice slightly, hoping the two police officers would hear, he added "And check out that body as well."

Lucy only nodded as she turned and moved herself away from the police officers who were now standing guard over Josh. She could not see him in the back of the car, assuming he had probably just lay himself down on the seat.

She contacted Harry to arrange for a team of agents from Alpha Command to come and help take control of the situation. Once she had made the necessary arrangements, she would follow and help Dave in the house.

Meanwhile, Dave made his way to the front door and found it unlocked. Having recovered his weapon, he had instinctively drawn the gun as he cautiously opened the door and began to make his way into the hall.

On the wall along the right hand side, there were assorted pictures of the family. Dave paused by one of them and saw the whole family, including the Home Secretary and his wife.

There were five doors around the hall, two on each side and one at the far end. Making his way along the hall towards the first of the doors on his right, Dave could see it was already open and led into the living room.

As he looked into the room, he could see a female body wearing a police uniform lying on the floor. As he stepped into the room to take a closer look, he found that the head had been completely turned round. He did not bother to check for a pulse as there was little chance the police officer had survived.

Stepping back in to the hall, Dave looked to the doors opposite. Both were currently closed and he assumed these were likely to be the bedrooms. He moved to the left hand door and slowly opened it. He carefully entered the room and found himself in what he believed must be Josh's room.

The bed did not look like it had been slept in for some time, but all around the room were food wrappers and empty jars of peanut butter. Obviously, although he had not suffered a full infection and mutation, he still needed the increased food intake which appeared to be a side effect of the infection.

"Harry's sending a team out immediately," Lucy said as she entered the room behind him. With a quick glance around the room, she walked over to the computer in the corner. Moving the mouse, the monitor came on and she looked at what was on the screen.

The first thing that struck her was the lack of password on the computer. She would have expected the son of an important member of the government to be a bit more security conscious. Nothing of importance sprung out, but she knew they would need to get this computer equipment back to Alpha Command to check out.

"Some appetite he's got here," she exclaimed looking around the room as she watched Dave checking the bedside cabinets. "We need to find whatever was being played to him as this is not normal."

"I've not seen anything obvious in here," Dave said. Moving bits of paper on the bedside cabinet, he said "No signs of needles or syringes in here. They must have been kept somewhere else."

"Let's try the next room," Lucy said as she moved to leave the room. "Your agents can sift through this room."

Dave nodded and followed her out of the room and towards the next room along. Dave took the handle of the door and opened it slowly. Even before he had opened the door very far, they were hit by a foul smell which caused them both to screw their faces up in disgust.

This was the main bedroom and as they both made their way in, they found a body lying on the bed. What used to be a white sheet was laid over it. Blood had seeped through and it was now stained a deep red. There were flies buzzing round which was not a good sign in Dave's book.

"Mrs Armstrong I presume," Dave said as he made his way around the bed.

Lifting the sheet back, Dave looked away in shock as the severely mutated face looked up at him. The mouth was wide open but had been contorted like someone screaming in panic. The eyes were bulging out of their sockets and the skin was peeling away from the face and neck. After a few seconds to recover from the shock, Dave laid the sheet back.

As he looked at Lucy, she did not appear to be quite as shocked by the find as he felt. Then again, she had seen many more mutated bodies than he had at this stage.

"Well, I guess that was more normal for what we expect from the alien infection," he said to Lucy, swatting a couple of flies away from his face. "That proves he was definitely trying something here."

Lucy had lifted the sheet lower down to look at the arm. She could see that there were signs of a number of needles having been stuck in her arm which confirmed that she had been used as a test subject.

"I agree," she said as she placed the sheet back where it had been over the arm.

"There's a door over there, I'm going to check it out," Dave said as he made his way around the end of the bed. "Let's see what's being hidden in there."

"Okay," she replied as she begun to rummage around the bedside cabinets and tables in the room. "I'll see if there is anything out here first."

Dave moved over the door and found that there was an electronic lock on the door, presumably linked to the number pad on the wall. There was no need for subtlety given that the owner was already dead.

He took out his weapon and shot the lock on the door. The charge dissipated through the lock with loud electrical crackle and it released immediately.

Behind him Lucy jumped at the sound, turning to see what had caused Dave to shoot his weapon off the way he had. As he pushed the door open, she saw that there the room beyond was dark, but they could see various small green lights to show there were probably a number of computers running in the room.

Intrigued, she started to follow Dave, who was now looking for a light switch on the wall inside the door. As he turned it on, both were stunned at what they found.

"I think we might have hit the jackpot," Dave said with a gasp.

"I think you're probably right," Lucy said, equally surprised.

Along the right hand and rear walls of the room were a range of pictures of people, all with bits of string tied to pins located on a map of the UK. Taking a closer look at some of the pictures, Dave saw that one of them was called Martin Pole, a leading dietician in the East Anglia region.

As he looked further round, he saw a pattern forming amongst all the people pictured.

"Lucy, it looks like we have a hit list of experts here," he said, pointing at a couple of them as he spoke. "They would all have the means and knowledge to help spread the alien infection in this country, if not the world. Talk about being organised."

Lucy was half listening, but was flicking through a file on the desk. She picked it up and handed it over to Dave.

"You better see this then," she said horrified. "It looks like a directory of those they have already tried to infect and the effects of it. Just from a glance, I think most have not taken the infection, but with only a couple of these guys running round, you're going to have some serious problems."

Dave picked up another folder and quickly opened at a couple of random pages. "My god," he suddenly exclaimed. "It looks like they have been working on modifying the nano-probes." Holding the folder so Lucy could take a look, he said "Look, they've been trying to test it with differing levels of exposure to see if they can control the infection."

Lucy leaned closer to Dave so she could see what he was pointing at. They were indeed testing their theories on what looked like forty or fifty different people.

"If they are trying to make a weapon out of this, then we've got to stop them," she said. She passed another piece of paper over and continued "It looks like everything is here, even the location of where they are doing the testing."

"Keep looking," Dave said. "You need to find evidence to prove if Ellis did actually send the email or not. If not, who did send the flaming thing? We need to stop that link so we can then try and limit the damage from both ends."

"Okay," she replied, turning back to the desk. "What about the computers? There may be more on there and I bet it's pretty well protected."

"When our guys get here," Dave agreed. "We'll get it all sent back to Alpha Command so we can analyse everything. We've got to follow the rules on controlling this evidence so it is secured. I think once we can put all this information together, we're going to have two steps. First step must be to verify if any of these possible infectees are running around the country or not. Secondly, we have got shut down that research base and stop them from trying to spread this thing any further."

Harry arrived by helicopter and made his way into the house. There were Alpha agents all over the place, bagging and boxing up nearly everything they found so they could return it all to Alpha Command.

He quickly spoke to one of the agents who directed him in the direction of the room where Dave and Lucy were still sifting through everything they had found.

As he passed through the bedroom, he paused to watch as two of the agents were putting Mrs Armstrong into a body bag. He'd seen pictures of mutated bodies before, and only days before had seen the burnt remains of the American soldiers from the airbase, but never had they been someone he had actually sat down to a meal with only a couple of months before.

Dave had briefed him on his way here as to what to expect, but as he entered the room, he could not help but be amazed at the scale of the detail and planning that had been undertaken here. It was going to take them some time to come to terms with what they had discovered and to plan on how best to deal with the new threat.

His mind turned back to the DPD in America. They were still fighting the threat over there and Johnson had requested that Lucy return to them within twenty four hours. While he was disappointed at the thought of her leaving and taking her expert knowledge and experience of the alien threat with her, he was also relieved that maybe he would fully get Dave's attention back on the work in hand.

"Right then," he said as soon as Dave had realised he was stood behind them. "I think it's time you got yourselves back for some rest, don't you?"

"Love to Harry," Dave replied as he continued to flick through another folder of papers, "but we've got too much here to sort out."

"It will wait," Harry said sternly. "That's why we have our agents here. They will take it all back to Alpha Command and you can start work on it tomorrow. In the meantime, you two might want to spend some time together before Lucy flies home in the morning."

Dave looked at Harry and then at Lucy with a look of sadness in his eyes, which he was trying to hide as best he could.

"We knew that this was only for a few days when I agreed to come here," she said, aiming the first remark more at Dave than Harry. "When's the flight home then?"

"Tomorrow morning, at eleven. You're going be met at Lakenheath air base apparently. There's no need to hide the fact from anyone as we've removed the threat we originally had. Now get yourselves out to the helicopter and go home."

Chapter 31

By the time they had arrived back at Alpha Command, it was getting very late in the day. It had been an exceptionally long day for the whole team.

Dave and Lucy headed back in to the command centre to gather the belongings that they had left prior to leaving for London that morning. Dave also wanted to go and see how Stuart was getting on in the infirmary.

He'd already heard via Harry that Stuart was fine, but felt he should at least go and give him a hard time about having got himself shot so easily. He knew Stuart would not hold back if it had been the other way around.

Before going to the infirmary, Dave decided to take five minutes out so as he could grab a quick shower. Tiredness was starting to rapidly creep up on him and he wondered whether he would even be able to stay awake this evening.

As he was getting changed into a fresh set of clothes, the television in the corner of the room caught his attention. As was normal in Alpha Command, the Sky News channel was being shown. They were reporting on the events that had occurred in London that morning.

"Al Qaeda Strike" read the headline across the bottom of the screen. Dave knew that while it was one of their favourite cover stories, it was also one of the easiest to get away with.

The journalist reporting the story was explaining how they had learned that a small team of four terrorists had been able to infiltrate the hotel and make an extremely daring attempt to kidnap the Home Secretary. They believed that the group were going to attempt to hold him hostage in exchange for the release of leading a leading Muslim cleric being held prisoner in the United Kingdom.

The journalist continued to explain that the plot had been thwarted by an undercover team of counter terrorist agents who had been able to make their way into the hotel shortly after the terrorists had made their move. As yet the reporter had not been able to find out as to how they had entered the hotel, but she promised to bring further information to the viewers as soon as they could.

The head line across the bottom of the screen changed to show "Home Secretary Murdered." The picture changed to show a photograph of the Home Secretary, reporting that he had been used as a hostage as they terrorists tried to escape, but had been killed in the crossfire as they tried to make their escape via helicopter from the roof.

Dave stood watching the screen as he began to wonder what the implications of the cover story might be. As part of the Alpha Protocols, they had to keep the alien threat as far away from public knowledge as possible, but they could well do without the attention this incident had drawn towards them.

While they had done their best to make sure none of the team had been caught on camera, he knew that they had experienced an element of luck as well. As he had noticed during the morning, the number of people who had gathered in the streets or were watching out of windows in the buildings along the road, any number of them could have had cameras or mobile phones.

Since they had left London to visit the Home Secretary's house, Dan had created a number of routines and viruses to search the internet for any references or pictures of the day's events. At least they could try and minimise any risk that there was.

Dave had already considered that he would need to take some time out over the next few days to review the mission reports. He also knew that he had to work doubly hard to improve the protocols so they would pose less of threat to their own operation in future.

There were also going to be a number of additional missions to plan and carry out over the coming weeks. They had already issued instructions to a number of their agents to start monitoring a number of targets who they believed were either already infected or had been targeted for infection in the Home Secretary's plans.

They also had the prospect of a large scale mission against a military base which they believed was located somewhere in the south western counties where there was documented evidence of testing of the alien nano-probes. Once the technicians got their hands on the computers and equipment that had been recovered, then they would be able to build a better picture of what they were looking at, what they would have to plan for.

A knock on the door caused him to jump slightly, bringing his focus back to the fact he was meant to be getting cleaned up so he could go and see Stuart in the infirmary. As he turned to look around to see who it was, Lucy's head appeared through the door.

Seeing that he was stood with just a towel around his waist, she took the opportunity to look him up and down. Getting a sudden case of embarrassment, he grabbed his t-shirt and rushed to put it on.

Smiling, Lucy asked him "Are you going to hurry up then? It's getting late and I want to go back and get cleaned up myself."

"I'll be there in a couple of seconds," he replied as he finished pulling on the t-shirt. "I was just watching the news about today. We're going to need to be a lot more careful in the future as the Al Qaeda story will get old very quickly."

"We?" Lucy asked. "You're going to be on your own from now on, so to speak."

"Thanks for reminding me," Dave said. "Now let me get changed and I'll be with you."

Having finished changing, Dave made his way out into the corridor to find Lucy was waiting just outside.

"Sorry I took so long," he said. "As I said, I got a little bit engrossed in the news on the TV."

"I caught some of it in the refreshment room while I was waiting," she said. "Now, are you ready to go and see Stuart?"

They walked down the corridor together and headed towards the infirmary. They would both visit Stuart together before they would spend a final evening together. Tomorrow Lucy would be going home, the end of an interesting few days. However, neither hoped it was not to be the end of what they both wanted to become a great relationship.

As they entered the infirmary, Stuart was already sitting up in the bed. "About time you got here boss," he said cheerily. "Can't you tell them I'm okay so I can get home?"

Dave turned to have a quick word with the doctor who was looking after Stuart. They quietly exchanged a few words before he returned to stand next to Stuart's bed.

He stood next to Lucy and put his hand on Lucy's shoulder, showing Stuart how close the two of them had become. Dave knew Stuart had realised that there was something between him and Lucy from the start, and wanted to just let him know he was right.

"I'm afraid you're going to have to be kept in over night Stuart," Dave said. "They are slightly concerned by some of the blood tests. The doctor wants to keep an eye on you just in case."

"Come on boss," he started to plead. "You can't let me stay in here tonight."

"Sorry mate," Dave said, trying to look as sympathetic as he could. As he leaned closer to Lucy, he added with a smile, "We'll think of you tonight."

Stuart lay back in the bed with a sigh. "Fine, you two go and have fun while I am stuck here all night. And whose bright idea was it not to put a television in here then?"

"Okay," Dave said. "Come on Lucy, let's go and have some fun then." As he led her out of the infirmary, they stopped in the doorway. Dave turned to look back at Stuart who now appeared to be sulking in the bed.

"Just make sure you put some bloody clothes on before you go home," he shouted back.

"One step ahead of you boss," Stuart called back, leaping out the bed. He already had a pair of jeans on, obviously expecting Dave to try and wind him up. "You're going to have to get up a lot earlier than that to catch me out."

"Good night Stuart," Dave called with a sigh as the pair disappeared into the corridor.

Having left STAR Park, Dave drove Lucy back to the hotel. They had decided to keep things simple for their last night together. They planned to have a meal within the hotel and then spend the evening watching a film or two in her room. Neither one had the energy to be going far tonight.

As Lucy had gone into the bathroom with the intention of having what she hoped would be a relaxing bath, she passed Dave the room key. This was so that he could let himself back in when he got back from the video rental shop which was just up the road.

As he wandered around the video shop looking for a DVD or two for them to watch, he found himself becoming exceedingly picky about the choice of film. In the past, he had been able to know what he wanted to watch without much thought. The last week had changed his view on films.

He picked up Independence Day, something which seemed to hold any appeal to him any more. Just how could that ever mirror the truth of what they had all been through in the past week, or even come any where close to the things they were likely to see from here on.

Neither did he really want to watch something that they would have to think about too much. He felt so exhausted from the day that he didn't think he would be able to get his brain out of first gear this evening. He was pretty sure Lucy would be feeling the same way.

He finally chose Domino and Sin City, hoping that Lucy had not seen either film. Given how tied up she had been by her own work for the past six months, he was convinced she would probably not have had the chance to have seen anything recently.

Arriving back at the hotel, he walked back through the corridors to Lucy's room. He thought that it was funny how nervous he felt right now given the amount of time they had spent together though out the past week.

He slid the card into the lock on the door and walked in. By the sounds of it, she was still in the bath. Not that he could blame her. If his injuries were anything to go by, he wondered how many bruises and cuts she had picked up over the past couple of days.

He gently knocked on the bathroom door and called out "I'm back with the films."

"Okay," she shouted back. "Give me another five or ten minutes and I shall be with you. Make yourself at home."

He thought about replying with a quick witted one line remark, but decided he was just too tired to think of one.

Dave walked into the room and placed the DVD's on the shelf next to the television. He turned it on and walked over to the bed. He took off his jacket, stopping himself from just dropping it on the floor. Instead he placed it carefully on the chair next to the bed.

"I'm not at home," he muttered to himself, shaking his head. He knew full well that his clothes seemed to prefer being hung on the floor most of the time. Whenever the cleaner he had come in, she would always leave notes for him about how to use coat hangers and washing baskets. Not that he had ever taken notice of any of them.

As he sat on the edge of the bed, he started to lift his feet up. As he did, he looked down at them and decided perhaps he should take his shoes off as well. Best he kept a good impression of himself with Lucy. She did not seem the type to appreciate shoes on the bed.

Lying back with his head against the pillows, he flicked through the channels on the TV. Many were still showing news reports of the events in London that morning, but he was not interested in what they had to say any more. They had been there and those involved knew the truth was far greater than most people in the country could ever deal with.

He found his eyes becoming heavier and decided he could not fight the urge to fall asleep. "Perhaps a five minute snooze won't hurt," he said to himself and let his eyes close.

Having finished her bath, Lucy pulled her dressing gown tight around her as she left the bathroom and entered the bedroom area. As she did, the television caught her eye as they started showing yet another news update with more information about the day's events.

The channel was showing a picture of the Home Secretary and his family. The reporter was outlining how his family had appeared to all have been murdered in their own home at the same time as the events that had been unfolding in London.

They still appeared to be accepting the story of Al Qaeda as those responsible.

About to ask Dave what DVDs he had picked up from the rental shop, she stopped as she saw that he was lying on the bed. She did not need to look closely to that that he was sound asleep.

She decided that she would go and lay on the bed next to him. Part of her wanted to wake him, while another wanted to just lay with him and go to sleep herself. She chose to lie next to him, hoping that it would be enough to wake him as she did.

As she lay down next to him, she carefully snuggled up alongside and laid her head on his shoulder. As she did, he seemed to stir slightly, but did not wake up.

As she lay looking at his face, she found herself relaxing, especially when he curled his arm around her. Within a few minutes, she herself had fallen asleep as well.

Chapter 32

Dave woke with a start to an unfamiliar sound. It must be an alarm of some sort he thought. Even before he had properly opened his eyes, he realised something was different this time.

The room was bathed in bright sunlight streaming through the partly open curtains. For the first time in several days, he had been able to sleep through the whole night without being woken up by some emergency or other.

As he tried to sit up so he could reach over to turn the alarm off, he found something was preventing him. In moving himself, whatever it was had started to moan and move closer into him.

He then realised it was Lucy, lying alongside him. She was laid with her head resting on his shoulder and her arm gently draped across his body. He soon remembered that they had been meant to be spending a last evening together before she returned home to Washington, but they must have both slept straight through it.

Having stirred from Dave moving, Lucy rolled on to her back, which then allowed Dave to reach over and turn the alarm off. As he did so, he took a look at the clock. He saw that the time was now just after nine in the morning. They would need to be leaving the hotel in a little under an hour to get her to the airbase at Lakenheath for her flight home.

He sat up and swung his legs over the side of the bed, finding that he was still fully clothed. Looking over his shoulder, he saw Lucy was now starting to wake up and looking back at him smiling. She was still in her dressing gown from when she had got out the bath the night before.

Her hair looked all messed up where she had laid on it all night after not having dried it thoroughly. Dave returned a smile as he sat looking at her and felt the pain of her imminent departure grow. Even now, looking as she did, he could not help but see why he was so attracted to her.

"Look's like we missed out on our plans for last night," he said quietly to her, sounding more than just slightly disappointed.

She smiled back and said "I know how disappointed you are, I am too. However, just your being here meant a lot after the past few days. There will be more chances to be together. Trust me when I tell you that we will win this fight."

Lucy suddenly felt slightly guilty having made that promise to him, and hoped she did not reflect this on her face. Deep down, she had started to fear that this was a fight that she would not see the end of, perhaps none of them would see the end of. She could not tell Dave this yet, she cared too deeply to do so. She felt he might loose a lot of his drive if she did.

Dave smiled as well and replied "Between our teams, we will save our world from whatever these visitors can throw at us. But I might not be able to save you from missing your plane if you don't start getting up right now."

Lucy laughed as she sat up and swung her legs over the side of the bed. It was time to get up and pack her belongings for the trip home.

Arriving at the airbase by car, Lucy was now able to see where they had been just three days before when they had recovered the alien craft. There was no sign that the Alpha Team had even been there and life appearing to be as normal.

On entering the air base, the guards at the entrance directed Dave to drive towards an area just off the main runway. One of them had met them when they had arrived earlier in the week, but he did not show any signs of recognising them. She thought this was probably for the best as they did not want to be answering questions about what had really happened.

As they drove round the buildings alongside the runway, both were slightly surprised to see a familiar looking plane taxiing into where they were headed.

"Air Force One, isn't it?" Dave asked.

"Only when the president is on board," Lucy replied. "And I doubt he would be here like this somehow. Maybe it's on a training flight or something."

As they pulled to a stop, they climbed out of the car and watched as the ground staff ran around the plane, undertaking the sort of jobs you would not normally see being done at a commercial airport as a passenger. The steps were moved up to the front door on the plane, while others were starting to refuel the plane further back.

As the door swung open, the first couple of passengers stepped onto the steps. Lucy was quietly surprised to see a very familiar face appear, closely followed by second.

As Bale and Johnson made their way down the steps, she walked over to greet them. She gave both men a quick hug and said "You don't know how relieved I am to see you guys."

Dave had followed behind and as he met Bale's gaze, Bale spoke to Lucy "I hope they've treated you well over here."

Turning to face Dave, and with a slight hint of anger in his voice, he continued to say "Mr Hunt, I hope you have taken care of Lucy for the past few days."

Dave gave a reassuring smile and replied "I've done everything I can to make her stay as comfortable as possible, given the circumstances."

He made no attempt to hide the smugness in his voice as he spoke to Bale. While he had been in the United States, he had seen how fond Bale had become of Lucy. While most had perceived it as nothing more than team bonding, Dave felt certain that he felt as much for Lucy as he did.

"And what do you mean by that?" Bale pressed, as he took a slightly menacing step towards Dave. The look on his face showed he did not like him and he was not afraid to show it.

Lucy turned to face Bale and asked "What's the matter with you? You said you did not know him before. Now I get the feeling there's something more going on here."

"It's not a story for today," he replied, still focused on Dave. "Maybe not even for this lifetime. Let's just say once you loose your trust in someone, it's not easy to win it back."

Lucy turned to face Dave and said "Can you tell me what he means by that? I doubt he'll give anything up to me all that easily."

Dave looked from Bale, down to Lucy and replied "He's right I'm afraid. It's not a story for today. But it's also not something that is worth worrying about either. This won't change anything between any of us, certainly not between you and me I hope. There are more important issues at stake to be honest."

Lucy was confused by the confrontation, but decided it was probably best to let it lie for now. Before she could say anything else to any of them, she was distracted by a pair of black cars approaching them from the same road that they had just approached the runway.

As they pulled up alongside, two men got out of the front car. The first of them she recognised immediately as Harry. The second one made his way around to the rear door on the second car.

She walked the few paces to meet him and held her hand out to shake his. "Hello Harry," she said as they shook hands. "It's nice of you to come and see me off."

"Thank you for your help Dr Tyler," he said. Looking just over her shoulder, back from where she had just walked from, he added "Dave, can you join us too?"

Dave stepped over to stand next to Lucy, with Bale and Johnson a few steps behind. They all waited as the second occupant of the car stepped out to greet them.

"Mr Prime Minister," Dave said, surprised to see him here.

"I just wanted to personally say thank you for everything you have done to help safeguard our country," he said. "Harry has been keeping me briefed on the events of the past few days, especially the discoveries made at our former Home Secretary's home. You've helped eliminate a threat that could have proved the downfall of our country."

"I'm afraid, the threat is far from over Sir," Dave said. "In fact, this is only the beginning. I am certain of that. I'm sure Lucy and her team will back us up on this, but we're in for a long, hard fight before this is over."

Beside him, Lucy was gently nodding. Johnson laid a hand on each of Dave's and Lucy's shoulders behind them and added "If it were not for people like these two, I am convinced we would have fallen to the alien threat a long time ago. Both teams, the DPD and Alpha, will do their best to ensure this planet is safe for everyone."

The Primer Minister held out a brown folder, with Classified written all over the front. As he passed it to Dave, he said "That is why I have given the Alpha Protocols clearance to use any resources, any funding, anything they need to take this fight to these aliens. No matter what it takes, no matter the cost, you are to win this war. This is our planet and I intend for it to be kept that way."

The Prime Minister returned to his car and started to climb in. Before he finished getting in, he looked at Dave and with a big smile, added "Just try not to destroy too much of it first."

As they watched the Prime Minister's car pull away from the runway, one of the ground crew approached Johnson with a message from the pilot that the plane was refuelled and ready to depart.

"Sorry guys," he said. "We've got to start making tracks to get back home now."

"Okay, just give me a couple more minutes," Lucy said back to him. Looking over her shoulder, she looked back to Bale. From the look on his face, she would need to push him to give her a moment alone with Dave before she left.

Johnson leaned in and offered his hand to Dave. "By all accounts, you've put together a good team here. One I look forward to working with so we can rid this world of the alien threat. If you can keep up the work of the past few days, I too believe we will definitely win the fight."

As Dave shook it, he responded by saying "Thanks. I hope you can have the same faith in my team, as you do in Lucy's."

"Good luck Dave," he said, turning to face Bale. "Come on, let's give them the time to say their farewells Mark."

Hearing Johnson call him Mark, Lucy knew he would take that as a direct order from a superior and get back on the plane. As she watched him, Bale took one more glare at Dave, before turning to climb the steps back on to the plane.

She resisted the urge to ask again as to what the problem between them was. She knew there would be plenty of time on the flight to work on Bale.

As they moved away, she turned her attention back to Dave. She stepped closer and placed her hand on his shoulder. She could tell he was more than a little disappointed by the fact she was now leaving to fly home, but she could not offer him anything more than confirming that she felt the same way.

"I promise to call you when I get back," she said. "I'm sure it won't be long till we can spend some more time together."

"I know. While we are doing what we need to keep this threat from destroying what we know or killing everyone, we will be together soon," Dave said sadly.

"Remember, you can always come and join us in Washington at any time," she said.

"Or you could join us here," Dave responded. "Whatever happens, I think I love you Lucy."

Lucy leaned in, having to stretch up slightly to reach and placed a kiss on his lips. Dave lifted his hand and placed it gently on the side her cheek as they kissed again. She then moved her head and they embraced tightly.

After a short while, Lucy said to Dave quietly "Sorry Dave. I really have got to go."

As he let the embrace go, they took the opportunity for one final kiss. Lucy stepped back away from him, wiping a tear from her eyes. As she did, she turned and climbed the steps behind her and into the airplane. Reaching the top, she stopped and turned to take a look back to him.

With a little wave, she turned and finally made her way onto the plane. As she did, one of the crew on board the plane swung shut the door at the same time as the ground crew began moving the steps away from the plane.

The sound of the engines powering up began to rise and the plane started to roll forwards. It began its short taxi towards the end of the runway.

Watching as the plane powered its engines and accelerated down the runway, Dave leaned against the side of his car. He watched as the plan took off and started its flight back home. He took one last look at the airplane as it disappeared into the clouds, only to be interrupted as his phone in his pocket began to ring. Quickly, he took it out of his pocket, irrationally hoping it was Lucy calling him already.

Looking at the screen for several seconds, he was disappointed to see it was only Stuart back at Alpha Command.

"Hunt here," he said, finally answering the call.

"Sorry boss," he said. "Our agents have located one of the candidates on the list of possible infectees. The DNA test on some hair they have recovered has come back positive."

"Do you know where he is?" Dave asked, focusing himself on the new issue at hand.

"Yes boss," Stuart replied. "And as soon as you get back here, we can prepare to send the team out to bring him in. Are you going to be long then?"

"I'm on my way. I'll be there inside the hour," Dave said as he finished the call. Before getting into his car, he took on last look back into the sky. Perhaps he was not going to have time to miss Lucy for long. The aliens would make sure of that.

With a sigh, Dave sat down in the car and closed the door. With a screech of wheels, he pulled off and began to make his way back to Alpha Command.

Back to whatever the aliens could throw at them.

Back to saving his country.

Epilogue

Two long days had passed since Lucy had returned to rejoin her team in the DPD back in America. Despite the Alpha Team having captured one infectee, Dave was still moping about Alpha Command, even though they had spoken at least twice each day.

Although many of their conversations were with regards to the alien threat as they worked to bring their different protocols together, they still found time for private talk here and there.

During the current call, the biggest piece of news announced was that the alien craft had now arrived at NASA. Lucy informed them that the whole team they had assembled to research it had been like big kids getting a new toy at Christmas, even bickering over whose turn it was to work on it. She was confident that they could start unravelling some of its secrets from his research very quickly.

Dave was providing an update on the work the members of the Alpha Team were doing as they worked through everything they had removed from the Home Secretary's office and house. The information they were collating was providing an in depth picture of the immediate tasks at hand for them.

They had started to prepare for their two main tasks which required their immediate attention. The first was to shut down and eliminate the hidden complex where research into weaponising the alien nano-probes was being undertaken. They had discovered that work was being undertaken on two projects.

The first had been to try and modify the nano-probes to help increase the abilities of their own soldiers. The second project was looking into how they could use the same technology as a weapon in the field. Why send the troops into fight if they could just drop a weapon that could kill as easily as a nuclear bomb, but not leave the destructive aftermath.

They understood that there will still obstacles for completing a successful trial, but that would mean there could be any number of infectees in the base, many of whom would be driven to escape and spread the infection.

Secondly, they needed to protect those named on the target list. While the majority of those who were infected in the trials appeared to be homeless people, picked up off the streets where nobody would miss them, those on the list would add untold knowledge and experiences to the alien agenda.

Dave was able to announce that in just under a week's time, the Alpha Team would be moving on the base. They knew the location of it and that it was going to be extremely well defended. They would have surprise on their side. Not the surprise that they would dare attempt a full on attack, but surprise of the resources available to them.

Despite still being a covert organisation, the Prime Minister had given the Alpha Protocols the freedom and the resources to do what they needed to eliminate the alien threat. They would do whatever it took, whatever the cost. The whole survival of the human race depended on them.

About the Author

David Francis was born in Dover, England in 1975, but has lived in Suffolk since the age of two. Having worked in the world of IT for over ten years, he has collected a number of certifications over the years, most recently the CISSP security award. Currently, he is an IT Manager for a software company based in Ipswich, Suffolk.

David has a keen interest in the world of sci-fi, particularly the worlds of Star Wars and Doctor Who. He regularly watches shows like Threshold and X-Files.

Away from work and sci-fi, David has a keen interest in a number of sports. He is an avid supporter of Ipswich Town Football Club, but also participates in sports such as football, running, tennis and cricket.

All of these interests have been used as the inspiration for writing **The Alpha Protocols**.

Printed in the United Kingdom
by Lightning Source UK Ltd.
116424UKS00001B/4-42